THE STONE OF KNOWING

THE STONE CYCLE BOOK 1

THE STONE CYCLE SERIES

The Stone of Knowing (The Stone Cycle Book 1)
The Cost of Knowing (The Stone Cycle Book 2)
The Stone of Authority (The Stone Cycle Book 3)
The Struggle for Authority (The Stone Cycle Book 4)
The Stone of Vitality (The Stone Cycle Book 5)
The Hope of Vitality (The Stone Cycle Book 6)

Companion Novelettes
The Seer: A Prequel to The Stone of Knowing (The Stone Cycle)
The Rending: A Prequel to The Cost of Knowing (The Stone Cycle)

THE STONE OF KNOWING

THE STONE CYCLE
BOOK 1

ALLAN N. PACKER

LUMINANT PUBLICATIONS

The Stone of Knowing
The Stone Cycle Book 1

Copyright © 2019 by Allan N. Packer

First edition (v1.7) published in 2019
by Luminant Publications

ISBN 978-0-6483051-7-0

Luminant Publications
PO Box 201
Burnside, South Australia 5066

http://www.allanpacker.com

Cover Design by Karri Klawiter
Map illustration by Brian Plush

'The Stone of Knowing' is dedicated to James, Melanie, Stephen, and Deborah, for whom it was created. Their enthusiasm brought it to life and saw it through to its conclusion.

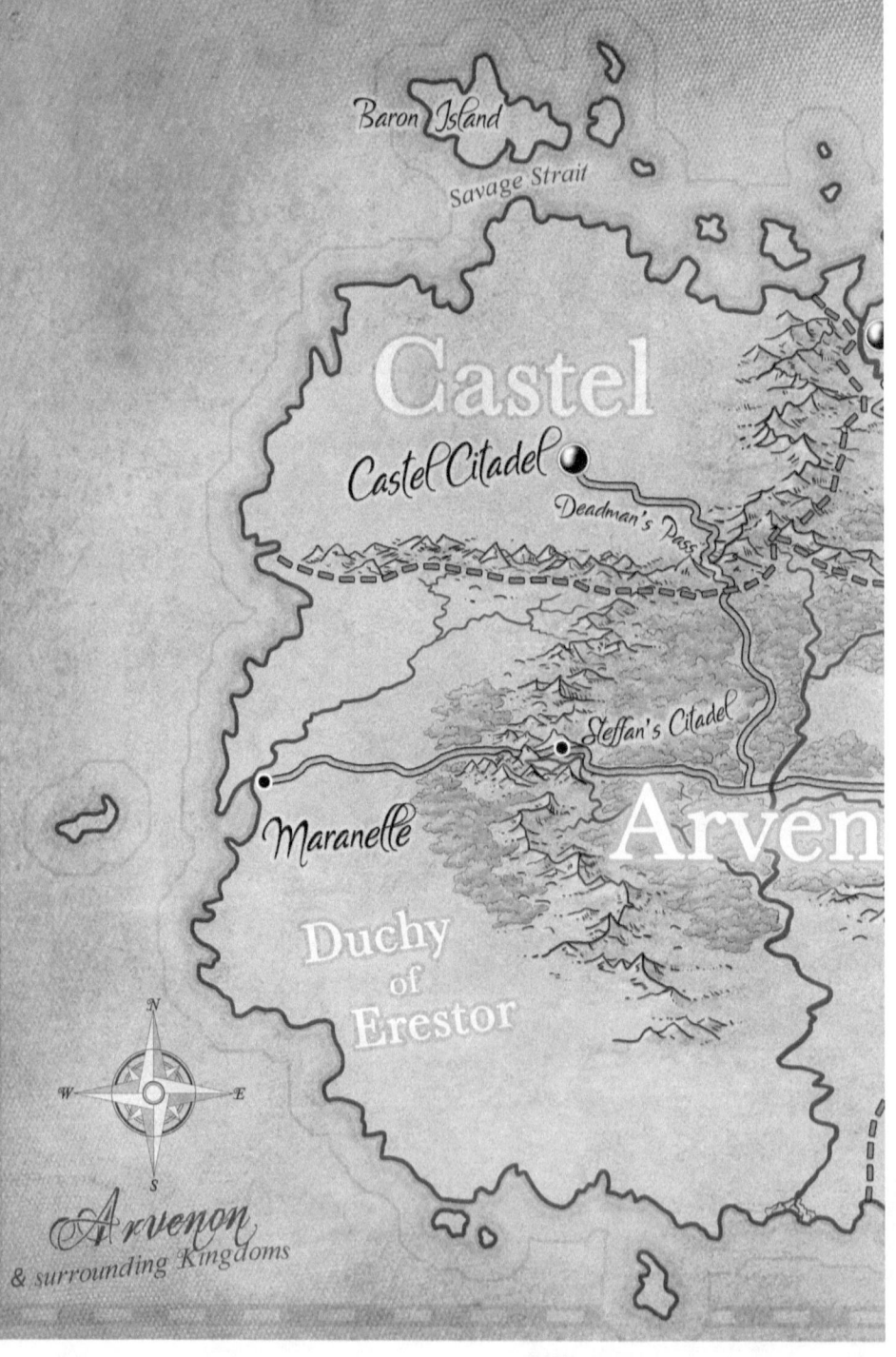

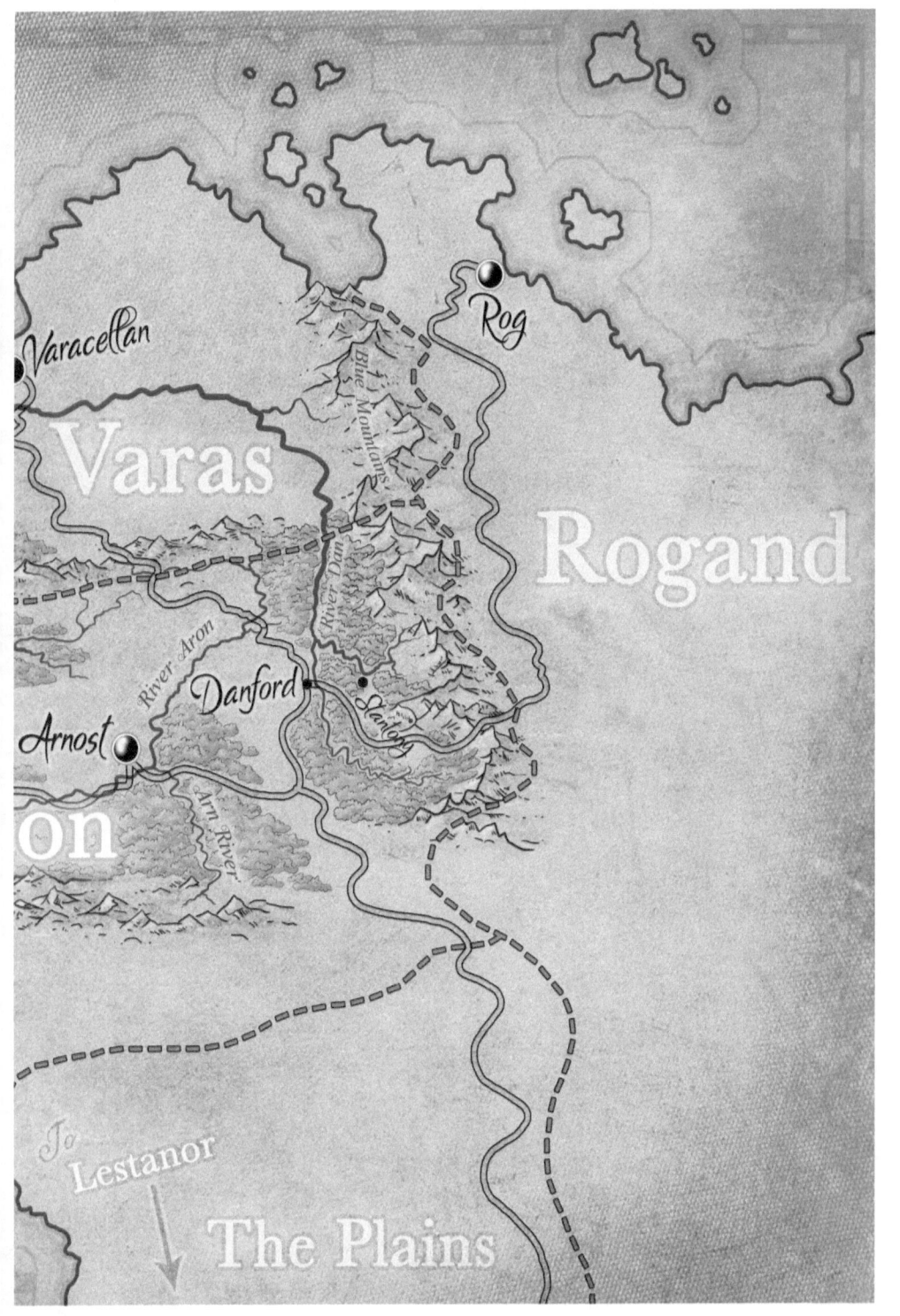

VOLUME 1—THE STONE

PROLOGUE

The king waited impatiently astride his horse, his thoughts dark and cold as the night that enveloped him.

For a brief moment the dazzling array of stars above captured his restless gaze, but he soon turned away. Staring at the night sky yielded no return. It wasn't worth his attention.

A torch bobbed toward him out of the darkness, the outline of an anxious servant gradually appearing beside it.

The man bowed low at his feet. "He has arrived, Your Majesty."

"Send him to me at once," growled the king.

The servant bowed again before scurrying away.

Before long a stallion pranced into view bearing a tall nobleman dressed in black.

The new arrival dipped his head as he drew closer. "The men are assembled, Your Majesty. I await only your command."

The sovereign scowled at the tall commander. "Remind me again," he demanded. "How does this plan benefit you?"

The rider barely hesitated. "Destroying our enemies and enlarging your kingdom at their expense is reward enough for me."

The king's eyes narrowed. He was well aware that the nobleman seized every opportunity to expand his own influence. This mission would be no exception. The commander had also sidestepped the question of plunder.

The evasiveness did not trouble the king. He himself would be the chief beneficiary in the end. He always made certain of that.

He studied the tall rider with a calculating eye for a long moment. Then he nodded once. "Do it."

Dipping his head once more, the commander swung his horse around and galloped away.

CRESTING THE RIDGE, the commander guided his black stallion forward until he reached the edge of the tree line. Far too many weeks had been spent moving his force into foreign territory undetected, but the time had come at last. He glanced irritably behind him as he waited for the last of the riders to take their positions in the shadow of the trees.

He stared down at the village below. The villagers had straggled home from the fields as the dusk deepened, and the laughter of children had stilled as the people disappeared into their crude dwellings.

There was nothing special about this place, no compelling reason to have lured the angel of death here rather than anywhere else that night. The slaughter simply needed to begin somewhere in Arvenon.

The tall nobleman stared out into the darkness. His presence here had a purpose, one he had carefully concealed from his scheming sovereign. The death and destruction he was about to unleash held no more interest for him than the particulars of the location. A prize beyond price lay hidden somewhere in this kingdom. His craving for it consumed him. It alone had drawn him here.

He turned to the horsemen waiting among the trees. "You all know what to do."

Dozens of torches flared into life, sending eerie shadows flickering from the horned helmets of the riders.

Rising in his stirrups, the dark leader raised a hand and thrust it toward the village.

"Destroy it all," he commanded. "Leave nothing alive."

1

Thomas found it on his way back toward the castle. The afternoon was drawing on and he was hurrying, but it caught his eye, and he quickly stopped and reached down for it. It was a small stone, almond-like in size and smooth to the touch. It lay gleaming in his palm, illuminated by the rays of the late afternoon sun.

Many times afterward he wondered how the stone came to be there and why he should have been the one to find it. But at that moment, the youth simply admired his new prize, captured by the striking swirls of blue and purple that covered its surface. He turned it over slowly in his hand. Then he tossed it into the air, once, twice, before dropping it carefully into the leather pouch at his belt. Retying the drawstring, he set off once again for home.

As the road drew him closer to the river, the orderly strips of cultivated land and clusters of cottages to his left began to fall away. Off in the distance he caught a glimpse of gray stone towers rising majestically over barren foothills. A sprawling town surrounded the castle with its lofty towers, and beyond the ford the road wound its way up to the ancient walls that encompassed the town.

To his right the last trees of the great forest advanced almost to the water's edge. Noticing the spreading gloom beneath their silent boughs, Thomas quickened his pace.

As he approached the ford, children's laughter drifted toward him from a nearby farm. A dog emerged from the forest ahead and set off slowly in the direction of the voices.

At the sight of the dog a wave of bitter memories welled up inside him. He had been up most of the previous night tending a sick grey-hound and the frail litter of tiny puppies put at risk by her illness. His efforts had drawn a rare compliment from his father.

Emboldened by the unexpected response, he again asked for a dog of his own. Once more his father had refused. "There are fifteen dogs across the courtyard," he replied impatiently. "Fine animals, too —the king's own hounds. The best in all Arvenon. What do we want with another one? I'll hear no more about it!"

Thomas sensed that this time the decision was final. His father would never understand. It didn't matter if there were fifty hounds across the courtyard. They belonged to the king. They were fine animals, to be sure. But they would never compare with any one of their lesser cousins if only it belonged to Thomas Stablehand.

He grimaced and returned his attention to the animal ahead. The dog seemed unaware of his approach. In fact there was something peculiar about its gait and the way it hung its head. It wasn't unusual to see underfed and unkempt mongrels about the town. But farm dogs mostly fared better, and plenty of small game inhabited the forest at that season. The animal appeared intent on joining the children. If it was a pet someone at the farm would take care of it.

Thomas soon overtook it. As he passed by, the dog finally noticed him. It looked up at him as his hand, probing absently, chanced upon the stone hidden securely in his pouch.

He gasped with fear and amazement. How could he have thought it was a dog? He shrank back in terror from the snarling face and ravening jaws of a wolf. The wolf's eyes burned into him—hideous, unnatural, and filled with savage hate.

Nothing else mattered except to escape those eyes. Knowing it was futile, Thomas turned and ran for his life.

He sprinted down the path, heart racing. His legs, already weary, quickly began to ache. A sharp pain stabbed his side. He risked a glance behind—the wolf was almost on him. Utterly terrified, he flew blindly from it.

Once he stumbled on the rutted path and almost fell. But he recovered and flung himself forward again.

His breath rasped painfully into lungs of fire. His world narrowed to the desperate pounding of his feet and the pain in his lungs and side. Inexplicably, the wolf had not run him down, but from its snarling it was right behind.

He cast around frantically for a haven, and a rough wooden farmhouse caught his glance. Three young children chased each other nearby. Their carefree laughter snapped him out of his mindless terror.

"Run for your lives! Save yourselves," he gasped. Startled, the children stopped playing and looked up.

They were not going to move in time. For a moment, Thomas forgot his own fear. Hoping to draw the wolf away, he veered toward a small barn, shouting and waving his arms to keep its attention. At first, the wolf continued to pursue him. Then abruptly it came to a halt, turning its slavering muzzle toward the children.

The children's mother appeared from nowhere and shooed them into the house, calling urgently for her husband. As Thomas came panting up to the barn he caught a glimpse of the farmer running toward the wolf with a pitchfork, a resolute look on his face.

Not until he was safe in the hayloft did it occur to the young stable hand that the farmer might need his help. Securing the stone and quickly tying off his leather pouch, he climbed down from his perch and picked up the nearest weapon—a long-handled ax. Heart thumping, he tentatively retraced his steps.

A cacophony of loud yells and frantic snarling drew him to the battle. Thomas arrived to see the creature writhing on the ground in its death throes, its life blood drenching the soil an angry red. The farmer stood leaning on his pitchfork. He was breathing heavily, a wild look in his eyes.

When he recovered himself, he turned to face Thomas. "Thank you, son!" he said. "I owe you my children's lives. The heavens be praised that you noticed the dog was rabid."

Dog? Rabid? Thomas stared at the animal in astonishment. It was indeed a dog. And the flecks of foam around its mouth supported the alarming conclusion. The farmer, now kneeling in some grass wiping his weapon clean, appeared not to notice his confusion.

Bewildered and feeling awkward, Thomas turned away, mumbling a goodbye.

The farmer stood up quickly. "Wait!" he urged, turning to Thomas and removing his cap. "There is little I can offer you by way of thanks," he said apologetically. "But tonight we will celebrate, such as we can. You shall feast with us at least."

Thomas shook his head.

"Come, now. Look at you. Skinny as a willow branch." The farmer winked at him. "My wife can do something about that," he promised, patting his own ample stomach.

"I must go." Thomas glanced anxiously at the sun sinking low in the sky.

"Ah, of course. Well, heaven must reward you, then."

Thomas took his chance and hurried off without a backward glance.

"Hey, I don't even know your name!" the farmer shouted after him.

"Thomas Stablehand," the youth reluctantly called back over his shoulder. For the first time he discovered that he appreciated his anonymity. He little guessed how much he would miss it in the days to come.

THOMAS WOUND his way through the streets of Arnost until the walls of the castle towered above him, blotting out half the night sky. The familiar smell of horses greeted him as he pushed through some heavy wooden gates into a spacious courtyard and then into the small three-roomed stone cottage that was his home. A cheery fire crackled in the hearth. Inviting smells wafted out from the cooking pot.

His mother, Marya, a diminutive person full of nervous energy, bustled about as though she expected the king for supper. She greeted him with obvious relief. "Where have you been, Tom? I almost asked your father to call out the bloodhounds after you," she scolded. "Did you enjoy your afternoon?"

He responded with a noncommittal grunt and set to work steadily at the huge plate of steaming stew she set before him. The ups and downs of life might shatter his equanimity at times, but very little affected his appetite. His mother attempted for a while to draw him into conversation, then gave up and left him in peace.

Thomas lay awake that night unable to put the afternoon's events out of his mind. He could picture the dying animal thrashing in agony on the ground. The rabies had exacted a heavy toll and its body appeared ravaged and depleted. That explained its slow reactions. But nothing accounted for the haunting wolf-eyes, still vivid in his mind.

It was the early hours of the morning before he finally managed to get to sleep. When he did, his dreams were filled with strange fore-boding. Wild and exotic creatures paraded menacingly before him, teeth flashing. Unfamiliar men appeared, their intentions for good or ill written plainly across their faces. Most enigmatic of all was a young woman, wild eyed and fiery, and impossible to comprehend.

He woke with the dawn, and stumbled out of bed bleary eyed and disoriented.

Later that day, Thomas returned to the stables from an errand to find a scruffy lad of about fifteen years of age waiting excitedly for him. The youth, Simon, almost lived at the stables, helping out with menial tasks whenever he was allowed. Today Simon greeted him so eagerly and with such wide-eyed admiration that Thomas began to feel uncomfortable. "I wish I'd been there to see it!" Simon enthused.

"See what? What are you talking about?"

"You know! The way you saved the farmer's children. Wrestling that rabid dog to the ground. And killing it with your bare hands!" Simon illustrated his words with an energetic re-enactment of the feat, complete with grunting and scowling.

"What?! Who told you that?"

"Everybody knows about it. Even King Steffan. You're a hero!"

"That's ridiculous! I wasn't even the one who killed it."

But Simon, his face shining, was gone, no doubt to spread the story even further.

CHANCE ENCOUNTERS with acquaintances among the townsfolk the following day confirmed to Thomas his new status as a hero. He quickly discovered to his intense embarrassment that the episode was assuming almost mythical proportions. He tried to reason with them, but his protestations had the opposite effect. Modesty befits a hero, and his denials were taken as further confirmation of his worthiness.

It appeared that an account of the incident had reached the castle, too. Plans were already underway to beat the bushes. Rabies was a serious threat to the farming community, and the dog was unlikely to be the only carrier. The king intended to personally lead a sweep through the outskirts of the great forest the next weekend. All able-bodied men were expected to participate. In spite of the risk involved, excitement was building in the town, and the talk was of little else.

Fortunately, there was plenty to do about the stables to distract Thomas. Both horses and hounds were being readied for the weekend's hunt, and since King Steffan would be visiting the stables in person, the stalls had to be cleaned out thoroughly and fresh straw brought in. Memories of the encounter with the dog-wolf still baffled Thomas, but he gradually came to the conclusion that the wolf must have been a product of his imagination. As for the stone, it lay forgotten in his pouch.

———

A SMALL PAIR of eyes capped by an unkempt mess of dark hair peered hopefully over the wall surrounding the stable courtyard. Keen to avoid more questions about his heroism, Thomas tried to ignore them. But the round little eyes looked so pathetic that eventually he could bear it no longer.

He nodded at the half-face. "Hello."

The eyes brightened, and a mouth and chin bobbed into view. "Are you very busy?"

Thomas relaxed. He could guess what was coming next.

The little voice was trying not to be too eager. "Can I ride the big war-horse again?"

Thomas struggled to keep a grin from his face. He carefully chose the steadiest old nag in the stables for the little urchins to ride, but they didn't need to know that. "I guess you can."

"And my friend, too?"

"If you don't disturb the horses."

"Oh, we won't! We promise."

It wasn't really convenient, but he knew how much they loved it. "Come back just before the sun sets. My father won't be around then."

Later, Thomas waited behind the stables for his little horsemen to appear. An old gray mare, suitably saddled, stood patiently beside him. Presently two shining faces emerged over the top of the wall. He helped the boys down and hoisted them onto the horse.

Dwarfed by the mare, they bounced up and down proudly, each brandishing a wooden sword fiercely in one hand and hanging on precariously with the other.

Thomas knew the boys saw him as an adult. That felt good. And yet another part of him envied them, perched jubilantly up there in the saddle. Did you have to leave fun behind when you grew up?

THOMAS WAS WORKING with his father checking that the horses were properly shod. He sensed that his parents had noted his withdrawn mood and were watching for his reaction to the stories that were circulating.

"You're quiet today, son," his father ventured.

It was a fair understatement. Normally they conversed a little when they worked together, but the youth hadn't offered him a word all day. Thomas heard the comment but didn't respond. In spite of all that had happened since, he hadn't forgotten their interaction a few days earlier and was still smarting from it.

Axel Stablehand didn't pursue it, and Thomas was grateful.

In spite of the denial of his fondest hope, Thomas had to reluctantly admire his father. From what Thomas knew of family history, Axel, one of a long line of stable hands, had been blessed with more ability than his forebears. He was generally regarded as efficient, reliable, and hardworking. In recognition of his skills he had been appointed master of the stables when the previous incumbent died some years earlier.

Thomas knew that his father hoped and expected the position would stay in the family. But he wasn't certain he warranted the confidence this implied, and he resented the steady pressure to achieve that came with his father's expectations.

THOMAS WAS CORNERED by his mother later in the day. "What's on your mind, Thomas?" she asked. "Is it the gossip about the farmer and the rabid dog?"

He shrugged, and she eyed him knowingly. "No, I didn't think so. You're upset with your father, aren't you? Because he won't let you have a dog of your own."

He didn't respond, but he didn't need to. She knew him too well.

"Don't be angry with him," she said. "He isn't trying to be unkind."

A grunt was the best he could manage in reply.

She wasn't willing to give up that easily. "Don't forget your afternoon in the countryside. You were running an errand for him, but he was just as interested in giving you an outing. He didn't have to do that."

Thomas wasn't placated.

"He's a tough taskmaster," she said, "and he expects a lot from his workers. But you know he's always believed there should be more to life than just toil when you're young, and he hasn't forgotten that you've been hard at work for a few years already. How many other seventeen year olds have fathers who give them an afternoon off once in a while?"

He still said nothing.

She threw up her hands in disgust. "I give up. The two of you are as stubborn as each other!" And with that she was gone.

Thomas knew his mother was right. He couldn't honestly say that his father was unkind. And he had appreciated the afternoon off.

But his pleasant excursion hadn't turned out as he'd expected. Life was starting to feel complicated, and he wasn't quite sure how it had happened.

2

Threatening rain clouds dominated the sky on the morning of the hunt, but they did nothing to dampen the enthusiasm of the throng gathered outside the walls of Arnost. A constant buzz of excitement lent the event a carnival atmosphere.

A cheer went up from the gates, and all heads turned in that direction. A mounted party emerged, led by King Steffan. The cheering spread as he progressed through the crowd, acknowledging his subjects with a wave.

Overawed, Thomas stared at the king as he passed. He seemed so strong and sure of himself. Not even the simple and practical garb he wore for the hunt disguised his regal bearing. As always, he stood out from the men around him.

The king and his party moved on and the attention of the crowd turned elsewhere. Thomas stood behind his father trying to look inconspicuous.

Almost immediately one of the king's stewards approached them.

"Good morning, Master Axel," he said. "The king requests that you present your son to him."

Although Thomas understood royal protocol well enough to recognize a command when he heard it, he still waited irrationally for his father to decline graciously on his behalf. Surely it would be inappropriate to trouble the king at such a time.

"It would be a great honor," replied his father, smiling happily.

In his daydreams Thomas had been presented to the king many times. Usually it was on the battlefield as he lay victorious but seriously wounded, struck down at the last after single-handedly defending his sovereign against impossible odds. Always he spoke gravely and respectfully, modestly declining the king's repeated offers of lands and titles.

Now, in his hour of need, he found his courage deserting him unforgivably. He envied his father's quiet confidence. The master's work often brought him into contact with the king, and he could picture them as he had seen them from a distance, calmly discussing the condition of the horses or making plans for renovations to the stables.

Thomas dragged himself behind his father like a condemned man led to the gallows. When they arrived they found King Steffan occupied. The strain of waiting soon drained from the youth any traces of self-assurance that remained.

Eventually the king, mounted on his courser, noticed them and looked down with a welcoming smile. "Ah, yes. This must be our stable master's lad. I hear that you killed a rabid dog with your bare hands."

Thomas stood with his head bowed as if scolded. His father nudged him gently, and he blushed deeply. "No, Your Majesty. It was the farmer I killed," he finally blurted out. "I mean the farmer did it. Killed the dog, I mean."

A hint of a smile flickered across the king's face. "I see. No doubt you did well enough. I have arranged for you to accompany the hunt on horseback. My Lord Denison, see that the steward finds a mount for young Thomas."

The stable master swelled with pride at the honor. Coming to the aid of his son, he thanked the king on his behalf. Thomas was led away and soon found himself astride a frisky mare, feeling as if the whole crowd was staring at him.

He knew King Steffan had the best of intentions, but he felt like a fish out of water. He longed to be among the commoners where he felt secure. He took what comfort he could from his skill in handling horses: at least he wasn't going to complete his embarrassment by falling off in front of the crowd.

THE CLOUDS WERE CLEARING, and the sun had climbed high into the sky when the last of the townsmen crossed the ford. The king had appointed marshals to oversee the crossing, and they remained behind to ensure that the enthusiastic group of children from the town stayed on the other side of the river.

The mounted party and the hounds had been first to cross. They were met on the other side by a grim-looking band of farmers armed mostly with pitchforks. The townsmen carried heavy wooden clubs or crudely fashioned spears and wore thick leggings of cloth or leather to protect themselves against being bitten.

The farmer had apparently been watching for Thomas and called out eagerly to him in greeting. Once the hunt was underway, Thomas's earlier feelings of awkwardness had begun to subside. Seeing the farmer brought the discomfort flooding back again. What about the stories that were circulating? Would he think Thomas had started them? Fervently wishing he was somewhere else, Thomas waved back half-heartedly and urged his horse on.

Once they penetrated the forest, Thomas gradually worked his way to the edge of the main group. At first the going had been easy, the trees being scattered and the undergrowth sparse. But soon the trees crowded in on the riders, forcing the horses to pick their way slowly among the waist-high brush. The townsmen and farmers struggled along behind as best they could.

Paths were infrequent here, and most of them led nowhere. Few people had cause to venture further than the outskirts of the forest, and there were no signs of habitation. The riders were constantly forced to duck their heads to avoid low-hanging branches.

Thomas soon wearied of it. He headed his horse away from the others toward a section of the forest where the trees were less densely populated.

He found himself moving through a stand of tall pines toward the green expanse of a large natural clearing deep in the forest. The sunlight filtered softly through the branches high overhead, and a gentle breeze brushed at the hair dangling across his face. He loosened the reins to allow the horse to crop on the plentiful clumps of grass growing in the clearing.

A slight movement attracted his attention. He glanced up. A fox stood among the trees across the clearing eyeing him curiously. It might never have seen a human before, or a horse for that matter. Thomas's mount moved, searching for new patches of juicy green, and he lost sight of the fox.

He sat quietly, soaking in the tranquility of the scene and relishing the chance to sit upright again. The beauty that surrounded him brought to mind the attractive swirls of color that covered his new stone. He unfastened his pouch and fished his hand down in search of it. Yes, it was still there. He withdrew the stone and examined it carefully, again struck by its unusual beauty.

He was in the act of returning it to its home when something made him look up again. The fox was gone. In its place crouched a snarling wolf.

He stiffened and stared wide-eyed at the animal. Those eyes—he could have sworn they recognized him. But the wolf was dead. And yet there never was a wolf. He shook his head, trying to clear his confusion.

The silence in the clearing, which he had taken for tranquility, suddenly seemed oppressive. The usual background of forest sounds was absent, and the birds were hushed. The whole forest appeared to be holding its breath.

Bristling with menace, the wolf took a step toward him. Thomas sat transfixed in the saddle, his heart pumping wildly. The horse, sensing his tension, lifted its head from the grass and shifted uncomfortably. The wolf moved closer. Thomas wanted to call out for help, flee, do anything. But he could only sit rigid, his breath coming in gasps.

As if it were reading his mind, his horse spun around and bolted for the forest. Thomas, too slow to regain his wits, connected heavily with the first branch the horse passed under. Still clutching the stone tightly in his left hand, he fell senseless to the ground.

He woke to find someone bending over him. An unfamiliar face, that of a young knight, swam unsteadily into focus. Thomas tried to lift his head and groaned. An unseen drummer pounded a relentless staccato in his skull. The knight looked at him with concern in his eyes. "Better lie still for a while," he said. "That's a nasty bump on your forehead."

"I'm all right," Thomas replied, trying to sit up. He almost swooned with the attempt, shafts of pain shooting up his left arm. "My arm!" he sobbed.

The knight leaned closer. "I think you've broken it," he said, probing the arm gently. "What's that in your hand?" he asked with sudden interest. Thomas, uncomprehending, made no reply. He gasped in protest when the knight moved his hand, working the stone from his grasp.

Thomas was totally unprepared for what followed. As the stone left his hand, the knight was transformed into a very ordinary looking man-at-arms. He must have been in his early twenties, with a shock of red hair protruding from beneath his small iron helmet. The young man held the stone up and gave a low whistle. "Very pretty," he said admiringly. "What is it?"

Seeing the stone in another's hand brought a sudden rush of energy to Thomas. "It's mine!" he exclaimed in anger. "Give it back!"

"No harm intended," replied the young man defensively. "I'll put it in your pouch," he volunteered, moving toward Thomas's unin-jured side.

"Make sure it's tied properly," snapped Thomas.

The soldier obligingly put it in the pouch and tied it very firmly, carefully avoiding the bad arm.

"What is it?" he repeated.

"A good-luck charm. A family heirloom," replied Thomas testily, surprising himself with the lie.

The soldier snorted ironically. "You can keep it!" he said with feeling, looking down at Thomas spread out helpless on the ground. He patted his sword. "This is the only good luck charm I'm prepared to trust."

Thomas groaned again and closed his eyes. The exchange had exhausted him and pain once again engulfed his senses. A dull ache had started in his arm, competing with the drummer for attention. Tears of self-pity welled in his eyes. How did he get himself into this mess?

Belatedly, he remembered the wolf coming for him. "What happened to the wolf?" he asked weakly.

The young soldier stood up and moved to his horse. "If you mean the fox," he replied, "I killed it. You appear to have an attraction for rabid animals," he added dryly.

Thomas frowned. Dogs which were wolves which were dogs. Knights who were ordinary men-at-arms. Wolves which were foxes. Was he going mad? A sudden fear pushed its way through his pain. Did he have rabies himself? Had he been bitten by the dog after all?

The young man noticed his agitation. "You needn't worry," he said, as though reading Thomas's thoughts. "I killed the fox before it got to you. Your horse alerted me. It came crashing through the trees and almost collided with my own horse. I decided to find out what spooked it and what had become of its rider. The fox found out what lances are used for," he concluded with satisfaction.

"I'm going to get help." He swung himself into the saddle and leaned forward, speaking softly to his mount. They moved off toward the trees.

"I won't be long. Keep your chin up," the soldier called back as he disappeared into the forest.

. . .

THE REST of the day was a nightmare Thomas hoped he would quickly forget. Olaf, captain of the King's Guard, was among the first to reach him. The captain decided Thomas's arm needed immediate attention. Ordering two of his men to hold Thomas down, he quickly reset the arm, immobilizing it with a splint made of hastily cut branches.

The fact that Thomas vociferously disapproved of the operation seemed to worry him not a whit. He wore the air of a man who had dealt with far worse. And Thomas, who felt roughly handled, received little sympathy. All who examined his arm remarked on how grateful he must be feeling toward the old captain for the fine job he had done.

They carried Thomas out of the forest on a crudely built stretcher. The going proved very difficult, and his bearers tipped him out twice before reaching open ground. It was late at night before he finally sank onto his bed in his own home, utterly weary and miserable beyond words.

THE AFTERNOON after the hunt Thomas's mother bustled into his room announcing a visitor. Thomas, moody and still in pain, was not inclined to be welcoming. To his surprise the young soldier appeared grinning in the doorway.

"May I come in?"

"Yes, of course. I...I'm Thomas," he replied awkwardly.

"I know. My name is William Prentis, but everyone calls me Will."

There was something infectious about his cheerfulness, and Thomas's spirits began to lift. "I never thanked you for rescuing me," he said.

"No need. Actually, I should thank you."

"Why?" asked Thomas, incredulous.

"Well, it's hard for a soldier to be noticed these days. There hasn't even been a decent border skirmish for years," Will said with disgust.

"Thanks to your escapade with the fox I managed to catch the attention of Captain Olaf."

Thomas grimaced at the mention of the old captain. "He's the one who nearly ripped my arm off!"

Will chuckled. "I guess it must have hurt. But you were in capable hands. The captain may not be gentle, but he's very experienced. I'd trust him to set my arm ahead of any of Arnost's so-called doctors.

"He's appointed me to the King's Guard." Will indicated the falcon crest, the royal insignia, on his new vest. "One day I'm going to be the captain."

The claim did not seem idle or boastful. Will's words were matter-of-fact. Seeing the intensity in the young soldier's eyes, Thomas believed it. He momentarily remembered his first impression of Will, that of a young knight, strong and self-assured, and found himself thinking that one day this man would make a fearsome enemy.

"My guess is we've seen the last of rabies for a while," Will ventured.

"Were any other rabid animals found?"

"No, only the two you came across. You seem to have a knack for finding them! How do you do it?"

Thomas blushed a little. "I don't know. I don't understand it myself."

Will stood up. "I must go. I have my first duty with the Guard soon. I'll come and visit again when I can."

With that he was gone.

DURING HIS CONVALESCENCE Thomas began to realize that the stone had something to do with his changes in perception. The realization first came to him in a thunderstorm.

A couple of days after the visit of Will Prentis, a storm rolled in from the west, and booming thunderclaps were soon spooking the horses. The night was pitch black; clouds blotted out the sky and neither the stars nor the moon were visible. Thomas was groping his way toward the stables when a huge sheet of lightning lit up the sky.

For a brief moment, every detail around him was plainly revealed to his sight. Then the lightning was gone, and his vision again went dark.

He remembered the image of the young knight, instantly replaced by the ordinary face of a young soldier. The transformation had occurred when the stone had been pulled from his hand. Could the stone have changed his vision, just as the lightning had done?

The stone lay securely in his pouch. That much he could tell with his right hand. Further investigation was impossible until his left arm became mobile again: Will had tied the pouch too tightly to undo it with one hand.

But how could a stone change what he saw? And where could such a talisman have come from?

A priest might know of such things. Thomas wondered uneasily, though, whether the church might regard it as black magic. He didn't like to think where that might lead.

No, he would keep it to himself for the moment. Only Will knew of its existence, and he seemed unaware of its significance. Indeed, although the two of them saw each other frequently in the weeks that followed the hunt, neither ever referred to it.

ONE MORE SURPRISE lay in store. A few days later his father, looking uncomfortable, came to his room. "Come outside, Thomas. There's something there for you."

Thomas followed him into the courtyard to find a small wicker basket on the cobblestones. Inside he saw a dark brown bundle of fur and an eager little face turned to him. He stared in disbelief.

"It's for you," repeated his father. Thomas, blinking back tears, turned to him, incapable of speech. "He'll be hungry. You'd better find him some milk," his father offered gruffly and moved off quickly toward the stables.

Thomas reached out his good arm to the puppy. The little mastiff whelp, probably no more than seven or eight weeks old, licked his hand, wagging its tiny tail frantically.

Overcome by a surge of joy, Thomas glanced up at his father's retreating form. Maybe his father cared about him after all. For as long as he could remember, his father had been quick to correct and rebuke, and slow to praise. He could not remember his father ever saying he was proud of him or pleased with him. He had certainly never expressed affection. He always felt a disappointment to his father, never able to measure up to the high standards a man had a right to expect of his only son.

In any event, being an invalid had its compensations: a broken arm and a lump on the head had achieved more in a few days than years of argument and pleading.

He smiled down at the puppy, which had curled itself into a little ball and closed its eyes. "Hello, Ben," he said quietly. "We're going to be good friends."

3

Having come off duty with time on his hands, Will decided to visit Thomas. The young stable hand might be unassuming, but the guardsman had quickly discovered that his new friend had some unexpected skills.

Will arrived in time to witness a vigorous assault by Thomas's mother on a broad expanse of dangling spiderwebs that had dared to appear above her doorway.

"Hello, Will." Marya beamed him a welcoming smile. "Thomas will be pleased to see you."

She grounded her broom. "It's nice that you've been taking such an interest in him. He's never had a chance to get to know any soldiers before."

"It's their loss, then," Will exclaimed. "Did you know he can mount a moving horse bareback, even with only one good arm?" He shook his head in wonder.

Her eyes went wide for a moment. Then a resigned look appeared on her face. "It doesn't surprise me," she said with a sigh. "He's always been good with horses."

"Where is he now?"

"At the stables. With the horses, of course." She rolled her eyes.

Will thanked her and headed toward the cluster of barns and stables that lay behind the house.

As he neared his destination, his attention was drawn to a small stockaded enclosure adjacent to the stables. A large bay stallion was screaming shrilly, rearing and flailing about with its forelegs. As Will watched, the middle-aged man hanging on grimly to its halter dropped the rope and fled the enclosure in terror. He escaped unscathed, but only barely.

Thomas emerged from a barn, and a disconcerted look appeared on his face as he took in the scene.

Curious to see what his friend might do, Will stepped quietly back out of sight.

Ignoring the man, Thomas slipped between the railings and entered the enclosure. The stallion neighed and watched him wide-eyed, its ears pinned back. Thomas approached the horse slowly, speaking to it soothingly until it gradually settled and allowed him to approach. He held up a small carrot and the horse nickered, peeling back its lips and accepting the treat.

The man looked on nervously. "Be careful!" he warned Thomas. "That animal just attacked me." He appeared thoroughly downcast. "I've never had a horse before. I was hoping to take this one back to the farm today, but it's completely unpredictable! Sometimes it lets me approach it, just like it did with you then. Other times it's totally wild."

He shook his head in dismay. "The animal is dangerous! I should never have let your father talk me into buying it."

"It's only dangerous because it's terrified," Thomas told him bluntly.

"What do you mean?"

"Which direction did you approach the horse from?"

"From behind, of course. If it sees me coming, there's no telling what it might do."

"And how are you planning to handle it when the horse behaves like it did earlier?"

"I yell at my children when they misbehave, and I'm not going to treat a horse any differently. I'd take a stick to it if it wasn't so savage."

Thomas shook his head. "You're doing everything wrong. It's not wild, and it's not unpredictable. It's scared. You're teaching it to be scared."

Thomas left the horse and returned to the railing. "Can I explain it to you?" he asked.

The older man looked uncertain, but he nodded slowly.

"Don't approach a horse from any of its blind spots," Thomas told him patiently. "If it can see what you're doing, it won't be so anxious. And you should never get angry with it. That will only scare it even more. You'll lose any trust you've built."

He paused, and peered at the man. Apparently satisfied that his words were being understood, Thomas beckoned to him. "Come with me, and I'll show you."

The man hesitated for a long moment, but then he took a deep breath and stepped back into the enclosure.

"Here," said Thomas. "You'll need this." He handed the man another small carrot. "Now, follow me."

The man trailed behind cautiously as Thomas once again advanced to the horse. Seeing their approach, the horse became restless again. Thomas spoke to it soothingly, motioning with his good hand for his companion to move more slowly.

When the man reached the horse, he tentatively offered it the carrot. He was even able to pat its neck. He still looked nervous but seemed much happier.

"Stay with it for a while," Thomas suggested. "Talk to it, but make sure you keep your voice calm and quiet. You can come back tomorrow and do the same thing. Let the horse get used to you."

Thomas turned to go, and the man thanked him gratefully.

After Thomas had left the enclosure behind, Will stepped forward and joined him. "That was nicely done, Thomas," he said with a smile. "You were kinder to the fellow than he deserved."

"I wasn't doing it for his sake," Thomas replied. "I was thinking of the horse."

Will grinned. "Either way, you did a good job." He pointed to the enclosure. "The two of them seem to be getting along like old friends."

Thomas shrugged. "I know what to do with horses. It's people I have trouble figuring out."

That drew a chuckle from Will. "How's your arm?" he asked.

"It's still sore." Thomas looked at him sheepishly. "Jumping onto moving horses doesn't seem to help it heal for some reason."

Will laughed. "We need to take your mind off it. Your mother's an outstanding cook—let's go see what we can wheedle out of her."

"I won't be seeing you for a while, Thomas. We move out in two days."

Will looked grave, but Thomas knew his friend had been longing for this. The whole of Arnost buzzed with excitement, and Thomas was caught up in it, too. "I heard some people arrived in wagons last night. Who were they? Many of them were wounded."

"Survivors from Danlenet. That's a small town near the Rogandan border. They say the whole border region is in turmoil. It was bad enough when the nomad tribes were plundering the outlying farms, but the attack on Danlenet must have been very well planned. The town was defended, but the townsmen never stood a chance."

Will lowered his voice. "One of the guardsmen overheard the captain talking to the king. They're wondering if King Agon of Rogand is behind this. King Steffan wants to find out what's going on. And he's going to teach the nomads a lesson they won't forget," he added with satisfaction.

Thomas gazed admiringly at Will. He looked every inch a soldier. "Will you be wearing armor into battle?"

"Me? Not yet." Will laughed. "The captain is the only guardsman with armor, and that's just a chain-mail shirt. Only the nobles and knights wear armor. It's too expensive.

"The King's Guardsmen are issued with thick buff leather jackets.

They'll protect against a sword cut, and they're much lighter and more flexible than armor. And we do have shields and helmets."

"I wish my arm was healed properly. I could come with you!"

Will looked startled. "You? You're a bit young. Besides, you'll never make a soldier; you're too gentle." Thomas, cut to the quick, felt his cheeks flame, but the young guardsman seemed not to notice. "And you're needed here. The King's Guard would be helpless without good horses, and you have a way with them."

The conversation sputtered on, but Thomas was far away. Long after Will had left he was still thinking up injured retorts to his friend's assertions. *Of course I can't fight! That's men's work. I'm needed to shovel manure.*

So that's all I'm good for. Well, they needn't think I'll be there to cheer them off when they leave. I'll be far too busy doing important work: mucking out the stables.

That night Thomas lay in bed tossing fitfully. He had no great ambition to be a soldier; for him the idea of battlefield glory was little more than an idle daydream. Nevertheless, he knew that few able-bodied males made it through life without being called upon, sooner or later, to defend the interests of king and country. Now, the only soldier he could call his friend—a soldier marked for greatness in the vision from the stone—had summarily dismissed him as unsuitable. He could still hear Will's words: "You'll never make a soldier; you're too gentle."

Grimly he vowed to himself that people would begin to see a new Thomas.

THOMAS PICKED at his evening meal, bone weary from the long hours of work. His arm, still not healed, had proven a frustrating restriction, and now it was throbbing painfully.

"Tarkess was still feisty when I left the stables," his father said.

At the mention of the war-horse, Thomas felt the blood drain from his face. A tight fist began to clench inside his stomach.

"Did the blacksmith have trouble with him?"

Thomas didn't answer.

"Well?" his father repeated, glancing up sharply.

Things deteriorated quickly after that. "You did take him to the blacksmith, didn't you?"

Again Thomas didn't answer.

"Do you have a tongue in your head? Answer me, boy!" his father raged.

"I started to take him, but he wouldn't settle down. You know what it was like in the stables. The horses can tell when something's about to happen, and a lot of them were restless. I couldn't manage him with only one arm."

"Did it occur to you to ask for help?"

"No one else was available."

"And so you forgot. One day, Thomas, you'll stretch me to my limit!"

Thomas squirmed uncomfortably, stung by the harshness of his father's reaction. He had worked as hard as anyone. His father had no idea how much his arm had ached all day.

The stable master pushed himself up from the table.

"Where are you going?" Thomas's mother asked anxiously.

"To get the blacksmith out of bed, Marya, where else? The king's destrier needs to be reshod, and I gave the job to your son. Only he forgot. I'm sure the blacksmith must be longing to reheat his forge." The sarcasm in his voice made Thomas cringe. "And who's going to pump the bellows?" The look he fired at Thomas felt like a physical blow.

"I'll do it!" he replied desperately.

"Do what, blow into it? Or wave your splint at it?"

With that, his father left. And with him went any opportunity for Thomas to make amends for his mistake. But it was no use anyway. His father was right—with one arm he was useless.

His father would pump the bellows himself, of course. The blacksmith's apprentice lived away on a farm somewhere; calling him was out of the question.

He longed to wait up for his father, to have some normal contact with him, even to apologize. But he went to bed. His mind was still churning restlessly when his father returned hours later, and dawn was lightening the sky before Thomas finally managed to get to sleep.

SWINGING his pitchfork ferociously with one arm, Thomas laid waste a pile of hay as the soldiers set out for the border.

The stable had been the scene of frenetic activity during the previous forty-eight hours as the stable hands prepared the horses for an extended period in the field. Now the stables were almost empty.

Ben lay quietly to one side, his little head resting on his paws and his eyes fixed on his master. No one else was anywhere in sight. Thomas might have been the only person in the whole of Arnost not at the muster.

His heart lay with the townsfolk cheering them off. But he had worked himself into a mood that reopened the wounds of his conversation with Will.

Thomas settled into a half-hearted rhythm, trying to persuade himself that his labors were essential.

Eventually he was joined by Simon. "Wasn't that amazing?" the younger boy gushed. "There were so many soldiers. Someone said there were five thousand!"

Thomas snorted derisively. "Five thousand? I hope they're in no hurry, then. Each horse will have to carry ten soldiers."

Simon was unabashed. "And did you see the king? His destrier was prancing around like it was standing on hot coals!"

Thomas grunted, his eyes narrowing. Obviously nothing had changed since the previous day, then.

"And did you see the way old Olaf's wife was carrying on?" Simon still babbled on excitedly. "Anyone would think it was his funeral. They say it'll be his last campaign."

Embittered by his thoughts, Thomas began to find Simon's chatter unbearable. "Simon, go away!"

Simon looked startled. "Why?"

"Because I have work to do."

"That's all right, I'll help you."

Thomas could see the eagerness in Simon's eyes. He knew how much the younger boy admired him. But then he pictured himself with Will and thought of the bitter medicine served him by his own hero. Maybe Simon needed some of it, too. It was about time he was toughened up to the harsh realities of life.

"Look, Simon," he said with exaggerated kindness. "A boy like you is just in the way around here. And anyway, you simply aren't cut out for this kind of work."

Even as the words left his lips he regretted them. He could see the hurt and bewilderment on Simon's face. But it was too late to turn back now. "You haven't got what it takes to be successful around animals. You're too...too scatterbrained."

His barb found its mark. Simon stared wide-eyed at him in disbelief, then turned and fled, his eyes flooding with tears.

Having attained his objective, Thomas found it brought him no pleasure at all. He tried to adopt an air of detached superiority. *Children*, he told himself. *They're so immature. Why do they have to take it so personally?* But it didn't help. He felt more wretched as time went on.

He was so lost in his thoughts he didn't hear his father approach. "Thomas, where have you been?"

He turned without answering.

"Your friend Will Prentis looked for you everywhere. He wanted you to take care of this for him."

His father held out a small necklace. Thomas stared at it stupidly. "Take it!" his father insisted.

Thomas took the necklace and examined it. He recognized it at once. It was Will's most treasured possession. It consisted of an ordinary-looking chain of fine but tough metal, securing a small ring of gold. Will had told him the ring was his only memento of his parents, both of whom had died when he was a small child.

"He asked me to tell you that if anything happened to him, he wanted you to have it." Thomas's father turned on his heel and left him to his musing.

He slipped the chain over his head numbly. An hour earlier he would have received it as a portent of hope, an unlooked-for affirmation of his value in Will's eyes. Now it hung heavy around his neck with accusation.

He headed off across the courtyard, kicking irritably at the loose cobblestones that lay in his path. The church bells in the town below began to clang their monotonous refrain, marking the departure of the king and speeding him on his way with the blessings of the church, such as they were, to encourage and comfort him. Thomas decided that if there was a God in heaven who ever deigned to notice him at all, it was probably only with contempt.

He was intercepted in his progress by an energetic ball of fur, tumbling enthusiastically about his feet. He reached down and gathered up the wriggling bundle, holding it to his breast. "Ben," he said unhappily, "you're my only friend in the world."

4

Steffan the Second, High King of Arvenon and until-now unchallenged overlord of the extensive kingdom won by his namesake five generations earlier, galloped over the crest of the hill, reined in his destrier, and called down a bitter curse upon his as yet unseen enemies. Will, riding behind the king in the vanguard of the troop, guided his horse alongside and angrily surveyed the devastation below them. Along the far bank of a small river were the charred remains of a village, still smoking.

Will already knew what they would find down there. They had seen it too many times in the weeks of frustration that lay behind them. Every living creature would have been slaughtered and many of the bodies horribly mutilated. Anything of value would be gone and the rest put to the torch. Yesterday a glance beyond the river would have revealed a golden sea of waving corn, almost ready for harvest. Today ash and blackened stubble choked the fields.

Following the lead of the king, the soldiers dismounted and rested their horses at the top of the hill. The need for urgency was past, and none of them showed any eagerness to explore the waste-land awaiting them.

Scouts were sent to examine the approaches to the village before the troop's horses confused the evidence. Will watched them go dispassionately. Nothing he had seen so far suggested their efforts would lead to anything useful.

Even attempts to determine the size of the raiding parties had been largely unsuccessful. There were few clues as to their numbers or identity. It seemed they were not only ruthless but well-disciplined. And so the rage and frustration had grown in Will and his friends until they were barely able to keep their anger in check. If ever they managed to draw their foes into open battle it promised to be bitter and furious.

They were not without eyewitnesses, though. Incredibly, there were often survivors, people away from the villages when the attacks began or a lucky few who somehow concealed themselves. But the survivors offered few insights. Naturally, their reports were exaggerated—horsemen everywhere, invincible and unstoppable, crushing all resistance with contemptuous ease. Depending on the witness, there were hundreds or even thousands of them.

All were agreed on one point, though: the raiders were plains nomads.

And yet it didn't make sense. Will had grown up in the southern border region and knew something of the nomad clans. The nomads proved ferocious enemies, to be sure, but somehow these raids seemed out of character with their peculiar code of courage. Surprise attacks, yes, but these continual furtive raids against almost defenseless villages?

Will expected the nomads would view such behavior as cowardly. Long before now they ought to have been demonstrating their prowess openly in battle. No, something didn't add up.

The scouts returned and reported to the king, and the soldiers were ordered to remount. They headed down the hill, forded the river and began to pick their way through the ruins.

The wattle and daub dwellings of the peasants had been almost totally destroyed. Sections of the manor house and church remained standing, having been solidly built of stone. In time, they could be rebuilt; except that the region was being steadily depopulated. Depopulated. Might that be the nomads' intention? And if so, why?

An urgent call from away to Will's left interrupted his thoughts. Along with a number of others, including the king, he headed in that direction.

One of the soldiers had discovered a small boy, perhaps four or five years of age, huddled in the remains of a building. The lad clutched something tightly to his chest.

He didn't seem frightened by them; he was quite unresponsive. Will thought him an appealing child, with his fair curls hanging softly about his head. He was plainly but adequately clothed, although his trousers were now filthy and his little jacket scorched. He had probably been his mother's pride and joy.

Then Will caught a glimpse of his eyes and shuddered. They stared vacantly, fixed on nothing. It was as though the boy had departed but somehow his body lived on. Will decided not to think about what he must have witnessed.

A friend of Will's from the King's Guard named Rufe Sarjant dismounted and approached the boy with a gentleness that belied his fierce demeanor. The giant guardsman spoke to him quietly, offering him food and drink from his saddlebags.

Although his efforts bore no immediate fruit, he was not deterred. He persisted patiently, attempting to coax a response from the lad. Will watched tensely, compelled by his friend's refusal to accept defeat. He longed for even a symbolic victory over their elusive foes.

After what seemed an age the boy began to stir as though waking from a dream. He looked about him, his interest slowly dawning. Will's spirits soared. Audible sighs escaped from others of the onlookers.

The boy searched the face of the soldier, his eyes coming to life. Apparently not finding whatever or whoever he was looking for, he shifted his quest to the faces around him.

But the awakening proved short lived. Slowly the light died from the boy's eyes. His face again became blank and lifeless. His spirit seemed to have retreated to some distant inner sanctuary, and he gave no further response.

Rufe, his face betraying his disappointment, picked the lad up and seated him on his horse. The motion knocked from the boy's grasp the object he had clasped so tightly. As it tumbled to the ground Will caught a glimpse of a small horse, delicately fashioned from wood. The force of the impact snapped off its head.

On losing the toy, the boy let out a haunting wail that sent a shiver up Will's spine. Rufe quickly retrieved the pieces. He returned them to the boy, who clutched them protectively and fell silent again, resuming his vacant stare.

Something snapped in the guardsman. "Why are we here, poking around in burned-out villages?" he asked loudly, trembling with anger. "We should be doing some burning and pillaging ourselves— out on the plains! It's time the nomads were taught a lesson." His stirring words drew grunts of assent from many of the soldiers.

Will shot an anxious glance toward the sovereign, who sat astride his horse nearby. It was immediately obvious to him that the king had heard Rufe's comments. Will was even close enough to catch a murmured response: "Yes, I think they're expecting us to do that."

He frowned, puzzled. What did the king mean?

King Steffan faced the soldier imperiously. "It's not your job to determine our strategy," he said sharply.

Rufe subsided immediately, a flush of embarrassment covering his face. He bowed his head in shame.

The king stood up in his stirrups and addressed his troops loudly. "I understand your frustration, men. Indeed, I share it. But hasty plans bring disaster more often than success.

"There will be a Council of War tonight. We will drag these barbarians into the open, I promise you. Then we will test their courage against soldiers instead of women and children!"

The king's ringing words were met with a few half-hearted cheers, but mostly silence. Will sensed that some kind of crossroads had been reached. The sullen looks worn openly by many of the men presaged trouble if something decisive didn't happen soon.

THE TROOP RODE WEARILY through the gates of Danford. Will rode alongside Rufe. The boy from the village was perched securely in front of his friend in the saddle. The lad, surrounded by the new sights and sounds of a large and prosperous town, stared impassively straight ahead.

"Look at 'em," Rufe tilted his head toward a group of townsfolk who eyed the soldiers disapprovingly. "We were conquering heroes when we first got here."

It was true. They had arrived to universal acclamation. With the marauders growing daily in boldness, trade had begun to slump disastrously.

"Yes," Will responded, "they expected a quick and easy victory."

At first the good citizens of Danford proved very willing to suffer the expense and inconvenience of billeting and feeding the soldiers. Now, nearly three months later, with no easy victories and not even a fight worth speaking of, the townsfolk showed signs of impatience. There was plenty of grumbling, although no open hostility. Not yet. But the mood of their hosts affected the soldiers' morale.

"I wonder which of this fine lot will care for our little friend here?" Rufe aimed a disparaging glance at the townspeople.

Will raised his eyebrows. "You're hopeful, aren't you?"

"Well, they'll have to. I can't look after him."

It touched on another sore point. The townsfolk were becoming alarmed at the steady trickle of refugees that threatened to become a flood if the raiding continued.

Danford was large, well-situated on the banks of the Dan, and protected by a centuries-old stone wall that encircled the entire town. It sat astride the main trading routes through the Blue Mountains to Rogand in the east, and south across the vast expanse of the Plains to distant Lestanor.

Danford had prospered in recent years. But these were uncertain times, and the wealthy rarely slept easily without the comfort of thick walls and well armed soldiers to guard them. Will guessed they would put up with the soldiers for a little while longer.

WILL STRODE through the darkening streets of the town heading for the Council of War. Receiving a summons had taken him completely by surprise, and he was working hard at suppressing his excitement.

He arrived to find the king already conferring with Captain Olaf and the captain of the cavalry reserves levied by the town authorities. Two of the king's knights arrived at the same time. One of them smiled welcomingly at Will and beckoned him over to a seat beside him. "Don't be nervous," he whispered sympathetically. "The king is not at all frightening to talk to."

Will nodded, hoping he appeared suitably overawed. What the knight couldn't know, though, was that the prospect of the evening filled him with eager anticipation.

"Let's get straight to the point," King Steffan began. "We will be talking tonight about a major change of strategy. I have invited one of our men to join us briefly." He acknowledged Will with a nod. "I understand he has considerable knowledge of both the nomad tribes and the Rogandans."

Will dipped his head respectfully in response. So that was it. Clearly the king kept his ear to the ground. He wondered how he had learned of his background.

"You have lived among the nomads and speak their tongue, I'm told."

"Not exactly, Your Majesty. After my parents died my uncle adopted me. He was a trader and we traveled across the Great Plains many times. Sometimes we stayed with the nomads. Communicating with them isn't easy: the clans speak many dialects, and some of them amount to totally different languages."

"Tell us something of these nomads. Can you give us any insight into them?"

Will's mind whirled. How could he capture in a few words the spirit of these remarkable people? Even here, in a cold room dimly lit by candles and the glow from the hearth, he could summon a picture of the sun beating down on the endless grassland, and the nomads, wild and free, galloping after the vast gianhi herds. He remembered sharing the jubilation of a kill with the hunters. And the wind blowing the dark tresses of a certain lithe nomad maiden...

He checked himself. "They are fierce, proud people, but generous, too, and bound by complex codes of honor. Raiding is not foreign to them—they're very practiced at it. They treat it as a game. Or maybe more a battle of wits.

"But this raiding seems different. I don't believe they would lightly begin hostilities on this scale; not without good cause."

The king pondered Will's words before responding. "The raiding is so...so systematic. And so far from their own territory. I've never heard of the nomads behaving this way before. Can you make any sense of it?"

Will frowned. "It's strange, Your Majesty. For one thing, the raiding parties must be reasonably large, possibly as many as a hundred men. Yet most of the clans are small. Very few could put fifty warriors into the field. And they rarely unite except in times of great peril. Or perhaps great opportunity..." He trailed off and became thoughtful.

The king's eyes narrowed. "What of Rogand? Do the nomads have dealings with the Rogandans?"

"Only with traders, Your Majesty. My uncle married a Rogandan, and the nomads treated her no differently from us. They see all of us as barbarians." His remark was greeted with snorts of incredulity.

The king waited for silence again. "And your aunt taught you to speak Rogandan?"

"Yes."

"You speak it fluently?"

"Yes, Your Majesty." Will had learned to be fluent, and the lesson had been bitter indeed. Never would he forget his aunt's hand reaching with malicious delight for the willow switch when he stumbled over his grammar, nor her mocking imitations of his accent.

King Steffan smiled at Will. "You have been very helpful. We may have need of your services again." And with that Will was dismissed.

Keenly disappointed, he headed back to his barracks. He'd hoped for much more. He couldn't even see he'd been of much use. Yet the king seemed satisfied.

It was a start. Three months in the field had not lessened his ambitions a whit. He felt brim-full of life and energy: young, strong, capable, and eager to demonstrate it.

One day his opportunity would arrive. He would grasp it with both hands.

WILL STOOD DESPONDENTLY among some trees on a hillside overlooking a small hamlet. He was beginning to wish he'd kept his mouth shut.

The morning after the Council of War King Steffan had called for volunteers. When it was made clear it would be a crucial and dangerous assignment, Will wasted no time in responding.

The king intended to split his force into three and station them strategically around the countryside. The King's Guard, the elite soldiers of the force, were to be split evenly among the three. Two volunteers would be sent to each major village and hamlet. At the first hint of trouble, they would race to the nearest soldiers and guide them back by the fastest route. Maybe, just maybe, they would get there before the raiders had left.

Will approved of the plan. He hoped it would offer him the chance to do something significant, and he sought out his assigned location eagerly.

That was a week ago. Now, watching the sun set lazily behind the treetops, he felt sure any exploits would be done a long way from this tranquil spot. He decided ruefully that staying with one of the main forces would have increased his chances of seeing action.

The temperature dropped quickly once the sun set. There was no cloud cover, and a full moon provided remarkably good visibility.

The dull clang of the church bell sounded across the valley, directing the villagers to their beds. In the half light Will could just see wisps of smoke coming from the chimneys of the cottages below. The villagers would be banking up their fires before settling down for the evening. It promised to be a cold and cheerless night up on the hill.

His partner, a wiry soldier named Garth, was nowhere in sight. A taciturn fellow, he obviously preferred his own company. They had agreed to take turns patrolling the main approaches to the hamlet. Garth had taken the first shift. If an enemy approached it should give them a little extra warning. If not, it might help them battle the boredom and the cold. Later they would keep alternate watches throughout the night.

Will suddenly thought of Thomas. It had been disappointing to leave without saying goodbye, and he wondered why Thomas had not been there to see him off. He reflected somewhat abstractedly that he had scarcely thought of his friend in the intervening weeks. He tried briefly to imagine life back in Arnost, but the pervasive chill pulled him relentlessly back to his dismal hillside. Hoping to prevent his feet from turning completely numb, he stamped them slowly and wriggled his toes inside his boots.

A movement away to his left stirred his alertness. Garth must be returning for some reason. Nevertheless he drew his horse further into the shadow of the trees and waited quietly, all his senses alert. A horseman moved quickly and silently in his direction.

As he drew closer, Will recognized the lean figure of his partner outlined in the moonlight, crouched forward slightly over his distinctive black roan. Will relaxed and moved into the open to be more easily seen.

When Garth spotted him, he spurred his horse on urgently. As he approached Will could see the tension in his face. "Horsemen!" he hissed frantically, "Scores of them! Massing on the spur behind us."

Will leaped into the saddle. "Get going! I'll try to warn the villagers, then follow you."

Neither waited for further discussion. Will raced headlong down the hill. He glanced back over his shoulder once, but Garth was already out of sight.

The king had made it clear that they should not attempt to defend the villagers—their role was to fetch the soldiers. But nothing had been said against warning the unprotected inhabitants, and Will meant to try.

Galloping into the village, he drew his sword and banged the flat of it hard against a large iron tub lying against one of the cottages. The noise was deafening in the quietness. Almost at once, cottage doors began to open.

"Fly! Enemies are upon you!" he bellowed, then spurred his horse through the village and up a slope into a stand of trees beyond. His route now lay back through the village unless he made a wide detour to skirt it. He decided to wait a few minutes, then slip through the village in the confusion.

Looking toward the hill opposite he saw dark figures, some carrying torches, moving swiftly toward the village. There were so many of them! He quickly tried to estimate their numbers—six score at least.

He looked down at the village again. The villagers were moving too slowly. A few hurried along the stream toward the edge of the woods, and a couple had escaped on horseback. But many of them still bustled about organizing children or possessions.

"Hurry, you fools!" he groaned in exasperation.

The first of the horsemen reached the village. At once flames sprang up from the thatch on the nearest houses. He saw one or two brave villagers confront the invaders. They were quickly over-whelmed.

Fires flared everywhere now. He watched in silent horror as a chilling drama unfolded below him, illuminated by the light of the spreading flames. The slaughter being visited on the villagers so appalled Will that his stomach began to churn. He bent forward over his horse and retched violently. Then a cold fury rose slowly within him, pushing from his mind his mission and his responsibility.

A heavily pregnant woman struggled up the hill toward him,

desperately trying to reach the safety of the trees. Before Will could move to help her, a nomad rode her down, decapitating her with one fell blow of his ax.

With a wild cry Will broke from his cover and swept down upon the raider. Startled, the man tried to defend himself. But Will hacked at him so violently he was forced from the saddle, bleeding freely from multiple wounds. Will leaped from his horse and fell upon him in a frenzy, venting all his pent-up rage over the ruined villages and wasted lives.

When he came to his senses, he looked around and saw that the raiders, their work completed, were withdrawing from the village. Heedless of his own safety he mounted his horse and charged after them, a fierce battle cry on his lips. But the roar of the flames drowned him out, and his approach went unnoticed. Riding up behind one of the last nomads left in the village he dispatched him with a mighty thrust and looked around for another.

Then abruptly he hesitated. Having slaked his immediate thirst for vengeance, his wrath began to abate, and his mind again became clear. Realizing with a start how close he had come to throwing his life away, he broke into a cold sweat.

There was little time to ponder his next move. It was clear now that King Steffan's new plan was doomed. Garth had not yet been gone an hour; the nomads would be far away before he even reached the nearest troopers.

Will rapidly weighed his options. They were few indeed, but one of them stood out with awful clarity. Destiny beckoned. Calmly and without hesitation he chose the path of peril.

Jumping from the saddle, he quickly stripped from the slain nomad his gianhi-skin cloak and rawhide leggings. After placing them over his own clothes, he jammed the grotesque horned helmet tightly onto his head. He looked up just in time to see the last of the nomads disappearing over the crest of the hill. Remounting his horse, he thundered off after them into the darkness.

5

Thomas flexed his arm and grimaced as the atrophied muscles contracted painfully. It was good to be free of the splint at last, though, and everything appeared to be functioning normally. The silky voice of Medlen, the town's senior doctor, flowed smoothly on behind him. Thomas turned to observe him with some distaste.

"Hmm. Yes." The doctor was nodding sagely. "I, too, greatly regret the inconvenience of the long recovery period, Ma'am." He bowed deferentially to Thomas's mother, who seemed flustered in his presence as always. "Had the injury been treated properly from the beginning..."

This theme had become boringly predictable over the course of Medlen's visits. Captain Olaf not being there to defend himself, the doctor seemed determined to squeeze the last drop from the old campaigner's supposed mishandling of the fracture. "...But I dare to hope that my careful treatment since will have proven efficacious." He lowered his eyes humbly.

Catching a glance from his mother, Thomas rolled his eyes heavenward and shook his head hopelessly. His mother, horrified, darted an anxious look toward the doctor and fixed Thomas with a threatening frown. The doctor appeared not to have noticed. Smirking unrepentantly, Thomas turned away again and began gingerly massaging his sore muscles.

Thomas couldn't wait to see the last of the opinionated physic. He saw little evidence that the man had contributed anything of substance to his recovery, though his mother set great store by the fellow and insisted Thomas follow his instructions to the letter. Even the messy sight of Medlen bleeding her son had not shaken her resolve.

Thomas had long since tired of the doctor's visits. He would have taken matters into his own hands had it not been for an incident involving his father.

He had been working late and didn't join his parents until some time after they had begun their evening meal. As soon as he arrived he could tell his parents had been arguing. And something in his father's manner warned him that more trouble was brewing. He waited nervously for the storm to break.

Axel had motioned toward Thomas's bad arm. "Isn't it about time you took that splint off, Thomas? How much longer are you going to persist with this idiocy?"

His mother had hastened to Thomas's defense. "The doctor gave strict instructions that the splint was to stay on until he is certain the arm is mended."

"Ha! That old fraud? The only thing he's qualified for is relieving people of their hard-earned money." He frowned at his son. "It's up to you, Thomas. He'll keep coming back, like a vulture to a carcass, as long as you let him. It's time you stood up to him. Are you a man or are you still a baby?"

Thomas, provoked by his father's challenge, had dug his heels in. He stabbed a finger angrily at the splint. "Do you think I want to put up with this a minute longer than I need to? It's easy for you to criticize the doctor. But I'm the one who will suffer, and for the rest of my life, if my arm doesn't heal properly!"

His father snorted. "Looks like you two and the leech have a very cozy arrangement going. All right then, have it your own way. But let me tell you, Thomas, you'll get nowhere until you face life like a man." He had plenty more to say, too, much of it hurtful and condescending, before he finally redirected his attack to the food.

Thomas had lost interest in the meal after that. As he sat there, angry and humiliated, he decided that the splint could stay for as long as the doctor wanted it to. Even if it meant being bled regularly. It seemed his only way of hitting back. Why did his father have to be so hard on him? These interchanges were always the same: Thomas's views and feelings didn't matter. And true to form his father had once again insisted on having the last word.

But now the day had finally arrived—the doctor had announced airily that Thomas's splint could come off. Perhaps the doctor had sensed that even his mother's credulity could not be stretched much further. Thomas was simply relieved that the charade was over.

"The voice of duty calls insistently. Others also await my ministrations, sadly not always with patience." The doctor exhaled softly, sighing his regret that business must so soon take precedence over pleasure.

But he did not move. He stood solemnly with hands clasped before him and head bowed slightly.

Thomas's mother stared at him blankly for a moment, then finally grasped what was required of her. "Oh, yes, Doctor. Your fee." At her words he bowed his head further as though such crass necessities were abhorrent to him. She reached hastily into a fold of her skirt, and a small leather purse appeared in her hand.

On impulse, Thomas fumbled with the drawstring of his pouch, freed it at last and reached in to grasp the stone. It felt cold to the touch as his fingers gently caressed its smooth surface.

He fixed his attention on Medlen and stifled a gasp. It was as though he had been wandering in a fog and the mists had thinned, offering a fleeting glimpse of an unexpected and foreign landscape. He felt certain that Medlen's mind had been laid bare before him for an instant. He glimpsed sights he knew he had never witnessed himself. Unfamiliar faces and scenes flashed by in his mind, and with a clarity never surpassed in his own memory. Insistent whispers in the doctor's own voice flooded his consciousness, and audible murmurings revealed secret musings and schemes. But Thomas realized he was not hearing these sounds with his ears. He sensed that Medlen's thoughts were somehow being exposed to his awareness.

Tantalizing as these impressions were, they were eclipsed by Medlen's absorption in the little drama he was acting out. Thomas saw the physic licking his lips slightly. He wondered how he had failed to notice the predatory set of the man's features.

Medlen stood silent and unmoving, and Thomas was sure that the doctor was responding instinctively to a familiar ritual. The man watched the coins being counted from the purse as a spider might lovingly anticipate the erratic progress of a small fly toward the web so patiently and tenderly prepared against such a visitation.

Coins changed hands. But still the doctor hovered. He cleared his throat significantly, and Thomas's mother awkwardly spilled a few more coins into his outstretched hands. Abruptly the ritual was over.

Thomas was suffused with a sudden shame. His parents' money had been squandered to gratify the swollen appetite of this calculating creature. He had blamed his father's goading, but he knew it was his own fault. He was the one who had allowed the farce to be prolonged.

"Thomas! What are you staring at?"

He snatched his hand from the pouch as though stung and turned guiltily away from Medlen. But the man had lost interest in them and moved toward the door, a faint smile playing across his lips.

Thomas hurried outside, eager to avoid conversation with his mother. The glittering intensity of the stone's power had begun to dazzle him, and his shame already seemed as pale and insubstantial as a shadow before the sun. He needed privacy, a quiet opportunity to explore the stone's potential unobserved.

Heading for the stables, with Ben trailing along behind, he caught sight of his father talking to Simon, who was mounting one of the horses. Thomas had seen little of the boy since the day of King Steffan's departure. Although he still came to the stables, he had made a point of avoiding Thomas, transferring his attention instead to the stable master.

Thomas noted enviously that the two of them appeared to be sharing some joke. His father appeared relaxed and happy. And, Thomas reflected bitterly, why wouldn't he be? Simon was not his son. There was no mountain of expectation for him to scale before they could enjoy one another's company.

Simon sat bolt upright in the saddle, a small figure against the gray bulk of the horse. A picture flashed into Thomas's mind of a young boy, proud and excited, atop a horse for the first time. He had been the one, Thomas remembered with a pang, who offered Simon his first ride.

Thomas's father disappeared into one of the stables. Thomas stood silently beside a tree, hoping he wouldn't be noticed. He took hold of the stone and focused his attention totally on Simon, who appeared quite unaware of his presence.

The effect was again startling, but completely different. This time he was unable to discern a dominant thought process. Instead, a restless and jumbled mass of emotions churned around him, like the turbulence where the thrusting spears of a waterfall cast themselves into the smooth surface of a lake.

But there were distinct patterns visible among the confusion of Simon's feelings. To Thomas's astonishment, the dominant underlying reality of Simon's life appeared to be deep unhappiness.

He had never thought of Simon as unhappy. Could it be that he was imagining it all? But the boy's misery washed over and through him, raw and painful. It called to his own inner gloom, pulling at him until he began to fear he would be engulfed by it.

He shut his eyes instinctively to block it out, and immediately it was gone. Relieved and startled, he kept his eyes closed until he had recovered himself. Then he tentatively reopened them. There it all was again, just as before. This time, though, he knew how to detach himself. He cautiously resumed his scrutiny, considerably sobered.

Somehow he sensed that Simon's home life lay at the heart of his distress. Thomas realized that he knew almost nothing about the boy's background. But he felt like he was staring into festering wounds of anger, fear, and despair—the merciless handiwork of other people.

Although he did not understand how, it became clear to him that Simon was an orphan. And that he lived with an old uncle, who provided him with food and shelter and plentiful cruelty and abuse as well. He sensed, too, with guilty recognition the scars of his own callous barbs. And he knew that his assertions had been far from the truth. Not only was Simon well suited to working with animals, his sojourns at the stables provided almost the only light in an otherwise dark and cheerless life.

Thomas closed his eyes again, seeking release from the intensity of Simon's inner turmoil and the unsteadiness of his own response.

The boy's plight evoked in him a strong response of sympathy, at the same time reawakening his own conscience. He knew he needed to make it right with Simon, to apologize for what he had said. He promised himself he would do it, and soon.

At the same time, a whole new world had opened before him, and it was hard to think about anything else. These new insights were unfamiliar, even threatening. Yet they were wildly alluring.

He opened his eyes to discover that Simon had finally noticed him.

A wave of emotion assaulted Thomas. The younger boy glared at him, radiating hostility, reproach, and envy. And there was something else Thomas could not readily identify, but which filled him with apprehension. It hinted at revenge, driven by the eager anticipation of spiteful satisfaction. The contact faded as Simon urged his mount forward and was lost to sight.

What was Simon up to? Having previously felt nothing but sympathy, Thomas now felt uneasy, and he struggled to untangle his own conflicting feelings. Simon had already become a rival for the attention and affections of Thomas's father. Could he somehow develop into a threat, as well? Thomas promised himself he would watch Simon more closely in future.

Noticing that Ben was distracted elsewhere, he set off walking, wanting to be alone for a while. Evidently the stone's gift might prove a mixed blessing. Thomas felt exhausted by its revelations and the questions they raised.

Again he wondered about the stone and its strange power. Where did it come from? What if it was evil? He dismissed the thought, unwilling to accept it. But he could not shake off the feeling that great evil might come of it. He wandered on aimlessly, lost in his thoughts.

The sun was slipping below the horizon when he finally turned toward home. He had decided he needed a rest from the stone for a while.

But not for too long. What incredible experiences! It was astonishing! Elation bubbled up inside him, and he let out an exultant whoop. What would people say if they knew he could see into their thoughts?

Yes, further investigation was clearly necessary. But more cautiously and discreetly next time. And some place where he would not be disturbed.

———

THE SUN ROSE SLOWLY over Arnost, touching the rooftops with its golden glory. Thomas, sitting alone on the edge of the market square, felt the caress of its first rays with their promise of warmth and new life. But the warmth could not penetrate deeply enough to banish the chill from his heart.

He thought of the occasion, almost three months previously, when he had first come to the square with the stone.

It was the second day after his splint had come off. His working day began soon after dawn, so he had arrived an hour earlier, knowing he would find others already there. He was filled with expectant curiosity. And he was not disappointed.

The stone had revealed more than he dreamed possible. He had heard of sailors happening upon strange lands, and he felt like an explorer stumbling upon a continent filled with astonishing wonders. He could not even begin to imagine all that had been waiting for him. Soon he was coming regularly, spurred on by the thrill of discovery.

As the weeks went by, he could sense he was adapting to the stone, or else it was adapting to him. Eventually he suspected he could almost read the thoughts of some as he observed them. He didn't understand how it worked, but thanks to the stone he somehow knew things, things that shouldn't have been possible for him to know. It was as if the knowledge, thoughts, and experiences of the people he observed had been transferred to him. These impressions could scarcely have felt more familiar to him if he had lived the experiences himself.

But his eagerness for secret knowledge diminished as inquisitiveness gradually turned to satiation. Yet he seemed powerless to stop. In recent days, as he left the square at sunrise he vowed to himself that he would not return. But each new dawn found him sitting in his accustomed position, shivering a little in the cool air and tightly clutching the stone in his hand.

What's happening to me?

He got up and set off with dragging steps back to the stables, putting the stone back in his pouch. His departure was not acknowledged by any of the merchants whose shops fringed the square. At first, the shopkeepers, bustling about in the pre-dawn half light, had eyed him curiously. One or two had even recognized him from the hunt and made friendly attempts to draw him out. He was determined, though, that his observations would not be disturbed, and his unresponsiveness had eventually defeated all comers. They soon learned to ignore him. Now, if anyone noticed his daily arrival and departure, they gave no sign of it.

Thomas walked slowly along the edge of the square, darting sidelong glances at the shopkeepers as he passed them. He caught a glimpse of Alf, the loud and bombastic butcher. His huge belly swayed from side to side as he waddled along. His face glistened with perspiration as he regaled some person unwise or unlucky enough to engage his attention.

Thomas passed the stall of Joe, the fuller. Joe was nowhere in sight, but Thomas could picture the old miser wearing his characteristic sour expression.

Next in line was a tiny stall run by Mother Joan, a snowy haired woman in the twilight of life who somehow eked out an existence selling pieces of embroidery. She sat in her usual position, her feeble fingers painstakingly stitching away the long hours in the market square. She always had a smile and a gentle word for everybody. Precious few repaid her in kind.

Lastly, he passed Frank, the flashy and extroverted cloth merchant. Frank appeared more interested in his customers than in his trade, especially the young, attractive women who frequented his stall, drawn as much by his eager flatteries as by his wares.

There were others, too. They had all become part of Thomas's world in a strangely disconnected way.

When he neared home, his mother spotted him and called him over. "Your father is looking for you. He's over in the kennels." She could not hide the concern in her eyes. "You don't look well, Tom. You need more sleep." He caught a tone of pleading in her voice.

He shrugged and headed off to the kennels. Although outwardly he made light of his mother's disquiet, her motherly attentions seemed his last link with normality. Will was far away and Simon was closed to him now, so he was grateful for her solicitude. Once again he was glad he had never tried to find out what the stone might tell him about his mother. It would have felt too much like a betrayal to pry into her secret thoughts.

He had never tested the stone on his father, either. The distance in their relationship had become a settled coolness since the king's departure, and Thomas wasn't sure he could cope with knowing his father's private thoughts about him.

His mother had good reason to worry.

What's happening to me?

He used to be happy once, before he found the stone.

At times he dreamed of being rid of it. Once he had even taken it to the river, searching out a place where the current flowed swiftly. He had toyed with the notion of casting it far out into the torrent so it would be swept from his life forever. But as he held it in his hand he was again entranced by its unusual beauty and sensed its latent power. It was the most precious thing in the world! He slipped it back into his pouch and hurried away. He hadn't repeated the attempt.

Thomas's father left him working alone in the kennels. Normally Thomas found his greatest contentment among the hounds, but today he was too troubled to enjoy it.

Only Ben was able to briefly distract him. Ben, well on his way to becoming a large and powerful mastiff, was utterly devoted to Thomas. Rolling around on the stable floor locked in a wrestle with the fawn colored ball of muscle, Thomas forgot his cares for a time.

As he lay resting afterward, he glanced affectionately at the dog. Ben had become Thomas's shadow. Thomas felt confident the animal would follow him almost anywhere; it was only with great difficulty he prevented the dog accompanying him on his daily pilgrimage to the market square.

He sighed deeply. Once again his thoughts had turned inexorably back to the square. Why couldn't he stay away? Going there afforded him little pleasure. Yet when he was honest he knew it gave him a sense of power and superiority. But although he fed off it greedily, it never satisfied him.

Before long he had begun to look condescendingly upon the vendors in the square. Fortunately they left him alone; he was not sure he could conceal his contempt for them otherwise. With the stone in his hand he felt he knew them better than they knew themselves. And he saw little that was worthy of admiration.

He knew that Frank was a lecher and an adulterer. And that Alf the butcher was barely more enlightened than the steers he carved up for his customers. Joe reminded him of a snake, coiled and ready to strike, lying in wait to poison and devour the unwary. The old man would sooner gain one coin by cheating than earn two by honest means.

Only Joan was the person she appeared to be: honest and cheerful. Yet he could not fully respect a person so poor who allowed herself to be consistently defrauded.

For the rest of the day Thomas worked half-heartedly at the menial tasks set him by his father.

Once he was interrupted by two small boys. He didn't need the stone to tell him why they were there. But he was unable to stop himself from using it.

Their shy faces gave little clue to the eager anticipation that flooded their minds. But their daydreams of horses and soldiers held no appeal for Thomas.

"Go away. I'm busy."

He relinquished the stone as he said it, unwilling to share in their disappointment.

THOMAS COULD NOT PUSH the boys from his mind. He had paid a price, too, in denying them their innocent pleasure. He faced at last the unpalatable truth: he had changed, and it wasn't for the better. The mysterious power of the stone had hopelessly ensnared him.

Yet he was so weary of it all. He had found himself immersed in an adult world he was not prepared for and did not understand. The motivations and passions of the people he observed often bewildered him.

Growing up had always seemed distant and hazy. Now it felt repulsive.

At first, stunned by the insight granted by the stone, he anticipated great revelations. But much of what he glimpsed was as trivial, selfish, and ordinary as the people he observed. So he came to see them as petty and hateful. At times, when he became party to little intimacies that he had no business knowing, he despised himself, too. He was becoming the worst kind of voyeur, peeping into people's minds.

What's happening to me?

THOMAS SAT UP WITH A START, waking from a nightmare that hovered just out of reach of his conscious mind. Dawn was still far off, but he had been waking earlier each morning, as though terrified of missing his distasteful appointment in the square.

He dragged himself out of bed and stretched his aching muscles. His head sagged wearily on his shoulders.

Seeking the reassuring feel of the stone, Thomas patted his pouch instinctively. His heart skipped a beat. The stone was not there! He clutched at the soft leather at the base of the pouch. The stitching had torn—his fingers poked through the gaping edges of a brand new hole.

Frantically he groped around his bed and under the blankets. There was no sign of the stone. He sent trembling fingers snaking over the rough flagstone floor and under the bed. It was nowhere to be found.

Fighting down his panic, he stumbled into the main room of the house and felt around until he found a torch. He lit it in the embers of the fire. Returning to his room, he began searching feverishly in its feeble light.

Before the sun rose he had turned his room upside down without success. Forcing himself to stay calm, he reviewed the previous day in his mind. He had spent time in the kennels and the stables and briefly visited the castle. And yes! He had exercised one of the mares in the grassy meadow beside the castle. And his father had sent him on an errand to the blacksmith in the town.

His heart sank. He could have lost the stone anywhere. But he had to start looking. Praying fervently for the dawn, he rushed from the house and headed for the kennels.

Seeing his master running past, Ben took off after him with a joyous bark, gamboling in front of him and leaping up excitedly. Thomas had to slow almost to a walk to avoid tripping over him.

Fairly dancing with frustration, Thomas cuffed the dog hard across the ears and ran on. Ben's bewildered yelp of pain pursued him fruitlessly across the courtyard.

Thomas searched all morning, refusing to entertain the possibility that his precious treasure was gone. His desire to be rid of the stone was forgotten, his whole being focused on reclaiming it. His parents might be wondering where he was, but that thought scarcely occurred to him.

As the day wore on, he realized he might have lost it forever. Reckless of the consequences, he cursed God bitterly. But the heavens were silent, and in time his anger passed.

As he retraced his steps from the blacksmith's, Thomas came to Arnost's small cathedral. Overcome with anguish he dropped to his knees by the roadside, ignoring the stares of the passers-by.

In the extremity of his torment he was confronted with his own motives. He saw that from the beginning he had used the stone irresponsibly. He had acted as if its powers were his by right and used them for his own selfish ends. He had distanced himself, too, from anyone who might have helped him escape the snare into which he had fallen.

Perhaps God was angry and punishing him. He begged and pleaded for a second chance. Everything would change if only the stone was returned. But still the heavens were silent. In time his remorse faded also.

Hours had passed before Thomas finally returned home. He arrived to an eager welcome from Ben, and the ready forgiveness of his faithful mastiff undid him completely. Too choked up to speak, he drew his dog close, making little effort to resist as the animal reached up energetically to lick his face. In receiving a generous love he didn't deserve, he found himself overwhelmed by his own selfishness. Filled with shame, he dragged himself away and went to bed.

. . .

THE DAYS TURNED to weeks and still Thomas searched everywhere for the stone. But there came a time when, almost against his will, his loss no longer consumed him.

His thoughts turned to other things. He acknowledged at last that he would probably never recover his treasure. It was, in fact, no longer his in any meaningful sense at all. Whether he accepted it or not, the stone was gone.

6

W ill leaned forward in the saddle and urged his mount up the hill toward the place where he had last seen the nomads. He topped the rise almost at a gallop, straining his eyes to see ahead in the gloom.

He could find no sign of the raiders. But his horse, no doubt alerted by its keener senses, abruptly swerved to one side and reared, almost throwing Will from the saddle. For a few moments the whinnying of horses and the angry curses of their riders filled the darkness. Will realized with alarm that he had almost charged directly into a large group of mounted nomads waiting silently just beyond the crest of the ridge.

Even before order had been fully restored, a harsh voice cut through the clamor. "It is Hocveg, I presume, who thus honors us with his presence." A sudden silence settled over both men and beasts. Something about the voice chilled Will to the marrow. He felt as though a cold blade had been passed across his flesh, setting his skin creeping.

"What have you found this time?" the cold voice mocked. "Some new toy to play with?"

The horsemen in front of him seemed to melt away. In the moonlight which filtered dimly through the trees he could make out a tall figure on a black stallion not twenty yards away. The man's horned helmet gave his silhouette an eerie appearance.

Although a response was apparently required of him, Will remained silent. He dared not speak lest he be discovered. He kept his head down, praying that he would appear either chastened or sullen, whichever best suited the character of the late Hocveg.

There was a long pause. "Bring me his helmet!"

A rider spurred his horse toward the astonished Will and snatched the nomad helmet from his head. Feeling naked and exposed he bent his head still lower, expecting every minute to be detected. But it seemed that all eyes were on the dark leader. The tall horseman seized the helmet from the rider, snapped off the two horns and flung them to the ground. The once-proud emblem appeared pathetic and emasculated as he held it aloft in the dim moonlight.

"Now put it back." He threw it dismissively to the rider.

The rider returned and thrust the broken helmet roughly onto Will's bowed head.

"He has been marked! Let him be spurned. He will be dealt with later," the voice promised with casual malice. The riders backed their horses away from Will as though he had the plague.

Will shuddered. Here was a very different kind of leader from either his own captain or king. But he had no intention of staying around long enough to find out what the tall Rogandan had in mind. For Rogandan he certainly was, nomad garb or not. Every word he had spoken was in that language. And it was his native tongue; his accent betrayed him to Will's practiced ear.

So the nomads were being directed by a Rogandan. And the man obviously expected to be understood, so at least some of them must have learned the language. What could it mean?

"How many are missing now?" The cold voice had resumed.

"Only one, Lord Drettroth," a rough voice answered in Rogandan.

"Find him and bring him back. And do not bring him back alive. His indolence has cost us precious time."

"Yes, Lord."

Three men rode back over the crest, toward the strange glow in the night sky that marked the passing of a village.

WHILE THE NOMADS WAITED, Will's mind raced as he assessed his situation. He shifted restlessly in his saddle. Then, with a sick feeling in his stomach, he remembered that nomads did not use saddles. They regarded them with contempt, learning to ride bareback almost as soon as they could run. Not only that, he wore a sword. The nomads rarely used swords, preferring axes and knives for close fighting.

He glanced about him furtively, feeling suddenly conspicuous again. But he saw to his surprise that the horses around him were saddled as well. And many of the nomads openly wore swords. He listened with new interest to the snatches of conversation going on around him. As far as he could tell, all were in Rogandan. The suspicion began to dawn on him that he and Lord Drettroth were not the only ones posing as nomads.

But before he could think this new information through, he was struck by another more disturbing thought. The search party was looking for a missing raider—what if they found Hocveg? And the bodies of two raiders were lying out there. What if they found them both?

Hocveg apparently had a reputation for looting; he would have been one of the last to leave the village. So it was probably Hocveg's clothing he was wearing now. But how had he left the body? Face down, it might be mistaken for a villager. But face up... He simply couldn't remember.

Will waited with growing tension for the raiders to return. He wondered if he could make a break for it if he was discovered. A quick glance revealed that he was now completely surrounded by riders, even though they were keeping their distance. His chances would be impossibly slim.

But with his acknowledgment of the apparent hopelessness of his situation was born a new determination. If he was going to die, he might as well make it worthwhile. His path to the tall leader was almost clear. If he was swift and lucky, he might just catch the Rogandan unprepared.

He carefully reached for the hilt of his sword and grasped it lightly, reassured by its solid familiarity. Twice tonight it had served him well. Ahead of it was the most important task of all.

Strangely, he found that his new resolve calmed him. As he waited he thought briefly of his hopes and dreams. Another would have to aspire to be captain of the Guard now. He thought, too, of Garth. He should have almost reached King Steffan's troops by now. But they would be too late. Will wondered if they would even know of his sacrifice. Perhaps a soldier would find his body up on the hill.

The horses stirred; the searchers were returning. He half lifted his sword free of its scabbard.

"Well?"

"We found him, Lord. He was dead already. Hacked almost beyond recognition. Malzakh has him now."

They had found the first one! He carefully eased his sword back into place.

"No villager could have done that." Will noted with satisfaction the apprehension in the man's tone. Let them sweat for once, the baby killers.

The dark leader must have noticed the man's tone, too. "Silence! The fool is dead as he deserves. May Malzakh bite him. Let us be gone." The riders, restless to be off, set off into the night, taking with them the body of their fallen comrade.

WILL and the raiders had been steadily riding for what seemed like hours. At first they had covered their tracks by riding single file until they reached a stream. They rode upstream for some time until they could leave the water without making tracks. The corpse of the raider was stripped and hidden in some bushes. Then they headed east toward the Blue Mountains. Will kept careful track of their bearings using the stars, a skill he had acquired while traveling with his uncle.

The extended period in the saddle offered Will an opportunity for reflection. The immediate danger had passed, and his spirits quickly rebounded. His current circumstances, while fraught with deadly peril, scarcely distressed him at all.

He had always been adventurous—foolhardy according to his uncle. He felt certain he had survived more life-threatening situations in his youth than half a dozen normal people might face collectively in their entire lifetimes. But rather than sobering him, it had given him a taste for the hazardous.

Even among the nomads he had been recognized as reckless. One of the clans gave him a name which meant "Lightning Rider." This time, though, he decided wryly, the lightning might fry him at last.

Will had wanted to be a soldier for as long as he could remember. He concluded early in life that it offered the best chance for someone in his position to make a mark in the world. Now he had what he wanted. And tonight he had killed for the first time—not once, but twice. It had been remarkably easy. He had expected that taking another's life would seem more difficult.

He even knew the name of one of his victims. Unexpectedly he found himself curious about Hocveg. Someone had invested years of time and energy, and perhaps love and affection, into raising him. Yet Will had snuffed out his life in a moment. It was so out of proportion. Were there parents or a wife somewhere praying to their Dark Gods for his safe return? Maybe even some children eagerly looking forward to the arrival of their father?

He pushed the thought from his mind. These men were barbarians, killers of the defenseless. They offered no consideration to their victims. They deserved none themselves.

He wondered what the men around him were thinking about at that moment. Were they, too, recalling their grim harvest at the village? Or were they simply anticipating a warm bed and a cup of ale? He fervently hoped their dreams tonight would be haunted by the screams of the dying.

No, these men deserved no mercy. If he could achieve it, he would cheerfully bring about the deaths of the lot of them. And he meant to try.

───────

"RUFE, Edgar wants to speak with you."

Rufe grunted noncommittally; he knew Edgar by reputation. Edgar might have been a relatively recent addition to the king's army, but he was already well known among his fellow soldiers, and for all the wrong reasons. "What does that troublemaker want?"

The soldier's eyes were alight, and he moved around impatiently. "It's important," he protested. "He'll tell you what it's about."

Rufe hesitated a moment, then shrugged and got up to follow the man. Why not? Any diversion would be welcome; there was precious little else to get excited about.

Rufe thought he could guess a little of what Edgar might be up to. They were stationed with one of the king's three forces in a small town called Stantony. In the previous week the soldiers had been summoned into battle only once, and the action had long been finished before they arrived. They were reduced once again to the infuriating role of inspecting the destruction.

Grumbling about King Steffan's new plan and the policy toward the nomads in general had not been long in breaking out. Inaction and frustration proved a volatile mixture. Lord Gramm, the commander appointed by the king, was reputed to be reliable and fearless, but he apparently lacked the skill to deal effectively with the restlessness.

The soldier led Rufe to a barn on the outskirts of the town. Edgar was relaxing in a comfortable armchair he had commandeered from somewhere, surrounded by as likely a band of cut-throats as Rufe had seen. Rufe's guide stationed himself watchfully at the barn door.

"Ah, Rufe Sarjant. Welcome." Edgar flashed him a charming smile. "No doubt you're curious about my invitation."

"You're brewing trouble, I don't doubt." Rufe spoke curtly, unimpressed by the ingratiation he thought he could detect in Edgar's manner.

"Not at all. Why would we want to involve you if we were planning trouble?" Edgar asked reasonably. "We're hoping to benefit from your advice. Maybe even your support."

"I'm flattered," Rufe replied coldly.

Edgar apparently decided to ignore Rufe's unsympathetic demeanor. "Will you hear us out?"

"I'm listening."

"Then I'll come straight to the point. A number of us witnessed your conversation with the king at the village."

So Rufe's suspicions were confirmed. It only remained to see where Edgar was leading.

"We agree wholeheartedly with what you said. It's time the fight was taken to the nomads. On their home territory for once. A force like ours could turn this whole campaign around in a week, maybe ten days."

Edgar paused, perhaps expecting a reaction from Rufe. Since there was none he pressed on. "If we took provisions with us we could move fast, sack a few nomad encampments, and return in time to trap the raiders on their way back to defend their own women and children."

"Why talk to me about it? Lord Gramm is the one you should be speaking to."

"Ah, Lord Gramm. Yes, a trustworthy soldier, to be sure. But entirely uninspiring. He isn't a strategist's armpit. He has enough trouble figuring out which day of the week tomorrow is. A more energetic man would have done something useful for his king by now."

Rufe wondered how far Edgar was prepared to go. "And where do I fit into all of this?"

"We wanted your opinion. You have a reputation as an intelligent man."

Out of the corner of his eye Rufe caught two of the men exchanging a smirk. So Edgar's flattery amused them, did it? Well, Rufe was no more taken in by it than they were. He might never match Edgar's animal cunning or Will's natural decisiveness. But he was no man's fool, either.

Edgar lowered his voice conspiratorially. "If we all give a strong lead together we can set things to right. The men respect you, Rufe." This was closer to the mark. Rufe was no natural leader, and Edgar undoubtedly knew it. But the men respected him, both because he was physically imposing and because they trusted him. It seemed that Edgar needed him for his credibility. "All we need is to borrow Gramm's force for a short time. He'll thank us when it's all finished."

Rufe Sarjant's credibility and Lord Gramm's troops; it appeared that Edgar had it all worked out. "And what would Lord Gramm be doing in the meantime?"

"Well, it might be possible to arrange for him to become, er, temporarily indisposed, let's say for a week or two."

"And what about his knights?"

"Leave it to us. We'll arrange something suitable."

This was treason. Rufe wondered if they were all rogues or if some of them were merely fools. Even if they succeeded, did any of them seriously believe King Steffan would thank them for taking matters into their own hands?

He had a feeling that Edgar's main interest was in looting. What a surprise it would be when Edgar and his cronies disappeared with the plunder sometime during the journey back. Some other dupe would be left to face the consequences. Someone like Rufe Sarjant, no doubt. They probably had the lead role in their little drama reserved for him.

Rufe would have liked nothing better than to expose the plotters. Without hard evidence, though, he was going to be running a big risk trying to outmaneuver treacherous men like these.

He wished Will Prentis was there. Will would know how to handle them. But he was far away in some backwater, most likely longing for some action. If only Will had listened to him. Anyone could see that the important events would happen here with the main forces.

"Can we count on you?"

For now, Rufe decided to keep Edgar on the hook while he tried to figure out what to do. "I'll think about it. But until I know exactly what you have in mind for Lord Gramm, you can count me out."

"Excellent! We'll let you know when our plans are in place." Edgar was grinning triumphantly. Clearly he thought Rufe was as good as in the bag.

Rufe left the barn aware that he was playing a very dangerous game. If he put a step wrong the consequences might be catastrophic.

WILL SENSED that the riders were nearing their home base. The men seemed to be sitting a little taller in the saddle and the pace had definitely picked up, even though they were now climbing steadily.

Their path soon took them into the foothills of the Blue Mountains and eventually onto a trail that had obviously seen considerable use in recent times. The trail was narrow, and the trees clustered thickly. They were soon forced to travel single file, relying on the horses to find the way since no moonlight penetrated the forest at all.

Will planned to follow the nomads to their base and then slip away unnoticed. One day the nomads would return to find King Steffan's soldiers waiting for them.

Clearly the time had arrived to start moving toward the back of the troop before it was too late. He decided to make his move as soon as they spread out again.

Abruptly he found himself out of the trees. The riders were spilling into a large clearing bounded by the forest on one side and on two sides by a broad sweep of a river which wound its way through the upper foothills. On the other side of the clearing, readily visible in the moonlight, lay a large wooden fortress. It was tucked into a bend of the river and surrounded on three sides by water. The clearing apparently resulted from the felling of the trees used in the construction of the stronghold. The site had been cleverly selected; the fortress had been invisible among the trees until he was upon it.

It appeared well enough constructed that a few determined men could hold off a small army for some time. Will was certain that no nomad would ever have built such a structure.

A command rang out. Two great gates opened, and the riders pressed toward the opening. Will was caught, unable to turn away.

As the riders milled around the entrance waiting to get inside, he found himself jostled among the rider-less horses led back from the village as spoil. He was startled to see a horse that he recognized, though at first he was unable to place it. Then with a thrill of horror he knew: it was Garth's black roan. And there was blood on the saddle.

For a moment Will was overcome by his aloneness. No one knew where he was; no one even knew he was missing. But there was no chance to dwell on it. Carried along by a tide of men and horses, he was swept through the gates and into the stronghold. The gates were bolted shut behind them. Will was trapped inside the fortress.

7

The last armful of planks landed with a clatter as Thomas dropped them onto the now-sizable pile. A large number of small sharpened hardwood plugs lay beside them; they would be driven through holes in the planks to secure them in place onto the crossbeams.

Thomas leaned back and surveyed his work with satisfaction, letting the sweat trickle freely down his face. He had been hard at it for two days now, and the end was in sight at last.

Seeing his master taking a brief break from his work, Ben trotted up with tail wagging, looking for attention. Thomas bent down and stroked him behind the ears. The dog grunted his appreciation.

The bent figure of Jeb lumbered into sight around a building, struggling with a handcart laden with steaming horse manure. He paused to catch his breath and nodded toward the barn. "Ah, looks a bit different now! What was it—a month ago? When it was knocked down by that wagon? Can't tell it's the same building."

Thomas had removed much of the roof thatch, dug out and replaced the damaged support posts, and attached new architraves and crossbeams. "My missus says you was up early this morning, young Tom." The old man's eyes twinkled in his weathered brow.

"There are other jobs that still need to be done."

"Ahh." Jeb nodded wisely. "Yes, always something more." He paused, his eyes patiently assessing the completed frame. "Well, it's a fine job, young Tom," he finally offered. He looked at the youth knowingly. "Did yer father set you to work at this?"

"No, it was my idea."

"Ahh. It'll be a fine surprise fer him, then. Yer father'll be proud of you when 'e gets back."

To his vexation, Thomas could feel himself betrayed by the spreading warmth of a deep blush. "It's nothing much really," he replied emphatically, "nothing much at all," hoping vehemence might override the contradictory message of his face.

A gentle smile creased Jeb's wrinkled features as he slowly bent to his handcart and resumed his labored progress.

Thomas turned back to the barn with Jeb's words echoing in his mind. `Yer father'll be proud of you.' He eyed his handiwork again, more critically this time. The sun, still low in the sky, dazzled him for a moment as it peeped through the clouds. He closed his eyes and let his thoughts drift...

"Hello, son, I'm back early." He imagined himself looking up to find his father beside him. Normally an unexpected appearance by his father would be unsettling, but this time a warm shiver of pleasure traveled down his spine. "By the Saints! Did you do this, Thomas? I know I've said often enough that you lack initiative, but I'm man enough to admit it when I'm wrong."

"It's nothing," he protested mildly. This time his face behaved itself perfectly. His father surveyed the almost-completed barn with a delighted smile, pulling at the posts and nodding with satisfaction as they firmly resisted the motion. The stable master looked down at his son with new respect in his eyes.

A breeze sprang up abruptly, chilling Thomas's sweat-soaked skin, and shattering the daydream of his father's return. A cloud moved across the sun, veiling it once more. Proud of him? Maybe there was a first time for everything.

But what difference did it make? Thomas faced the bare outline of the barn—another solid day's work would complete the task. He reached down for the first plank with a sigh. He was tired.

THE MORNING WAS ALMOST SPENT and only the roof remained to be done when Simon sauntered casually into view, an open smirk on his face. Ben leaped up to greet the newcomer, his tail wagging eagerly. Simon ignored the dog.

The sight of the youth raised a familiar set of uncomfortable questions for Thomas. He had promised himself he would make things right with Simon, but he'd never made the attempt. What could he do to mend things? Would it even be possible now?

The coward in him insisted it would be wiser to just keep his distance. He knew that wasn't right.

As he wrestled with his conflicting feelings, Thomas couldn't escape the simple fact that he should have spoken to Simon long ago. So much damage had been done when he allowed himself to be dazzled and distracted by the stone. He hadn't been the only one who paid a price for his foolishness.

He remembered his earliest experiences with the stone. The depth of Simon's pain had been one of its first revelations. He had glimpsed the bitter legacy of other people, and seen that he himself had intensified Simon's misery with his cruel and thoughtless words.

Thomas took a deep breath. "Simon, I've been wanting to talk to you," he said awkwardly. "I wanted to...I wanted to say I'm sorry."

"Sorry for what?"

"For the way I spoke to you. Back when the soldiers left for Danford."

Simon's face was an impassive mask.

Thomas remembered again the rawness of Simon's pain. "I didn't mean it," he added. "What I said back then."

Simon immediately snorted in disbelief. "You said what you were thinking. Don't try to pretend now that you didn't mean it!"

Thomas's heart sank. He was telling the truth, but how could he convince his former friend?

An unyielding expression came over Simon's face. "I didn't come here to argue," he said. "Your father gave me a message for you. He couldn't find you when he was leaving."

"What message?" Thomas asked in surprise.

"He wanted you to knock down this barn and clear the site before he gets back tomorrow. He doesn't want a barn here anymore."

Thomas frowned. "Surely you're not serious."

Simon shrugged indifferently. "Believe it or disbelieve it. It's your choice. But don't say I didn't tell you."

Thomas furrowed his brows. "If he gave you that message, why wait until now to deliver it?"

"I saw you pulling down the roof and timbers a couple of days ago and assumed he must have seen you after all and told you himself," Simon answered innocently. "It only just occurred to me that you didn't know."

Thomas looked at the younger boy uncertainly, suddenly doubting himself. What if the message was genuine, and Simon had deliberately withheld it until the work was nearly finished? Over the last couple of days Thomas had occasionally noticed him watching from a distance. His behavior now made sense.

"Anyway, you still have plenty of time," the youth continued. "This scrap heap shouldn't take long to clear away." Simon sniffed contemptuously at the fruit of Thomas's prodigious labors.

With great difficulty, Thomas held his peace.

The smirk returned to the younger boy's face. He turned his back on Thomas and ambled off.

After a time Thomas sat down, head in his hands, miserable and disheartened. He had made an attempt—finally—to fix his mistake, but it had been too late. It was abundantly clear that Simon had no interest in reconciliation. He wasn't going to forgive him.

Thomas hadn't forgotten, either, that the stone showed him more than just Simon's distress. It had also revealed that Simon was actively seeking revenge.

Where would it lead? Thomas could no more avoid Simon than he could avoid the stables. Both of their lives were centered there.

And now a new decision had been forced upon him. A crucial decision. What should he do about the barn? He had to assume that Simon was telling the truth, even if his timing had been motivated only by spite.

With an effort, he put Simon from his mind. He needed to think clearly about the problem before him.

He could understand his father wanting to remove the barn three days ago—it had been a useless eyesore. But would his father want him to demolish it now? Surely that would be pointless and wasteful. His father might even accuse him of lacking initiative again if he simply obeyed blindly.

What should he do?

He turned it over and over in his head, struggling to reach a conclusion. Finally, knowing he needed to settle it, he called an end to his agonizing and made his choice. Picking up a bundle of thatch, he headed for the ladder.

THOMAS'S FATHER discovered the barn soon after his return late the next afternoon. Thomas, walking behind him, saw him stiffen abruptly and stare at the structure standing bright and renewed in the sunlight.

Seeing it again brought a thrill of pride to Thomas. Breathless, he waited for his father's response. After a time his father turned to him, and Thomas, smiling expectantly, was stunned to see his face white with anger.

"What is the meaning of this?"

"I, I..."

"Did you do this?"

"Yes. I thought I would surprise you."

"Surprise me? Well, you have succeeded beyond your wildest hopes!" Eyes flashing, the stable master bent toward him and spoke slowly and distinctly. "Perhaps you didn't get my message." Thomas recognized a dangerous tone in his father's voice.

"Yes, I did. But..."

"Including the part about not wanting a barn here anymore?"

"Yes." Thomas felt physically sick. He forced out a response. "I thought you'd be pleased."

"Pleased?" his father shouted. "How could I possibly be pleased? You ignored my instructions and did exactly the opposite!"

Thomas could not manage a reply.

"This will have to be removed. You realize that, don't you? And since you built it, you can pull it down. Is that clear?"

Thomas, his head bowed, could only nod. He turned to go. In doing so he noticed a familiar figure disappearing behind a nearby building. His humiliation was complete: Simon had witnessed the whole interaction.

THAT NIGHT THOMAS did not appear for the evening meal. Marya, normally talkative, had very little to say. But she bustled about so relentlessly that Axel was finally driven to exasperation. "What on earth is wrong with you, woman?"

"Thomas is what's wrong with me." She turned on him like a hen cornered in defense of her chicks. "What did you say to him?"

"Nothing he didn't deserve. I left a message for him to pull down that damaged barn. But no, he had his own ideas. He rebuilt it instead."

"Maybe he didn't get your message."

"He got it all right. He admitted as much."

"Maybe he got it after he'd already started."

"Maybe. But that hardly excuses him."

The stable master's wife had found her voice at last. "You don't know how hard he worked while you were away. Up well before dawn, and barely pausing for breath all day. It was all he could do to raise the food to his mouth each night." She pointed an accusing finger at him. "And he was doing it for you! Can't you see that?"

"Well, he has a strange way of being helpful."

"What did you say to him about the barn?"

"I told him to pull it down." Axel refused to meet his wife's eyes.

She stared at him in disbelief. "Pull it down! You can't be serious! Why can't you think of him for once? How do you think he's feeling right now?"

"How should I know?" he replied obstinately.

But Marya knew her man, and she pressed home the attack. "Are you telling me you can't find a use for a solid little storage barn?" she asked incredulously.

"I don't know. Well, maybe. Perhaps I could." He still would not meet her eyes. "It appeared solid enough," he finally muttered.

"Go and tell him, then!"

"All right, all right. I'll tell him first thing in the morning."

His wife softened, like a flower blooming with the melting of the snow in spring. She came to him and draped her arms about his neck, cooing happily in his ear.

"By the Saints, Marya, will you stop fussing?"

Grinning at his discomfort, she left him to finish his meal in peace.

EARLY THE NEXT morning Axel appeared grim faced in the doorway.

"Did you speak to Thomas?" Marya's face was eager.

"No, I couldn't find him. But there's no longer any point."

Her face clouded. "Why not?"

"The barn is gone. He must have pulled it down during the night." The stable master raised his arms heavenward in hopeless appeal. "The senseless stupidity of it! Why can't he think for once instead of just reacting?"

He glanced once at his wife, then turned and hurried outside, away from the grief in her eyes.

THOMAS WANDERED AIMLESSLY through the town, letting his feet take him where they would, but carefully avoiding people.

After a time he found himself in the oldest part of the city.

Dilapidated houses crowded into narrow streets fouled with rubbish and effluent. Repelled by the place, he steered a course away from the sights and smells assaulting his senses. His instincts told him, too, that this was not a place to be found alone. Not even in the daytime.

He did not welcome the return to reality. He preferred the empty numbness that had pervaded him since the previous night. Soon after dark he had set upon the barn, almost blinded by tears that flowed uncontrollably. When there were no more tears he attacked it with a savage energy fueled by bitterness and anger. In time that passed, too, and his nerveless fingers completed the destruction mechanically. Then he sat down inside one of the stables, the faithful head of Ben cradled in his lap. At dawn he had stolen away, knowing only that he wanted to be alone.

Although Thomas was unfamiliar with this part of the city he was confident he was heading in the right direction. Thankfully, there were few people about, just a few children playing amidst the reeking muck. As he passed a particularly ill-favored residence, a figure detached itself from the doorway and stepped directly into his path. He froze.

A gaunt and wizened face thrust expectantly toward him and yellow eyes, gleaming with a mad light, peered intently into his. A thin arm shot out, and a bony hand grasped him by the wrist.

"It's him, it's him! At last!" The old man danced and capered about in triumph, never for an instant letting go his grip on Thomas's arm.

Thomas tried to pull free. But the old man was remarkably strong for one who appeared so frail. The wrinkled face drew nearer. A hoarse cackle sounded from the grinning lips, and Thomas, disgusted, noticed saliva running freely down his unkempt beard and onto his filthy tunic.

A child appeared in the doorway and ran back inside crying, "Mama, Mama! Grampaw's got out again."

The old man looked at Thomas shrewdly. "He'll try to make you give it to him, he will." He pulled at Thomas's arm urgently. "You mustn't let him have it. Not for anything!" Thomas stared back wide-eyed, wanting to escape yet gripped by a strange fascination.

A large woman bustled into the street, jaw set grimly, and waddled determinedly toward the old figure. She grabbed him firmly by both shoulders and pulled him bodily away from Thomas.

"Get back inside," she yelled. Then, with forced politeness, "Please pay him no heed, young man. He's always trying to accost people in the street." She tapped her forehead significantly as she shoved him back into the house.

"No! No!" shrieked the old man. "This is him, I tell you! He's the one from my dreams. There's more. I've got to tell him..."

The voice trailed off as the door slammed shut behind him. The sound of blows and more yelling carried into the street. Thomas turned away in revulsion. Shaken and confused, he hurried toward home.

8

Will sat with his back to the wall of the stockade, enviously watching the raiders feasting heartily around a huge fire. He was cold and hungry and his eyes drooped with weariness, but he was determined he would not remain idle in whatever remained of the night.

The small garrison had evidently made preparations against the return of the raiders for there was ale and freshly roasted meat in plenty as soon as the horses had been attended to.

Will kept his distance from the others and was relieved to find they continued to avoid him. Indeed he was beginning to think they had forgotten him entirely when someone tossed a hunk of roast meat in his direction. He retrieved it gratefully, brushing resolutely at the dirt that covered it when it landed. The flesh was only partially cooked, and the best meat had apparently been eaten already, but he bit into it hungrily, pausing only to lick off the juices freed by his exertions.

No one offered him any ale, and he tried to convince himself it was a good thing. Certainly he needed a clear head tonight.

. . .

HUNCHED up against the cold watching the revelers, Will found himself becoming impatient. They had long since tired of eating, but the ale still flowed freely, and they showed no signs of moving away from the fire, which had begun to die down. He guessed they wouldn't be sleeping in the open tonight; not when there were buildings at hand to offer shelter from the cold. Even though he knew it was irrational, he found himself frequently glancing at the sky, watching anxiously for any lightening of the darkness. But it had to be at least four hours before dawn.

His restless mind had already come up with a scheme. It was daring and risky, and he needed darkness to give it the best chance of success. If only the Rogandans would move off to sleep.

There was no longer any question that they were all Rogandans. Will had not heard any other language used since joining them, and any remaining doubt was dispelled as they feasted: their bawdy songs branded them more effectively than any coat-of-arms could have done.

Will's thoughts were interrupted by the appearance of Lord Drettroth. There had been no sign of the tall leader since they entered the stockade. Perhaps the Rogandan lord was above feasting with lesser mortals. Or maybe he knew his presence would inhibit the revelry, for a hush came over the scene as soon as the soldiers registered his arrival.

One man, too drunk to notice what was happening, lifted a wobbly voice in a crude tavern song. His solo might have been amusing had it not attracted the deadly gaze of Lord Drettroth. The man's companions, at first nudging him frantically, backed away from the hapless soldier. At last he realized his peril. He looked around expectantly as though hoping for a miraculous deliverance. Finding no help in sight, he sank to his knees as if to plead for mercy. But the excitement along with his drunken stupor must have been too much, and he finally pitched forward, senseless, landing flat on his face.

It probably saved him. The Rogandan lord, after regarding him icily for a moment, turned his attention to the others. They were now as silent and attentive as mice watching a barn owl.

"You have feasted well, men." It was a statement rather than a question. "Now you must rest, for tomorrow night we set out for the town of Danford." A murmur arose at his words, but the men were quieted by an imperious flick of his hand.

"Yes, their king has been slow to take our bait. So we must send a message that even a simpleton like him can understand. He seems reluctant to ride south against the clans. Nomad raiders in the streets of Danford might help make up his mind." A rumble of approval broke out from the assembled soldiers.

"We must be fast and efficient. Some of our men posing as merchants are already in the town. They will overwhelm the guards and open the city gates.

"You know what to do! But there will be no plundering. Kill and burn, but do not plunder, on pain of death. As always, there is to be no speaking at all, except for the nomad battle cries you have learned.

"Once the streets are flowing with blood we will leave as quickly as we came. No one must be left behind.

"If you are foolish enough to fail, you will taste my wrath." He stretched out a finger toward them and slowly swung it around, fixing the men huddled before him with an unearthly glare that shone with a terrible light of its own.

A tremor passed through the assembly like a ripple spreading over the surface of a lake. Then his voice dropped almost to a whisper which carried clearly in the stillness. "If you do well, you will be rewarded."

The gathered throng was silent. None dared to stir or speak. But more was required of them, for thunder gathered slowly on the brow of their master, exaggerated by the flickering firelight which played strangely across his angular features.

Then one or two cheers broke out, breaking the silence and charming away the growing storm. Scattered at first, the sound quickly swelled to a crescendo, an awful paean of praise for the terrible overlord. Their leader raised his arms exultantly as though invoking the affirmation of his Dark Gods, too.

Will sat numbed and unable to move. The scene he had just

witnessed unnerved him. The horror in store for the comfortable citizens of Danford appalled him. And yet the nightmare would be only just beginning. So much depended on him.

"Go now. Rebuild your strength. Tomorrow there will be entertainment. And then there will be glory."

At the mention of entertainment a number of heads turned in Will's direction. For an instant, panic threatened to engulf him. He barely checked himself from leaping up and dashing blindly for the gates. Instead he lowered his head between his knees to fight off his dizziness.

Then the moment passed, and he mastered himself again, grim and more determined than ever in his resolve.

When he looked up again Lord Drettroth was gone, back into the darkness from which he had come. The men jumped up and scurried off like frightened sheep to their shelters. Soon only Will remained, staring fixedly into the glowing embers of the dying fire. His hope flickered like its last flames, but his spirit was unbowed and unbroken still.

No one had stayed to guard the outcast Hocveg. After all, what could he do? Even if he escaped, how could he survive in the wilderness without a horse or hunting weapons? Apparently Hocveg was fully expected to take his chances with tomorrow's entertainment.

Well, they were in for a surprise. He pulled the broken helmet from his head, stood up, and threw it high over the wall. The sound of a splash carried to him faintly on the night air. Looking around he selected another from among those abandoned by the men in their haste and planted it defiantly on his head.

WILL SWAYED UNSTEADILY atop the stockade walls for a moment, then with a sharp intake of breath he jumped. He hit the ground hard, tumbled forward, and lay motionless, listening for the footfall of the guard patrolling on the wall above. When the guard had passed he moved stealthily to the river. After hesitating briefly he eased his body into its icy waters and struck out confidently for the other bank. After reaching it he disappeared into the trees on the other side.

HALDEK GOT up and reluctantly dragged himself away from the fire and his cup of ale. The guardhouse at the gates was hardly comfortable, but at that moment it seemed very appealing.

He had to check on those fool guards once in a while, though. Otherwise one of them would find a quiet corner and put his feet up. If Lord Drettroth ever caught a guard asleep on the job there would be no second chances for the half-wit. That would be bad. But he, Haldek, would be held responsible. The consequences of that didn't bear thinking about.

Life would have been much easier if Lord Drettroth would only stop turning up unexpectedly at odd times of the night. In fact the later and the darker it was, the better he seemed to like it. But no one in his right mind inquired too closely into the habits of their strange master.

Haldek sighed and clumped slowly up the ladder onto the walkway circling the top of the walls. He paused at the top and glanced down into the stockade. The great fire was little more than glowing embers now. All was quiet. The soldiers were no doubt sleeping soundly after their earlier carousals. He turned back to the wall and decided to stay put. If the guards were doing their job they would be along soon enough.

He gazed out over the wall into a sky brilliant with stars. The full moon, low in the sky now, illuminated the open space beyond the walls, picking out the stumps of the felled trees. The clearing appeared to be populated with tiny standing stones, silently watching and waiting.

Often, on lonely nights on the wall he found himself half-expecting to witness some dark and sinister ceremony. He shuddered, only partly from the cold. What in the name of the Dark Gods had he done to warrant being banished to this forsaken hole? He rubbed his hands together vigorously, trying to restore the feeling that yielded slowly to a creeping numbness.

Where were those guards? He turned and glared along the walls, finally making out a figure moving toward him.

Haldek noticed the man's shoulders drooped despondently. A wave of irritation washed over him. These men didn't know what sentry duty was. Compared to his years on the battlements of Agon's castle in Rog, this was a carnival. Apart from the isolation, anyway. And the primitive quarters. And the eeriness of the clearing in the moonlight.

He softened a little in spite of himself and greeted the sentry almost warmly. "Anything happening?"

"No." The sentry yawned hugely and tightened his shoulders against the chill. "I thought I heard something in the river earlier, but it must have been fish. Or maybe a bear."

Shortly the other sentry joined them, and all three leaned over the wall without speaking. Banished from home and familiar routine by his circumstances, Haldek allowed his imagination to carry him away.

But a startled gasp from the second sentry interrupted his reverie. "What's that moving over there?"

"Where?"

"Over there, by the trees!" The man pointed away toward the edge of the clearing.

Something was moving. The standing stones were coming to life. Gripped by an awful fascination, Haldek stared fixedly, unable to tear his eyes away. He couldn't tell what it was in the moonlight, but it was definitely coming toward them.

Haldek squinted, trying to identify it in the gloom. It was walking upright. But it appeared to have horns. A horrible thought came to him—could it be a demon?

The horned silhouette moved into the shadow of the walls and disappeared from sight. Haldek and the sentries stood motionless, holding their breaths to catch the slightest sound. Then, from before the great gates, they heard a voice: "Open, in the name of Agon!"

Haldek stood dumbfounded. After a pause the voice called again. "By the Dark Ones, is no one awake in this place?" It was definitely a human voice, weary and with an edge of desperation. And the words were Rogandan.

Haldek found his voice at last. "Go on, you fools! Don't just stand there!"

The men burst into life and hurried down off the wall to the gate. Haldek roused two other guards from the guardhouse. Together they took up positions inside the gate, weapons and burning torches in their hands.

"Open it!" Haldek commanded. The men unbarred the gates and swung them slowly inward.

A young man dressed as a nomad stumbled inside. He stood shivering before them, and Haldek saw that his clothing was soaked through.

"Who are you and what is your business?"

"I have come with an urgent message for Lord Drettroth."

Haldek glared at him suspiciously. "What is this message and who sends it?" he challenged.

The stranger bristled. "My message is for the ears of Lord Drettroth alone," he snapped, "as is the identity of the sender. I would not pry too closely into Lord Drettroth's business if I were you. He is not known to be a forgiving man."

Haldek could find no argument with that. "Where, then, is your horse?"

The man's face was grim. "My horse went lame two days ago. I have been forced to walk through this accursed wilderness. It was many leagues before I found a suitable ford across the river, and even then I became soaked." He paused, his chattering teeth emphasizing his plight. "Haven't you got a fire somewhere?"

Haldek hesitated. The fellow's accent was unfamiliar; he couldn't identify it. But he seemed genuine. And if Lord Drettroth learned that an important messenger, already delayed, had been hindered by Haldek...

He nodded to the guards. "Close the gates." He gestured toward the guardhouse. "Come with me."

Once inside, the stranger rushed to the fire with all the desperation of a drowning man clutching at a floating branch. For some time he stood before it in his dripping garments. He looked more like a half-drowned animal than a human.

Finally he spoke. "Can you have a horse prepared? I expect Lord Drettroth to send me back immediately with a reply."

Haldek was aghast. "Send you back like this? You're in no condition to go anywhere!"

The man looked genuinely surprised. "Has Lord Drettroth discovered compassion during his months in the wilderness?" Haldek gave no answer, so the man went on. "I'll be fine once I get some ale into me." He looked hopefully at Haldek.

"Ale? Yes, you certainly look like you need some."

Haldek felt ashamed—only a few months in this accursed place and already he had forgotten common courtesies. He personally drew a large mug of ale from a barrel in the corner. He carried it to the man, who eagerly followed its progress across the room. He took a long pull. Then he closed his eyes and let out a deep sigh.

The recuperative effect was immediate. "The horse," he said, assuming a businesslike manner. Haldek nodded to one of his men who headed for the door. "Make sure it's a fast one. And I'll need provisions in the saddlebags," he called after the sentry's retreating form.

The resilience of the young man amazed Haldek. He had been well chosen.

"I must speak to Lord Drettroth."

"Now? It will be dawn in only an hour."

"I said my message was urgent!" The man's eyes flashed angrily. "You will answer to Lord Drettroth if you delay me."

"Of course."

Haldek did not find the idea of rousing Lord Drettroth an attractive one. He glanced at the other men and guessed from the tension in their faces they were thinking the same thing. But this was one job he was not going to delegate.

"I will take you to him now." The other guards visibly relaxed.

They set off toward the buildings on the far side of the stockade. As they drew level with the remnants of the great fire, the man turned to him and gently placed a hand, still trembling slightly from the cold, on his shoulder.

"Listen," he said, his voice softening. "Do you think Lord Drettroth will be pleased about being woken from his sleep?"

Haldek shook his head emphatically.

"Then let me do it. If he is angry I won't be here to remind him of it for long. Just take me to the guards outside his building."

There was sense in the man's words, and the sentry found the idea dangerously appealing. But he knew his duty. Surely the stranger was mad if he thought Haldek would leave him to approach Lord Drettroth alone and unannounced. He shook his head dismissively and resumed his journey.

A pair of burly guards challenged them as they approached the lord's cabin.

"This man has an urgent message for Lord Drettroth," Haldek responded importantly.

One of the guards stepped forward. "Now? You want to see him now?" he asked incredulously. "You're braver than I thought, Haldek!"

Haldek bristled. "I said it was urgent."

"He'll have your guts for bowstrings."

"Let Lord Drettroth decide that," Haldek replied confidently, feigning a self-assurance he didn't feel.

The guard shrugged. "It's your funeral. Both of you leave your swords here."

They handed the swords to the guard, and his companion ran his hands roughly over their clothing, checking for hidden weapons.

"Wait here." The first guard disappeared into the building. He returned after a seemingly interminable delay. "Lord Drettroth will see you now."

Haldek stepped into the building, trying by a supreme act of his will to stop his body from shaking. The stranger followed him, cool as ice.

Two oil lamps on a low table filled the room with a dim light. A fire in one corner sent glimmers of light chasing after the shadows on the walls. Lord Drettroth awaited them, dark and inscrutable.

"Your reason for disturbing my rest must be pressing," he growled. "I hope so, for your sake."

Haldek gave in to the tremors that shook his frame. "This m-man has come with an urgent message, L-lord," he stuttered. "He insisted it would not wait."

Lord Drettroth turned to the man and surveyed him coldly. "I am expecting no message. Who sent you?"

Instead of answering, the man glanced significantly in the direction of Haldek and the guard. Lord Drettroth gestured impatiently. "Leave us."

Haldek stepped outside, relieved to be gone from the presence of his dread master. The guards positioned themselves before the door again, and he leaned back against the wall of the building.

The shutter of the window beside him lay slightly ajar. He found he could just make out the conversation inside. After a brief struggle between fear and inquisitiveness, his natural curiosity won out. He quietly leaned closer to the window.

"I bring greetings from Agon, High King of Rogand, Overlord of the Dukedom of Nakos, Master of the Idrenian Isles, and soon-to-be Emperor of the known world. To his loyal and beloved servant, Lord Drettroth, Commander of..."

"Enough of this! Where is Agon's message, curse you!"

The messenger cleared his throat. "Due to its sensitivity, His Majesty entrusted it to my memory rather than write it down."

"Hah! So how am I to be sure that this message is from the king?"

"With respect, My Lord, who else could have directed me to your fortress in the midst of this wilderness?"

"Do not be clever with me, young fool. Were you not the king's messenger, your life would be instantly forfeit for such impertinence.

Be sure I will remember you when I return to Rog. What is this all-important message, then?"

"King Agon is concerned about the progress of the raiding."

"So he is concerned is he? Our king is concerned? I am touched. But he did not send you here to tell me that. Get to the point!" Lord Drettroth's voice had taken on a dangerous tone. Haldek held his breath.

"His Majesty gives you one month more," the messenger said bluntly. "If your mission is not accomplished within that time, he regrets that it will be necessary to replace you, or recall you and your troops."

Haldek had heard enough. He eased himself away from the window and leaned toward the guards. "I will await the messenger at the gate," he whispered. Retrieving his sword, he sped away toward the welcome glow of the guardhouse by the gates.

THE MAN RETURNED after what seemed an age. Haldek was unable to read him. "Did it go badly?" he asked, offering another cup of ale.

The man accepted it gratefully, and soon a little life returned to his face.

"I'm to leave immediately. He wants my visit to be treated with the utmost secrecy." The man hesitated. "At least I think that's all he meant."

"Meant by what? What did he say?"

"He said that if he ever hears of me again, the man who mentions it will be flayed alive."

"You'd better go, then," Haldek said anxiously. "If he finds you here at dawn there'll be hell to pay."

"You're right about that," the man replied with feeling.

"The horse is ready." Haldek clapped him on the back and propelled him to the door.

Once outside, the man moved to the horse swiftly and prepared to mount it.

"Wait," Haldek called suddenly.

The man froze, his foot in the stirrup.

Haldek approached him until he was close enough to see his face. "May the Dark Ones look kindly upon your path," he offered quietly.

The man's startled eyes stared back at him for a moment. Then a warm smile slowly softened his burdened visage, like a first glimpse of the sun after many days of storm clouds. "And also upon yours!" He swung nimbly into the saddle.

The guards opened the gate once more, and he was gone.

An awful thought thrust itself upon Haldek: no one was patrolling the walls. The visit of the messenger had absorbed him so totally he had neglected his main duty.

"You two, get that gate closed. The rest of you get up on the wall. Now! Oh, and one other thing: if there's as much as a whisper about this messenger, I'll personally roast the man responsible over a slow fire. The fellow doesn't exist, and his visit never happened. Is that clear?"

They nodded obediently and went about their tasks.

WILL HALTED his horse at the edge of the clearing and looked back. He ought to have been elated. But already his fingers and toes were numb with the cold, and a long and crucial journey lay ahead of him.

His thoughts were drawn to the gatekeeper; in another place and time they might have been friends. He raised a hand in farewell and felt sure he could dimly make out an arm raised in reply from the walls.

But there was no time to lose. He glanced up at the sky, noting the telltale signs of the approaching dawn. Digging his heels into the ribs of his horse, he set out on the ride of his life.

9

The sights and smells of the town sometimes appealed to Thomas and occasionally overwhelmed him. But every year they combined in a dizzying assault on the senses called the Feast of St. Michael.

Thomas was convinced the whole world descended on Arnost for the Feast. Stalls lined every street, and hawkers crowded the market square. Dried fruit from Lestanor, exotic spices from the distant Simion Isles, and cleverly wrought metal goods from Rogand tempted the eager throngs that engulfed the town like a human tide.

Lords and ladies pampered themselves with rare luxuries. Peasant farmers traded their produce for much-needed farm implements. And, whatever their station in life, all feasted heartily, for food and ale were plentiful and inexpensive.

Everyone was saying the crowds were smaller than usual this year. Thomas heard his father suggest that the unrest in the border region was having an effect, along with the absence of the king from Arnost with so many men. The general mood was still one of celebration, though. The trouble at the border seemed a long way off, and the king's soldiers were there to deal with it now.

Thomas hadn't noticed any difference. To him the whole experience was just as exciting as ever.

"Enjoyin' the Feast, Thomas?"

The familiar level tone of old Jeb's voice sounded through the hubbub in the market square.

Thomas swung around eagerly. "Course I am, Jeb!"

A gentle smile creased Jeb's steady face. The man seemed rooted in solid rock. Not even the excitement of a Feast penetrated his calm.

"What about you, Jeb? Don't you enjoy it, too?"

"Me?" Jeb looked mildly surprised, as if the idea hadn't occurred to him before. "Yes, lad," he replied in his deliberate way. "I'm glad of the break."

"But why does it have to be so short? Three whole days gone already. And today's all but over."

"Ah, best not to think about that," the old man replied simply.

"I try not to. But I can't help it. Only three more days and the Feast will be finished."

"Don't waste yer time talking to an old man, then, young Tom. Be off with you, and have yer fun." As if to reinforce his advice he turned and, with a single wave of his weathered hand, was gone.

MEANDERING through the hawkers in the market square, Thomas noticed a crowd gathering nearby. The banners of the cobblers' guild waved proudly above a huge decorated wagon.

As he hurried over to join them the chatter of the onlookers ceased. All eyes were on the wagon. He craned his neck hopefully but could see nothing. Bending almost double, he burrowed determinedly into the solid mass of people, ignoring the ensuing growls of disapproval. He emerged at the front in a perfect position to watch the morality play that had just begun.

Battle had already been joined. Satan, richly clad in a magnificent gown of crimson and black, was enticing a poor shepherd boy to steal from his master.

A mound of newly baked bread covered a nearby table. Satan

casually selected a loaf. He set it down within easy reach of the hungry shepherd, who eyed it nervously.

The Tempter gazed at the youth pityingly and shook his head. "You work so hard! And he gives you so little to eat." He paused to let his words sink in.

"How long since you've tasted bread like this?" He indicated the loaf. It was so fresh from the oven that steam still rose from its golden-brown crust.

His silky voice took on a wheedling tone. "It smells good, doesn't it? Why don't you try it?"

The lad stared at the loaf longingly. A trembling hand reached out uncertainly. He was almost touching it.

Satan glanced around furtively before lowering his voice. "It's only one tiny loaf. He won't miss it. Go on, take it!" he insisted.

Close by a horde of demons hovered expectantly. Gloating in their hideous masks, they stood poised to drag the fallen youth away to everlasting torment. The onlookers, thoroughly alarmed, shouted encouragement and warnings.

Just when all seemed lost, the shepherd rallied, and directed a desperate last-minute appeal heavenward. Two saints climbed into the wagon. Hands clasped, they knelt to pray.

Soon a shining Jesus-figure simply dressed in a white robe appeared and banished the demons. Satan, shaking his fists in impotent rage, turned and fled. The shepherd boy followed Jesus with eyes alight, his hunger forgotten.

The onlookers erupted in cheers. Thomas shouted with them until hoarse.

THE PLAY OVER, guild members hitched horses to the wagon and marched proudly off behind it to repeat the play elsewhere in the town.

As the crowd dispersed Thomas drifted off toward the stalls just beyond the square. On the first day of the Feast his father had given him a small handful of coins. If he intended it as a peace offering,

Thomas's non-committal grunt in response must have offered him little satisfaction. Nonetheless, Thomas was pleased with the gift. Money commanded respect, and the coins earned him the right to walk among the stalls with head held high.

All but one still lay safely in the pouch at his waist. The missing coin was now in the keeping of an old peasant woman. Thomas had exchanged it for a large piece of honeycomb dripping with sweet nectar. He had spent a whole day savoring it in anticipation before the purchase; the reality was impossibly fleeting by comparison.

He could spare no more coins, though. The rest should be just enough to buy a bolt of bright cloth for his mother. Thomas had already wandered wide-eyed for hours among the bewildering array of options, and he was no closer to a decision. But there was plenty of time.

HE WAS STILL SEARCHING, totally absorbed, when an angry yell rose above the background babble of voices.

"Stop him!"

Thomas swung around in time to see a wooden cart upended into the street. A grim-faced boy erupted from the chaos. He dodged through the crowd frantically, a large loaf of bread tucked firmly under each arm.

"Stop him! Thief!"

A burly stall-keeper stepped into the boy's path. The youth tried desperately to evade him, but the man's two powerful arms ended the flight.

The baker arrived, red faced and panting. His finger stabbed accusingly at the boy. "He stole my loaves!" he gasped indignantly. "Tipped over my cart!"

His captor wrested the loaves from his grasp and returned them to their owner. The lad's eyes glared back defiantly out of a gaunt face. But his thin body trembled in the stall-keeper's firm grip.

He was hustled away toward the market square. Shouts of "Make way! Thief!" preceded him. The crowd caught up the cry, and it spread quickly. "Thief! They've caught a thief."

The angry crowd jostled and buffeted the lad. Thomas followed, curious to see the outcome. He could not grasp why anyone would be stupid enough to steal, especially so soon after the cobblers' guild drama. Surely the lad must have been aware of it.

The inevitable punishment was well deserved. Yet the frail youth seemed so pitiable he could not help feeling sympathy for him.

Town officials readied the stocks and secured the ankles of the luckless thief. The crowd subjected him to a continual stream of jeers and occasionally blows. He bore it bravely for a time. Eventually, though, he buried his face in his hands, his bony frame wracked by heaving sobs.

Unable to witness the humiliation further, Thomas turned away in distress. Silently he vowed that he would never yield to temptation, no matter how sorely he was pressed.

HEAD HELD high and lips pursed in a cheerful whistle, Thomas pushed through the merrymakers and set off for home. The pouch at his waist no longer jingled with coins, but he had every reason to be satisfied. He had bargained a good price for the large piece of deep blue cloth now clutched possessively in his hands.

Although the vendor had grumbled, Thomas saw his coins forced into an already bulging pouch. With six good days of the Feast behind him the man could probably afford to relax his price a little.

Almost clear of the main mass of people, Thomas found a small crowd pressed into a square. A performing bear? There were certainly bears at the Feast again this year—his father had seen one. Anxious not to miss any action, he elbowed his way eagerly toward the front.

Surprisingly, the crowd readily let him through, closing silently behind him. The youth popped into the open to find himself face to face with an old friar. Deep-set and brooding eyes locked on him briefly. Then the disturbing visage turned away.

Snow-white hair and an unkempt beard flowed restlessly around the man's face, caught up in a sudden gust of wind. He fixed his gaze heavenward. So intently did he stare that Thomas followed his gaze, half-expecting to see some marvel descending on the wings of a gathering storm.

Nothing unusual appeared. Thomas creased his forehead and regarded the friar in puzzlement. Plainly dressed in rough burlap and leaning on a sturdy wooden staff, the man could have been a prophet of old. As if to complete the image, he rounded sternly on the onlookers, spreading his arms grimly over them.

"Repent of your avarice! Turn away from your licentiousness." His thin voice grew in strength, and his hands shook. "Repent! Before it is too late.

"Darkness awaits you. You call down doom upon yourselves. The Feast of St. Michael? You dishonor his sacred memory with your gluttony and drunkenness! Do you expect to answer only to yourselves?" The old man pinned the crowd with flaming eyes. No one dared move.

"Cold, hard-hearted folk! What of the widows and the orphans among you? How many of you care for them? Which of you place the Eternal God above your appetites and desires? Do not think to escape the fires of hell should death take you." Several of the bystanders trembled, eyes wide with dismay.

"Turn away from the wrath to come! Seek mercy before justice befalls you."

The prophet glared around him, and a shaking finger picked out Thomas. "Think not that you will be spared. Your hatred and rage prepare you only for damnation."

Shaken and abashed, Thomas bent his head and shuffled his feet. When he finally risked a snatched glance, the friar's attention had shifted elsewhere.

Thomas grew restless. The old man's warnings clearly applied to someone else. How could he have been foolish enough to stop here?

He stole another glance at the friar. Seeing the man looking in his direction he rapidly shifted his gaze downward again.

The dire warnings rumbled on like thunder rolling through the hills. Head down, Thomas found his mind wandering. The bare and callused feet of the old prophet captured his attention. Travel-hardened toes poked out from the hem of his tattered robe, and Thomas observed that the toenail of his right big toe was missing. The toes bobbed up and down rhythmically. He hadn't noticed before, but the man was slowly swaying backward and forward like a sapling bending in a stiff breeze.

The strident voice ceased abruptly, cutting short Thomas's investigations. He looked up. The friar leaned heavily on his staff, head bowed, his fire extinguished. He appeared frail and tired.

Along with almost everyone else, Thomas grasped his opportunity and slipped away.

Strolling home in the sunshine clasping the precious cloth to his heart Thomas found the apocalyptic warnings of the old friar gradually fading from his mind. He savored in anticipation his mother's reaction to the gift. He had never before had an opportunity to give her anything substantial. He was confident she would be delighted. There could be no doubt about her surprise.

Once he reached home he decided not to go straight inside. An occasion like this needed to be shared. Though his best friend wouldn't understand, he could still participate in Thomas's pleasure. He headed for the stables, calling for Ben.

When he found Ben he also found Simon. The dog's chin nestled appreciatively in Simon's lap while the boy's left hand deftly stroked under his muzzle and behind his ears.

Thomas had been fool enough to think nothing could mar his enjoyment of this occasion. He flashed a grim look at his rival.

With his right hand Simon tossed a small object in the air, catching it before it fell. He tossed it again, and it spun in the air, flashing in the afternoon sunlight. Thomas froze. Could it be? Surely it was impossible! Once again the tiny object sailed into the air. He peered intently, neck craned forward and eyes narrowed.

For a moment the world stopped. "You stole it!" he gasped. "You stole it from me."

Simon stared at him, uncomprehending, but unmoved. "What are you raving about?"

"How *dare* you!"

Thomas's focus narrowed to the object of his hate before him. First he had snatched away the attentions of Thomas's father. Now it was Ben.

Worst of all, he had dared to steal Thomas's precious treasure. Once Thomas had been all-seeing. Now he was blind.

He abandoned himself completely to the fury which rose within him. A red veil spread behind his eyes and briefly blinded him. Then he leaped at Simon.

Ben sprang aside with a bewildered yelp. Thomas grabbed Simon's right hand, prizing open his clenched fingers. Simon fought back savagely.

Momentarily possessed of a superhuman strength, Thomas wrested the stone from his opponent with a jubilant bellow. Grasping it triumphantly, he attacked the younger boy ferociously, desiring only to hurt him. The two rolled across the floor of the stable, striking and clawing at each other.

Bruised and bloodied, Simon tore free of Thomas. Picking up a stick he struck out at the older youth, landing a painful blow across the arm.

This was too much. Thomas snatched up a pitchfork lying nearby. Pushing aside all thought of the consequences, he raised it and lunged.

Simon barely managed to avoid it. He turned and fled. Tail between his legs, Ben slunk away.

Thomas stood still for a very long time. Eventually he moved, wincing with the pain from his arm and numerous scratches. Blood trickled down his face and dripped off his chin. He opened his hand. The stone was still there, fouled with blood.

He turned absently and noticed the bolt of cloth for his mother. It had been trampled during the fight. He bent slowly and picked it up.

Grime and fresh horse manure had changed its color from a deep blue to a speckled dirty brown. Blood stains mingled with the dirt. He regarded it numbly.

On his way to the well to clean up Thomas passed old Jeb. Ashamed, he kept his head down, hoping Jeb wouldn't speak to him or notice his appearance.

Having washed himself as best he could, he tried to restore the cloth to its original condition. His efforts were in vain. Several large stains remained, and there were two small but noticeable tears in the middle where it had apparently been ground under foot. He couldn't give it to his mother now.

Thomas wandered aimlessly into the street, trying to push from his mind a vivid image of a lunging pitchfork. He couldn't go home. Simon would have been there first, of course. His father would be furious.

There would be a heavy punishment. He could weather it. But he could imagine already the disappointment in his mother's eyes, and he knew he had no resources to deal with that.

It dawned on Thomas later that the stone had revealed nothing to him, either of Simon during the fight or later Jeb.

It was the same stone. He knew it as well as his own hand. But it took only a few minutes in town among the revelers to drive home the harsh reality: the stone was utterly useless.

10

In the distance Will noticed a lone woodcutter at work among the pines on the fringes of the forest. Until now he had seen no one since leaving the forest stronghold, and the need to check his direction had become pressing. He headed toward the man eagerly.

Seeing another human lifted his spirits considerably. The journey had been demanding and uncomfortable, and he had driven himself unmercifully. People meant warmth and shelter, and both he and his horse needed rest.

As the sun rose he had gradually warmed up. Despite his sleepless night he had felt refreshed and energized. He made good progress while the sun climbed into the sky and paused briefly at noon only to rest the horse. Again he had reason to thank the Rogandan guards; his saddlebags overflowed with fresh bread, dried meat, and even a skin filled with ale.

Early in the afternoon, though, a fine rain set in, and before long it had soaked him thoroughly. Then a steady breeze sprang up out of the east and chilled him to the bone. He needed to dry out and sleep for a few hours before pressing on.

Soon the Rogandans would ride for Danford. They needed to arrive fresh enough to fight, so it did not seem possible that they could be in position in one day. Will's head start should allow him plenty of time to alert the nearest troops at Stantony and still get inside the walls of Danford first. The 'nomads' would get a taste of their own medicine.

The woodcutter spotted Will while he was still some distance away. To Will's vexation, the man dropped his ax and sprinted off into the forest before he could call out, soon disappearing among the trees. The young soldier quickly realized that following him was hopeless.

It dawned on Will that he must look like a nomad. He had kept the gianhi-skin cloak—it had a way of retaining his body heat without making him sweat. Even the horned helmet still sat in place. It had proven surprisingly effective at keeping the rain off his head.

He dismounted and pulled off the cloak and helmet, tossing them in frustration into a nearby clump of bushes. Then he thought better of it. Retrieving them, he stowed them carefully in his saddlebags, making sure they were out of sight.

As he was remounting, a hoarse cry rang out. He looked up to see two mounted men and several others on foot heading determinedly in his direction. Apparently the woodcutter had not been working alone. The men were armed and clearly meant business.

Will decided quickly that now was not the time for explanations. Trying to outrun them made even less sense. He turned his weary mount toward the forest and dug his heels into its flanks.

"Have you given our conversation any more thought, Rufe?"

Rufe had been called from his bed back to the barn commandeered by Edgar. Edgar seemed casual and relaxed. But his companions were like taut bowstrings. Something was brewing.

The small group of plotters had been conspicuous by their

absence in the last couple of days, but Rufe knew they would not have been idle. And after considering and rejecting many desperate schemes, he was no closer to blocking them. He felt hopeless and powerless and yet strangely responsible for the looming disaster.

That it would be a disaster he had no doubt. Why hadn't King Steffan dealt with the nomads more effectively? His failure had all but handed Edgar his opportunity.

Rufe decided his only option was to stall Edgar. "You haven't told me your plans for Lord Gramm and his knights."

"Trust, Rufe, trust," Edgar chided. "How can friends help each other without a little trust?"

Rufe did not reply.

"So you're still undecided?" Edgar asked.

Rufe nodded.

"Well, you can join us in a toast at least." Edgar nodded to one of his friends, and a mug of wine was thrust into Rufe's hands. "To the speedy downfall of the nomad raiders."

Rufe hesitated, unwilling to rely on Edgar even for a mug of wine. Where had it been pilfered from?

Then he shrugged and drank deeply. The wine seemed good on the way down, but left a bitter aftertaste. Just like everything about Edgar, he reflected grimly.

Rufe headed back to bed determined to find a way of stopping Edgar. But sleep overtook him before he had even begun to think about it.

———

THE SOUNDS of pursuit had faded away. Tall, stately oaks surrounded Will on all sides, and their leafy green canopy shut out the sky. The forest was almost completely silent. Warm drafts of air soothed his aching limbs, but he knew he could not afford to relax until he was clear of the trees.

His detour had already cost him several hours. At first he planned to hide until his pursuers had left. When it became clear they did not intend to give up the search, he decided to try to find a way around them. Now he was entirely lost.

As the daylight slowly failed Will happened upon a stream gurgling merrily along a deep gully. On the far side he could just make out a faint path in the half light. By the time he managed to find a suitable place to descend into the gully and cross the stream the path was barely visible.

No obvious token indicated which direction to take or even whether the path led anywhere at all. He debated with himself for a while then turned his horse upstream.

The path followed the stream for a while then turned away, skirting a dense tangle of fallen trees choked by thick undergrowth. The ground sloped steadily upward as the path wound its way around the hillocks. Soon the sound of the water had faded away altogether. Then the path turned sharply, and the stream abruptly reappeared. Droplets of spray danced gloomily in the fading light to the ceaseless music of a small waterfall.

Will paused beyond the waterfall and watered his horse before drinking deeply himself. Continuing in the dark seemed pointless, so he searched around for a comfortable place to lie down. Having tied up the horse to the branch of a fallen tree, he settled down for the night just off the path. His dwindling food supply he left untouched; it might need to last longer than he had expected.

A succession of attractive scenarios had paraded irresistibly before Will since leaving the Rogandan stronghold. All of them strongly featured honors and rewards for the man who so bravely saved the great town of Danford.

Now he berated himself for his foolishness. Never before had reality seemed to smile so intimately on his idle fantasies. And never before had his need for clear headedness been so urgent. He resolved henceforth to shun daydreams as a luxury that a man of action could ill afford.

The darkness was almost complete. Will sighed and closed his eyes, determined to rest.

A slight movement of air past his cheek roused him. His horse nickered loudly. A pale flash of white disappeared up the path as he looked up.

It seemed so insubstantial he wondered at first if he had imagined it. But his horse had sensed it, too.

Could it have been an apparition? A nameless dread worked its way up his spine, making his scalp crawl. Suddenly he felt vulnerable.

Will sat without moving for a long time. At last he could bear it no longer. Taking on an army would be better than waiting for a phantom to reappear. He untied the horse and set off up the path.

Negotiating the path in the dark took all his concentration. It continued to wind its way about, sometimes near the stream and sometimes away from it.

He would have missed the house but for the familiar smell of smoke from a wood fire. The dwelling had been built only a short distance from the path, but hidden from direct sight among the trees. All was silent apart from the quiet gurgle of the water and the throaty 'ribbit' of frogs, which faded away behind him as he moved further from the stream.

Still leading his horse, Will blundered around the rough wooden walls of the cabin, blindly searching for a way in. His fears had receded into the background with the anticipation of hot food, companionship, and a place by the fire.

An ominous voice from within the cabin stopped him cold. "Trespass in the haunted wood at your peril. Worse things than death may await you."

For a moment Will's fear welled up again. Then he called out boldly. "You will not readily drive me away from a warm fire with such words. I am cold and weary and need shelter for the night. I'll take my chances." It didn't hurt to be prepared, though. He quietly drew his sword.

An urgent mumble of voices carried to Will while he waited. Eventually a thin line of flickering light appeared as the door opened a crack. "Come in, then, if you dare."

Will sensed that the rough tone was forced, an awkward addition that did not belong to the voice. He quickly tied the horse and stepped toward the door.

"Not the sword. That stays outside!"

Will opened his mouth to protest, then shrugged. Sometimes you simply had to trust your instincts. He sheathed his sword, unstrapped the scabbard, and leaned it against the outside wall of the cabin. Then he stepped up to the door.

The crack widened, revealing a small room dimly illuminated by firelight and a couple of sputtering candles. He stepped in and looked around curiously. A few rough items of furniture barely relieved the starkness of the cabin's single room.

But his immediate attention was drawn to the occupants. A middle-aged man stood warily by the fireplace. His narrow gaze followed Will's every movement while his hand fidgeted beside the handle of a long-bladed knife. Huddled on the far side of the cabin sat an old woman. A cloak covered her stunted and misshapen body and a shawl held close about her head hid her face entirely. Her posture suggested she was a hunchback.

Will's travels had brought him into contact with many strange people. He could readily imagine what the idle ignorance of superstitious villagers might make of a hunchbacked old crone. It wasn't hard to guess why they had hidden away in the heart of a 'haunted' wood.

Finding himself in a home, even a rude one, made him acutely aware of his fatigue. "May I sit?"

A wooden chair lay unused beside the old woman, but the man nodded toward a low stool at the opposite end of the room. Will slumped onto it gratefully.

"Do you have any hot food? I will gladly pay for it."

The man bent to a metal pot suspended over the fire. His eyes scarcely leaving his guest, he scooped a generous portion into a wooden bowl. He handed it to the weary soldier along with a lump of bread.

Will took it eagerly and ate, scooping it out with his fingers. The stew seemed to contain lumps of fish, and he couldn't remember when he last enjoyed a meal so much. He cleaned out the bowl with the bread, not looking up until it was all gone.

"I must be gone well before dawn. I am a member of the King's Guard and I have urgent business in Stantony." He paused. "And I must avoid the local villagers." Neither of his hosts responded, but he could tell he had captured their interest.

"Can you guide me to the edge of the forest and direct me toward Stantony?"

The man spoke at last. "It is not possible. I have a game leg, and my...sister is unable to guide you." His face was unyielding.

"But you must! I will never find my way in the dark. And my errand is pressing."

There was no further comment. Will could see the man's curiosity had given way to stubborn determination.

"Can you at least wake me, then, three hours before the dawn?"

"We will wake you." This clearly presented no problem; most likely they would be glad to see the last of him.

The man apparently wanted to say more. Choosing his words carefully, he said, "It cannot benefit you to speak of your visit here. If you have any...gratitude for our hospitality, any respect for our solitude, you will leave us in peace." His face was stern, but he could not wholly suppress a tone of pleading from his voice.

"I'm sure I can be well away from here without needing to talk to anyone," Will replied. "If you guide me," he added significantly.

Will could see that the man was torn between the desire to be rid of him as expeditiously as possible and the need to remain secure in their haven, far from prying eyes. He decided to help them with their decision.

"I was pursued deep into the forest by a woodcutter and his friends. I think they mistook me for a nomad raider."

The man frowned in annoyance; the woman appeared shaken by the news.

"If I spend tomorrow wandering around the forest, they may find me. And you, too."

The man looked at Will darkly, then shot a glance at the woman who had become restless and distracted.

"All right," he growled. "You have your way. We will guide you as you ask."

Will could no longer ignore his exhaustion. Whether or not his hosts would play false, he needed to sleep. He mumbled his thanks and cast himself down on the floor.

HE WOKE to someone shaking him roughly. He squinted up into a face outlined by the flickering light of a single candle. Then he realized where he was. Surely he had only just laid down.

"It is time. You must go."

Will sat up reluctantly and rubbed his eyes. A warm skin had been placed over him while he slept, and he found to his surprise that his sword lay beside him. He stood up and strapped it on.

Will's horse snorted a welcome as they emerged from the cabin. The man hobbled around the side of the house for a moment and reappeared with the saddle. Will recalled with shame that he had gone to sleep without first taking care of his mount. It appeared that his hosts had made good his omission. He moved guiltily to the horse's side and tightened the girth straps.

Whatever the reputation of these people, they had treated him with kindness and respect, even though he was a complete stranger.

The man thrust a loaf of bread into his hand. "My sister will guide you."

Surprised, Will looked around for the woman. He glimpsed her dimly through the morning mist standing nearby. Fumbling in his pouch, he removed several coins and pressed them insistently into the hand of his host. After mumbling a brief protest, the man accepted them willingly enough.

As they prepared to leave, the man approached his sister and spoke quietly in her ear. She nodded impatiently and headed for the path, glancing back to be sure Will was following. She led him further upstream, then turned away across a clearing onto another fainter path.

The woman proved nimble enough in spite of her deformity. With a horse in tow, Will was hard pressed to keep up with her. It quickly became apparent to Will that he would never have found his way without her help.

She led on without pause until the first faint lightening of the sky heralded the coming of the dawn. The trees had thinned noticeably.

Soon they passed through a final patch of very dense woodland and arrived at the edge of the forest. Rolling hills dominated what could be seen of the distant skyline. The woman would go no further.

"Which way is Stantony?"

She did not speak, but pointed to a road, barely visible off in the distance.

He mounted his horse and looked down at her earnestly. "Thank you. You have done more than you can know by helping me. When my task is complete, if it is in my power, I will help you and your brother."

As he walked his horse clear of the forest, a voice called softly after him, "Fare well, king's man!"

He turned back, utterly astonished. For the voice was not that of an old crone, but the sweet tones of a girl who would soon be a woman.

But she was gone. He caught a last glimpse of her gliding off into the trees, and remembered the flash of white disappearing past him in the forest.

He set off without delay, his thoughts distracted by his guide. What lay behind that closely drawn cloak? Was she a witch, able to change her age and shape at will? Or simply a youth playing at an old crone? And if so, why? Intrigued and dissatisfied, he rode reluctantly away from the answers.

He had almost reached the road when he noticed three horsemen riding down from a ridge that overlooked the entire area. They chose a route which would soon intersect with his own. As they drew closer he saw that two of them were youths and the other scarcely more than a boy.

After a hurried consultation, the boy separated from the others and galloped back along the road in the opposite direction. The lad leaned forward over his horse, urging it to greater speed, but could not resist glancing frequently back over his shoulder.

Hoping to avoid them, Will kicked his heels into his horse's flanks. In response they spurred on their mounts and soon cut him off.

The youths—one slight and fair haired, the other taller and riding a skittish bay stallion—were armed, and as they approached they drew their swords importantly. Will had no intention of allowing them to delay him for long. He slowed his horse to a stop, drew his own sword and lay it across his knees. The eyes of the fair haired youth widened, and he glanced nervously at his bigger companion.

"Throw down your sword, stranger, or we will not answer for the consequences," the dark haired youth commanded.

"Is it always your custom to greet travelers in this way?" Will asked evenly.

"We know who you are," the youth sneered in response.

"Yes, you can't fool us," blurted the fair haired one. "We know you've been with *her*." He shook his sword indignantly. "We saw you. You're a nomad, no matter how *she's* made you look."

"I have no time for superstitious foolishness," Will replied scornfully. "I have an urgent errand for the king that cannot be delayed. Move aside!"

The fair youth glanced anxiously after his departed friend. Guessing they had sent for help, Will spurred his horse at them, determined to break through and trusting in the speed of his horse to outdistance them.

But the dark haired youth swung his horse into Will's path and swiped at him with his sword. Will barely ducked in time. He was immediately forced to raise his own sword to deflect another blow.

Warming to the task, his opponent soon rained blows on him. The youth had clearly been trained to use a sword, and Will was forced to parry vigorously. He was too eager to be dangerous, but the tall youth would be a competent swordsman one day.

Will thrust half-heartedly, unwilling to hurt him. But it was becoming evident he would not break free without taking the initiative.

Encouraged by his friend's boldness, the fair haired youth pressed in on Will from behind. Seeing his enemy momentarily distracted as a result, the larger youth aimed an energetic blow at Will's head. Will reacted too late to parry the stroke effectively. Glancing off his own sword, the blade gouged a deep tear down the length of his cheek.

Will's free hand flew to his face in disbelief. In a few moments, this credulous young fool had done him more injury than a stronghold full of Rogandan soldiers in a whole night. Blood flowed freely from the stinging wound.

His assailant paused, almost as surprised as him. Then, a new light in his eye, he returned to the attack. His friend advanced confidently from the other side.

Riled now, Will charged his attacker. He wanted to hurt him, to return pain for searing pain. He lunged for his sword arm, intending to take him out of the fight. But the youth's bay lurched forward, carrying its rider full onto the point of Will's sword. He reeled back, crashed to the ground, and lay still.

The fair haired youth gaped at his friend, wide-eyed with horror. Then he wheeled his horse and galloped off as though pursued by an army of demons from hell. His sword quivered point down in the ground, discarded in his haste.

A quick examination with his hand convinced Will he had suffered nothing worse than a flesh wound. He turned back to the fallen youth. Seeing him lying in his blood brought Will a deep pang of remorse. The youth had done nothing worse than trying to defend his home against a supposed invader. Such needless waste.

Why did it have to end like this? He shook his head, frustrated and angry at the senseless stupidity of it.

The youth had brought it on himself. Yet that knowledge failed to satisfy Will's need for self-justification. It was two nights—could it truly have been so recent?—since he had killed the two Rogandans. Anyone would excuse him for that, and his countrymen would unanimously praise him. But this?

If only he could have those few minutes over again. He wrestled unhappily with his thoughts. Never in his life had he found himself so bound in the grip of shame.

Harsh cries aroused him. A group of horsemen, riding hard, was almost upon him. Their armored leader rode a powerful charger and wielded a battle-ax. He was tall and dark haired. When he saw the fallen youth he bellowed out a roar of fury. Will hastily sheathed his sword still bloodied and urged his horse to a gallop.

Hurried glances over his shoulder showed the dark haired leader pursuing him closely. The others had fallen behind. Spurring his horse unmercifully, the ax man was gaining ground steadily.

Will kicked his mount hard in the ribs, and it sprang away with renewed energy. Another glance a few moments later showed his pursuer slipping behind. Carrying a heavy man in armor, the charger could no longer maintain its burst of speed.

The man bellowed and wept in frustrated rage. Finally abandoning the pursuit, he sent a despairing curse racing after his fleeing quarry.

Long after every sign of the chase lay far behind, the words still haunted the troubled young soldier: "His blood is on your head! Forever! For EVER!"

RUFE WOKE TO BRILLIANT SUNSHINE. He sat up and groaned. His stomach wanted to violently escape his body. He'd clearly overslept, yet no one had roused him, and there was no sign of other soldiers. The large barn in which he slept, normally a hive of activity in the morning, was strangely silent and empty.

Where was everyone? Lord Gramm always inspected the soldiers early each morning. Something must be going on. Had the soldiers been summoned to a village? If so, how could they have gone without disturbing him?

Or worse still, had Edgar finally made his move? A nasty suspicion crept in on him—Edgar's wine last night must have been drugged. Thoroughly alarmed and furious at being so easily duped, Rufe pulled on his boots, strapped on his sword and hurried outside. He squinted in the sudden light. His shadow clung closely to his body —he had almost slept the morning away.

Almost immediately he met two of Edgar's henchmen. They greeted him casually, but their manner said they had been waiting for him.

"Are you with us?" The tone was deliberately matter-of-fact even though the question was blunt.

Rufe sensed that a great deal hung upon his reply.

"Yes, I'm with you." Rufe could not remember a time when he had so consciously and deliberately set out to deceive someone. But he had built a reputation as a man of his word, and he could see that the soldiers accepted his answer at face value.

The men visibly relaxed. Rufe wondered what had been planned for him had he responded differently. He glanced at them with contempt. It would take more than this pair to dispose of him.

"Come with us. Things are moving along very nicely. Gramm is out of the way, and Edgar is whipping up the rabble right now in the town square. The nomads will soon be in for a big surprise."

Rufe set off after them, racked with indecision. What could he do? He looked at the men walking hastily ahead of him and decided there might be a simple way of buying more time.

He quickened his pace and caught up with them. Positioning himself between them, he placed his arms loosely around their necks. He responded to their startled looks with a genial smile. Then he abruptly squared his shoulders, stepped back and drew their heads together with a single fluid movement of his powerful arms. With a sickening thud the two men slumped senseless to the ground.

Rufe bent down and put his ear to their mouths. Yes, they were still breathing steadily. One at a time, he picked them up in his great arms as a father might carry a child, and shifted them back to the barn, carefully laying each of them on a palliasse. After stopping for a moment to admire his handiwork, he once again headed for the town square.

RUFE CAUTIOUSLY CIRCLED the soldiers on the edge of the square, bending low to remain inconspicuous. Hands on his hips, Edgar stood on top of an old wooden cart in front of the soldiers. He was working them gradually and persistently, like a man breaking a horse.

But a few stubborn dissenters were not yet convinced.

"What about Lord Gramm and his knights?"

"How many times do I have to tell you?" The hard edge in Edgar's voice suggested his patience was wearing thin. "They're ill. All of them. I can't help it if their food doesn't agree with them.

"Mind you, it serves them right if you ask me," he added, dropping his tone sarcastically. "They wine and dine like kings every day while we survive on scraps."

Rufe knew it wasn't true, but a spontaneous growl of agreement from the crowd indicated Edgar had struck a chord. He pressed home his advantage. "But I'm not interested in feasting. I want to strike a blow for my king!

"The nomads have had it all their own way. It's time we took the fight to them. We're the king's soldiers. But are we cowards?"

Edgar's challenge evoked a loud chorus of denials. He almost had the crowd where he wanted it, and Rufe could think of nothing to do or say to stop him. Soon it would be too late.

Rufe concluded reluctantly that it was too late for him to intervene effectively. No one could stop Edgar now except Lord Gramm.

The lord must be somewhere nearby, probably drugged and under guard. Rufe hurried off, on the lookout for another soldier who was not at the meeting. As he ran he mumbled a fervent prayer that Lord Gramm would be conscious when he found him.

· · ·

A BUZZ of voices rose on the far side of the square. A lone horseman appeared, picking his way through the crowd toward the center of the square. The voices fell silent as he passed through their midst, and all heads turned to follow his progress. Steam rose in clouds from his horse. Judging by its step it was almost spent, although it still tossed its head proudly.

The rider's face bore a gaping wound, and his eyes probed the crowd with restless intensity. Many soldiers stepped back involuntarily when they saw his appearance.

The man drew his horse to a halt just before the wagon where Edgar glared darkly down at him, annoyed at the interruption. He looked up, and even Edgar flinched when confronted with his ruined visage.

"Where is the commander?"

"What business is it of yours?" Edgar replied.

The rider eyed Edgar coolly before answering. "Raiders have attacked the village I kept watch over. My task is to alert the commander."

Someone called out. "It's Will Prentis. From the King's Guard."

A hubbub arose. There were loud cries of "To horse!" Men began arguing and milling around in confusion.

"Be silent, you idiots!" Edgar roared over the din. "Do you want another fool's errand to a burned-out village?"

"Wait!" The rider's clear voice rang out. "He is right. The village is destroyed. It is already too late."

Edgar seized his opportunity. "Listen to this man. There is nothing more to argue about. We must ride for the nomad encampments at once. We will plunder them as they have plundered us."

"No! Listen to me." The rider rose in his stirrups, and his voice carried commandingly. He turned to Edgar. "Who placed you in authority here?" he challenged loudly.

Edgar scanned the crowd and nodded to several men who immediately pushed their way toward the front. The other soldiers backed away. The rider swung his horse around and drew his sword. It was caked with dried blood. Edgar's men surrounded him, though they hung back warily.

"Your task," Edgar called out, "was to raise the alarm as soon as your village was attacked. And yet you say it is too late to save it." He pointed accusingly at the rider and addressed the crowd. "This man's village was destroyed while he escaped with a flesh wound. I say the raiders chased him, and he hid until they had gone. He is a coward and a traitor who deserves to die."

Edgar's men closed in, probing for a weakness.

11

Silent as a cat, Thomas padded through the dark and drafty corridors of the castle. During the winter months, every fireplace hissed and cracked, pitting blazing fire against the creeping chill. At this time of the year many of the fireplaces were deemed unnecessary, though, and the cold seeped slowly from the enclosing walls, setting Thomas shivering and longing for sunshine and the open air.

Whatever the season, the castle bustled with life and energy, even with the king away; Hilda the Grim, who oversaw the kitchen hands, pageboys, and chambermaids, saw to that. Sudden woe befell any idle hand coming into range of her ever-restless eye. But the castle was so vast and its corridors so labyrinthine that not even Hilda could oversee it all at once. That morning Thomas had seen no sign of her, not even the scurrying of her minions at the rumor of her approach.

He had been sent by his father with a message for the Hunt master. Ferreting the man out proved a challenge worthy of Hilda herself. Thanks to the cleaning girl who pointed out the old hunter's refuge, though, Thomas had finally tracked him to his lair. He startled the master out of a peaceful midmorning nap.

His message delivered, Thomas set off to find the castle entrance and the relative warmth of the stables. His journey took him through unfamiliar and lightly trafficked sections of the castle. At one point, he paused beside a narrow window that offered a distant glimpse of the river and the forest beyond it.

He fell to thinking about the carefree afternoon, seemingly years ago, when he had found the stone. The Thomas of those days was long gone, largely as a result of that discovery. And what did he have to show for it? He was confused and often unhappy, he had made a bitter enemy, and the power of the stone was lost to him.

Thomas had seen very little of Simon since their fight in the stables. For some inexplicable reason Simon had not told his father about his attack with the pitchfork, or even about the fight. Whether he was saving it until he could extract the maximum revenge, or whether he had some other motive, Thomas couldn't tell. Simon had not forgiven him—of that much he was certain—although that didn't help him suppress the shame of his own behavior.

His musing was interrupted by the welcoming crackle of a huge fire, issuing from the open doors of a large room. Although he had only seen the room on a few occasions, Thomas recognized it at once —the king's personal audience chamber. After a furtive glance into the chamber, he stepped inside and pushed the doors partly closed. The fire roared encouragingly just inside the doors, and he positioned himself before it, gazing about him in admiration.

A large table stood in the center of the room, surrounded by many elegantly carved chairs. The largest chair, almost a small throne, faced him at the far end, commanding the table.

Full suits of ancient ceremonial armor stood tirelessly at attention along both main walls. His father had brought him here once as a small child, and Thomas had taken some convincing that the suits did not conceal real knights. Even now he couldn't help shooting sudden glances at them, half expecting to surprise them in some tiny movement.

Imposing as they were, though, the suits of armor were not the main feature of the room—the chamber was dominated by huge wall hangings. Twelve tapestries adorned the walls, each featuring the deeds of a different king. The history of Arvenon appeared to be woven into the giant hangings, but Thomas could not name even one of the kings. He was disappointed to find no tapestry depicting Steffan II, the current ruler.

The largest and most lavish showed a young man astride a restless charger, the light of battle in his eye. A desperate struggle raged below him. His hand was raised high and behind him an eager troop of horsemen restrained their steeds with difficulty, waiting for his hand to fall.

It was his face that captured Thomas. The weaver had portrayed a young man with the air of one born to rule. His face showed a determination that reminded Thomas of Will. And with the imminent prospect of battle and perhaps death, the youthful warrior exuded a calmness that Thomas envied.

"Impressive, isn't it?"

Thomas leaped in alarm at the sudden voice. He whirled, wide-eyed. An old man stood behind him, gazing upward at the hanging. The man seemed vaguely familiar, but Thomas couldn't place him. He wore simple attire—not as lavish as might be expected of a noble, although certainly not the attire of a serving man, either. Thomas had been so absorbed he hadn't heard the man enter the room.

"Do you know who he is?" The old man smiled inquiringly at Thomas, inclining his head upward to indicate the youth in the giant tapestry. Thomas shook his head.

"It's Steffan the First. Our current king was named for him."

The man seemed unconcerned at Thomas's intrusion. Emboldened, Thomas decided to try to satisfy his curiosity. "What's going on?" he asked, pointing up at the hanging.

"The tapestry shows the Battle of Samoth, fought almost one hundred and fifty years ago. Arvenon was a smaller and weaker kingdom then, struggling to survive against the larger and more aggressive Kingdom of Rogand.

"The king, Rufus II, fought two inconclusive battles against the invading Rogandans, before he was finally brought to bay near the village of Samoth."

The old man's reply raised more questions than it answered. But he appeared to be in a talkative mood, so Thomas decided to wait and see what else he had to say.

"The Arvenian forces were outnumbered five to one, and the battle went badly for them. The king's only son was mortally wounded almost at once.

"The battle wore on into a second day. By midmorning, the king's son finally died, and the Arvenian army was on the brink of collapse. Just when it seemed the battle would be irretrievably lost, Steffan arrived. That moment is depicted on the tapestry before you.

"Steffan was the newly crowned king of Erestor, a small neighboring kingdom allied to Arvenon. He realized that if Arvenon fell, Erestor would be next, and he didn't hesitate to throw his full support behind Rufus. Erestor's army was small, but it included some of the finest cavalry ever seen up to that time."

The old historian had warmed to his task, and Thomas listened, fascinated and totally engrossed.

"Steffan's arrival was unlooked for by either side, and his horsemen swept through the right wing of the Rogandan army like a scythe. Rufus somehow rallied his surviving troops and attacked the enemy's left wing. It, too, quickly folded. Then the Rogandan center found itself under attack from two sides on narrow fronts. Most of the Rogandan soldiers milled around in confusion, unable to get at their enemies.

"The issue was decided just before sunset. A detachment of Erestorian archers arrived at the battlefield, and immediately began raining a deadly hail of arrows into the Rogandan ranks. The invaders held for a while, then turned and ran. Steffan's cavalry cut them down as they fled, all the way to the River Ange. Only the darkness saved them from total destruction. As it was, only one in three returned to Rog to face the wrath of their king.

"Rogand's power was broken, and Arvenon knew peace for many years."

"But didn't you say that Steffan was king of a different country?"

"Yes, I did. Rufus was gravely wounded in the final stages of the battle. The king had fought so well, only to see his son killed and his line ended on the day of his greatest victory.

"But he had a daughter. He offered her hand to Steffan there and then. Steffan accepted it, and Rufus proclaimed him the new king almost with his dying breath.

"Once it became known, there was dissent within the kingdom, of course. But the marriage brought legitimacy to the new rule, and Steffan combined the kingdoms and quickly strengthened and extended them. Most important of all, he proved to be a wise and just king, much loved by all. Just like our own king."

Thomas decided that while his luck held, he would keep the man talking. "Who are the other tapestries about?"

"The greatest kings of Arvenon, before and after Steffan. The tapestry to the left of Steffan's depicts Rufus II. Steffan himself commissioned it, in honor of the deeds of his late father-in-law."

"Who is that one to the right?"

The old man didn't answer. He held up his hand for silence. Voices could be heard in the corridor outside, rapidly becoming louder.

"You'd best be off." He pointed to a small door at the far end of the room. Thomas scurried through it, pulling it shut behind him just as the approaching voices reached the main doors of the chamber.

As the door closed, he heard a respectful greeting, "My Lord Duke, I see you have arrived already..."

And then it hit him. The old historian was the Duke of Erestor, the king's uncle, and, in the absence of the king, the regent of the kingdom! No wonder he knew so much about the Arvenian kings—it was his own family history. Thomas was mortified.

He had seen the duke many times, but mostly from a distance, and always before today dressed in a manner befitting royalty. He felt the blood rush to his face as he realized that he had not bowed to the duke. Worse, he had dared to speak to him, and hadn't done so in an appropriate manner. He hadn't even thanked him, a courtesy due to any commoner, much less a duke. He shivered at the thought of his father learning of the conversation.

He set off along the corridor before him toward a door at the far end. It was closed, but he opened it slowly and peered through it into a small antechamber. Two more doors lay to the left and the right, and another stood open opposite. Through the far door he could see what appeared to be a major corridor of the castle.

Thomas headed quickly through the antechamber toward the corridor, anxious to be gone. Before he reached it, though, he again heard voices in the corridor outside. One, loud and strident, he knew at once, and realized to his alarm that he was on a collision course with Hilda the Grim.

Hilda would want to know why he was sneaking around the castle, where he had been, where he was going, and who he had been bothering. He glanced at the doors on either side, chose quickly, and went through the one on the left, praying as he did that the room would be empty.

His prayer was answered, not only in the affirmative, but far beyond his expectations. In a day of marvels, he had stumbled on the most marvelous thing of all: a mirror. He had heard of its existence and knew what it was called, but had never seen it till now.

It stood almost as tall as him, mounted on a frame of exquisitely carved mahogany. It was truly a gift befitting a queen. Thomas knew without needing to be told that he did not belong in this room.

Nevertheless, he was drawn to it like a moth to a flame. He gazed in wonder into the mirror, clearer by far than any still pond on a calm day, and saw a tousle haired, gangly youth staring back at him. Although his mother had asserted it a hundred times, it nevertheless surprised him to see strong traces of his father in his own face.

As he stared, his curiosity was aroused: what would he look like when he was a man? Perhaps things would improve for him. Maybe he would be happier then.

He recalled his first glimpse of Will. The stone had transformed the young soldier from an ordinary man-at-arms into a knight, a vision that surely revealed Will's destiny. Could the stone show him something of the future of the pale youth before him in the mirror?

He reached down into his pouch and fumbled around, finally grasping the stone in his right hand.

Nothing happened. It wasn't surprising—the stone was now useless, after all—but he was still disappointed. He continued to stare absently into the mirror. Then the image seemed to shimmer, and a subtle change became apparent. It took him a few moments to identify it; the image before him had scarcely altered.

It had something to do with the eyes. He peered intently into the eyes and staggered backward in disbelief. The madness in the eyes. His eyes. His wolf's eyes. How could he bear it?

He instantly released the stone, and his eyes were as before. But it was too late. He could not undo what he had witnessed.

These eyes did not presage rabies. They spoke to him of the ruin of hope, the death of normality, the triumph of insanity in his life.

He fled the room and the castle in utter dismay.

12

ufe's search had finally paid off. A solitary soldier stood outside a small barn on the outskirts of the town. He appeared alert and nervous. The barn doors were shut and barred. Rufe debated with himself for a moment before deciding to risk a bluff. He walked purposefully toward the soldier.

The man tensed instantly, his hand flying to his sword hilt. "What do you want?"

"Edgar sent me. You're watching Gramm, aren't you?"

"So you're with us?" The soldier's hand relaxed again. "Why did he send you?"

"He thought you might need to be reinforced."

The man looked worried. "Is there trouble?"

"No. Everything's going according to plan."

As he said it he sent his huge fist crashing into the soldier's jaw. The man slumped to the ground and lay still. Rufe hastily unbarred the doors and threw them open.

Once his eyes adjusted to the dim light inside the barn he saw prostrate forms laid out everywhere. After a quick search he found Lord Gramm and went straight to his side. The noble lay senseless, but breathing steadily. Rufe shook him firmly, but to no avail. His knights lay strewn around like wheat stalks scythed by a reaper. Edgar must have drugged them heavily.

His heart skipped a beat at the sheer audacity of it. But Lord Gramm could not punish those responsible if he didn't know who they were. And Edgar was shrewd enough to keep even his own accomplices in the dark. Knowing Edgar, someone had already been set up to take the blame.

Rufe quickly despaired of arousing even one of them. Then he heard a low moan coming from a corner of the barn. He headed toward it hopefully.

The sight that awaited him stopped him in his tracks. Several young men lay together, many of them severely wounded. Appalled, Rufe approached more closely. He recognized a squire of one of the knights. The squires must have put up a fight.

He discovered the source of the moans. A young man, ghostly white from shock and loss of blood, stirred weakly. He seemed to be drifting in and out of consciousness.

Drugging Lord Gramm and his knights was treasonous folly. But the brutality before him was beyond everything. Confronted by the pale, motionless young forms, Rufe's feelings of powerlessness vanished like an early mist before the sun. The urge to make Edgar pay became so compelling it felt almost like physical pain.

The insistent needs in the barn tugged at his heart. But every other fiber of his being drew him irresistibly into the eye of the storm brewing outside. He rushed out of the barn and sprinted toward the square.

His first glimpse of Edgar revealed him talking to a stranger on a horse. His spirits leaped when he recognized the man as Will Prentis. But what were they saying? He pushed to the front at the same moment Edgar pronounced judgment. Rufe caught a brief glimpse of Will's ruined face as his friend swung his horse around, surrounded by his attackers. Then he reached the cart.

Edgar finally spotted the giant guardsman. Fear showed on his face, and he called loudly for help. But he was too late.

Rufe vaulted into the cart before Edgar's sword had cleared its scabbard. Edgar had time for one hasty swing. Rufe blocked it with a lump of wood from the cart and kicked him hard in the midriff. He doubled over, and Rufe brought both fists crashing down onto his head.

He turned to the astonished crowd and indicated Edgar's prostrate body. "This...this *fool* drugged Lord Gramm and locked him in a barn."

They stared back uncomprehendingly. Most had drawn well away from the ring that closed around Will. Perhaps they hadn't heard him over the confused buzz of voices.

But Will's attackers heard. Several of them wavered, their faces betraying first shock and then horror. Fully half of the group slunk away and melted into the crowd. That left five. Two of them rushed at Rufe. The rest redoubled their attack on Will.

Still the crowd wavered. Rufe glared at them in disgust. He bent down to Edgar's limp body, heaved it up and hurled it at the two men clambering onto the cart. One of them was knocked to the ground. The other dodged it and pulled his friend to his feet.

Rufe drew his sword and leaped off the cart. He was dimly aware of one of Will's attackers going down. Then he charged howling at his enemies.

Furious, he flailed about with great slashing strokes, taking fierce delight in the frantic dodging of his opponents. His superior strength and reach forced them onto the defensive.

But he soon tired. And his opponents fought with the savage desperation of doomed men.

One of them got behind him. Suddenly he was fighting for his life. The sword became slippery as a cold sweat loosened his grip. Then he steadied himself, feinted toward one of the men, and dodged free. Sobered, he placed his back to the cart and struck out with renewed energy.

Other guardsmen joined the fray at last, and his attackers once again lost the initiative. Small knots of men struggled back and forth around the cart.

Within minutes it was over. Two of Edgar's remaining cronies had thrown down their swords. The other three lay dead. A soldier of the King's Guard lay beside them.

Rufe turned his back on the carnage and looked around for Will. He soon spotted him striding purposefully in his direction.

Will Prentis had always been his friend. Now they had fought together, alone and against the odds, and prevailed. Resolutely ignoring Will's damaged cheek, Rufe smiled a welcome. Will sprang past him onto the cart without even acknowledging him. Open-mouthed, Rufe stared after him.

Will stood to his full height. "You men. Gather round. Now!" The soldiers obeyed slowly, avoiding the bodies. Bewilderment showed on their faces.

"Listen to Rufe Sarjant. You need to hear what he has to say." Will turned to him at last and beckoned him up.

Rufe smiled up at him warmly. "I'm glad you're back, Will."

Will merely nodded. "Make it brief," he said bluntly.

Rufe scurried up onto the cart. This was a day of surprises. He pushed aside his questions and faced the men. "I found Lord Gramm and his knights. They're in a barn near here. Unconscious, all of them. They should recover after Edgar's drugged wine wears off. Some of their squires may not be so fortunate.

"It seems Edgar had plans for us. He talked about revenge against the nomads. But I think he was more interested in looting them."

Rufe began to warm to his task. "I suspect..."

Will cut him off cold. "I need five volunteers. Men who can't ride fast or fight hard."

No one stepped forward. Will turned swiftly to Rufe. "Choose them when I'm finished. And make sure they're reliable. They must tend the wounded, guard the traitors, and explain everything to Lord Gramm when he recovers."

He inspected the crowd, frowning. He seemed to be assessing them. "Thanks to Edgar's treachery our numbers are reduced and we are without our leaders. We must do the best we can."

He drew himself to his full height. "I have come from the nomad stronghold." Exclamations of amazement and disbelief greeted his words. Rufe gaped at Will, utterly astonished. He felt as though he was seeing him for the first time.

Will raised his hand for silence. Such was the force of his presence that the soldiers obeyed without hesitation. He swung around to Rufe. "My saddlebags. Get out the nomad clothes."

Rufe jumped down and retrieved them, tossing them up to Will.

He held them high. "The men who wear these are not nomads. They are Rogandan soldiers, led by a Rogandan lord. I speak their language and passed myself off as one of them.

"They want to provoke our king to fight the nomads. Even now they ride for Danford. They plan to sack the city. If they succeed, the king will be forced to turn on the nomads. You can imagine the rest." He pointed down at Edgar's still form. "This greedy fool would have played right into their hands."

"Why should we believe you?" someone in the crowd called out. "Maybe you're lying like Edgar."

Rufe reacted without thinking. "You're the ones beyond belief," he shouted, jumping up beside Will. "You listen to a self-serving liar. But you can't recognize the truth when it's shoved under your noses. Well, anyone who says Will Prentis is lying can argue it out with me." He thrust out his chest and glared at them belligerently.

This earned him a brief smile from Will. For a moment his friend seemed less aloof. Then he turned back to the soldiers, and his voice rang with authority.

"Choose quickly. The fate of our kingdom hangs in the balance. I will ride to Danford, even if I must face the Rogandans alone. Who will dare to ride with me?"

Rufe stared first at the crowd then back at Will. The soldiers stirred restlessly. Will's challenge hung in the air, his marred face confronting the soldiers like a rebuke. Yet he seemed completely calm. Rufe could not suppress an irrational notion that even if no one joined him, Will would somehow beat the Rogandans single-handed.

Will had changed. He may have become distant and unreachable, but he wouldn't have to ride alone.

Rufe stepped forward. "I will ride with you," he said quietly.

Will nodded an acknowledgment. Still he waited, arms folded across his chest. There was complete silence.

Then one soldier stepped out from the crowd. "I will, too."

Another followed. "And I."

"Me too."

Just as a falling rock dislodges others, the momentum gathered. The lone voices became a chorus and the chorus an avalanche of cheering.

Will tolerated their enthusiasm for no more than a minute. He held up his hand one last time. "Get your horses and weapons and return here at once. We must ride as we've never ridden before."

As they dispersed Rufe heard him add under his breath, "And pray that we arrive in time."

THE SOLDIERS at first made good time. They rode north swiftly through the open country surrounding Stantony, before swinging west to ford the broad river that wound lazily across the plain.

Will and Rufe led the way to the other side and turned to wait for the others. The water, just three feet deep, flowed gently, but the ford was narrow. There was barely enough room for two wagons to pass in the middle. The soldiers pressed toward the crossing, which soon degenerated into a confusion of splashing horses and shouting men.

Will jumped his horse back into the river and swam it across, scrambling up the opposite bank. Rufe heard Will's voice through the din, calling the men to a halt. The chaotic surge toward the river ceased abruptly, and the ford cleared. Will's voice rang out again, shouting instructions. As if by magic, a disciplined column of soldiers began crossing four abreast.

Will followed and led them west again without pause or comment. They climbed for almost an hour into rising foothills and crossed a pass, descending again into undulating terrain that stretched as far as the eye could see.

Every now and then the column of soldiers stretched out too far, and Will dropped back and urged on the laggards. Increasingly he glanced up at the sun, sinking slowly over their left shoulders, before frowning ahead across the hills.

Finally, returning from one of his trips down the line, he drew his horse alongside Rufe's.

"We're moving too slowly," he announced. "I'm going to ride ahead. I've already selected twenty men with fast horses."

Rufe's jaw dropped. As if to emphasize Will's words, several riders moved forward resolutely. Rufe recognized among them some of the best fighters in the troop.

He looked back at Will, dismayed. The soldiers had regained their sense of purpose since Will arrived. What would happen now?

"Who'll lead the troop if you leave?"

"You."

At first Rufe thought he was joking. But Will's face showed otherwise. Rufe was so flabbergasted he was unable to respond. All his life kings or lords or knights had been there to give the orders. Nothing had prepared him for this.

"I can't lead them!" he finally blurted out.

"Why not?"

"Because...because I don't know what to do."

"All you have to do is get the men to Danford as quickly as possible," Will replied. "If you find the Rogandans there, attack them without delay. If not, get inside the gates and defend them."

"The men won't follow me."

"Of course they will. If they'll follow me, they'll follow you."

Rufe shook his head, frowning. "It isn't the same." Will made it sound so straightforward, and he felt like a stubborn child trying to complicate a simple chore. For Will, leading seemed as natural as breathing. But it wasn't that way for him. "I don't have your qualities."

Will had been listening patiently, as though Rufe's objections would vanish once he was allowed to express them. But now he spoke pointedly. "There isn't time to consider personal feelings. Our mission is too important. The whole kingdom might be on the brink of disaster."

Rufe wanted to protest, to point out the obvious shortcomings that disqualified him. But when he opened his mouth, nothing came out.

"You needn't worry. I'll let the men know." With that, Will trotted back down the line again, calling out to the men as he went.

Rufe was stunned. The matter had been settled before he could even consider it as a serious option.

Will returned after a few minutes. "I've spoken to the men," he said. "You're in charge now. I'll see you in Danford!"

He raced away, followed by his select group of soldiers. His final instructions reached Rufe faintly over the drumming of hooves: "Keep the men moving!"

Will's hand-picked soldiers rode hard. They soon dipped out of sight behind the hills ahead. Each time they reappeared they had dwindled in size until Rufe could no longer see them at all.

Once Will had gone Rufe realized how much he had been depending on him for purpose and direction. Now he felt utterly alone.

With Rufe at their head, the main body of troops rode on in silence. Cresting a ridge, Rufe looked back and noticed that the line had stretched out too far again. He headed back to urge the stragglers to quicken their pace, fully expecting to be ridiculed. To his surprise, they responded obediently.

Will had taken complete command of the troops before leaving Stantony and no one had raised as much as a murmur. That was amazing enough. But the soldiers' meek acceptance of his sudden delegation to Rufe was nothing short of astonishing.

Rufe still wasn't quite sure how it had all happened. But one thing stood out very clearly: Will Prentis had become difficult to refuse.

"THERE, BEYOND THOSE HILLS."

Rufe's gaze followed the soldier's pointing finger out across the seemingly endless prospect of rolling hills. Yes, he could just make it out: a tiny strip of silver reflecting the late-afternoon sun. The River Dan. Beside it lay the town of Danford. Their goal was at last within reach.

Rufe strained ahead for a glimpse of Will and his troop. But he knew it was irrational. They were long since out of sight.

After hours in the saddle, both men and horses showed their weariness. But Rufe could not shake off a mental picture of a sea of nomad-clad horsemen sweeping away Will and his tiny force. The time had come to pick up the pace.

WILL's troop charged through the last village before the walled city of Danford. Only the barking of a dog marked their passage. They swept onto the final stretch of road past an abandoned cottage, disturbing some hens which ran squawking under an old wagon overgrown with weeds. Then all was quiet except for the drumming of hooves.

Will halted his men under the cover of the last stand of trees before the walls of Danford and peered out into the dusk. The gates had already been closed for the day. All appeared peaceful.

"Wait here. I'm going to see who holds the gates."

Will removed his helmet and drew his cloak around him to hide his sword. Head down and slouching forward in the saddle, he headed toward the gates. To all appearances he was just another weary traveler, his horse plodding with fatigue.

The night-watchman challenged him well before he reached the wall. "The gates are closed. Be off with you!" The words were carefully articulated, but the speaker could not disguise a heavy accent.

"But I need shelter for the night." Will glanced back over his shoulder. "You can't turn me away! It isn't safe out in the open."

Coarse laughter greeted his statement. Apparently he had said something amusing.

He wondered if their sense of humor had a limit. "It's rumored there are nomad barbarians abroad tonight."

The laughter ceased abruptly.

A spear whistled through the air and quivered in the ground beside him. "Begone!" His horse laid back its ears and tossed its head wildly. Will swung the animal around and galloped away from the gate. Echoes of renewed laughter chased him out of earshot.

He pulled his horse up inside the safety of the trees. "They've taken over the gates already. We don't have much time."

"Are the gates closed?" one of the men asked.

"Yes, although they've left the portcullis up." Will looked around him and cursed. "They probably aren't strong enough to hold off a determined assault, even by twenty men. But we have no ladders, no ropes, nothing. Not even a horn to alert the people inside."

A soldier spoke up. "Could we get the portcullis down? Cut the ropes that hold it up, maybe? That would keep the Rogandans out."

Another answered. "Not a chance. One of the guards showed it to me when we were stationed here. It's raised and lowered by heavy chains. Neither the winder nor the chains are even visible from outside the walls."

Will's mind churned as the darkness deepened. He glanced away toward the distant hills, little more than an outline against the sky. Rufe and his men were out there somewhere. He prayed they would arrive in time.

Someone broke the silence. "If the portcullis is up, we can get inside it."

"How does that help us?" Will demanded.

"We won't last long outside the walls once the Rogandans arrive. But maybe we can defend the tunnel between the gates and the portcullis."

"Yes, and spend our time dodging boiling oil from the gate-house," another voice chipped in sarcastically.

"No, wait. It's worth thinking about." Will had no better ideas. And a desperate situation called for desperate measures. "Don't forget their task is to open the gates, not defend them. They won't be boiling up a vat of oil. Anyway, supplies like oil and rocks aren't stored at the gate-house. They're only taken there during a siege." Will sincerely hoped he was telling the truth.

"But we can't just ride in. The minute they see us coming they'll drop the portcullis. After their friends get here and finish us off, they'll wind it up again and let them in."

Will pondered for a minute. "Then we'll have to make sure they don't realize twenty men are at the gates until it's too late."

"How do we do that?"

"A while back we passed an abandoned wagon. We'll hide inside it. Once we get it past the portcullis we can use it to barricade the entrance." He jabbed his finger at several of the men. "You four, go back and get it. And be quick about it!"

THE DAN WOUND its way like a glittering serpent through the plain before them. The troop had broken free of the hills at last.

Without slowing, Rufe twisted around in the saddle and reviewed the column stretched out behind him. After weeks of frustration and idleness Will had promised them a real opportunity to do at last what they came for. There had been so many false alarms, though. Would the Rogandans be there?

He felt certain they would. And the soldiers thought so, too. Glancing back at them he could sense the expectancy in their ranks, the suppressed nervous excitement. The setting sun caught their spear tips and set them flickering like dancing fireflies. It was an impressive sight. The king's soldiers were riding to war.

Once they reached level ground, still a league or more from the town walls, Rufe drew them up to speak to them. The deepening dusk masked their faces, but tension charged the silence. For some of them this would be their first real fight. It was no practice drill with blunt swords—the Rogandans were hardened killers. But the men would find what they needed. They were the king's soldiers.

Rufe was not afraid. Whenever fear came visiting he simply called to mind the image of a witless boy, alone in a razed village.

Even the heavy burden of leadership had begun to melt away beside the imminent prospect of vengeance.

"If Will Prentis is holding the gates against the Rogandans," he called out, "stay together until we reach them. Press the Rogandans toward the walls. Don't let any of them escape!

"And stay silent until they spot us. We have the advantage of surprise—let's make the most of it. We may never get a better chance to destroy them.

"The King's Guard should stay close to me." He drew his sword and held it aloft. "For the king and for Arvenon!"

The men roared it back. "For the king and for Arvenon!"

Rufe Sarjant spurred his horse toward the distant walls. The ground trembled as eight score horsemen galloped after him into the gloom.

RUFE HEARD the fighting before he saw it. The ringing clash of metal on metal and the cries of battle revealed a struggle immediately before the gates. He urged his weary horse to a final effort and charged toward the press, his men close behind.

A burning wagon blocked the entrance, its flames dimly illuminating the struggle. On the far side, a perilously small number of dark forms held at bay the raging nomad-clad soldiers of Rogand. Dozens of hand-held torches weaved a frantic rhythm through the air as the frustrated raiders crowded into the entrance trying to reach the defenders. But the flames kept them back, and the entrance had been blocked so effectively that only two or three men could attack at once.

At the sight of his enemy an involuntary roar exploded from Rufe's lips. Behind him the roar grew in volume, swelled by scores of other voices.

For a moment the fighting stopped as startled heads turned away from the walls. A ragged cheer went up from before the gate, then died as the Rogandans renewed their assault with reckless ferocity.

A line of horned horsemen swung around to face the new threat.

They barely had time to turn before Rufe's soldiers crashed upon them like a tidal wave, shattering the line. Rufe plunged through into the heart of the Rogandan troops with the guardsmen surging into the gap behind him. His weariness forgotten, he pressed urgently toward the gates.

Horn-helmed heads beckoned on every side. Rufe's sword danced among them. A fierce joy flooded through him, energizing his wildly swinging arm.

The Rogandans gave ground reluctantly. But the king's soldiers would not be denied. Cheering wildly, they swept aside the last raiders and broke through to the defenders.

First to reach the wagon, Rufe leaped from his horse and ran to find Will. The fighting had been heaviest here, and he picked his way appalled among the ghastly debris of battle.

Then he stopped cold. Before him lay Will Prentis, his lower body crushed beneath a fallen horse. The flickering light revealed his final agony, preserved in his contorted face. Rufe trembled violently and uncontrollably. His mind became numb.

Somehow his feet returned him to his horse, and he found himself back in the saddle. He stared unseeing, first toward Will and then to the battle still raging around him. The trembling slowly faded, replaced by an icy calm.

He looked out upon his enemies, and a deadly wrath mounted within him. Then, as violently and indiscriminately as a volcano spewing fire, he erupted.

Rufe spurred his horse savagely. Ears flattened and nostrils wide, it propelled its giant rider into the thick of the battle.

None could hold their ground before him. He soon formed the vortex of a whirling turmoil of destruction. Friends and foes alike fell back in terrified confusion before his berserker fury.

How long it continued he could not tell. But there came a time when his enemies had all fled or perished. Dimly he became aware of a nagging sense of pain and loss. Then he remembered where he was, and grief flooded over him.

People with torches emerged from the town and began searching out the wounded. Rufe heard his name spoken in awed tones by other soldiers, although none approached him.

He had no desire for company. His terrible passion was spent, and a confused sense of shame began to nag at him. Tired and downcast, he slipped away into the darkness alone to wrestle with his feelings.

13

The days had shortened, and the air held a new chill when the king finally returned to Arnost with his army. A huge crowd cheered their arrival, and this time Thomas was a part of it. Olaf led in the King's Guard, and Thomas searched everywhere for the distinctive red hair of Will. To his bewilderment, he saw no sign of him.

The king followed his Guard, waving to the crowd. But he seemed grim faced to Thomas. Others noted it too, and many expressed surprise. Hadn't the king's soldiers won a great victory at Danford? Some began whispering darkly of an end to peace and a beginning of troubles.

To his growing disquiet, Thomas had discovered nothing of Will. He had plenty to distract him, though—he was fully occupied in the stables attending to the horses that returned with the king the previous day. Many were in poor condition. His father had been absent for much of the afternoon and finally returned just after sunset.

"Have you heard about your friend?" his father asked gruffly.

"Which friend?" Thomas replied warily, uncertain about what might be coming next.

"The guardsman, Will Prentis. The one who left you his chain."

"No. Have you seen him?" Thomas couldn't conceal his eagerness.

His father shook his head. "He came back in one of those covered wagons. Seems he was badly wounded in the battle at Danford. He's quite a hero, I'm told."

"Wounded?" echoed Thomas, torn between alarm and pride at the news. "Where is he?"

"In the barracks, I imagine."

THOMAS SET off for the barracks, surprisingly reluctant to meet with Will now that the time had come. He had been stalling for a couple of days, not because he wasn't eager to see his friend, but because he was unsure of his welcome. A lot had changed in the short months since the king left for the border region. Thomas's life had changed irrevocably in that time, thanks to the stone. By all accounts Will's had, too.

Will Prentis's name was on everyone's lips since the soldiers returned to their families. Of course, Thomas knew better than to believe without question the reports spreading like wildfire through the town. His own experience had taught him that wagging tongues love to exaggerate. There was always a kernel of truth underneath, though, and it seemed that Will had somehow been responsible for saving the town of Danford. His serious wounds added further weight to his reputation.

The victory at Danford had left its mark on all of the soldiers. It was obvious even to Thomas that they had returned from their campaigning with a new confidence. It wasn't exactly a swagger— more an air of robust self-belief. And Will wasn't the only subject of idle conversation. People also spoke in awed tones of another guardsman, a one-man army called Rufe Sarjant.

As he approached the low stone building that housed the King's Guard, Thomas fingered Will's chain anxiously. If Will didn't want to see him, returning the memento at least gave him an excuse for being there.

When Thomas asked for directions to Will Prentis, the soldier on duty dismissed his request peremptorily. "He's not available."

"I need to return something to him."

"Then give it to me."

Something in Thomas rose up at the soldier's imperious tone. He shook his head stubbornly. "No. He entrusted it to me."

The soldier looked down at Thomas skeptically. When it became obvious that the youth was not going to leave, he shrugged. "What's your name?"

"Thomas. Thomas Stablehand."

The man called across to another soldier. "Hey, Red. Go see if the chief wants to speak to a Thomas Stablehand."

Confronted with this evidence of Will's new status, Thomas's stubborn bravado evaporated. He shrank back, trying to be inconspicuous. The soldier, meanwhile, totally ignored him.

The inevitable rejection felt like an age in coming, and Thomas fidgeted uncomfortably, debating with himself about slinking away unnoticed. He had been a fool to think Will would be willing to see him.

Eventually, the soldier called Red reappeared. To Thomas's surprise, the man addressed him directly. "He'll see you. Come with me."

The soldier on duty scowled at him. "Make it quick," he commanded. Thomas scurried after Red, leaving the sentry muttering loudly about the chief never getting well with people pestering him all the time.

Red left him without introduction at the door of a small but cheerful room. A fire crackled importantly opposite the doorway, and sunlight streamed through a small window. A man lay on a low bed talking quietly to a giant guardsman.

Thomas hung back just outside the doorway. The man looked up and beamed a welcoming smile. Thomas started as he realized that the scarred visage belonged to his friend Will.

"Thomas! Come in. It's good to see you again at last." He eyed Thomas approvingly. "You've grown up since I last saw you." He winked at the other soldier. "We'll have to find a place for him in the King's Guard before too long." Thomas, still wounded from their last conversation, was too astonished to reply. Now he felt even more discomfited.

The other soldier excused himself. "I'll see you tonight, Will."

"Thanks, Rufe. I'll look forward to it."

At the sound of the name, Thomas again started. The burly guardsman caught his expression, and Thomas saw a shadow pass across his face, a fleeting look of pain. Then he was gone, striding off down the passageway.

Thomas stepped into the room awkwardly. "I brought your chain, Will."

Will accepted it gravely. "Thank you for keeping it safe." He slipped it around his neck. "But now I want to hear all about your doings. What have you been up to with the horses? What's been happening in Arnost all these months?"

The unexpected warmth of Will's welcome and interest soon thawed Thomas. Their conversation rambled on, and he quickly rediscovered his old pleasure in the company of his friend. They skirted the recent past, it was true, but that seemed to suit Will as well as it suited Thomas.

As he was leaving, Will insisted that he visit again, frequently. Thomas felt sure he meant it.

"But I don't want to tire you out. The guard outside said that too many people were pestering you."

Will laughed out loud. "The men seem to have taken it upon themselves to protect me. The truth is that I've hardly seen anyone except Rufe since we arrived back in Arnost.

"Pestering me?" He laughed again, heartily, almost as if rediscovering laughter. Thomas didn't need the stone to tell him that Will hadn't done much laughing in recent days.

"You're good for me, Thomas. I need a lot more than just armies and battles in my world. Come again, and make it soon."

Thomas left the barracks with a new smile on his own lips. He couldn't remember when he last felt so content. Even the scowl of the sentry didn't shake him.

"WHAT HAPPENED when you reached the gates of Danford, Will?"

Thomas had seen a great deal of his friend in recent days, but he had rarely found him in much of a mood to talk about the battle. Today Will had been more forthcoming, and he was determined to make the most of the opportunity.

"We approached the gates in an old wagon. Most of the men were hidden in it. The Rogandans controlling the gates tried to scare us away, then when that failed, they threw spears at us. One of the men was wounded in the leg. But we made it into the passageway between the portcullis and the gates, and upended the wagon to block the entrance.

"They tried everything to dislodge us. Their options were limited, though. They couldn't make too much noise, in case they roused the people inside Danford."

"Why didn't you make noise yourselves?"

"We tried, believe me. But no one heard us, and the Rogandans kept us busy dodging arrows and spears from above.

"Eventually Drettroth and the main body of raiders arrived, and things really livened up. The Rogandans inside the gatehouse tried dropping fire on us, but it only set the wagon alight. That made it even harder for Drettroth's men to get at us. They tried opening the gates to attack us from behind, but one of our men almost made it into the city to rouse the guard. They didn't try that again. I guess they decided to just wait for Drettroth to finish us off.

"Our situation was desperate. We were being picked off one by one. Around that time I was trapped under a horse and lost consciousness. I remember nothing more about the fight.

"I woke up the next day with my legs crushed, and the king's personal physician fussing over me. But I'm told that Rufe arrived just in time."

"What about our soldiers inside Danford?"

"Once the main battle started, I suppose the people in the city were finally roused. They say that the Rogandans held out for hours in the gatehouse. But they were all killed eventually.

"Drettroth lost half his force killed or wounded in the battle. But the important thing was that his plan was completely exposed."

"Are we at war with Rogand, then?" To Thomas, the prospect was more thrilling than frightening. He didn't doubt for a minute that the Rogandans stood no chance against Will Prentis and Rufe Sarjant and all of King Steffan's soldiers.

"Not yet. King Agon sent emissaries claiming that Drettroth had acted alone, without his authority. The king knows that isn't true, though. It's probably only a matter of time. Don't spread that around, by the way. There are enough rumors already."

"I won't!" Thomas vowed eagerly, flattered to be holding an important confidence.

There was one other question on Thomas's mind. He hesitated for a while, then curiosity won out. "Is it true that Rufe Sarjant is a berserker?"

Will frowned. "That's a harsh title for a man like Rufe."

"I think so, too," the youth added hastily, seeing Will's reaction. "Rufe seems so gentle." Thomas had, indeed, seen plentiful evidence of Rufe's thoughtful concern for Will during his recovery.

"He's the kind of person who'd rather help people than harm them," said Will.

Thomas nodded wisely. "I guess people just made it up."

Will shook his head emphatically. "No. I didn't witness it myself, but if half the reports are to be believed, Rufe accounted for almost as many of Drettroth's raiders as the other soldiers together."

So it was true. Rufe was a man of contradictions. "I wonder why he became a soldier."

Will shrugged. "I don't know. The choice might have been made for him; he's descended from a long line of soldiers." Will stretched an absent finger up to his face and smoothed the scar on his cheek. "Either way, sometimes life takes unexpected turns." He gazed off into the distance, as if deep in thought. "Everyone's good at something," he finally concluded. "Unfortunately for Rufe, he happens to be very good at killing."

IN THE WEEKS THAT FOLLOWED, Thomas became directly involved in Will's convalescence, and the soldiers gradually came to accept his presence in the barracks. Mostly, though, the two of them went riding together.

"Walking causes me considerable pain," Will told him. "It's easier when I'm riding, because the horse takes my weight instead.

"The problem is that I need to completely relearn my riding technique. I always relied on my legs to guide the horse, especially when both hands were occupied. But I don't have much strength in my legs now. I need you to help me develop a new way of riding."

"I'm happy to try," Thomas promised him. "I'll need my father's permission to spend time away from the stables, of course."

With the king himself frequently checking on Will's progress, the request was readily granted by Thomas's father. It seemed that Will could have pretty much anything he wanted, within reason.

By the time a month had passed, Will's confidence in the saddle had been fully restored.

"I'm ready to fight on horseback again," he said. "When it comes to horses, Thomas, you're a master."

Rufe Sarjant was also impressed. "I wasn't sure I'd ever see Will assured in the saddle again," he admitted.

Other soldiers had witnessed Will's improvement, too, and Thomas began to develop a reputation for his horse skills. Thomas was more than delighted with the affirmation, although he was careful not to show it.

Soon after, it was announced that Will Prentis had been appointed second in command to Olaf, captain of the King's Guard.

The appointment was wildly popular among the soldiers. The Danford veterans—the soldiers who had followed Will on the epic ride to the Battle of Danford—felt they had a special claim on his leadership. These men were the envy of every other soldier. Everyone wanted to serve under him.

To the king, busy locating and training soldiers as fast as he was able, Will provided an ideal rallying point.

THEIR HORSES GRAZED NEARBY as Thomas sat with Will beside the river. "How did you get the scar, Will?"

The question was casual, but the reply was terse. "When you fight, you expect to get wounds."

Presuming that his friend was sensitive about the effect of the scar on his appearance, Thomas promised himself he wouldn't mention it again. He said no more, contenting himself with tossing pebbles into the river.

It was Will who broke the silence. "Being a soldier is not what you think, Thomas. People get killed, people who shouldn't."

"You mean the villagers? That wasn't your fault. Besides, if it wasn't for you, more of them would have died."

"Not just the villagers. Sometimes..." Will hesitated, seeming to choose his words carefully. "A soldier does things...things he doesn't intend." He shrugged helplessly, as though it was too hard to explain.

"I know just what you mean." Thomas desperately wanted to prove his maturity, to show that he understood, too. "It doesn't just happen to soldiers. I've done things I didn't intend as well." The words were out before he realized what he was saying.

Will, his interest aroused, turned to him curiously. "What's happened, Thomas? Tell me about it."

Thomas, flustered, didn't know how to respond. Will continued to stare at him, saying nothing, but clearly expecting an answer. What was he going to say? He had to say something, or Will would think he was boasting to impress him. The silence was becoming uncomfortable.

"I...Well, it was a few months ago. You see, there was this thing. I found it. A stone, I mean. A little stone..."

He hadn't planned it—the idea of telling Will would never have occurred to him—but once he started, there was no turning back. Hesitantly at first, then with growing abandon, Thomas spoke, and the story of the stone poured out. As he spoke, he took to his feet and began pacing around, unable to suppress his agitation. The story burst out, like a river swollen by the spring thaw bursting its banks. Apart from the fight with Simon, he held nothing back. Will did not interrupt him.

The relief of getting it out was more than he could ever have imagined. It was only when the pressure had been released that he became consciously aware of it.

Finally, the flow stopped. He sat down abruptly, exhausted and panting a little.

Will, his face inscrutable, still said nothing. Thomas began to worry, his relief giving way to fear that his friend would think him mad.

Finally, Will spoke. "You're not lying, Thomas. That much is obvious to me. But even so, it's a difficult story to believe!"

He stared at Thomas thoughtfully for a time. "Let me see your stone," he finally commanded.

After a moment's hesitation, Thomas reached into his pouch and retrieved the stone. He handed it to Will, who took it and examined it closely.

"I remember it," he announced. "A family heirloom, eh?" He aimed an ironic grin at Thomas, who felt his cheeks flush in embarrassment at the reminder of his old lie.

Will held the stone and gazed fixedly at Thomas, frowning. "I can read your thoughts," he exclaimed in surprise.

Seeing the alarm on Thomas's face, he chuckled, and tossed the stone back to Thomas. "I was only jesting," he reassured him. "But the look on your face, Thomas!"

Then slowly he became grave. "I'm sorry. I can't begin to imagine what it must be like to have lost such a power after having it. So you really see nothing at all with it now?"

Thomas shook his head mutely. He cradled the stone in his hand, and looked at Will. The scar again caught his eye, and without intending to, he found himself staring at it. At once, as if in a dream, he saw through the scar to a distant scene. A young man lay on the ground. He frowned in concentration.

"What is it, Thomas? Do you see something?" Will's voice sounded far away.

"Yes. It's a young soldier. With dark hair. He's lying face down. I think he's dead; there's blood everywhere. There's a tall man with a battle-ax."

A stinging slap across his cheek jerked him back to the riverbank. A second slap knocked the stone from his hand to the ground. The furious face of Will hovered inches from his own, the scar livid. Will's eyes were wild with rage, and an accusing finger jabbed emphatically and painfully into his shoulder. "Don't...you...EVER..." Will spat, "do that again."

Then he turned on his heel and hobbled away to his horse. He mounted and rode away without a backward glance.

Thomas stood, shaking uncontrollably, and watched him until he had disappeared. Then he numbly retrieved the stone and secured it. He paced aimlessly up and down the river, distressed and restless.

When he had finally recovered himself enough to ride away, he left with a tight knot in his stomach and a feeling of utter hopelessness.

To Thomas's total astonishment, Will appeared as usual for their next ride. He behaved as if nothing had happened.

Only once did he refer to the previous incident.

"I believe your story about the stone, Thomas, if it's any comfort to you. But don't ever try it out on me. Understood?" The words were spoken mildly enough, but danger lurked behind them.

Elated, Thomas agreed eagerly. It seemed to him a very small price to pay for the restoration of their friendship. He felt like he had just been released unexpectedly from a deep, dark dungeon.

The vision of the young man left him bemused. Whether it was real or imagined, present, past, or future, he had no inkling. Could it signal the reawakening of the stone, or had it simply been imagination? Why had Will reacted so sharply?

The stone continued to show him nothing whenever he tried it. Unable to find any way of unraveling the mystery, he eventually abandoned the attempt.

NEITHER OF THOMAS'S parents had much to say as they ate their evening meal. Thomas, more interested in eating than in talking, didn't care at all.

One thing had been nagging at him, though. Spoon halfway to his mouth, he paused long enough to ask, "Do you know where Ben is? I haven't seen him today for a while."

There was no response. Ignoring the question, Thomas's father said, "A child was savaged by a dog in the town today."

"Did the hounds get out again?" Concerned, Thomas again paused briefly in his assault on the food. "I'll bet it was Toby. That animal's savage; something needs to be done about him."

"It was Ben." His father's tone was so casual that at first Thomas wasn't sure he had heard properly.

"What?"

"Ben mauled a young child."

Thomas's spoon dropped to the table with a clatter. "You can't be serious. It couldn't have been Ben."

"It was Ben. The child's mother described the dog exactly. Simon told me himself."

Thomas's heart skipped a beat. "He's lying," he blurted. He couldn't control the shrillness in his voice.

His father frowned. "Why would he lie about it?"

Thomas's mouth clamped shut; what could he possibly say? A chill of dread crept over him.

"It wasn't the first time, either." His father's tone allowed no contradiction. "Ben attacked Simon during the Feast of St. Stephen. I saw the wounds myself."

So that was Simon's game. Thomas felt the blood drain from his face. He could scarcely breathe. "I promise I'll keep a closer eye on him from now on," he managed.

His father shook his head with finality. "You can't have an animal attacking people. I overlooked it the first time, Thomas, against my better judgment, because I knew how much you cared about the dog. But no more. I put him down this afternoon."

Thomas propelled himself from the table, knocking over his stool. He ran from the house, into the deepening gloom, sobbing his rage and grief. The uncaring stars stared down at him.

Simon's revenge was complete.

14

L ife changed dramatically for Thomas in the weeks that
followed. The changes had been in turn astonishing, exciting, frightening, and utterly disheartening. After the initial
disasters were in the past, though, he dared to hope that his new life
might even prove rewarding.

It was Will who was responsible for his change of direction. He
had appeared one afternoon as Thomas exercised some horses,
waiting patiently until he had finished.

"You have a lot of skill with horses, Thomas. You seem to understand how they think. I know very few others who can handle them
so naturally."

Thomas had felt himself blushing deeply at the compliment.

"I need your help," Will had continued, his face becoming serious. "We're training soldiers as fast as we can, and they need to learn
to ride and handle horses."

Thomas was astonished. "Why should you need help with that?
Surely all of your recruits can ride already."

Will shook his head firmly. "No, they can't. Many of them are sons
of poor farm laborers who don't own horses. A lot of them have no
idea how to get into the saddle, much less ride. And if they were

responsible for the care of their own horses, the animals wouldn't last for long.

"It's becoming a major problem, and it's slowing down our training. I've spoken to your father, and he understands the urgency. He's willing to release you, so you can help us out."

"But they'll never listen to me! I'm not even a soldier."

"No, but you're a horseman. And one of the best I've seen. You'll be fine."

"But..."

Will waved his hand dismissively. "It's important, Thomas. The king needs this army."

And that was that. Thomas started the next morning.

IT DIDN'T TAKE MORE than a single day of training before Thomas's worst fears began to be realized. He had no experience of command, and his students were quick to take advantage of his lack of confidence. Grumbling at his instructions soon turned to loud complaints. His voice became more and more shrill as he tried to get them to listen. By noon on the second day, most of them were openly ignoring him and even mocking him. Worst of all, almost no progress had been made in teaching them the horse skills they needed. Thomas had not been able to hold their attention for long enough to teach them anything. He was discovering the hard way that teaching is not possible when a student is unwilling to learn.

He had never been more unhappy. He was a total failure, and he knew it. At that moment his father's lowliest job as an unskilled stable hand felt out of the reach of his capabilities.

Then, at his lowest ebb, the situation miraculously changed.

It was late on the second day of training. One of the students had been hopping around, wild eyed, squawking like a chicken in a mocking impression of Thomas yelling. He finally came to a halt, panting from his efforts, but rewarded with riotous applause from the others.

Thomas stood speechless, fighting back tears of anger and frustration. Then he looked up and saw Will standing nearby, silently watching. He had almost certainly seen the entire performance.

Will hobbled purposefully toward the youths. He was soon spotted, and a buzz of excitement swept through their ranks. They instantly fell silent, standing aside respectfully to make way for him. The contrast could not have been more marked. Thomas's heart sank even lower.

Will addressed them calmly, without raising his voice. "All of you want to become soldiers." Heads everywhere nodded eagerly. "I'm told that some of you hope to join the King's Guard." Will paused and surveyed the throng of enthusiastic faces. Dismayed, Thomas felt certain they would instantly stand on their heads if their captain asked it of them.

Will lowered his voice slightly, and the recruits leaned forward. "I'm sure you're all aware that soldiers of the King's Guard are skilled horsemen. Do any of you fit that description?" he asked mildly.

He turned toward Thomas, acknowledging him with a nod. "You're fortunate to have Thomas to teach you. He's the best chance you have.

"And in case you didn't know, I'll be asking him for recommendations for the Guard. He won't be suggesting your name unless you have excellent horse skills, unwavering discipline, and a positive attitude." He paused to let his words sink in. Thomas could see some of the recruits beginning to color.

"Oh, and one other thing. Thomas happens to be a friend of mine. When you treat him with respect, you're treating me with respect." Then Will's voice took on an iron edge. "If I should find any of you showing him disrespect, I'm going to take it *personally*."

He wheeled, and left them gaping after him in stunned silence.

Thomas realized that his next move was crucial. Stung by the way his students had belittled him, and remembering Will's reaction on first seeing him mount a moving horse bareback, Thomas made a quick decision. Walking briskly to the nearby enclosure, he selected a horse without a saddle or bridle and slapped it on the rump, guiding it into the open. He clicked his tongue, and the horse moved off at a brisk walk.

Thomas ran along beside the horse, took a firm grasp on its mane and, after a quick skip, vaulted up onto its back. Then he steered it with his legs, heading back toward his students. A couple of them watched open-mouthed. The rest were uncharacteristically silent.

He brought the horse to a halt, and remained on its back, towering over them. "It's your turn. Who's ready to try that themselves?" Every one of them remained silent.

Thomas turned to the ringleader among his students. "Well?"

His former tormentor had nothing to say. He looked down, shuffling his feet, unable to meet Thomas's glare.

Thomas slid down from the horse's back and moved to one side. "If you want to learn to ride as well as I can, then join me over here. Right now. I won't be wasting any more time on the rest of you."

Most of them joined him immediately. None of the others were far behind, although swallowing their pride was clearly a struggle for some of them.

Thomas didn't give them time to think. He sent them off immediately to find a horse of their own, and he kept them working hard without a break until well after the normal time for their evening meal.

He had no further trouble after that.

Even before he had finished with the first group, he began training a new set of recruits. No repetition of Will's speech was ever necessary. Thomas didn't need it.

THANKS TO HIS STUDENTS, Thomas soon became aware that idle tongues around the town had found a juicy new topic for gossip: the royal succession. Almost a year had passed since the attack on Danford and the border towns. But the new army that had been steadily building before their eyes offered a constant reminder to the townsfolk of the uncertain times that lay ahead. The king was greatly loved, and his loyal subjects expected to see his line continue. Where, then, was his heir?

According to rumor, the king would soon depart on a mission to bring home a bride. The king's uncle, the Duke of Erestor, would act as regent until he returned.

———

THE SWEAT TRICKLED FREELY down Thomas's brow as he plunged the pitchfork into another bale of hay and hefted it into the air. He was definitely getting stronger, he decided, but the thought offered little comfort at the end of another long day with still more work ahead. He glanced briefly at the ruddy glow of the sunset and then returned to the haystack.

"WHY DO YOU DO IT, THOMAS?" his mother fussed. "You have a job, an important one. It isn't necessary to work in the stables as well. You'll get sick if you keep this up." His father ignored the glance she shot in his direction. She was hopeful indeed if she expected help from that quarter.

Thomas ignored the question, too, and sank onto a stool. He picked up a spoon and began poking at the steaming gruel she placed in front of him.

Why did he do it? He wasn't sure himself. It certainly wasn't to prove something to his father; that would be a futile waste of time. His father acted as though his exertions were only to be expected. He'd certainly never encouraged Thomas to slow down, much less stop.

Was he trying to prove something to himself? Or was he simply clinging on to the old, the familiar? Too weary to be long bothered with trying to figure himself out, he plodded his way through the bowl of food before him.

. . .

"You've done wonders with them, Thomas." Will stood beside him, openly admiring Thomas's second group of recruits as they wheeled and trotted in formation. "What have you taught them?"

"The simple skills, mostly. Caring for their horses and learning to understand their needs. Controlling them, and learning to ride without using their hands."

"And there've been no major injuries. That's an achievement."

"Well, I've taught them how to fall without breaking a limb, of course. But you've forgotten the miller from the first group. That break was a bad one—I'm not sure he'll ever walk properly again." Thomas hung his head at the memory.

"Don't blame yourself for that, Thomas. I saw what he was like myself. A lot of these youths are terrified of their horses at first. But those who can't master that fear will never learn to ride safely. We can be grateful he survived the fall."

Will turned to Thomas, a thoughtful expression on his face. "Don't be afraid to ask, even demand, more from these lads, Thomas. Not all of them will be capable of it, but some will rise to a challenge."

Will left Thomas basking in the warm glow of his praise. Somehow, Thomas reflected, Will knew how to get the best out of his men. He never interfered or told Thomas how to do his job, just offered a timely word of encouragement or a well-placed suggestion.

How had Will guessed that he would be so well suited to this kind of work? It was now clear, even to Thomas, that he had a gift, not only of handling horses, but of passing on the skill to others. As his confidence increased, so did his effectiveness and his enjoyment in the role.

The next day Thomas initiated extra training for the more capable recruits. Before he had finished with them they could ride bareback confidently, control a horse without a bridle, and mount and dismount from a moving horse. No one from the first group was selected for this honor. If Will ever noticed, he never mentioned it.

Thomas's charges were now more than ready to learn to fight on horseback, a skill that he could not teach them. Nevertheless, he had won their respect. Beginning with past students from the second group, his former trainees sometimes found time to visit him, both to laugh behind their hands at the newest recruits, and to ask for advice on the finer points of horsemanship.

WITH THE ADDITIONAL demands of his advanced class, Thomas no longer found time to help his father. His father never commented on it. But he noticed. More than once in Thomas's presence, he observed pointedly how helpful Simon had become around the stables, and how he could no longer manage without him.

With difficulty, Thomas held his peace. Simon belonged in the past, and he was determined to keep it that way. He didn't want to think about Simon. Doing so led to memories, painful memories. Memories of loss. Memories of a blinding red passion and a strange and frightening desire to wound and kill.

And he could not think about Simon without thinking about the stone. Since the incident with Will the stone had lain undisturbed in his pouch. For the first time in many months Thomas was truly contented, and he had little desire to risk that for any reason. The stone was as unpredictable and mysterious as it was powerful. Even apparently closed to him, it had somehow managed to threaten his friendship with Will, the friendship he valued more than any other. So he left it alone and untouched.

The stone was not absent from his mind, though. Far from it. He imagined it brooding in his pouch, like a snake, coiled but still deadly. At best he and the stone were observing a truce. He didn't question its potential to visit trouble upon him still. Nevertheless, he doubted that he could bring himself to part with it.

STEFFAN the Second of Arvenon frowned, unable to hide his displeasure. He stood at the window of his apartments in Castel Citadel and glared out in frustrated anger toward the mountains in the distance, beyond the fields where banners fluttered above the tents of his army.

From the moment of his arrival here in Castel, everything had proceeded favorably, very favorably indeed. The marriage negotiations had been quickly concluded, and only the nuptials remained to be celebrated. A treaty between Arvenon and Castel had met with approval on both sides and was in the process of being drawn up.

Now there were unexpected delays. King Istel, at first eager to conclude the arrangements, suddenly could not see his way clear to give up his daughter Essanda until after her nineteenth birthday, another three weeks away.

Steffan did not want to be so long away from his kingdom in these uncertain times. And if, as promised, he remained after the wedding for a further two weeks before escorting his bride to her new home, the risk of bad weather interfering with the journey would steadily increase. Snow sometimes came quite early to the mountains, and the journey south might become unnecessarily hazardous.

He exchanged glances with Lord Bottren, a high-ranking nobleman and close friend who had journeyed with him from Arnost. Then he turned his attention to Count Gordan, a cousin and confidant of the King of Castel. The count was about his own age and seemed to share his outlook on life and also many of his views on issues of strategic policy. He had seen much of Gordan throughout the negotiations, and found himself liking the count and hoping he would become both a good friend and a useful link between the courts of Castel and Arvenon.

"I just don't understand the delay, Gordan," he said frankly.

The count sighed. "There is no hidden agenda, Your Majesty. The reason is simple, and personal. Now that the day approaches, the king finds it more difficult than he expected to say goodbye to his daughter. She reminds him so much of his beloved wife. I'm sure it would not be an issue had he not lost the queen to the fever five years ago."

"And why has my request been refused to spend time with the princess?"

Gordan winced. "Our customs are, perhaps, different from yours, Majesty. The king expects that you will have the rest of your life to enjoy the company of the princess. Who will, of course, soon become your queen."

There it was again—this time the king was certain of it. A brief look he couldn't identify had flashed across Gordan's face. The count would deny it, but the topic of the princess clearly made him uncomfortable for some reason.

What had he been missing about the girl? She was certainly young, almost eleven years his junior, but by all accounts she was intelligent and accomplished beyond her years. Her looks were much less important than her lineage and her childbearing potential, but there had even been hints that she was very attractive. Those hints were becoming increasingly difficult to believe.

It was all beginning to seem too good to be true. So far he had seen the princess only briefly and at a distance, so heavily appareled in finery that he was not confident he would even recognize her in different circumstances. If only he had been allowed to spend some time in her company, surely his questions would have been answered.

"She's not mad, is she, Gordan?" The question had been plaguing him, and it just slipped out.

The count looked genuinely astonished and alarmed. "Mad? Of course not! How could you suggest such a thing, Your Majesty?"

The king decided to let it drop for now. Another issue had been weighing on his mind, and he might as well get that out in the open as well. "I know of the Rogandan threats, Count Gordan. Do they have any bearing on the sudden hesitation of King Istel?"

Gordan's face hardened. "Our policy in Castel is not dictated by the threats of Agon, Sire." When the king did not reply, he steadied himself and went on. "You clearly have unprecedented access to the state secrets of Castel. My compliments to your agents," he offered ironically, bowing low.

"I can assure you that my agents are working only on behalf of Castel, not against it. Our kingdoms are soon to be allied by marriage and by treaty, Count. You can always count on us for support."

The count bowed once again. "Thank you for your kindness, Your Majesty. I will convey your words to My Lord the King."

He excused himself and left.

"What do you make of it, Bottren? Did I go too far?"

The nobleman paused thoughtfully for a moment before answering. "No, Your Majesty. I don't think there's any harm in letting them know that King Istel's hesitation troubles you deeply. Or in hinting that we know more about their affairs than they might have guessed."

"Keep our agents looking into this business of the princess. I want to understand what's behind it."

"Certainly, Your Majesty."

The king cast his gaze once more to the distant mountains. "Agon appears to be spreading his tentacles far and wide. But he's hopeful indeed if he thinks he can bully kingdoms this far from Rogand."

"Let us not underestimate Agon, Sire. He is a ruthless and ambitious man. And he has demonstrated a talent for the unexpected. I fear he might have surprises in store for us all yet."

"Thank you for the reminder, Bottren. You're right, of course. I will be giving a great deal of attention to the problem of Rogand just as soon as the issues with Castel have been resolved and my marriage is behind me. Indeed it cannot be denied that this marriage has itself been partly prompted by the ambitions of Agon."

He dismissed the nobleman and stretched out on his bed, allowing his mind to wander. Affairs of state paraded restlessly through his mind. Of late such thoughts had increasingly been displaced by hopeful brooding around affairs of the heart. The two streams swirled about in his head, competing for his attention.

"I KNOW the wedding delay has tested your patience, Steffan." King Istel's voice had taken on a soothing tone.

Steffan bowed. "I'm sure Your Majesty has had his reasons."

Istel sighed. "Please do not suspect me of fomenting intrigues.

There are none. My daughter celebrates her nineteenth birthday in one week. The following day she will become your bride.

"Forgive the sentimental foolishness of an old man. It is hard for me to give up my beloved daughter, even though this marriage has my full blessing.

"Perhaps, too, it is difficult for me to embrace change. As you know, I married a woman twenty years my junior, and even now my son is only twelve years old. I have been surrounded by the young, and I try to keep pace with them, but every year it becomes harder."

Steffan bowed again. "One week will pass quickly."

"I thank you. But there is another matter I wanted to discuss with you."

Steffan could not help noticing that as usual King Istel did not dwell for long on the topic of the princess.

Every attempt to ferret out the mystery surrounding his future bride had been frustrated. Men who had much to say on other subjects found little of substance to contribute when the princess was mentioned. It almost seemed as though the nobility of Castel had formed a conspiracy of silence around the subject. He was committed to the marriage, because he needed the alliance. But it was becoming increasingly apparent that his bride-to-be was not exactly what he had been hoping for.

"Every trader coming from Rogand reports that Agon's soldiers are on the move," Istel continued, a grim look on his face.

Steffan nodded. "We have received the same reports."

"And my agents tell me they appear to be heading west. You have been building an army, Steffan. I fear you will soon find yourself in need of it."

Steffan decided to be blunt. "Will Castel stand with us?"

Istel did not hesitate. "We will. Our army does not compare in size with your own, much less with the hordes of Agon. But we will fight with you if you are attacked."

Steffan scanned the face of his future father-in-law. He seemed sincere and in earnest.

"I will be frank," Istel continued. "Castel needs this alliance. If

Arvenon is overwhelmed, Castel cannot expect to stand for long." The king could not hide the concern in his voice.

Throughout the negotiations, the strategic needs of both king-doms, in addition to the Arvenian succession, had always formed the basis for the alliance. But now Istel had stated his vulnerability openly and more directly than ever before. Steffan wondered at the reason for this further frankness.

"And there is one final thing. We have recently received disturbing news from one of our agents." Istel seemed to be choosing his words carefully. "He has stumbled upon evidence that one of your nobles—unfortunately he has not been able to identify which one—has held discussions with Agon."

Steffan's immediate response was disbelief. What kind of game was Istel playing?

The Castelan king was watching his face carefully. "This agent has proven very reliable. Always. He has never failed us." He seemed genuinely concerned. "I am truly sorry to be giving you this information."

Could it be true? Steffan frowned deeply. His court was so far away, and he had been held up here, unnecessarily, for so long.

"You have been planning to remain here for two weeks after the wedding before returning home. At my insistence." Istel looked worried. "Perhaps you should return sooner. If you leave one week after the wedding, the journey through the mountains might be easier, too."

Istel clearly took this alleged threat seriously. Steffan decided he would send a message to the duke. Just in case. His uncle would know what to do.

Steffan left Istel's audience chamber more confused than ever. Why delay the wedding? Why insist he remain in Castel after the nuptials? What was Istel hiding about his daughter?

And how could he benefit from telling Steffan about the claims of treachery? It would only reinforce Steffan's eagerness to return to his own kingdom earlier.

There was much to think about. Commoners saw the king as all powerful. But there were so many situations over which even a king had little control.

King Steffan, plagued with questions, surrounded by unknowns, and far from home, faced the truth and admitted it to himself. King though he was, he felt uncertain and vulnerable.

15

———

Thomas and Rufe sat side by side in a small tower room, soaking up the rays of the midmorning sun that streamed in through a high window. The castle was a cold place at the best of times, and the weather was gradually becoming cooler. The sunlight offered a pleasing addition to the warmth from the fire in the grate. They sat in silence. Rufe was comfortable with silence, and Thomas liked him for it.

The tower room had long been a favored hideaway for Will and Rufe, an occasional refuge from the many pressing demands on their time. The room was sufficiently remote to be private, but it took some steady climbing to get there. At first Rufe had pressed Will to choose a more accessible location, but Will insisted on hobbling up the long flight of steps, almost in defiance of his injury.

From the time Thomas first learned about the retreat, both men made it clear that he was always welcome there. Nevertheless, many weeks had passed before he found the courage to join them regularly.

The fact that they thus honored him astonished Thomas. Of late even the soldiers, not known for showing deference to anyone but their own, had been treating Thomas with respect. He put it down to his friendship with Will. But if he could have known it, the reason had much more to do with his own growing reputation as horse master. He was developing into an effective leader, and it was obvious to everyone except himself. Once again he attributed his success to Will, and in particular to Will's early intervention on his behalf.

But whatever the reason for it, he derived much simple delight from the fact that his opinion, his counsel, and even his company were actively sought by the two people in the world he most admired.

Thomas leaned back in his chair and allowed his mind to wander. He tried to imagine the king and his embassy far away in Castel. Had the marriage negotiations been successful? A messenger had arrived from Castel early this morning if rumors could be believed. Perhaps there would be news. If so, Will would be certain to know the details.

At some point Thomas knew he would be expected to marry, too. How was he supposed to make that happen? If you were a king, you sought a suitable alliance, and sealed the agreement with a marriage. A wife was included in the deal. But it didn't work that way for commoners. The castle boasted some attractive young women, to be sure. One or two happened to be very attractive indeed. But Thomas couldn't think of a single reason why any of them would be interested in him. In the presence of girls he somehow lost the ability to speak. If a girl was particularly attractive he sometimes couldn't even think straight.

These woeful thoughts were banished by the arrival of Will, accompanied by Tolin, the dour quartermaster general of the king's army. Tolin, slightly flushed from the climb, entered the room with voice raised and gesturing emphatically. Tolin was one of the few soldiers willing to disagree with Will, who didn't seem to mind at all —in fact he seemed to appreciate it.

"You should be out there with them, Will. Rufe, too. Sending a thousand men into the countryside without their leaders is like asking a child to ride a horse without a bridle."

"They're hardly leaderless, Tolin," replied Will patiently, pausing at the door to catch his breath. "Count Ranauld is an outstanding leader, and doesn't need any help from us. Several others are developing nicely, too. They just need a chance to establish themselves, and they'll do that better without other people yapping at their heels all the time."

Seeing Tolin's mouth open for a rejoinder, Will quickly steered the conversation elsewhere. "When can we expect more horses?"

Thomas suppressed a chuckle as Rufe aimed a wink in his direction. Will certainly knew how to handle the old veteran. When it came to stores, supplies, weapons, and all the necessities of provisioning an army, Tolin's knowledge was nothing short of awe-inspiring. And it didn't take much to get him talking about the subject.

"We've got ten more due in later today. Someone will need to meet them at the city gates. Someone competent this time. That last groom was a disaster—we don't need spooked horses stampeding through the market again."

Tolin jerked a thumb pointedly in Thomas's direction. "Why can't you send Thomas?"

Will raised an eyebrow inquiringly at Thomas.

"I don't mind. I'll go meet them," he replied, trying to sound matter-of-fact even as he felt himself coloring at the compliment. He had no teaching today—most of his competent students had joined Count Ranauld's training exercise, and since it was market day the rest had been given the day off.

Thomas stood up to go. "Any news of the king?" he asked, pausing at the door.

"A messenger came today from Castel," Will told him. "The negotiations went well. Wedding preparations have been proceeding, and the marriage should take place within days. The king will probably stay on for a while afterward, and return with his bride before winter sets in."

"And what of Olaf and the soldiers?"

"Olaf has been received with great honor, and the King's Guard are quartered with him in the castle. The rest of the men are camped outside the city walls."

"Ridiculous." Tolin never seemed reluctant to offer his opinion. "It made no sense taking a force that size to Castel. What was Olaf thinking?"

Will shook his head. "It wasn't ridiculous at all. The king certainly didn't need two thousand of his best men to protect him from bandits on the road. But there's no harm in showing a potential father-in-law that his daughter will be well protected. Or in reminding him of the benefits of a strong ally. Rulers of small kingdoms never sit easily on their thrones in troubled times."

The conversation rambled on. After a while Thomas, his curiosity sated, took his leave and headed for the city gates. The horses would be welcome; it seemed like the growing army could never get enough of them. Will had convinced the king he needed a mobile force, so the king sent agents ranging far and wide looking for suitable mounts. A steady stream of horses had been arriving ever since, creating ongoing challenges in feeding and stabling them.

No one knew when this army might be needed. But Will did not expect the day to be long delayed, and he did not intend to be caught entirely unprepared. The level of activity around the castle had increased dramatically, placing extra demands on everyone who worked there. With the constant arrival of new horses, Thomas knew his father must be pushed to the limit as well. The worry in his mother's face confirmed it. But the young horse master's own role consumed all his attention, and that was entirely to his liking. He no longer had any desire to help his father.

THOMAS MADE his way to the main gates of Arnost. He passed through them, beyond the pair of guards who stood idly on each side of the main entrance. They ignored him, just as they ignored almost everyone who came and went. Their role was to maintain order, not to grant or deny access to the city, and they hindered no one who went peacefully about their own business.

He took up his position just outside the walls, beside the main road that led through the gates. From here the road was visible far off into the distance, but he could see no sign yet of the horses.

Thomas had chosen a good location to wait. He stood there fascinated by the endless tide of humanity that ebbed and flowed through the city gates. Men and women, merchants, commoners, and the occasional minor noble mingled together, some loud and energetic, others heads down and with no interest in any affairs but their own.

Observing people never ceased to fascinate him. Careful observation could reveal a great deal to a practiced eye. As he well knew, a treasure trove of insights and secrets lay concealed inside every person, buried too deep for even the keenest observer to glimpse. Nevertheless he harbored no lingering desire to return to the days when he used the power of the stone to peep into the souls of the unsuspecting. Nor had he forgotten the mirror and the awful madness in his own eyes. He was willing to go to great lengths to avoid any fulfillment of the stone's prophetic vision.

He could now acknowledge that he had abused that power. Perhaps, from the security of at last having something worthwhile and significant to do with his life, it was easier to be honest with himself. Or perhaps it was because the stone was closed to him. Either way, he was not proud of the way he had acted, and he liked to think that he would do it all very differently if he had his time over again. But there was no point wasting regrets on the past. He had more than enough responsibility to occupy him in the present.

He glanced across the plain that stretched south and west beyond the city walls. A wide variety of stalls always spilled out into the fields on market day; on this particular occasion a cattle market seemed to be the main focus. Small clusters of the animals could be seen everywhere, surrounded by curious onlookers, and the sound of lowing drifted toward him across the fields.

In the far distance on the road he thought he could see a small group of horses. But it could just as easily be cows. He returned his attention to the people around him.

Thomas soon discovered that he was not the only person standing around at the gate. A tall grim-looking man occupied a position across the road from him. He had been there for some time with no apparent purpose. Thomas studied the stranger closely. He had become adept at doing so surreptitiously, facing elsewhere and looking sidelong at his subject, then rapidly shifting his gaze forward if the person under scrutiny happened to glance in his direction.

Something about the man seemed not quite natural, but at first he couldn't put his finger on it. People didn't usually stand around in a public place for no reason. Some, like the guards, found themselves there because of their work. Others, like him, were waiting for someone or for something to happen. And a few idlers could always be seen hanging around a crowd. None of the usual reasons seemed to fit, though.

Eventually he figured it out. He felt sure that this man was working hard at looking inconspicuous. His curiosity now thoroughly aroused, Thomas studied him even more closely.

The man wore a long greatcoat that fell to his ankles. The weather, while cool, definitely did not warrant such a thick garment. A quick scan of the crowd revealed a few others similarly attired and similarly engaged. As he watched, a driver momentarily lost control of his cart. It swung off the road and knocked into one of the men. The man reacted instinctively, reaching up to grab the startled driver and yanking him off his cart. Then the man subsided as quickly as he had erupted, and released the driver with a rough apology, "Sorry, friend. No ill intended." He spoke with a strange accent.

Thomas tore his eyes away from the scene and stole a glance at the first man, who stood watching the incident with a look of fury plain on his face. Then the anger vanished, and his face again revealed only careless passivity. So complete and rapid was the change that Thomas had to tell himself that he had not imagined it. Then the man turned and looked directly at him, and this time Thomas was not sure he had diverted his gaze quickly enough.

Fully alert, but anxious not to be discovered, Thomas shifted his attention back to the road. He could now clearly see a group of horses being led by a few men on horseback, not far off and making their way toward the city gates. He sighed and shifted his feet, feigning boredom and impatience. But the strange men occupied his attention entirely. He felt sure that during the scuffle he had caught a brief glimpse of a sword under the foreigner's coat. What could it mean? His thoughts swirled frantically around the possibilities.

After what seemed like an eternity, he risked another sidelong glance at the first man. His attention was elsewhere. Without consciously planning it, Thomas reached down for the drawstring of his pouch and groped in for the stone. Its power flared instantly, and he stared open-mouthed. The intruders were Rogandan. They might disguise their garb and their speech, but no secret could be hidden from the stone. Their true purpose was laid bare, and what he saw chilled him to the bone.

Then he discovered that the man had become aware of him, fully aware, and he read his death in those eyes. He realized with a start that he had been staring openly, his guard lowered and his pretense at indifference exposed.

At this crucial moment the long-awaited horses arrived. He took in the situation in a moment. A young man, not much older than himself but richly dressed, appeared to be in charge of the party. Three other older men each led three horses with halters behind their own mounts.

The young nobleman led a single horse—a bay mare. The mare was not saddled, but it had reins rather than a halter, suggesting that the young man had recently been riding it bareback.

Thomas seized the opportunity. "You've arrived at last!" he exclaimed loudly. "Come with me, and I'll show you to the stables."

He quickly took the reins of the bay mare from the surprised young nobleman and swung up onto its back. The mare shied away, pulling against the restraint of the reins. The noise and bustle of the crowd was clearly spooking it. Thomas spoke quietly to the animal, and it settled again.

Taking the lead, Thomas rode quickly through the city gates looking neither to the right nor to the left. No one tried to prevent him. It was slow going trying to force a way through the densely packed throng that crowded the road to the castle.

Once well clear of the gates, Thomas dismounted and returned the reins to their owner. "You'll find the stables just below the castle.

Ask for Axel, the stable master. I'm sorry, but I must leave you—I have an errand of pressing urgency." Without waiting for a reply he pushed his way into the crowd.

After several minutes of frustrating struggle Thomas had made very little forward progress. The milling throngs were clogging the road hopelessly. He peered behind him and saw that the group with the horses had advanced almost as much as he had.

Then an idea came to him. Pushing through the crowd in the opposite direction, he made his way back to the horses. The young nobleman was working hard to keep the mare under control, and doing admirably given the circumstances. Eyes bulging and ears laid back, the horse pulled this way and that struggling to free itself.

Taking the reins of the mare once more, Thomas leaped onto its bare back and pulled back savagely on the reins. The mare reared, almost throwing him, and screamed in protest. All eyes turned in his direction. He urged the horse forward, leaning down and slapping it hard across the ribs. The crowd scattered as horse and rider plunged forward, barely missing a cart and almost trampling several people. He shouted a warning at the top of his voice as the horse careered wildly up the road, the crowd parting magically before it. The mare charged on, completely out of control, and it took all of his skill to keep his seat.

The horse slowed only when the road drew to an end at the castle. Then, panting and quivering, it came to a complete halt. He slid off its back and, handing the reins to a surprised guard, ran into the castle courtyard yelling frantically for Will.

Half the castle was in an uproar by the time Thomas finally managed to locate Will. He found him at the stables, talking to the stable master.

Breathless and agitated, Thomas came to a stop and stood doubled over panting stupidly, unable to speak. His father eyed him for a moment as a man might gaze at a carnival curiosity, then turned his back on him and resumed his conversation with Will.

"I must speak with you, Will!" Thomas blurted, finally recovering himself enough to interrupt them.

His father faced him. "As you can see, Thomas," he said, speaking with exaggerated patience, "Will is busy right now." He again turned his back on his son.

"But this is urgent!"

"And so is my conversation," snapped Axel, spinning around, visibly annoyed now. "Your rudeness is intolerable! If you must behave like a child, do it elsewhere so we can finish talking in peace."

Thomas bristled. Of all people, why did Will have to be with his father at that moment? But nothing mattered except for the urgency of the situation. Calming himself, he spoke again, forcefully, and directly to the young deputy captain. "Will, I must speak with you. Right now. It cannot wait."

Will turned to him, then glanced back at the storm brewing on the face of the stable master. "What is it, Thomas?"

"I must speak with you alone."

Thunder appeared briefly on his father's face, then he abruptly turned on his heel. The storm receded into the distance.

Will cocked an eyebrow quizzically at Thomas. "It seems you have my full attention," he observed.

Thomas did not hesitate. Like water from a burst dam, his story poured from him, beginning with his suspicions of the strangers and ending with the alarming revelations of the stone. He spoke rapidly and concisely, skipping over unnecessary details but omitting nothing of importance.

Will did not interrupt him. As he listened, a deepening frown furrowed his brow.

Thomas at last finished his account and paused, breathless.

"You've done well, Thomas. Very well indeed! But there is much to do." Will punched his hand in frustration. "I've been blind! Stupid!"

He set his face to the castle and hobbled toward it as fast as he could manage. Spotting a soldier, he shouted to him, "Get me Rufe Sarjant. Hurry, man!" Wide-eyed, the fellow took to his heels, disappearing into the castle courtyard.

Rufe's huge frame soon appeared, and he quickly joined them, curiosity evident on his face. Will drew him aside, beckoning to Thomas to join them. A small cluster of soldiers gathered nearby, peering uneasily in their direction.

"Rufe, listen carefully. I need you to go with Thomas to the city gates. Take as many soldiers as you can mount quickly, but do not delay. When you get there, Thomas will point out a number of men. Kill them all. Don't let any escape."

Rufe threw a surprised glance at Thomas. "Can Thomas really be certain who deserves to be put to death?" he asked doubtfully.

"He can," Will replied flatly. Seeing continuing hesitation in his friend's eyes, he added, "There's no time to explain now. Don't fail me in this, Rufe!"

That was enough for the giant guardsman. He sprinted toward the gathered men, calling loudly for horses.

Thomas stirred, the anticipation of the impending action affecting him strangely. For the first time he felt like a man, and yet also newly aware of his own mortality.

"I'm going to need a sword."

Will shook his head emphatically. "You won't be doing any fighting. You're no soldier—you wouldn't last two minutes."

An old wound, buried deep, stirred uncomfortably.

"We cannot afford to lose you," Will continued, real alarm in his voice. "You're much too important!"

The old scar vanished from his consciousness, forgotten.

Rufe reappeared astride a horse and leading another. Thomas took the offered reins and swung into the saddle. Only seven soldiers had quickly found mounts; others would have to follow as quickly as they could.

Rufe set off immediately, heading away from the castle. Taking a deep breath, Thomas dug his heels into his horse's flanks and followed.

THOMAS SHRANK INTO A DOORWAY, not wanting to watch but unable to tear his eyes from the terrible ritual of death before him. It was not going well for Rufe and his men. Four of them lay dead along with all four guards from the gate, and between them they had accounted for only one of the Rogandans. Another had died at the hand of Rufe.

Rufe, positioned behind a small cart, battled grimly against two men. All three of his remaining soldiers stood desperately at bay, outmatched in skill and visibly nearing the end of their strength. Even as Thomas watched, one of them went down, and his victorious opponent moved to join the fight against one of the others. At this critical moment three new soldiers arrived from the castle and plunged into the battle, restoring the balance at least for a while.

The Rogandans had been ready for them when Rufe's little group rode up to the gate. Thomas had barely pointed out the first of the foreigners before they found themselves under attack from all sides. The attackers showed a callous disregard for commoners—several bystanders lay unmoving on the ground, unable to flee quickly enough to get out of the way.

The Rogandans were few in number—Thomas had counted eight —but they were battle hardened and well armed. Their long cloaks hid more than swords; Rufe's men found their thrusts turned aside by chain mail, and they had only small shields for their own protection.

Rufe had at once been set upon by three attackers who quickly realized he was the leader. Only his longer reach kept him alive in those first frantic moments. He had backed up to a wall to avoid being surrounded, bellowing loudly, "To me!" The gate guards, standing stupidly at their posts and watching open-mouthed, sprang into life and headed for Rufe. The distraction gave him the chance to catch one of his attackers off guard. He ran him through the throat.

A guard from the gate pinned a Rogandan against a wall with his spear. The man's mail coat protected him as he twisted this way and that trying to get free. A second guard came at him from the side, dancing back and forth as the frustrated Rogandan aimed blows at him. The whole pantomime would have been comical but for its deadly intent. Eventually they succeeded in bringing him down.

That was the high point of the battle—everything had gone horribly wrong since. The Rogandans were simply too ruthless, too well trained, and too strong. Where were Will and the other soldiers?

Thomas watched tensely as Rufe rained blows on his two opponents. He felt sure his friend would prevail. But the other soldiers?

Then he noticed a movement out of the corner of his eye. One of the Rogandans had brought down his opponent and was heading in his direction! He knew the man—it was the one he observed at the gate—and the man had clearly recognized him, too. He began backing away fearfully and discovered to his horror that he had no safe path of retreat. Battle raged on both sides, and a dead end alley lay behind him. He desperately tried to open the nearest door, but it was shut fast and barred.

The Rogandan closed in. Thomas edged away, heart pumping wildly. He blundered into a discarded basket, stumbled, and fell heavily, hitting his head. For a moment the whole world spun before his eyes, but as his vision cleared enough he saw his attacker almost within reach, a mocking smile on his lips. Thomas shrank back in helpless terror as the man raised his sword to strike. But the blow never came. The Rogandan stopped short, a look of surprise flashing across his face. A red-tinged spearhead protruded through his neck. He went down hard, twitching violently, then lay unmoving.

Thomas, his head pounding, looked up dazedly. An image of Will on horseback swam into view, concern on his face. Seeing Thomas unhurt, he paused only for a minute.

"Get yourself to safety, Thomas. Now!" he commanded, pointing to a horse wandering nearby. Then he turned away, shouting instructions. A large group of soldiers plunged into the battle. Thomas saw two more Rogandans go down, then the remainder fled into the back streets with soldiers in hot pursuit. Will didn't wait for the outcome but spurred his horse through the gates. Two noblemen and a sizable group of soldiers followed him.

Thomas picked himself up and staggered toward the horse. Mounting it, he turned his back on the destruction and headed for the castle.

16

To Rufe it felt like an age had passed since the fight at the gates of Arnost. In fact it was no more than a few hours. He peered uneasily across the river, trying in vain to detect movement on the far shore in the moonlight. How many more times could his men deny the Rogandans the passage of the ford? He knew another attempt would not be long delayed. He passed the back of his hand across his eyes. How good it would be to rest, to sleep. When would this night of blood and death come to an end?

His thoughts returned again to Will. The young deputy captain had returned to the city soon after the Arvenian soldiers had finally dispatched the last Rogandan at the gates. Rufe, exhausted from the struggle, felt only relief that the threat had been dealt with. But Will had realized that this incursion was merely the beginning. Rufe found himself quickly summoned to a conference with Will and the duke.

Will addressed himself to the regent. "This is not Danford over again, My Lord. The Rogandans have not come here to raid. I believe they intend to occupy Arnost. I'm confident we will soon discover that an army is hidden somewhere nearby."

The duke appeared doubtful. "Where could anyone hide an army near here without us knowing?"

"Surely not in the woods across the river," Rufe had said.

Will had been far ahead of them both. "I've given it some thought," he said. "The only likely place is the Dark Forest, just across the Arn River. It's vast and unpopulated—you could easily hide an entire army in there. But it's only two hours hard riding from Arnost."

"What do you propose?"

"The only place an army could easily cross the Arn River is a small ford on the main road east. I'm confident that two or three hundred soldiers with enough archers could prevent a crossing. With Count Ranauld away from the city we do not have enough men available. But we should round up as many as can be found, and send them to the ford. They can act as though they're involved in a training exercise.

"The Rogandans won't realize yet that their men at the city gates have been discovered. Hopefully they won't do anything more than observe our soldiers. In the meantime, we must send men to find the count. Without some of his thousand, we will have no hope of holding the ford for long."

"Will you lead the men to the ford?"

"I will go with them, but Rufe should lead the defense. If the Rogandans are there, I will return immediately. There will be much to do if Arnost is to remain safe."

Rufe did not feel equipped to take charge of the defense, but he knew Will well enough not to waste his breath protesting. The regent moved quickly to put the plan into action.

Will had been vindicated. Once they arrived at the ford, watchmen soon spotted observers in the woods across the river carefully monitoring their movements.

The pretense at a training exercise had worked, too—almost. Everything had gone smoothly until some of Rufe's men became a little too enthusiastic, stopping and searching every wagon that happened to cross the ford. The true situation must have gradually become apparent to any interested observer.

The Rogandans attempted a crossing before reinforcements arrived, and it had been a near thing. Small groups of mounted men with concealed weapons had ridden into the ford and quickly discovered it openly held against them. A determined assault in force at that moment would certainly have carried the day. But the cautious approach of the Rogandans cost them crucial moments, and reinforcements sent by Ranauld galloped up even as they were massing for their first serious attack.

In the long hours that followed, Will had joined Rufe and his men twice. Each time Will brought a few more soldiers to join the defense along with wagons full of spears, fresh clusters of arrows, and spare bowstrings.

His presence alone was worth hundreds of fighters. While he was there the men's spirits lifted visibly and weary hands gripped their weapons more tightly.

Once Rufe asked him what he had been doing, but Will deflected the question, simply saying that he was needed elsewhere and reminding Rufe that holding the ford was enough for him to be thinking about. Will was right, of course. He always was.

The sound of axes carried into the night. During the current lull in the fighting Rufe's men were hard at work strengthening a long wooden palisade he'd ordered built. He needed it to protect his men, and particularly his archers, from enemy arrows.

Although his archers were few in number, they had played a critical role in preventing the Rogandans from forcing the ford. A deadly hail of arrows rained down on the attackers each time they entered the ford, felling men and horses and staining the water red.

The crossing soon degenerated into a bloody chaos. The Rogandans could make no use of their superior numbers. Sending in more men would have been pointless.

The river was broad and the water thigh deep at the crossing. The shallow section was little wider than a single wagon, and it doglegged twice before reaching the near side. The river flowed across it swiftly. Smooth stones large and small lay underfoot, slippery with moss, making it impossible to cross quickly. The ford could safely be navigated with ample time and due care. Forcing a passage against a determined enemy was another matter entirely.

Soldiers who lost their footing were quickly swept away downstream. Those who couldn't swim drowned, and many who could swim were dragged under by the weight of their gear. The wounded had no chance at all.

Any who made it through the confusion were ridden down on the far bank by horsemen with lances or met by a determined line of soldiers charging with spears lowered. Enough had made it across, though, to steadily reduce the ranks of the Arvenian defenders. Arrows from across the river found their mark, too, resulting in a constant stream of casualties even when no assault was underway. The palisade had offered some respite between Rogandan sallies.

Rufe's defensive strategy might have been simple, but he applied it with firm resolve. So far it had worked. Rufe himself was first into battle and last to retire. He wasn't Will, but the men followed him willingly enough. Too many good soldiers had followed to their death today. There were so many Rogandans. Before the daylight failed he had seen the opposite shore and the woods beyond it crawling with them.

On his last visit Will left him with the words, "I need you to hold until daylight, Rufe." He meant to do it. But unless the Rogandans withdrew or the king's men abandoned their defense of the ford, before long few of his soldiers would be left to defend Arnost.

The enemy soldiers attacked heedlessly, like cattle driven to the butcher. Will had warned him about it. "Don't expect them to give up," he said. "They're led by Drettroth."

"How do you know?" Rufe had asked.

"I can sense it," Will replied. "And the signs are there. Have you wondered why the Rogandans at the gates didn't just slip away when they had been discovered? That's Drettroth. He's not interested in explanations or excuses. His soldiers succeed, or die in the attempt."

. . .

"RUFE! COME QUICKLY!" A scout beckoned urgently. He hurried toward the man.

"What's happening?"

"They've been building rafts below the ford. Dozens of them!"

Rufe groaned inwardly. It had been too much to hope that the Rogandans would be satisfied with an endless series of failed attempts on the ford. He peered across the river. The moon offered light enough to faintly see the activity on the far bank.

A river crossing by raft would be extremely difficult and unpredictable. The river was too wide and the current flowed too swiftly to offer any certainty about where the rafts would land. But the Rogandans could rely upon an overwhelming superiority in numbers. Rufe could not ignore the threat posed by the rafts. He would be forced to divide his force or risk being outflanked.

"How long do you think we have before they launch?"

"It's difficult to be sure. Maybe an hour. But no more."

Before Rufe had time to take any action, though, another soldier alerted him to a large body of horsemen riding in from the direction of Arnost. Moments later Will himself arrived at their head. The news spread quickly and loud cheering erupted from Rufe's men. Best of all, Will had brought with him as many soldiers as Rufe already had. He seemed to have developed a habit of showing up just at the crucial moment. How did he do it?

Will located Rufe, and the two leaders stood together for a long moment without speaking. The moonlight revealed a Will weary to the point of exhaustion. Clearly he had not slept this night. But that was equally true for them all.

Rufe felt great satisfaction at the prospect of facing battle with his friend rather than alone. He was relieved, too, at the thought that his captain would now take charge of the defense.

"They've built rafts," Rufe told him.

Will nodded in the dark. "I expected that."

Somehow his friend always managed to stay one step ahead. "How did you guess?"

Will shrugged. "It's what I would have done," he said simply.

"What do we do?"

"I've made some preparations."

Several wagons arrived as they watched, and men quickly began unloading them. Count Ranauld also arrived and joined the two men.

Will drew them both aside. "Rufe, I need to call on you for one more effort. When the Rogandans launch the rafts they will make an all out attempt to secure the ford. The rafts are little more than a diversion, and I will deal with them. But I need you to hold the ford. They'll throw everything they've got at you.

"I also need you to demonstrate your tactics to the count. He will relieve you, and he needs to understand exactly how you've managed so effectively to beat back a vastly superior force for all these hours.

"Once the immediate attacks have been dealt with, Rufe, I want you to take all your men back to Arnost. Make sure they get food and especially sleep as soon as you get there. Check that the defenses of the city are sound, then get some rest yourself. Don't keep pushing yourself. I'll be depending on you when I get back, and I need you alert and refreshed."

"What about you? You're exhausted, too!"

"Don't worry about me. I'm no longer needed elsewhere, so I can finally try to help out here. I'm determined to make sure that Drettroth is denied passage of the river until noon tomorrow. After that I'll get out fast, and everyone with me. When you return, make sure that the duke is clear that all of his preparations must be completed by noon."

"I understand." Pushing down his weariness, Rufe set off immediately to explain the defenses to Ranauld.

RUFE'S MEN waited patiently for the attack. They had forgotten their weariness in the excitement of the arrival of Will and his reinforcements. Ranauld's new reinforcements waited with them, tense and nervous in anticipation of their first action.

Much distant shouting accompanied the launch of the rafts across the river. The eyes of the Arvenians were drawn to the broad sweep of river below the ford. Many shapes moved slowly in the dim light, out over the surface of the water. There must have been almost two hundred rafts, each bristling with a small thicket of spears that glinted in the moonlight. So many! Flights of arrows flew through the sky from the defenders to meet them, but the watchers saw dark shapes raised against the missiles. The Rogandans had prepared a huge wooden shield to protect each raft.

Then came a surprise. A small point of light arced slowly through the air toward the rafts. It came down directly onto a wooden shield raised above a raft, and burst as it landed. A splash of light flared out as it spewed liquid fire. The fire ran across the shield, setting it ablaze, and down onto the raft and its occupants. The shield was quickly thrown overboard. Small figures could be seen writhing on the raft, covered with flames. Some cast themselves into the river. Screams of pain carried across the water.

The defenders watched in amazement as more and more tiny lights sailed through the air toward their targets. Some landed on the water, sputtering before disappearing beneath the surface of the river. Others fell onto the rafts, spreading fire and terror among the attackers.

Rufe's men did not cheer. The scene was too terrible for any response but silent horror. But new hope rose in them. They already trusted Will completely and depended on his leadership. They had heard the stories from the Danford veterans, and knew their leader somehow had the knack of arriving at the critical moment and turning disaster into victory. Now they were witnessing it for themselves. The battle for the ford would become a new story of legend. And they were part of it.

When the Rogandans released their expected attack on the ford, a deafening roar rose up from the defenders. They had hurled back attack after attack at great loss and almost to the limit of human endurance. But now they determined they would never be overcome, whatever the cost and no matter what the enemy threw at them.

The battle raged on, and slowly a night of blood and horror passed and gave way to a dawn of unspeakable weariness.

. . .

Rufe and his men reached the city walls soon after dawn. They rode through the gates slowly, utterly spent but proud and erect. The wounded followed close behind in wagons.

The countryside around the city was no longer recognizable. No farmhouses or buildings of any kind remained, and smoke still rose from burned fields and dwellings. They had ridden through a wasteland.

Before they could pass in through the gates they had to make way for a few wagons leaving the city laden with women, children, and the elderly. They soon discovered that a long line of such wagons had already departed, heading west or south, away from the fighting. These were the last.

Rufe discovered that the city had been emptied of everyone except soldiers and those few able-bodied men and women who had stayed to provide for their needs. All the cattle from the market had been rounded up and herded into the city. Any usable supplies had quickly been gathered from every farm within miles. Anything that remained had been put to the torch.

An enormous amount of crucial preparation had been carried out, and in a remarkably short period of time. Rufe began to under-stand what Will had been doing in the hours before he returned to the ford. He also realized why it hadn't been possible to immediately send all of Ranauld's men to reinforce the defenders.

Drettroth must have hoped to take the city by surprise. Now he would find it held in strength against him. He must have expected to supply his army from the rich farmlands surrounding Arnost. Instead he would find a barren wilderness. If he expected to starve the city into submission, he would eventually discover that it had been well stocked and its hungry dependents sent elsewhere.

Rufe suddenly thought of Thomas. Without his alertness they would certainly have been overtaken by a terrible disaster. He decided to seek him out as soon as he had an opportunity.

He located the Duke of Erestor and delivered Will's message. The regent had not been idle. The last wagons had departed. Adequate supplies had been gathered. Final repairs to the city walls were almost complete. The duke may have weathered a few too many winters, but he was a capable man and had the situation well in hand.

Having seen to the welfare of his men, Rufe took the opportunity to snatch a few hours sleep.

THE SUN WAS high in the sky when he woke. There was no news of Will. Noon came and went with still no sign of the captain or his men. Rufe was bent on gathering some men and heading back to the ford, but the duke overruled him. "Will knows what he's about," he said calmly. "He'll be back when he judges the time is right."

Two more hours passed before a line of wagons rolled slowly into view. The duke sent out mounted soldiers to escort them in. Rufe met them at the gate, eager for news.

"We left the captain several hours ago," one of the wagon drivers reported. The man carried a leg wound, bound with bloodied bandages. He spoke through clenched teeth, struggling with pain and pale from loss of blood. It was obvious that every man capable of fighting had remained at the ford.

"The Rogandans managed to get a few rafts across the river, a long way downstream, out of our sight. Our scouts discovered them before they reached us, and we managed to drive them off. But they attacked the ford again at the same time. We held on, but lost a lot of men. The captain sent us off as soon as it was safe to leave. That was midmorning. He was determined to hold until noon."

THOMAS JOINED RUFE, and they waited together with growing anxiety as the afternoon drew on. Rufe paced restlessly along the city wall, muttering to himself. More than once he was determined to mount a horse and head off alone to find out what was happening. Thomas talked him out of it with difficulty.

Late in the afternoon more wagons appeared in the distance, moving slowly. Before they reached the city a group of horsemen came into view, far behind but heading for the city.

Rufe ran from the wall, calling loudly for men to join him. A mounted party quickly formed and galloped away from the walls. When they reached the wagons, a few men detached themselves from the group and climbed onto the wagons. The wagons picked up speed, and before long the gates opened to receive them.

Rufe and the other horsemen dwindled slowly into the distance. Who would they encounter? Would it be Will, with whatever remained of his force? Or the first contingent of the victorious Rogandans? Now it was the turn of Thomas to pace anxiously along the wall. The horsemen met and merged in the distance. Thomas could not tell if they met as friends or foes.

After what seemed like an age, Thomas could make out a large body of horsemen. They were hundreds strong, surely too many for Will's party. Had Rufe now been lost as well, undone by his rash impatience to rejoin his captain?

But now behind this group an even larger body of men could be seen, spreading out across the plain. As the first group drew closer, riders could be seen looking back over their shoulders, and urging weary mounts to greater efforts. It was Will and his men! Rufe must have joined them.

They arrived in good order and passed proudly through the gates. Will and Ranauld rode with them, both apparently unscathed. Ranauld led them in.

Will waited at the rear, not entering the city until all his men were safely inside. His arrival was greeted with noisy jubilation by the men on the walls, and the sound of cheering rose on the afternoon air.

BEFORE THE SUN set an immense army had spread out across the plains before the city and could be seen setting up camp. The city was invested. The siege had begun.

Men gazed in awe at the vast extent of the enemy encampment.

Then they looked around them anxiously, trying to assess the strength of the city walls.

The Rogandan losses at the ford, great as they were, appeared to be about as significant as a few broken ears in a cornfield. But however strong the enemy army might be, the watching soldiers took great heart from the return of Will Prentis. Where Will led, men would follow. And no matter the odds, they were certain he would lead them to victory.

VOLUME 2—THE SHAKING

17

The Duke of Erestor banged his fist down hard on the table and glared angrily at the Council members seated before him. The hubbub gradually died down, and all eyes turned in his direction.

"May I remind you, My Lords, that our situation is difficult enough already without us bickering with each other? Any sane person," and with this he locked eyes with the pompous Lord Sinnett, who colored and quickly lowered his gaze, "can see that all available manpower is needed for the defense of the city. Each of us has servants to see to our basic needs. Beyond that we must all make sacrifices for the sake of our mutual security. Do I make myself clear?"

He paused for a long moment. The nobles had gone quiet.

Will, standing behind and to the left of the duke, glanced at the assembled lords. They were a reduced group in more than numbers. Several of the more astute nobles, like Bottren, Dongan, and Owein, had accompanied the king on his delegation to Castel. Others, such as Gorein, Storr, Burtelen, and Leile, had hurriedly departed for their holdings in the south and west to strengthen defenses and raise armies. Many of those who remained were essential neither to the king nor to the kingdom. Yet even as their relevance diminished, by some mysterious logic they had apparently deduced that their importance had increased.

Good men still occupied seats at the table, but sadly they were now outnumbered by lesser brethren. Count Ranauld briefly caught his eye, disgust evident on his face. Will kept his face impassive.

The duke rose to his feet and cleared his throat. "As you are aware, we have been very fortunate indeed to have at our service Will Prentis, the deputy captain of the King's Guard." He nodded to Will. "I am today confirming him as commander of the army. As of now, all soldiers in Arnost will come under his direct authority. I am appointing Count Ranauld," and the duke paused and bowed in his direction, "to act as his deputy."

Loud murmuring greeted his announcement. A nobleman answering to a commoner? It was unprecedented. The duke raised his voice and talked them down. "Our king holds Will Prentis in very high esteem, and before he departed he advised me to strongly consider such an appointment should the need arise." He paused to let that sink in.

"Any of our soldiers will readily confirm," he continued, "that he has long been commander in all but name. He commands the complete loyalty of every one of our soldiers, and I expect no less from each of you.

"I need hardly remind you," he concluded, "that without the commander's extraordinary efforts over the last two days, every one of us would be dead or enslaved."

Will could not help noticing the subtle emphasis the regent placed on his new title, reinforcing his status.

The duke paused again, and directed his gaze pointedly around the table, offering a challenge to anyone who dared take it. No one said a word.

Then the silence was shattered as Count Ranauld surged to his feet, his chair skidding noisily back across the stone floor behind him. His voice rang out as he raised his goblet high. "To the commander!" One by one the others stood with him, a few without hesitation, others more slowly.

At last only the Earl of Pisander retained his seat. The earl, who ran the king's foreign spy network, lived for intrigue. He also had a high view of his own importance. Leaning casually back in his chair, he studied each nobleman's face in turn. Will's eyes he ignored. Then slowly he rose to his feet, raised his goblet and aimed his gaze in the direction of Will. "To the commander," he averred firmly.

———

THOMAS TOOK A DEEP BREATH, steadied his nerves, and strode through the door. He had not been alone with his father since before the incident with Will, and he was not looking forward to it.

A few hours ago his mother Marya had left the city in a wagon, heading for safety with most of the other women. She hoped to join her brother and his wife, living far away south on a farm with three children that Marya had never seen.

His mother had not gone willingly, though. She desperately wanted to remain with her husband and her son. Axel, reinforced by a decree from the duke, overruled her protests. Thomas felt sure that his father did not want to be separated from his wife, either. But he was a practical man, and her safety was his highest priority.

Thomas found his father seated at the table preparing food. He glanced up briefly when Thomas entered then returned to his work.

The youth was determined to make an attempt at peace. "I'm sorry I interrupted your conversation with Will."

His father did not respond for a while. Then he said, "When you were a little boy you were bitten by a horse."

Thomas, who had heard this story many times, was curious that his father chose to mention it now.

"The wound wasn't dangerous, but it took a long time to heal. You were very upset. Your mother believed you would never want to go near horses again. She thought the incident shocked you most because you loved the horses and couldn't understand why one of them would want to hurt you.

"I believed there was a chance your interest could be recaptured. I spent many hours with you, helping you to overcome your fear. At first you were resistant, but gradually you regained your confidence, and you began to rediscover your love for them."

Thomas hadn't heard this before. He listened intently, his interest stirred.

"I taught you first how to recognize their moods, and later how to manage them whatever mood they were in. You were a fast learner. I taught you to ride, too. You were the youngest rider I ever saw."

"I know you taught me to ride," Thomas acknowledged. Nevertheless his father's comments were a revelation to him. He hadn't been aware that his father had a role in the development of his unusual ability to read and respond to horses. It gave him a lot to think about.

"You were good with horses and a hard worker. I always hoped you would succeed me one day," the stable master continued. "I remember the day I presented you to the king. I was proud of you.

"You used to be happy back then." He sounded wistful. "I don't understand what happened. Everything changed."

His father was right—it had all changed. Because of the stone. But how could he explain it to his father? He wouldn't be able to make him understand.

"Back then you wanted to be with me—with your mother and me. Now you only seem to care about Will Prentis and Rufe Sarjant and their friends."

Shamed by his father's words, Thomas didn't know what to say. It was all true. They had grown apart, and it was his fault. And to think that his father might be sad about it—he hadn't expected that.

"You've become a different person, Thomas. You fought with Simon, didn't you?"

Thomas looked down, then finally nodded uncomfortably. "Yes." He wanted to tell his father it was Simon's fault, but he couldn't honestly say that.

"Why would you do that?" His father seemed baffled. Then he glanced at his son sharply. "He told me you attacked him with a pitchfork. Is that true?"

Thomas felt himself coloring. How could he possibly explain? *Simon had my stone!* His father would not understand, and he couldn't blame him.

He saw his father's eyes narrow in anger and disappointment. For a while neither of them said anything.

"There was a time when you used to treat me with respect." His father started up again, and his voice had taken on a harder edge. "I don't like what you've become, Thomas. Yesterday I finally understood that you care nothing for me."

"I said I was sorry." Thomas finally found his voice again. "But I needed to interrupt you—it was urgent!"

"It was obvious to me that your message was urgent—when I finally found out what it was. It wasn't the interruption that showed your lack of respect. It was your refusal to deliver the message in my hearing. What possible reason could you have for doing that?"

He had paid such a heavy price for the stone. Now, as he felt the full impact of his father's words, he began finally to grasp just how much it had affected their relationship. For the first time Thomas actually considered sharing his secret with him.

"There was a reason. A good reason."

"Well?" His father spread his hands inquiringly. "What was it?"

Now he came to it, Thomas could not imagine how to begin to explain the whole complicated, messy story of the stone. Nor could he imagine how his father would receive it. He stood there wrestling with his thoughts and feelings. Should he make the attempt? He couldn't decide, so in the end he managed only an evasive non-answer. "It's difficult to explain."

His father aimed a look of disgust at him. "It doesn't seem difficult to me. It's very simple: you care nothing at all for me, or for your mother."

This accusation was so untrue. He cared deeply about his parents. And it was so unfair. From the way his father behaved at times, Thomas could just as easily claim that he cared nothing for his son.

"You're a very important person now. Too important to have anything to do with the likes of us."

He looked at his father in disbelief. Could he really have misunderstood him this much?

Thomas had found himself, entirely to his own surprise, doing a job that counted for something, and he wanted to do the job well. He also wanted his efforts to be noticed and appreciated, and he couldn't pretend otherwise. But it had never entered his head that he was more important than his parents. He simply didn't think like that.

His father's barbs drove from his mind any thought of telling him about the stone. He felt only anger and hurt.

Then came the final injury. Simon appeared in the doorway of Thomas's bedroom, a mocking smile on his lips. It was obvious that he had been listening to the conversation. Worse, his father was not surprised to see Simon—he had known that he was there. And Thomas had actually considered revealing the secret of the stone.

How *could* his father say all this to him in the presence of Simon? Now it was his turn to wonder what possible reason could excuse such behavior.

"Oh, Simon will be sharing your room from now on," his father informed him casually. "His uncle has gone south for safety, and Simon has no one else to stay with."

Thomas stood there speechless. Seeing the look on his face, his father said curtly, "If you don't like it, you can always go stay with your friends in the castle."

Thomas said nothing. He pushed past Simon into his room, gathered his few possessions, and left.

———

BELLS RANG LOUDLY, and the gathered throngs cheered deliriously as King Steffan of Arvenon strode purposefully and majestically into the cathedral, between two long lines of armed men standing importantly at attention. The men, selected from his own guard, stood resplendent in their dress uniforms.

Doubts still ravaged his mind. To add to the uncertainties about his new bride, there was now the disturbing fact that he had received no word from Arnost for several days. New messengers had been sent, but they had not yet returned.

All these distractions the king pushed from his thoughts. He reminded himself of the reasons why he had sought this alliance. Each of them remained pressing. He was committed now, and he was determined to go through with it. Today was his wedding day, long considered and long anticipated, and it deserved his complete and undistracted attention. If there were problems to address in Arvenon they could wait until the following day. If Istel had been playing him false in some way, he would deal with it later. And deal with it firmly.

He made his way to the front of the cathedral, with Lords Bottren and Owein following close behind. A bishop in a flowing gown and tall miter greeted them and showed them to their positions.

A trumpet fanfare heralded the arrival of the princess and her retinue. After a stately entrance accompanied by rapturous applause, she made her way slowly to the front of the church. Steffan watched closely, trying without success to get a clear glimpse of the young woman behind the thick veil that covered her face. Her gown was a stunning white waterfall of lace, glittering with diamantés. His eye was drawn from the exquisite veil, topped with a diamond tiara, down to the long string of pearls around her neck supporting a large sapphire pendant. The overall effect was dazzling. Steffan pulled himself to his full height, gazing admiringly upon his regal bride.

Trumpets sounded, monks chanted, and choirs sang. The bishop solemnly intoned the rites. The bride and the groom exchanged vows promising love, honor and fidelity until death parted them. He spoke boldly; she so faintly he could barely hear her. Then he placed a ring on her delicate finger.

The bishop spoke of the joys and trials and the rights and respon-sibilities of marriage and parenthood. Steffan, half-listening through the distractions of the day, was struck by the simplicity of the message. The prelate painted a picture of the basic hopes and needs of human life. His homily would have been equally at place in the wedding of the poorest and most humble couple in the kingdom.

Amidst the pomp and splendor of the royal wedding, the bishop was choosing to remind the groom that the basic benefits of life did not exist merely for the pleasure of kings. Steffan heard the entreaty and silently promised himself that he would not forget it.

The bishop offered words of blessing, and it was done. A triumphant fanfare rang out as he led the bridal couple to a balcony and presented them to the enthusiastic crowd, who waved banners and cheered wildly. King Steffan found himself caught up in the joy of the throng, and smiled back in unfeigned delight.

Finally the wedding party, invited guests, and a large contingent from among the nobility of Castel, proceeded to a massive hall in the castle where a sumptuous banquet had been laid out. The tables groaned under the weight of an overwhelming assortment of food both local and exotic, beautifully presented. Round loaves of bread made from fine-ground flour stood piled high on wooden platters, still steaming, fresh from the oven. Every kind of meat had been prepared, from fish, fowl, and whole pig carcasses to the finest cuts of venison and beef. An unparalleled selection of fresh and dried fruit competed with sweetmeats, honey cakes, and delicious desserts for the approval of the revelers. The best wine from Lestanor flowed freely as well as copious quantities of the excellent local ale.

Harps and lyres offered a soothing background to the feast, and pipers waited at the ready for later in the evening when guests might wish to dance.

Steffan had been warned in advance that Castelan custom prohibited the bride from removing her veil until after all the celebrations were complete. Further, since for that day she was exalted above all others in honor as she was in beauty, she was not expected to speak but simply to bask in the attention and admiration of all. So she remained demure and silent throughout the feast that followed the ceremony.

This was no intimate family occasion. Ambassadors from all the neighboring kingdoms had attended the wedding and were present at the feast. Each of them came in turn to the bride and groom throughout the meal and presented fine gifts and fine words.

The Rogandan ambassador managed to be particularly insufferable, delivering a speech full of empty sentiment in words dripping with honey and a tone dripping with sarcasm. The man returned to his seat and sat smugly surrounded by toadying ambassadors of lesser status who hung on his every word. Whenever Steffan glanced in his direction, he raised his chalice and proffered an exaggerated bow.

As the afternoon and evening wore on, the celebrations became increasingly tiresome to Steffan. The desire grew in him to dispense with partying and to escape the nobles and ambassadors who vied for his attention. More and more he wanted to be alone with his bride, to converse with her at last and to see her face.

He took every opportunity, though, to study his father-in-law. King Istel imbibed freely and celebrated more and more loudly as the wedding supper proceeded. Occasionally, however, Steffan caught him staring at his daughter with a look akin to anguish.

The night was well advanced before Steffan's frustration finally came to an end. He left the revelers and the banqueting hall and was ushered to his wedding chamber. Servants respectfully helped him out of his ceremonial garments and into comfortable attire of smooth silk before bowing deeply and leaving him. His bride was, he knew, somewhere nearby being likewise prepared. He waited, eager and impatient, for her arrival.

SOLDIERS on the wall ducked involuntarily as a large rock sailed over their heads, crashing into a house behind them in the city. Will stood on a battlement beside the gates, watching. The Rogandans probably did not know that the houses close to the wall were unoccupied. He was more than happy for them to waste their shots demolishing houses instead of focusing on the wall.

More challenging were the fireballs the attackers had launched, starting fires and keeping his soldiers busy trying to put them out. At least one large blaze was still burning out of control, and a pall of smoke hung low over the city.

In the first couple of days of the siege Will had set the defenders to work building their own catapults. They built especially large ones with the result that their engines had greater range than those of the Rogandans. For now. The defenders also had an unlimited supply of ammunition to quarry from the rocky outcrop on which the castle was built.

The Arvenian soldiers had quickly put the catapults to good use, forcing the Rogandans to hastily remove their new encampment and re-site it further back out of range. A few even larger catapults were now under construction in Arnost. Will didn't want the besiegers to become too comfortable.

For the Rogandan catapults to reach the city, they were forced to operate well within the range of the defenders. One lucky shot from Will's men had already destroyed a Rogandan engine, and most of the enemy soldiers had been hastily pulled back for their own protection.

From his position atop the wall, Will raised his hand, then lowered it. The gates swung ponderously open, and a large group of mounted soldiers issued out and galloped toward the Rogandan catapults. Most of them engaged enemy soldiers, but a few rode up to the catapults and quickly poured oil over them. Other soldiers then threw torches onto the catapults. Within moments all of them were ablaze.

The Arvenians wheeled and galloped back to the city even as groups of Rogandan cavalry formed behind them. They raced through the gate, and it swung shut in the faces of the pursuing Rogandans, who were met with a hail of arrows from the wall and quickly retreated.

The defenders jeered and shook their fists at the fleeing Rogandans. They shouted with delight at the sight of the burning catapults.

The sally had bought the city some time, and it was good for morale. But Will was under no illusions. Before long there would be other larger engines to take their place. And they would be well defended next time.

Will's thoughts went to the king far away in Castel. Was he aware that his capital was under siege? Messengers had been sent, but it was difficult to know if they had been able to get through.

But what exercised Will most was the inaction of the Rogandans. Their catapults kept the pressure on the defenders, to be sure. But Drettroth had more than enough men for a direct assault on the city. Why was he not attacking? And in the unlikely event that the Rogandan lord was content to simply starve the city into submission, he certainly did not need an army this size to maintain a siege. What was he planning to do with the rest of his soldiers? There were far too many unknowns, and it made Will uncomfortable.

The duke joined him on the wall, interrupting his musing. "I see your sally was successful, Will."

"Yes, My Lord. It has given us some breathing space, at least for a while."

"How are the men?"

"In good heart. A lengthy siege will test their resolve, though."

"Some of the lords are pressing for a Council of War. They want to know what we're planning."

Will raised an eyebrow quizzically. "What do they expect, My Lord? It will take a very large army to lift this siege. We do not have anywhere near enough men to do it."

"I know. We will meet with them and try to help them see reality. Unfortunately, few of them have any comprehension of the ways of war."

The duke sighed. "Most of them are more of a hindrance than a help. A rock from a catapult damaged a small part of the servants' quarters of the Earl of Pisander earlier today, and he has taken the opportunity to demand a new and more luxurious dwelling.

"I fail to understand why he didn't leave when he had the chance. His holdings are within my own Duchy of Erestor, west of here. He would have been safe there, and he is of little use in Arnost. His spies cannot reach him while he's locked up in here."

Will shrugged sympathetically. "I do have a proposal I could present to the Council, My Lord. People are usually easier to manage when there is some kind of a plan."

The duke looked at him doubtfully. "We must preserve the king's army if we are to preserve his city."

"My plan does not put the army at risk."

The regent frowned at him. "Don't expect me to approve any plan that puts you at risk. The men believe in you, and I depend on you. I cannot afford to have anything happen to you."

"I understand, My Lord."

The duke offered no further comment.

This particular issue was far from settled, though, and Will had the feeling that the regent knew it as well as he did. Perhaps, like his commander, the duke was simply planning to choose his timing carefully before picking a fight.

18

The afternoon dragged on interminably. Thomas hefted another heavy stone and lugged it to the wall, puffing and blowing as he went. He loathed this work, but he could think of nothing better to do.

He could hardly have felt more miserable. Only a few days ago he had been on top of the world. As horse master he had an important role, a job he loved and excelled at. Now his students patrolled the wall or put out fires; the army had little use for horsemen during a siege. Back then his free time had been spent relaxing with Will and Rufe. Now both men were so busy that he rarely caught a glimpse of them.

The pinnacle for Thomas had been his discovery of the Rogandans lurking at the city gates. His quick reaction had played an important part in saving the city. And the stone, inert for so long, had responded in his moment of need and exposed the designs of the invaders. Now his intervention seemed small and insignificant, overshadowed by the heroic defense of the ford and the drama of the siege. And he had since found the stone closed to him once more.

On one of the few occasions he had seen Will, his friend had noticed that he was bored and inactive.

"Perhaps your father could use some help at the stables," he had suggested.

But Thomas would not go back to the stables. He had wasted no time finding something else to do. Builders were hard at work strengthening the wall, and he soon found himself helping them.

The work was difficult and dangerous, the more so when the Rogandans began lobbing rocks the size of ponies over the wall. The stone mason in charge of the section of wall where Thomas was working became increasingly upset and irritable as time wore on. Thomas soon became a target. "Can't you work faster?" "Are you deaf? I told you to put it over there!"

When Thomas made a mistake mixing mortar, the mason lashed out unmercifully. "Don't you know anything? You're worse than useless! You create more work than you're doing."

Shoveling manure at the stables would have been preferable to this. But Thomas knew that he could face neither his father's accusing silences nor Simon's smugness. He decided he had little choice other than to persist.

Life had an uncomfortable way of turning on you just when everything seemed to be going well. And given the circumstances of the siege, it seemed highly unlikely that any further changes would be for the better.

"WHAT ARE we doing to break this siege, My Lord?"

"Why are we just sitting here while the Rogandans pillage our land?"

"When will the king return from Castel with his army to relieve us?"

The duke endured the carping of the nobles with increasing annoyance. Finally he held up his hand. The clamor continued unabated.

"Silence!" he bellowed, a look of fury on his face. "I shall dismiss you from this chamber and this Council if you continue to behave in this way."

Some of the nobles appeared affronted, but the noise subsided.

After a few moments of silence, the Earl of Pisander spoke up. "I think my fellow nobles are simply wondering if our excellent commander has prepared a plan for dealing with the Rogandans."

"The city walls are solid, and we have enough men to defend them, My Lord," Will replied calmly. "My plan is to ensure that the Rogandans stay out, while we remain safe inside."

"A safe plan indeed, Commander. No one could accuse you of being unduly adventurous." A couple of the nobles snickered. "Do you have no thought of taking the fight to the Rogandans?"

"Our estimate is that the Rogandans have twenty thousand men in their army. We have almost twenty five hundred—barely enough to protect the city. I would be a poor commander indeed if I committed our soldiers to battle against such odds without a very compelling reason, My Lord."

"Are you afraid to fight unless the odds are in your favor, Commander?" Pisander asked quietly.

Will, who had thus far never managed to engage in any fight where the odds were in his favor, did not bother to reply.

"If you think he's afraid, why don't you issue him a formal challenge, Pisander?" Count Ranauld broke in, his voice icy calm.

"Don't be ridiculous, Ranauld. You know that a nobleman cannot duel with a commoner."

"That problem is not insurmountable. I am his Second In Command. Issue the challenge to me. I would be delighted to defend his honor."

Pisander went pale. "Come, My Lord. You entirely mistake me. I meant no slight on our gallant commander. Everyone knows he has no cowardly bone in his body. I was merely hoping to learn if he might have some plan of action."

"As a matter of fact I do." All eyes turned immediately to Will. He looked to the duke for permission to speak. The duke frowned, but inclined his head.

"We need to find out what Drettroth, who leads the Rogandans, is planning to do. His army is very large, much larger than he needs for a siege. And he was never planning a siege, anyway—he expected to take Arnost by surprise. I suspect that Arnost was only ever intended to be a stepping stone, and that he has other plans for this army."

"How do you propose to uncover Drettroth's plans," retorted Pisander, "given that our best agents have uncovered nothing? Are you planning to write to him and ask for the details?"

Will ignored Pisander's sarcasm. "I'm proposing to visit the Rogandan camp myself and learn what I can."

The duke was on his feet in an instant. "Certainly not! It would be suicide."

"My Lord Duke," said Pisander reasonably, "surely we should at least hear the commander out."

"How could you possibly get in there undetected?" Ranauld protested.

"There are twenty thousand men milling around out there. No one can keep track of them all. I speak Rogandan, which means I should be able to bluff my way out of any difficult situation."

"But even Rogandan soldiers have duties to perform," protested the duke. "A soldier doesn't just wander around wherever he wants."

"I'm not planning to go as a soldier, My Lord. I'll go as a priest. Their armies never go anywhere without them. And no Rogandan soldier would dare to ask questions of a priest."

"But what if you meet other priests?"

"I know something of how they behave. When I was young, my friends and I used to imitate the priests. I was thought to be pretty good at it."

"When do you propose to do this?" asked Pisander.

"I'll go tomorrow night as soon as it's dark. There's a place where I can easily be lowered over the wall. I'll find my way to Drettroth's tent, discover whatever I can, then I'll be out of there before dawn."

"It's a bold plan," Pisander admitted. Others around the room murmured their agreement.

"It's far too risky," asserted Ranauld.

The duke had the last word. "I'll never allow it," he said flatly.

Nevertheless Will was determined to go. He fully understood the risks, and the thought of being caught was too awful to entertain. But an attempt had to be made. And he was confident that the duke would be brought to see the sense in it.

Of late Will had discovered, to his wonder, that in the end people mostly acceded to his requests and embraced his proposals. Perhaps it was because he had developed a reputation of making suggestions that were more than usually useful. Perhaps people believed in his luck.

Confident that he would be proceeding with his plan, Will began serious preparations for his foray into the Rogandan camp even before receiving agreement from the duke.

His confidence was soon tested. The duke sought him out not long after the conference. The regent appeared harried and frustrated.

"Pisander has been bleating in my ear since the minute the meeting ended," the duke complained. "He insists that we must find a way to get information. He says that his agents are either missing or outside the city and unable to report. Frankly, even if they all suddenly appeared tomorrow, I wouldn't set much store by anything they had to say. They somehow managed to completely miss the arrival of twenty thousand Rogandan soldiers in the Dark Forest."

The duke sighed deeply. "He's right, though—we do need information. But not at the cost of your life, Will. This plan is madness! I will not let you walk alone right into the middle of the entire Rogandan army."

"I understand your concern, My Lord. Believe me, I have no desire whatsoever to fall into the hands of Drettroth either. We have met once before, and I doubt that he remembers the meeting warmly," said Will, a grim smile on his face.

"But what is he planning to do with all those men?" he continued. "I can't imagine he'll leave them sitting here for long. Nor can I see him waiting out a siege. If we don't get some idea of his intentions soon, My Lord, we might not have another opportunity. He'll leave enough men here to keep us quiet, and disappear off with the rest to who knows where."

"But even if we discover his plans, what can we do to prevent them?"

"We can find a way to get messengers through the Rogandan lines to warn other cities that he's on the way. Given enough time to prepare, they might be able to avoid capture. Drettroth will be forced to tie down more of his forces laying siege, or waste men storming heavily defended walls."

The duke did not want to be convinced. "Even if you're right, why does it need to be you?"

Will shrugged. "Who else speaks Rogandan fluently, My Lord? Who else even knows what Drettroth looks like?"

Hearing no response from the regent, he added, "And who else would be willing to make the attempt?"

The duke could not deny the need to discover Drettroth's plans, and he had no answers to Will's questions. He left with his face betraying his frustration.

Before twenty-four hours had passed, the regent had acquiesced. Will did not ask for or expect his enthusiastic blessing; he knew that would be too much to hope for.

A SOFT TAP at the door of his apartments stirred Steffan into life. "Enter!" he commanded.

A servant woman appeared at the door and bowed low. "Her Majesty, Essanda, Queen of Arvenon, and Princess of Castel, awaits your pleasure."

"You may send her in," he replied, trying not to sound eager. He leaped to his feet, ready to greet his bride.

The woman bowed low again and backed out of the door.

A few moments later Queen Essanda entered the room. The

contrast between her earlier impregnability and her current appearance could not have been more marked. They had dressed her in a flimsy gown of transparent material, and every line and curve was fully revealed in the candlelight.

Steffan stood with mouth agape and stared. Everything instantly became clear—the reason behind the secrecy, the hesitation of the king, the awkwardness of the Castelan nobles. He had been preparing himself for the unexpected, but he hadn't been anticipating this. How had they managed to keep it hidden? A mixture of emotions assaulted him: disappointment, anger, shame, pity, but most of all astonishment.

"Do I displease My Lord?"

Her trembling voice startled him out of his reverie. He looked at her face and saw a small tear starting on one cheek. Compassion rose within him. He remembered that the princess, too, had feelings. She surely deserved his consideration.

He moved to the four-poster bed and sat down. Patting the bed beside him, he said to her gently, "Come and sit here."

She obeyed at once, and placed her dainty hand into the larger hand he offered her.

"How old are you, child?" He put the question as delicately as he knew how.

"I am fourteen," she said importantly. "It was my birthday yesterday."

Steffan could think of nothing to say. At almost thirty years of age, it had taken time to reconcile himself to a bride of nineteen. Nothing had prepared him for marriage to a child, barely pubescent.

"I know what is expected of a wife," she offered calmly, blushing faintly. "My nurse explained it to me."

He winced, then hurried to disguise it. He knew men who would not hesitate to bed such a wife. But he would never do it.

"In my kingdom we do not usually marry a girl until she is a little older," he began tentatively.

"That is usual in my father's kingdom, too," she returned. "But Pappa explained that it was important for me to marry now."

She looked up at him with her big round eyes. "I have always known that my father would choose me a husband to help his kingdom," she said gravely. "I am willing to do my duty to my father. And to my husband."

Unable to think of anything to say, he remained silent. What should he do? He needed a mature bride who could deliver and mother an heir. He could arrange to have the marriage annulled, and return her to her father. But how could he return home empty handed?

It had not been easy to find a suitable bride. Essanda seemed a perfect choice: from royal stock, shaped by similar customs and even speaking the same language. Where would he begin looking again? How eager would the next king be to hand over a daughter if he backed out this time? And what would the idle tongues of the gathered ambassadors do with the scandal?

And these difficulties, great as they were, were far from the only considerations. In such uncertain times, Arvenon needed dependable allies as much as Castel did. How could the new alliance possibly survive an annulment?

Steffan began to see that Istel had cleverly steered him into a position from which it would be difficult to escape.

Essanda had waited patiently through his long silence, but now she looked up at him uncertainly. "I overheard Gordy—I mean My Lord Gordan—talking to my father. He said you would be angry at first. But he said you are a good man, and that you will treat me kindly." Her big eyes peered at him entreatingly. "Will you be kind to me?"

As he gazed back into her calm and hopeful face, admiration stirred within him. He could not begin to imagine what this situation must mean for her—a carefree child one day, wife to a strange husband from a foreign land the next. Her childhood had been ruthlessly stripped away, replaced by the stern prospect of a life of duty as queen and mother.

Heavy expectations had been placed on her young shoulders. Far too heavy. Yet somehow, in spite of her frailness and vulnerability, she managed to radiate courage and determination.

"Yes, I will be kind to you."

He realized as he said it that he had made his decision. She would remain his wife in name, and one day become his wife in practice. Arvenon would have to wait a while longer for an heir.

"Count Gordan is a wise man," he noted. To himself he added bitterly, *But he has betrayed my trust and squandered the respect I held for him.*

He turned toward her and took both of her hands. "You are my queen now, Essanda. But I will not yet ask you to take on the full responsibilities of a wife. That must wait until you are older. Do you understand?"

She nodded.

"But it will remain our secret. You must tell no one. Can you remember that?"

Again she nodded, a serious look on her face.

Galling as this situation was, it wasn't difficult for Steffan to see how it had come about. In spite of a long history of friendly relations, Arvenon and Castel had engaged in very little direct communication in recent decades. During the reign in Arvenon of Steffan's grandfather, King Leonid III, the Castelan succession had been contested. In an attempt to strengthen their case, both of the claimants had sought to secure Leonid's endorsement. He had steadfastly refused to interfere in the affairs of another kingdom. The eventual winner had resented his lack of support, and the two kingdoms had grown apart as a result.

These quarrels had seemed little more than ancient history to Steffan when he found himself searching for a bride, and apparently King Istel had seen it the same way. Nevertheless, Steffan was now paying a heavy price for the long isolation.

"I don't understand it," he mused. "Why did Actan never mention your age?"

Lord Actan's lands bordered Castel, and he had informally acted as Arvenon's ambassador since before the reign of Steffan's father. Actan died only weeks before Steffan's first approach to King Istel, leaving no heir. Had he remained alive, he would certainly have briefed Steffan fully. But why had he never mentioned details of the royal family earlier?

Her soft voice broke in on his thoughts. "Perhaps he did not think it was important." Then abruptly she smiled, and dimples appeared in her cheeks. "He was nice. He used to give me sweetmeats."

Essanda's reply startled him. Steffan, thinking aloud, had not been looking for an answer. He especially would not have expected a child to offer such a response. She was almost certainly right, though.

Still speaking largely to himself, he added, "I wonder that none of the other ambassadors ever mentioned it."

"Perhaps they thought you knew already."

It was indeed the logical conclusion, but still surprising from a fourteen-year old. Steffan began to look at the girl with new eyes. He had heard she possessed wisdom beyond her years—maybe some of what they told him was true.

Then her little mouth formed a pout. "I don't like some of the ambassadors," she asserted.

"Why not?"

"Some of them are bad men."

"Which ones?"

"The Rogandan lord is *horrible*." Her face wrinkled in disgust. "Do you know he said terrible things about you and your kingdom?"

"He said terrible things to you about me?"

"Oh, no. He was talking to someone else. I was nearby, but he didn't think I was paying attention. He thinks I'm a half-wit.

"I'm not, though," she said seriously. "I just sit quietly and look somewhere else, and people seem to think I'm not there. I learned that from my Pappa. He says that peacocks strut to attract attention, and eagles soar to avoid attention."

The girl was full of surprises.

"What did the Rogandan say?"

"He said, 'Let the Arvenian fool marry the half-wit child. Very soon we will deal with him and his upstart kingdom. Then Castel will not last long, either.'"

"Are you sure that's what he said?"

She looked offended. "Of course I'm sure. My Pappa says I have a very good memory."

"Did you tell your Pappa what he said?"

"Yes. I tell him everything I hear the ambassadors say. And what the nobles say, too."

Steffan immediately found himself very interested indeed in what the girl might be able to tell him.

Long into the night they sat side by side on the bed talking, her delicate form dwarfed by his sturdy frame. When her yawns outnumbered her words, he picked her up tenderly and placed her into the large bed, tucking her in and bending down to kiss her on the forehead. Then, taking a feather pillow and a quilt, he stretched out on the floor at the foot of the bed.

There was a great deal to think about, and it was almost dawn before he finally surrendered to sleep.

THE SKY gradually darkened until only a faint outline of the distant hills remained. In Erestor, far to the west beyond those hills, the sun would have just disappeared into the ocean. The duke stood on the wall and gazed off into the night, pierced by a pang of homesickness. When would he stand again on the battlements of his castle in Maranelle and smell the fresh salt air and watch the fishing boats glide home on the evening tide?

He sighed and turned his attention once more to the Rogandan encampment. The lights of countless campfires twinkled across the plain. He knew how deceptive the peaceful scene below really was. Reality yielded a grim and very different picture. Whenever armies faced each other the angel of death hovered patiently somewhere nearby.

A torch appeared on the steps leading up to the wall. The giant frame of Rufe followed close behind it and with him a strange figure the duke did not recognize. The stranger was clad in a dark hooded cloak of homespun wool. A wide black leather belt loosely encircled his waist, and black leather shoes covered his feet. The face beneath the cowl was painted with long streaks of deep blue. The effect was singular and disturbing.

The stranger was Will Prentis. The transformation in his appearance was nothing short of astonishing.

"I would never have recognized you," the duke acknowledged, assessing him closely in the torchlight.

"It took some time to get it right," Will said casually. "My red hair would have given me away, so I dyed it black. Provided I can remember the right greetings and chants, I can't imagine any way I could be detected."

"I hope you're right," said Rufe worriedly.

"You're like an old mother hen," Will laughed. "Don't worry, Rufe, I'll be back at the gates well before dawn. Just make sure someone is there to let me in!"

Rufe personally lowered him over the wall. Will disappeared slowly from sight as Rufe steadily played out the rope. Eventually the rope went slack, and a couple of quick tugs from below signaled that Will had made it safely to the ground. Rufe retrieved the rope, coiling it as he drew it back in.

The duke went off to his bed to get some sleep. Rufe settled down on the wall to wait.

Cocks crowed in the city, heralding the dawn. The sun rose slowly, ushering in a new day of life and toil, and dispensing its rays impartially to Arvenians and Rogandans alike. But Will had not appeared, and the steadily growing light revealed no sign of him anywhere near the gates.

The duke reappeared on the wall as dawn was breaking. He placed his hand comfortingly on the shoulder of the giant guardsman. "Don't worry, Rufe. He's simply been delayed. He always comes through in the end."

But the morning drew on, and still they waited. Afternoon came and went and yielded to a new evening. A whole day had passed without a single attack upon the city. The entire countryside seemed to be holding its breath.

The missing commander did not appear, and their hope began to fade slowly with the light.

Something had gone wrong. Badly wrong.

19

Steffan ambled happily hand-in-hand with his mother along a beach in Erestor, the fresh sea breeze playing with her long dark hair. Then, for no apparent reason, a fisherman standing beside his boat picked up a mallet, and began rapidly laying into the side of his vessel. A staccato hammering sound punctuated each stroke. The odd behavior was accompanied by an urgent voice, "Your Majesty! Are you awake, Your Majesty?"

The king emerged groggily from his dream and opened his eyes to the half light just before dawn. The voice and the hammering continued, more insistent than before.

He groaned and sat up, his back aching from lying on the floor. He struggled sleepily to his feet and made his way to the door.

When he opened it he was greeted by an apologetic Lord Bottren. "I am very sorry to disturb you, Sire. But there is important news. King Istel has learned that Rogandan soldiers now occupy the mountain pass that leads south into Arvenon."

Steffan exclaimed loudly in anger.

"There is more, Your Majesty. Before the pass was closed a messenger came through from the duke in Arnost. A large Rogandan army has now besieged the city."

Steffan looked at his friend in disbelief. "It has come so soon." He bowed his head for a moment, covering his face with his hands. Then he straightened again. "Agon chose his timing well," he observed bitterly.

"King Istel has convened a Council of War. It will commence as soon as you arrive."

Steffan returned to his room and dressed quickly. Essanda still slept, and he moved about quietly so as not to disturb her. He slipped away to join Bottren as dawn lit up a sky heavy with rain clouds.

Led by a Castelan retainer, they made their way to a modestly sized audience room in the castle. The room was dimly lit by small windows high on one wall and warmed by huge logs crackling loudly in a large fireplace. Steffan could make out King Istel and a small number of Castelan knights and nobles. Count Gordan sat beside the king. The light was too poor to easily read their faces, though, and he wondered if that suited his new father-in-law on the morning after the wedding.

The other Arvenian lords, Owein and Dongan, had already arrived and were seated at one end of the table.

"Welcome. Your Majesty, My Lord," King Istel greeted them, nodding to each in turn. "It gives me regret to rouse you in this way so soon after our joyous celebrations, but a common enemy threatens both of our kingdoms."

Steffan held his peace. He knew he was going to need to choose his words carefully. Having suddenly found himself at war, he could not afford the luxury of fully indulging his anger over Istel's deception.

"I assume you have been briefed, Steffan?"

"I have," he affirmed.

"Please be seated." The king indicated two unoccupied chairs beside Dongan.

Steffan did not move.

"Is there a problem?" Istel's voice was even.

"I will be frank, Your Majesty and My Lords. We find ourselves in dark days, in greater need than ever before of true friends and trustworthy allies. We have made a treaty and pledged ourselves to each other for good or ill. Yet all parties have not approached this alliance with equal candor, and the conduct surrounding the birth of our accord has threatened its very existence. You have conspired together to take advantage of our trust and deceive us." He made no attempt to disguise the anger in his voice.

A number of the Castelan nobles shifted uncomfortably. Bottren looked startled, and Owein and Dongan rose from their seats. Gordan's face was unreadable.

"Please, please," said King Istel placatingly. "Let us not be hasty, Your Majesty." He stood slowly to his feet. "I presume you are referring to my daughter's age. That is a minor matter which time will soon mend. Let me assure you that I myself..."

Steffan cut him off cold. "I know what you intend to say, King Istel. I don't doubt that your speech has long been prepared. You will, from your own experience, sound the praises of marriage to a woman many years your junior. You will extol the virtues of your daughter and remind me of her lineage, her qualities and her great potential. You will assert that the deception is of no consequence. And you will remind me that our kingdoms have the best chance of weathering the coming storm if we do it together. Spare me your words! I do not need them to help me choose a course of action. I have already decided."

"What do you intend to do?" Istel asked directly, his voice betraying his uncertainty.

"Essanda will remain my queen." Several of the Castelan nobles exhaled audibly. "And she will stay here in Castel until she is older." King Istel sank heavily into his chair, unable to hide his relief.

"But it will be on my terms. She will have her own apartments, as befits a queen of Arvenon. Lord Owein will remain here to oversee her continuing education and preparation. I request that Count Gordan be placed in charge of her security." The count looked to his king, who readily bowed his head in acquiescence.

"There remains the question of access to her family." Steffan could see Istel stiffen. "She will have unrestricted access to her brother. Access to her father will be subject to the condition that neither our marriage nor issues of state will ever be discussed between them." Istel slumped back into his chair. Once again his relief could not be concealed.

"Do not think, though, that I will forget your deception, My Lords. Your conduct in the days to come will have considerable bearing on the decisions I take once this immediate crisis has passed."

Istel was clearly unable to speak. Gordan rose to his feet on behalf of his king. "Your response is very gracious, Your Majesty, and we thank you sincerely for it. I know I speak for His Majesty and all his nobles when I say that Castel will stand firm with Arvenon, whatever troubles may lie ahead." He bowed deeply to Steffan.

Steffan acknowledged his statement with a curt bow of his head. "With your permission, I would like to request a brief conference with the Lords Gordan and Owein before we begin the Council, Your Majesty."

"Of course." Istel rose slowly to his feet and stood bent before the table, leaning on his hands. He appeared old and tired. "I, too, thank you, King Steffan. We have both been put to the test, and you have shown yourself to be the better man." Then he straightened and faced Steffan squarely. "I swear to you, though, that I will prove a truer kinsman than I have a friend."

Steffan bowed and withdrew with the two lords. When they were alone he turned first to Owein. "When I am absent from here, as I surely will be soon, I charge you with the responsibility of caring for the queen. She is barely fourteen years of age, and has much to learn to prepare her for her role.

"She is an intelligent girl, though," he observed. He fixed Gordan with an ironic gaze. "She has also provided me with as much useful information in a few hours as the best agents of Castel and Arvenon could uncover in several weeks."

Gordan colored slightly, and bowed low to cover it. "We will work hard to ensure that information flows much more freely from Castel in the future, Your Majesty."

"I will look forward to it," he replied tartly.

Then Steffan addressed the count with a gentler tone. "Gordan, I believe you have a special relationship with Essanda."

"She is as dear to me as my own life, Sire," Gordan acknowledged.

"Then while she remains in Castel I place her security in your hands. If you wish to undo some of the damage you have done yourself in my eyes, you will not fail me in this."

"She will not suffer harm while breath remains in my body," Gordan vowed.

"Then let us return to King Istel's conference. We have a war to win, and Agon has the initiative."

WILL MOVED AWAY from the wall and took stock of his surroundings. The moon rode high obscured entirely by clouds, leaving the night comfortingly dark. He did not expect Rogandan soldiers to be located anywhere nearby, but he could not rule out the possibility of night patrols.

He closed his eyes and focused his thoughts inward, immersing himself in the imagined world of the Rogandan priests. It didn't hurt to be well prepared.

He expected it would take a while to locate Drettroth's headquarters. Once he had done so, he needed to quickly find a suitable place to hide within earshot. How he would accomplish all this was far from certain, but he felt sure that opportunities would present themselves at the right moment.

Above all, he knew that he needed to appear confident and inconspicuous, just another priest going about his business. With his heart pounding in his chest, he set off boldly toward the nearest line of campfires.

He had gone only a few paces when dark figures erupted all around him. Before he could react at all, a gag had been stuffed in his mouth, his arms pinned, and his hands trussed. It was over in barely two heartbeats.

"Exactly as the traitor promised!" A harsh voice laughed with satisfaction.

His captors bustled him through the outer line of Rogandan campfires, barking a rough password when challenged. Will's mind whirled as he was hurried on deeper into the encampment, struggling to adjust to the disastrous change in his circumstances. Most galling of all was the knowledge that he had allowed himself to be betrayed.

They drove him forward unmercifully, pushing and shoving roughly if he fell behind, until they had almost traversed the full extent of the Rogandan camp. Finally they reached what appeared to be their destination.

He was pulled to a halt outside a strongly guarded tent. The tent stood at the top of a low hill with a commanding view of the surrounding encampment. After stating his business to a guard, one of his captors briefly disappeared inside. He soon re-emerged, beckoning for Will to be taken in.

Will found himself thrust into a spacious tent, well lit by many clusters of candles. Lord Drettroth sat in a large and comfortable chair, his teeth bared in a self-satisfied smile. Beside him stood a thickset brute with bulging muscles and a demeanor of arrogant self-confidence. He radiated pure evil, and the casual malice in his face made Will's blood run cold.

The guard forced Will to his knees, and on a signal from Drettroth his hood was thrown back and his gag removed.

"Ah, Commander," Drettroth said mockingly. "It is so good of you to pay me another visit. I have often wanted to renew our acquaintance since our last all-too-brief meeting.

"Yes, do not fear," he added. "I know who you are, in spite of your vain attempt to disguise your appearance.

"Search him thoroughly," he commanded the guards. Many hands probed him roughly, covering every inch and seeking out anything he might have secreted in a hidden pocket. They found nothing. Drettroth nodded at the door, and the guards left.

"Forgive me, I have not introduced you to my own commander."

He turned to the other man. "Luzik, this is the recently appointed commander of the rabble of Arvenon. He goes by the name of Will Prentis, I am told. A commoner, like you.

"I see he has acquired a scar since I last saw him," Drettroth mused. "That is certainly in keeping with a priest of our Dark Gods. The scar seems lonely, though, don't you think, Luzik?"

Luzik came forward and grabbed Will's chin roughly in one fist. Will averted his eyes as the evil face drew close to his own. Luzik's rank breath almost made him gag.

"I see what you mean, My Lord. But that can soon be mended."

Luzik whipped out a knife and slashed it viciously across Will's other cheek, then wiped it clean on Will's robe before putting it away. Blood ran down Will's chin and dripped onto the floor of the tent.

The man stepped back to peruse his handiwork.

"Untidy lout!" he shouted. "You've befouled Lord Drettroth's clean floor." He slapped Will so hard on the side of the head that he fell over sideways.

Luzik dragged him back onto his knees again, and he knelt there, dazed and wretched. Warm blood trickled out of his ear, and a loud ringing dulled his hearing. His face stung from the open wound on his cheek.

"Twice you have interfered with my plans," Drettroth spat. "You will not receive a third opportunity."

Then he relaxed, and his voice took on a genial tone. "But I forget my manners. You must have many questions. I understand that you came here hoping to learn something of my plans.

"Before we examine what I have in mind, though, I regret that we will need to excuse Luzik. He has business to attend to. But I can promise you a much closer acquaintance with him tomorrow evening."

Will did not like the look of the smile the two men exchanged.

Drettroth turned and nodded to his commander, who got up to go. As he walked out of the tent he backhanded Will across the head again, knocking him to the ground once more. He leaned down closer to Will's still-ringing ear.

"That's just a small taste, scum!" he growled, his voice dripping with venom. Then with a parting leer he left.

"Guard!" Drettroth called peremptorily. One of the sentries came into the tent and bowed.

"Untie the hands of our guest. And give him water. We don't want him wilting before tomorrow's entertainment."

The guard untied him and left the tent, returning with a skin of water that he threw across to Will.

Drettroth stood, and with exaggerated courtesy waved Will to a chair beside a large table covered with maps. After a moment's hesitation, Will pulled himself off the floor and went to the chair, taking the skin with him.

Drettroth leaned across the table and selected a large map. It covered Arvenon, Castel, and the other kingdoms that flanked them. The map stretched south as far as the border of Lestanor.

He waved his hand over the seaward region of Arvenon, to the west. "Once I have annexed Arvenon, the Duchy of Erestor will become a separate country again. Historically it never belonged to Arvenon anyway. It will be ruled by one of your own nobles—after he has delivered Arnost to me as promised.

"He will not be popular, I fear." Drettroth chuckled. "He will be expected to recruit for me a large detachment of the fabled Erestorian cavalry. And you do have some excellent archers—I felt as though they were making a special effort to impress me at the ford. I'll be needing a company of archers from Erestor as well."

Drettroth again bared his teeth in a grimace he no doubt intended as a smile. Will wondered how he could speak so lightly of an event that resulted in the loss of so many of his own men.

"All of these recruits are going to see a great deal of heavy fighting," the Rogandan continued regretfully. "I wouldn't wonder if few ever return to honor their new ruler.

"And then there is also the annual tribute to consider. The new ruler will have to squeeze very hard indeed to extract that much gold from his subjects.

"He will find a way, though. Or I will replace him with someone more energetic."

Will was appalled to think of the price that his countrymen would pay for this treachery. And the traitor was an utter fool if he truly thought he could negotiate to his own advantage with the Rogandans.

Who could it be? Will rapidly ran through the possibilities. Pisander came at once to mind, with his connection to Erestor and his arrogance. But it could be anyone.

Then an awful thought occurred to him—could it be the duke? Surely not. The notion was absurd. He refused to even consider it.

"We are here." Drettroth stabbed a finger at a point on the map that boasted a tiny illustration of a city and the label 'Arnost'.

"If you had my men at your disposal, where would you take them next?"

Drettroth's smug inquiry sounded more rhetorical than genuinely curious. Will didn't bother to answer.

"West to Erestor? North to Castel? Both at once?" Drettroth sighed deeply. "It is difficult to choose between so many delightful alternatives," he lamented. "But I have made my decision. I will be sending some of my men west to Erestor. Others will stay here. In the morning, though, I, along with a large contingent of my army, will depart southward for Ranwood.

"Once we reach Ranwood some of my men will go on to Stonehold. I'm told it's a solid little fortress. Very poorly defended, though. My scouts have advised me that people are coming and going as if there was no war going on at all. These townspeople will soon discover otherwise.

"Ranwood and Stonehold will become important bases for securing Arvenon. Along with Arnost, of course."

Drettroth's self congratulation made Will squirm. To the Rogandan lord, this appeared to be a game. It wasn't just boasting—Drettroth was taunting him. He was playing with Will as a cat plays with a mouse. And there was no reason to hold back. He was freely handing out vital information, but there was nothing Will could do with any of it.

"Once Arnost has been yielded to Luzik on my behalf, he will remain for a time to carry out a very special task that I have given him. I intend to make an example of Arnost. Even you will have a role.

"I have been told how much your soldiers depend on you. Imagine how disheartened they will be when your lifeless body is discovered outside the gates of the city, horribly disfigured. The story will spread quickly, I'm sure."

Will worked hard to keep his face impassive. The truth was that he felt sick to his stomach.

"As for the soldiers in Arnost, they have opposed me, so all of them must die. None will be offered the privilege of serving in my army.

"Sadly, the citizens of Arnost will suffer a similar fate. The streets will run with their blood, except for a lucky few who will be allowed to flee in every direction to proclaim the fate of those who dare to oppose me."

So Drettroth did not yet realize that few people remained in Arnost except soldiers. He did not know everything, and the reminder gave Will new heart.

"Are you a religious person, Drettroth?" Will asked on impulse.

His question brought Drettroth up short. The brow of the Rogandan lord began to darken in anger at his captive's insolent familiarity. Then abruptly he threw back his head and laughed.

"You are a remarkable young man. Perhaps you have decided that I can do nothing worse to you than I am already planning. You are quite right, of course.

"But still it is a curious question. Why would a fly caught in a web ponder the metaphysical standing of the spider?

"I could almost wish you were leading an army for me. I am far too accustomed to being told what men think I want to hear—not one of my men is bold enough to say what he really thinks.

"But I could never trust you." He rounded on Will. "You must be Rogandan by birth—how else could you speak our language so well?

Why then are you leading an Arvenian army? What made you turn on your countrymen?"

Seeing he could expect no answer from Will, Drettroth shrugged. "No matter. I know of an effective way to deal with traitors."

Will wished his betrayer in Arnost could hear this conversation.

"But I have not answered your question. Perhaps you have heard the rumors." Drettroth raised an eyebrow questioningly.

Will knew of no rumors and must have looked blank because Drettroth quickly continued.

"Apparently not. Some of my men have suggested that I was once a priest," he explained. "Such talk has no foundation in fact, although it is true that I have made a careful study of the Dark Gods.

"I have little time for the priests and their arcane rituals," he said with disdain. "They bore me.

"But I do believe in the Dark Ones," he averred fervently. "I have seen far too much to doubt their existence."

A haunted look came into Drettroth's eyes. "Do you believe in Malzakh the Destroyer?" he asked.

Will hesitated for a moment, then shook his head.

Drettroth's teeth showed in a grim rictus. "You will!" he promised. "Oh, you will. And very soon now."

Will averted his face in denial. He sincerely hoped that the Dark Gods were nothing more than an evil figment of Rogandan imagination. He flatly rejected them on the basis that such a horrible travesty of the purpose of life and death could not possibly be true.

Will could not help thinking that the nature of the Dark Gods went a long way toward explaining the character of the Rogandans. They believed that Nehrvina the Awful gave them life. When they were full of years she also took it back. Nehrvina satisfied her ravenous hunger by devouring the spirits of her children when they had thus been released.

Malzakh the Destroyer neither gave life nor took it away. He simply preyed on those who died an untimely death. Nothing but eternal terror awaited his victims. He did not devour their spirits entirely, but instead endlessly feasted on them in turn, allowing the passage of time to restore what he had taken before rending them again.

The only release came for those whose untimely deaths were especially undeserved. In time Nehrvina claimed back their souls, stealing them away when Malzakh was distracted, and consuming them herself.

The priests promised some relief, however, for the faithful who were lucky enough to be taken by Nehrvina. As a reward for a lifetime of worship, the Awful One placed their spirits for a time in Paradise, a place of unlimited pleasure, without pain or suffering. It was no eternity of bliss, though; eventually all must succumb to her insatiable appetite.

With such uncertain alternatives awaiting them, it was little wonder that the fear of death cast a constant pall over the lives of the Rogandans. Much of the energy they brought to life was spent in an effort to avoid dying.

And there was little incentive to behave well, apart from the fear of retribution from rulers or revenge from the wronged. They believed that the same fate would overtake the most depraved and the most decent, provided they lived to the same age. An early death was therefore the only real evil.

Not surprisingly, these beliefs made them indifferent soldiers. Rogandan rulers had responded by encouraging a popular sect which taught that death in battle was entirely undeserved, and that soldiers would therefore escape eternal torment in the clutches of Malzakh. Further, they would immediately be admitted to Paradise if their service was sufficiently wholehearted.

Nevertheless the shirking of Rogandan soldiers was proverbial. That was probably why Agon appointed leaders like Drettroth and why he in turn cultivated a thug like Luzik. With nothing but terror awaiting them beyond the grave, a more immediate source of terror was needed to drive Agon's soldiers forward into battle.

No, Will did not believe in the Dark Gods. His aunt had believed, though. He remembered the fear in her eyes as her final fever grew. As the prospect of an untimely death became ever more apparent she had even belatedly tried to appease Will. Unwilling to forget the depth of her cruelty toward him, he had reacted to her deathbed overtures with disgust. She deserved the fate she anticipated.

Will glanced across at Drettroth. "I myself intend to cheat Malzakh," the Rogandan lord asserted determinedly. "May his dreadful hunger instead be satisfied by the enemies of Rogand!

"Every true Rogandan believes in the Dark Gods. Except perhaps for Luzik. He is no believer—power is the only god he worships. He, too, will learn to see things differently in time, perhaps before many more winters have passed." He bared his teeth in a nasty smile.

Drettroth yawned hugely, and Will had to suppress himself from imitating his captor. "It is becoming late, and I have a long day ahead of me tomorrow. And I fear that I am keeping you awake.

"I regret that this will be our final meeting. I leave for Ranwood in the morning, and you must wait here for the return of Luzik.

"I trust that you have enjoyed our time together. If not, I am sure when you meet the Destroyer you will find yourself wishing that my hospitality had been greatly extended."

He bowed mockingly to Will and left the tent.

The candles in the tent burned low. Will tried to sleep but sleep eluded him. His face throbbed from the wound on his cheek, and all night he lay restless and regretful, tortured by the consequences of his own stupidity. The duke and Rufe had been right. He had been a fool to make this attempt. Even if he had not been betrayed, there was little chance he could have found his way to Drettroth's tent and learned anything useful in the course of one night.

There was a fine line between bravery and bravado, and he had crossed the line. He had leaned on his luck once too often, and now it had run out.

THE SUN ROSE AGAIN, and almost an entire day passed. Will had many weary hours at his disposal, and he took the opportunity to berate himself at his leisure. His courage dwindled away completely as the day progressed. He knew he had no hope.

He thought of his friends. The duke and his soldiers would grieve for him, but Rufe would miss him the most.

He thought, too, of Thomas, and wondered what would become of him and his stone. He remembered the day by the riverbank when he had slapped the stone from his friend's hand. He hadn't fully believed the story about the stone until Thomas described the dark haired youth lying dead in a pool of blood, and the father with the battle-ax. Then he knew it must be true. He wondered if Thomas realized that Will himself had slain the youth.

Yes, he had regrets. But for the most part his life had been full and rich, even if it had been short. He had aspired to lead the King's Guard, and he had become commander of the king's army. For a couple of days, anyway.

Now it was all ending. The same foolhardiness that propelled him to such heights had now become the cause of his downfall.

From the moment that Drettroth departed Will could hear guards constantly all around the tent, but no one approached him or even spoke to him. Occasional furtive glances outside showed that the tent was surrounded by men dressed in the same garb as Luzik. Will guessed that they were members of Drettroth's personal guard, or possibly Luzik's. He had no doubt that they knew what to do should the 'priest' attempt to escape.

When he became hungry he searched the tent thoroughly for food but found nothing to eat. He rationed the skin of water carefully to make it last until evening, even though he knew there was no real point to it.

The sun had sunk low in the sky before Luzik returned. He could hear the Rogandan commander shouting orders and the sounds of heightened activity outside. Still no one came for him, so he went to the entrance of the tent to see for himself what was happening. Being careful to stay out of sight, he peered cautiously outside.

"Round up more men," he heard Luzik calling to other members of the guard. He could see a crowd of soldiers beginning to gather around the low hill where the tent was sited. No doubt they were being called together for the evening's entertainment. A regular dose of random violence would cultivate their fear of Drettroth and his cronies.

"And make sure no priests are among them." Luzik jerked a thumb meaningfully in the direction of the tent. No doubt Luzik didn't want awkward questions when Will's turn came and the onlookers got to see a priest being put to death. Perhaps Luzik thought he could avoid any confrontation with the priests even while showing his soldiers he wasn't afraid to lay hands on one of them.

Then Will noticed a couple of captives, bound and standing miserably off to one side of the hill. They appeared to be Arvenians— probably peasants who were unlucky enough to be in the wrong place at the wrong time.

Moments later the first of the peasants was brought to Luzik. He stood silently before the muscle-bound monster. Will could see the fear on his face, but he did not plead for his life. Luzik's sword flicked back and forth until blood was flowing freely. Still the man made no sound. Disappointed, Luzik drew back his arm and cut him down as casually as a man might swat a fly.

The second peasant was pushed forward. He fell to his knees, begging loudly for mercy with a tremulous voice and many tears. Luzik probably did not understand a single word of Arvenian, but he took the fellow's meaning well enough and seemed delighted by his behavior.

Luzik began dancing around the man, leaning in closer from time to time to inflict wounds that caused pain but not death. Will prayed that the man would cease his noise and shorten his misery. But the fellow did not understand, and his pleas redoubled, punctuated now by wails of pain and terror. Luzik intensified his dance, glee evident on his face.

Then out of the corner of his eye Will noticed one of Luzik's guards capering around in a mocking imitation of his leader. Although the fellow was careful to stay out of Luzik's line of sight, the guards nearest the tent had seen it, too.

"Look at Suveg!" one of them whispered. They watched his antics for a moment.

"Thinks he's so clever, Malzakh bite him!" said the other.

"Ridiculing Luzik openly? He's a half-wit!"

"He's always hated Luzik."

The gathered soldiers didn't seem to have noticed Suveg, but most of Luzik's guards were now watching him instead of their leader.

"Look! Luzik's spotted him. Now he'll get it!"

The guard was right. Suveg desisted from his dance, but a moment too late. Luzik stood rooted to the spot, staring at him.

Luzik plunged his sword into the captive without ever taking his eyes from his mocker. The frantic pleading gave way to a long rattling sigh, and the captive's voice finally ceased.

Suveg took his leader's meaning. He stood uncertainly for a moment, then he turned and fled.

"After him!" Luzik bellowed. "Do not lay a finger on him, though. He's mine."

Guards took off after the man, Luzik following close behind.

"I'm not going to miss this." One of the two tent guards disappeared in the same direction, closely followed by his companion.

Will poked his head outside the tent and looked around. The soldiers still remained in position around the hill, bored and restless, but not moving away. None of Luzik's guards were anywhere in sight.

They had left Will unattended. He'd been offered a chance. A fool's chance, maybe, but still a chance. His courage flickered back into life. He probably had no more than a minute to act on it.

He stepped outside the tent and faced the soldiers. Every eye turned in his direction. They stood silent, watching to see what he would do.

He filled his lungs and thrust his arms wide. Then he opened his mouth to the sky and an unearthly sound issued forth from deep in his throat. The eerie noise grew in strength, carrying clearly in the late afternoon air.

As one man the soldiers fell to their knees and bowed low to worship.

20

The soldiers grumbled under their breath as members of Luzik's personal guard rounded them up and herded them toward the commander's tent. They had long since tired of these messy exhibitions of Luzik's barbarism, but none dared to risk his wrath by openly showing it.

Haldek went with them, reluctantly as ever. Not for the first time he wondered what he was doing camped outside a foreign city, surrounded by thousands of others who didn't want to be there either. It didn't help that they were led by men they universally feared and despised.

They had fought one battle so far, and it had been brutal. Haldek lost friends at the ford. Good friends. He himself had been driven multiple times into the attack, and he knew beyond doubt that he was very lucky to still be alive. How many other such battles could he survive?

The Arvenians had fought like demons. Their reckless ferocity unnerved him. Didn't they fear Malzakh? Perhaps they served a different god who was more merciful than the Destroyer.

His mind wandered back to his years of sentry duty, first at Agon's castle in Rog, later at the stronghold in the wilderness, then back at

Agon's castle again. Patrolling a wall at all hours of the night was never comfortable, but he now realized that he'd had it easy. He would choose sentry duty every time over fighting in battle. Only partially disabled soldiers and old men patrolled Agon's walls now, though. Every able-bodied man had been pressed into service in Drettroth's invasion army.

The soldiers bunched together, their eyes on Luzik. Haldek found himself right at the front of the crowd, almost directly in front of the action. Two peasants had been found for Luzik to play with. How could the ugly brute think it made him look good to carve up defenseless farmers in front of a crowd?

The first man died calmly and with real grace. Perhaps Nehrvina would honor his courage and rescue him from the Destroyer.

The second man showed himself craven. As Luzik toyed with the fellow, Haldek tried to imagine what it would be like to be trapped in such circumstances. He wondered how bravely he himself would die.

In the middle of it all, Luzik's attention abruptly shifted elsewhere, and he and his men vanished over the other side of the hill, apparently chasing one of their fellow guards. Haldek did not entirely understand why they had left, but it appeared that Luzik was settling an old score. The show seemed to be over for the evening, though, and Haldek waited impatiently for the commander to return and dismiss them.

Then a priest stepped out from the tent. Haldek groaned inside. Priests were even more frightening than Luzik.

Everyone knew that you didn't mess with them. They interceded with Nehrvina on behalf of the faithful, and if you found yourself in Malzakh's clutches you were going to need all the help you could get. Equally important, as a reward for their service the priests were destined to become gatekeepers in Paradise. If you were ever lucky enough to arrive there, you'd better hope you could find one of them willing to let you in.

Haldek spotted dried blood on the priest's face and cloak. He had apparently cut himself on one cheek, and he had a scar to match it on the other cheek as well, long since healed. It was unnatural the way the priests did that to themselves.

The man spread his arms and uttered the Call to Fear. Along with every man present, Haldek fell to his knees to worship. He did it without a second thought.

After the multitude had made obeisance, the priest cried out, "Rise, faithful servants of the Dark Gods."

The soldiers rose to their feet.

"All Hail, Terrible Nehrvina, Giver of Life and Dread Receiver of the Spirits of the Dead," intoned the priest.

"All Hail!" echoed the soldiers faithfully.

"Grant your servants long years in the land, to worship Your Awful Majesty."

"Long years!" they echoed fervently.

"Should our lives be cut short, deliver us from the feared hand of your Merciless Brother, we beseech you."

"Deliver us!"

"All Hail, Nehrvina!"

"All Hail!"

"All Hail, Nehrvina!"

"All Hail!"

The priest was warming to his work. He thrust his arms high to the heavens, and his voice rang out strong and true. The soldiers responded with increasing enthusiasm to his energetic delivery of the familiar ritual.

"All Hail, Fearsome Malzakh, Terror of the Living Spirits of the Dead."

"All Hail!"

"Satisfy your great hunger with the spirits of our enemies."

"Our enemies!" the soldiers cried.

"Do not imprison our spirits, but release us to your Gracious Sister, we humbly pray."

"Release us!"

Haldek bellowed heartily along with the rest of them, his spirits rising.

Then he noticed that Luzik had returned along with his guards. The commander at first seemed puzzled as he took in the scene, then angry. But after a moment he came and stood to one side of the priest, facing him with arms crossed and a smile of amusement on his face. He appeared to regard the holy ritual as a joke and the priest as nothing more than a clown.

Haldek stared at Luzik with a profound sense of violation. The sadistic leader was rightly feared by every soldier, but why should he be allowed to show disrespect to the gods?

He glanced around him. The priest continued to intone the ritual at the top of his voice, and the soldiers still responded wholeheartedly. But Haldek could see that others had noticed Luzik's behavior, too, and they were not pleased either.

The liturgy came to an end. Then, unusually, the priest threw back his head, and the strident Call to Fear rang out once more. The soldiers fell obediently to their knees and again bowed low.

Haldek raised his head and saw that everyone was not bowed as they should be. Luzik remained on his feet, his smile now more mocking than amused. Half of his guards had knelt with the soldiers. The others clustered nervously behind their leader.

The priest's arms began to shake violently. His eyes rolled back in his head until only the whites were visible. Haldek knew that the gods granted this kind of ecstatic trance only to the most devoted of their priests. He had seen it a couple of times before. In each case the priest had become the mouthpiece of the gods and pronounced some truly frightening judgments.

Those guards who were still on their feet fell trembling to their knees and bowed low to the ground. Luzik, though, appeared to be thoroughly entertained by the priest's behavior. He gave the impression that he couldn't wait to see what was going to happen next.

The priest slowly turned to Luzik and fixed him with his unseeing white eyes. Then a quivering finger moved slowly in the direction of the commander and singled him out.

A terrible voice issued from the throat of the priest. "Do... you...*believe*?"

Haldek waited breathlessly for Luzik to give an answer. The question seemed to take the commander by surprise. He opened his mouth, then glanced around at the expectant soldiers and shut it again.

What would he say? If he answered "Yes," then he must explain his insolence in standing during the Call to Fear. If he answered "No," his life was instantly forfeit.

Luzik gave no answer. He evidently sensed a dangerous mood in the men. Haldek felt it, too—a simmering anger was slowly bubbling its way to the surface.

"*Do...you...believe?*" the priest demanded.

Still there was no reply.

"Malzakh has been scorned. He is wrathful," the priest announced ominously.

The commander reached down for his sword, then snatched away his hand as a low growl escaped from hundreds of lips. Let him dare to lay a finger on the priest. Haldek licked his lips involuntarily at the prospect of witnessing—even participating, he thought recklessly—in the commander's demise.

The priest thrust out an arm imperiously toward the soldiers. "A mina!" he commanded.

He was going to invite the gods to pass judgment. Now it was certain that someone would die. A ripple of fear ran through the crowded mass of soldiery. Haldek looked at the face of the commander and thought he sensed a whiff of panic. Luzik had lost control of the situation. Malzakh hovered nearby, and the commander seemed to sense it.

A soldier pulled himself to his feet and placed a tiny halfpenny coin in the hand of the priest. The mina was the most common of coins, with a snake on one side, representing the gods, and a mouse on the other, representing the people. The priest was calling upon the gods to choose between himself, as their representative, and the rest. Surely the gods would vindicate the priest.

"Reveal the source of the blood guilt, Mighty Destroyer!" the priest cried, tossing the coin high into the air.

Every head came up to follow its progress. It fell to the ground and rolled a short distance before stopping. Several soldiers scrambled after it, and one raised it from the earth with trembling hands. "The mouse!" he cried.

Gasps escaped from the throats of hundreds of soldiers. The gods had pointed to the people.

"A peka!" demanded the priest.

A penny was thrust into his hand. One side held the head of the king, Agon, and the other a walled town. Haldek swallowed nervously as the priest invoked the name of Malzakh again and spun the coin high into the air. If it revealed the head of the king, then the guilt lay with the leaders of the army. If it revealed the town, then the masses were implicated.

Whole regiments had been put to the sword when such a coin toss went against them. Every man present held his breath as the penny fell to the earth.

Once again soldiers surrounded the fallen coin and bent over it, though none dared to pick it up. "The king," a voice called at last, and the men erupted in relief at their escape.

The priest's arm swept commandingly across Luzik and his men. Dozens of soldiers sprang up and encircled them at a distance, ready to prevent any escape.

"The coin," the priest commanded. A soldier retrieved it and handed it to him.

One last time he invoked the name of the god. One last time he flung the coin high. This time it must choose between the leader and his men. If it revealed the walled town, every one of Luzik's guards must die. If it revealed the king, the commander himself would become the victim.

The door of escape still remained ajar for Luzik. Haldek glanced across at the commander and saw him tense but rooted to the spot. He must have been a gambler—he was taking his chances. The priest had risked his own life on a toss of the coin, and Luzik appeared willing to do the same.

The coin spun lazily through the air, turning over and over. It landed, rolled, and came to a halt. Soldiers approached it reverently. Haldek's heart skipped a beat as one of the men raised his head to the eager throng. "The king!" he cried triumphantly.

"No!!! This man..." Luzik's cry of fury was drowned by a mighty roar as soldiers, and even his own guard, pressed forward to seize him. Fear lent him tremendous strength, and he burst free, only to be tackled to the ground by a writhing knot of enraged men. The soldiers would not be cheated.

Luzik's sword was removed and his arms pinned to his side. Haldek cheered with the rest of them as Luzik was dragged forward to face the priest. They stuffed a gag into his mouth, and men laughed in scorn at his frantic stifled attempts to speak.

Soldiers forced Luzik to the ground, and he lay struggling on his back with arms and legs pinned from every side. Although he twisted and turned he could not break free.

A curved blade was pressed into the priest's hand. His white eyes fluttered as he raised his hand to the sky.

"Receive your trophy, Dread Malzakh!" he cried, and the knife plunged down, once, twice, a third time.

Luzik's muffled screams of terror faded to a gurgle and ceased. Men cheered themselves hoarse. Hardened soldiers clung together, and some wept openly.

The sun sank abruptly below the hill, and Haldek became aware that he was cold. The soldiers began to disperse, their passion spent. Justice had been done, and they left satisfied.

A hand grasped Haldek's shoulder. He spun round and found himself looking into the eyes of the priest, now deceptively normal. He started as he saw a look of recognition flash across the priest's face. It made no sense, though. He didn't know the man—he had never seen him before.

"I need your help."

The priest, whose presence had been so commanding, now appeared weak and frail. He pointed, and they set off through the spreading dark in the direction he indicated, the priest leaning on Haldek's arm for support.

"You must take me to...to the gates of the pagan city."

"Surely not, holy one!" Haldek protested.

"Do not question the will of the Dark Ones," the priest returned weakly.

Haldek subsided and led him on meekly through the dark. The request of the priest baffled the soldier, but he knew better than to question one who had the very ear of the gods.

They moved ever more slowly as their journey progressed—the priest seemed spent after his ecstasy and his appeal to the gods. He leaned more heavily on the arm of Haldek. Occasionally soldiers looked at them curiously, but no one approached them.

After what seemed like hours they came at last to the final line of watch fires. A sentry challenged them rudely.

"You dare to question a priest?" Haldek retorted incredulously. The sentry mumbled an apology and waved them through.

They stumbled on until the gates of the city towered above them. The priest finally released his hold on Haldek's arm. "Leave me now," he commanded, his voice feeble with exhaustion. Haldek obediently stepped back away from him.

The priest took an uncertain step forward, then abruptly swooned and slumped senseless to the ground.

Haldek took one look at him, then turned tail and fled from the gates in terror.

21

Will woke to the cheerful sound of birds singing outside his room. Sunlight streamed in through a window over his bed. He had no idea where he was, and for a moment he could recall nothing of the immediate past. Then it all came rushing back: his capture, the conversation with Drettroth, his sleepless night and long day of waiting in the tent, the confrontation with Luzik, his invocation of the Dark Gods.

He realized he must now be in Arnost. He did not know how long he had slept, but his weariness had not left him entirely. His eyes still hurt, too, and he rubbed them gingerly.

He sat up and examined himself. The priestly robe had been removed, and he had been washed clean, but the scent of death seemed to linger in his nostrils. He had gone to the Rogandan camp an unbeliever, but he knew now beyond doubt that the Dark Gods were real. Had he simply brought down an evil man—well deserving of death—by his own bold cleverness and three lucky coin tosses, or had he been the unwitting tool of the Dark Gods, following a purpose and a plan beyond his comprehension?

He felt again the blade in his hand, rising and falling, rising and falling. He had called down the Dark Gods, and they had responded.

He knew that the ecstatic trance had somehow gone beyond his own skillful pantomime. He remembered the fierce joy that suffused him as he struck Luzik, and knew that it had not been natural. He remembered the commander writhing in terror beneath him, an unbeliever no longer. He had wielded the knife on Malzakh's behalf, and he felt sure that Luzik knew it.

When it was over, he had been close to collapse. Without the help of the Rogandan soldier he knew he would never have made it back to the city. How strange that he had turned to the very person who helped him at the Rogandan stronghold in the wilderness. The man did not recognize him, of course. The scars, the robe, and above all his masquerade as a priest ensured that.

He had been left utterly spent, sapped of all strength. His lack of sleep did not account for his weakness. The brush with the Dark Gods seemed to have drained away his life energy, leaving him exhausted and empty. And darkness had seeped in to fill the void.

Even now the horror of it all still filled his mind. In the fresh light of day, Will wondered how he could ever be clean and free from the darkness again. He covered his face with his hands.

A knock on the door broke across his grim thoughts.

"May I come in, Commander?" The duke stood in the entrance way, smiling down at him.

"My Lord Duke!" He bounded out of bed, and immediately sank back down again, unable to stay upright.

"Are you wounded?" the duke asked, concern on his face.

"No, My Lord, just a little lightheaded," Will replied, feeling foolish.

At that moment the cathedral bells began to peal loudly. Will looked out of the window, alarmed. "What's happened?" he asked.

"You've returned," said the duke with a smile. "Every person in the city is celebrating."

Will stared at him in disbelief. "They're ringing the bells for me?"

"They would have rung them earlier," the duke confirmed, "except I insisted they wait until you were awake."

"How long have I slept?"

"All night and half a day. It's early afternoon."

Will groaned. "We have so little time! We cannot afford to delay." He stood again, more slowly this time. "We need to convene a meeting of the Council, My Lord, so that I can share what I have learned. And I need to see Rufe Sarjant. And Thomas Stablehand. I fear I won't be able to stay here for long."

The duke frowned. "Don't expect me to approve any new forays into the Rogandan camp," he said decidedly. "Given the time you were gone and the condition you were in when you were found, I'm guessing we're lucky to have you back at all."

Will made no reply.

"What happened in there?" the regent demanded.

Will felt a shadow pass across his eyes. "I will not willingly talk about the details, My Lord. But you are right about being lucky. I am fortunate to be alive.

"I do know what Drettroth is planning now, though, and we must find a way to prevent him."

The duke nodded. "I will call together the lords as you request. We will meet before the day ends. I will also call for Rufe and Thomas. But first you must tell me what you have learned about Drettroth."

"Gladly, My Lord."

Will quickly told of his conversation with Lord Drettroth and the departure of the Rogandan lord with a large part of his army. He outlined Lord Drettroth's plans and made it clear that no town or city in Arvenon remained safe. The circumstances around his capture and subsequent escape he barely mentioned. He said nothing either of Luzik or of the traitor. But he asked the duke to double the guard on the city gates immediately.

When Will had finished, the duke studied him closely for a long moment without speaking. "I can see you have not told me every-thing, Will," he concluded. "Far from it. Nevertheless, I trust you, and I will allow you to choose your own time for speaking more freely.

"And in spite of my resistance to what seemed to me a fool's errand, I freely acknowledge that you once again proved to be right. You made it back, and with the information you went there for."

Will responded with a tight smile. "I do recognize that it was foolish of me to make the attempt, My Lord, and I promise you I will be more cautious in the future."

"I am gratified to hear you say it," the duke replied.

"You passed lightly over your escape," he continued. "Yet it is obvious to me that much more could be said. Rufe reported that he heard a disturbance in the Rogandan camp at sundown, not long before you appeared.

"He never gave up hope, you know. He watched all night, all day, and into the next evening. It was he who found you at the gates. He saw you arrive, and he thought he saw a Rogandan soldier helping you. The fellow bolted the minute you arrived at the gate."

Will's thoughts were drawn once more to the Rogandan. It had been so surprising to encounter him again.

"I imagine there is a tale here well worth the telling," said the regent. "It seems your legendary luck has brought you through again, no doubt with the help of your own considerable resourcefulness.

"I will arrange for food and refreshments to be brought to you. Give yourself time to recover before you attempt anything more. I will send for you when the Council has been convened. And I will arrange for Rufe and Thomas to come to you soon."

"I am grateful, My Lord."

The duke paused and studied Will again for a moment. "I don't know what lies behind your other request, but the guard on the city gates will be doubled at once, and they will be instructed to be especially alert."

Will thanked the duke again, and bowed deeply as he left the room. He did not believe for a minute that the regent could be the traitor. But he knew instinctively that it was never wise to assume anything.

Already he was planning his next moves. He must leave the city as soon as possible and find a way to get to Ranwood and Stonehold ahead of Drettroth's army. He would entrust the preparations to Rufe.

But first he needed to expose the traitor. The city would never be safe until he did. For that task he needed the help of Thomas and his stone.

"CHOOSE FOUR MEN, Rufe, and make sure they're ready to leave at a moment's notice," Will commanded. "I need hardy travelers and good fighters, equally proficient with the bow and the sword. And excellent horsemen, too." The rapid flow of instructions left Rufe looking dazed.

Thomas had rarely seen Will so grim. He wondered if his friend might be angry with him for some reason.

"Thomas will choose the mounts later, including a spare. I want seven horses, Thomas, built for endurance but capable of speed," Will continued sternly.

A man in the livery of the duke entered the room and bowed. "I bring a message for the commander from the regent," he announced importantly. Will stepped aside to receive the message.

Rufe leaned over to Thomas with a grin on his face. "Don't take it personally, Thomas. I've seen him like this before," he confided. "It seems to happen whenever he gets himself a new scar."

He again assumed a serious countenance as Will dismissed the duke's messenger and rejoined them, but still managed to fire off a wink. Thomas, grateful for Rufe's cheerful encouragement, couldn't suppress a smile.

Will caught him smiling and looked back and forth between the two of them for a moment, his expression unreadable.

"I've just been called to the Council of Lords," he finally told them. "I need you to accompany me, Thomas."

"Me?" Thomas asked incredulously, certain he must have misheard.

"Yes. I'll explain more on the way there."

They set off with Will leading, striding along with restless determination in spite of his limp. "When we get to the meeting, try to stay out of sight, Thomas. Don't say anything. If anyone asks what you're doing there, I'll handle it.

"I'm bringing you to the Council for a reason. One of the lords is a traitor." Before Thomas even had a chance to register his shock, Will plowed on. "I need you to find out who it is. Use your stone."

"But...the stone...it isn't reliable!" Thomas sputtered. "Usually it doesn't show me anything at all."

Will brushed aside the objection. "You found out about the Rogandans at the gate."

"Yes, but that was an accident. I mean, I didn't control it. It just happened."

"Well, I don't have any other options. I must find out who it is. And I'll need you to help me get some proof, too."

Thomas, already nervous at the thought of appearing at the Council uninvited, now became thoroughly alarmed. Will's expectations were completely unrealistic.

"Don't worry about it," Will said casually, apparently guessing at his thoughts. "It'll work out."

Thomas followed Will dejectedly, like a whipped cur trailing its master. Fortunately, when they arrived at the meeting no one even noticed Thomas—the attention of the lords was entirely upon Will. Such a hubbub greeted his arrival that the duke was forced to rise to call them to order.

"My Lords," he shouted. "Please! One at a time."

As the din subsided, the Earl of Pisander spoke up. "I am sure I speak on behalf of us all when I say that it is gratifying to see your safe return, Commander." The other lords echoed the sentiment, and Will acknowledged it with a bow.

"Commander," began the duke, "please tell us what you learned at the Rogandan camp."

"My Lord Duke, My Lords." Again Will bowed. "Almost the first thing I learned was that there is a traitor among us. I was betrayed."

His statement was greeted with an uproar. Once again the regent called them to order, but this time it took longer for calm to be restored.

"That is a serious charge, Commander. Do you have proof?" one of the nobles asked, frowning.

"Not yet, My Lord."

"Did you learn the name of this supposed traitor?" another asked.

"No. His name was not mentioned," Will admitted.

"I don't have time for this!" Pisander said disgustedly, rising from his chair with open contempt on his face.

"Do you have another more pressing engagement, Pisander?" asked the duke pointedly. Pisander glowered, but he sat back down.

"Perhaps you could tell us something of Drettroth's plans," suggested the duke.

Will accepted the duke's change of direction and began outlining what he had heard. As Will spoke, Thomas fiddled with the drawstring of his pouch, trying to remain inconspicuous. He finally got his hand into the pouch and grasped hold of the stone. He scanned the faces in the room, willing the stone to show him something, anything. It was useless.

Will continued, with frequent interruptions and interjections. Now that he had made his accusation, the goodwill shown him at the start of the meeting had greatly diminished.

In spite of the urgency of discovering the traitor, Thomas found his mind wandering. One of the nobles was regularly popping something into his mouth when he thought no one else was watching. Thomas watched more closely, trying to catch what it was. It looked like dried dates. Thomas had seen such delicacies at the market. They were rare and expensive—from Lestanor or somewhere like it. Where would a noble find dried dates during a siege? He must have hoarded a supply.

Another of the nobles constantly scratched his scalp. Thomas harbored a perverse satisfaction at the thought that even lords suffered from head lice.

A third noble, the man the duke had called Pisander, was hiding something in his cloak. Thomas started. How did he know that? He released the stone and saw nothing. He grasped it again, and once more the impression became clear. He was sure of it. He focused all his attention on the man.

Pisander continued to participate in the conversation, but Thomas perceived that one thing only dominated his mind—the parchment secreted in his cloak. It worried him, and it excited him, and his thoughts returned constantly to the urgent need to keep it safe and undetected. Above all he feared losing it.

And there was something more on the edges of his mind. Thomas could not establish the precise reason, but Pisander wanted the meeting to end, and to end quickly. There were pressing things he needed to do.

"I'm sure this is all valuable information if you're a soldier. But I can't see what relevance it has to us," Pisander was saying. "I propose that the commander and the duke—and Ranauld, of course—go away and discuss it together. Come up with a strategy, and call another meeting later for us to consider it." He rose once again from his chair as though the matter was now settled and the meeting at an end.

"Sit down, Pisander!" the duke ordered irritably. "The meeting will not finish until I say it's finished."

Thomas looked across at Will, trying desperately to catch his eye. Will's attention seemed to be fully engaged in the interaction with the nobles. He was looking everywhere except at Thomas.

Other nobles had become restless, too. It appeared that soon the duke would call the meeting to an end. Thomas became desperate. He coughed.

A couple of the lords looked in his direction, but still Will did not notice him. "Who's he?" one of them demanded, pointing at Thomas. "What's he doing here?"

All heads turned in his direction. Remembering the murderous scrutiny of the Rogandan intruder at the city gates, Thomas had the presence of mind to snatch his hand from his pouch before meeting anyone's eyes.

He looked up and found Pisander staring at him suspiciously, eyes narrowed. "Boy!" Pisander called. "What do you have in your pouch? Bring it here at once. Something of mine went missing recently. Something valuable. It's small, but it's an heirloom."

The mention of the word *heirloom* aroused Will's attention immediately. He looked across at Thomas sharply. Thomas stood still, nervous and shaking, his eyes fixed pleadingly on his friend.

"I'm speaking to you!" bellowed Pisander. He rose from his chair and began moving toward Thomas. Will got there first.

As he drew close he shot Thomas a questioning look. Thomas leaned in swiftly to his ear. "He's got something hidden in his cloak!" he whispered urgently. "A parchment."

"Who?" asked Will blankly.

"Him! Pisander!" hissed Thomas as the earl stormed up to them.

Will positioned himself in front of Thomas. Pisander glared at him, but Will refused to budge. He addressed the regent without ever taking his eyes off Pisander. "My Lord Duke," he said calmly. "May I suggest that everyone returns quietly to their seat?"

"Get out of my way, you upstart commoner!" spat Pisander.

"Return to your seat, Pisander!" commanded the duke. "Or if you prefer, my guards can arrange it for you," he added caustically.

Pisander stood staring venomously at Will for a moment, a look of pure hatred on his face. Then he turned to go. As he did, he stabbed a finger directly at Thomas. "Your turn will come!" he promised. Thomas could not keep himself from trembling.

Will walked across to the duke and spoke quietly into his ear for a long minute. The duke nodded, and Will returned to his position in front of Thomas.

"The commander has a request," the regent announced. "I expect every one of you to comply with it."

Will wasted no time. "My Lords, could each of you please remove your cloak and place it on the table in front of you? The cloaks will be briefly examined, then returned to you shortly."

His words caused a sensation. Several nobles were on their feet in an instant, complaining loudly about the insolence of the request. Pisander shoved back his chair and drew himself erect. "I will not tolerate this any longer," he announced and strode purposefully to the door.

Will nodded to the guards standing at either side of the door, and they crossed their spears, preventing the noble from leaving. "This is an outrage!" he fumed.

"Remove his cloak," Will commanded. A comical struggle ensued between the writhing earl and four guards as they attempted without success to remove the garment. Pisander protested vigorously at the top of his voice throughout the entire process.

After watching for a few moments, Will walked over to the guards. "Hold his arms," he commanded. They did so, holding the earl steady as Will poked his hand methodically around the folds of the cloak. Pisander became increasingly frantic as the search progressed, shouting threats at Will, the guards and even his fellow nobles, who observed the proceedings wide-eyed but did nothing.

Finally Will withdrew his hand triumphantly and held up a large parchment. Pisander went pale, but bellowed even more loudly, "How dare you! Return that to me this instant. That document is sensitive. It is to be seen only by the king!"

Will handed the parchment to the duke, who opened it and began reading to himself. His face grew hard, and he rounded on Pisander. "So is this how you demonstrate your allegiance to your king?" he asked quietly.

Then he addressed the assembled nobility. "My Lords, I will read this letter to you, and you can draw your own conclusions."

"No!" Hearing Pisander start up again, Will gathered up the earl's cloak and shoved the end of it into his mouth. An urgent mumbling continued, but the bellowing ceased.

"*To the Earl of Pisander,*" the duke began. "*Now that we have your commander in our custody, we are entirely satisfied as to your good will. He will be dealt with appropriately.*

"*This letter is your guarantee of safe conduct when our forces take over the city. Show it to my commander, Luzik, when you open the gates to him as promised. Your reward will be delivered only when Arvenon is entirely under our control.*"

"The reward in question," Will broke in bitterly, "was to rule Erestor as a Rogandan puppet. Drettroth plans to make it a separate kingdom again. Pisander was expected to raise armies for Drettroth and bleed the duchy dry to pay tribute to Agon."

The duke resumed reading from the letter. "*One final matter,*" he continued. "*I am searching for a small trinket that was stolen from me and taken to your country. It is a small stone, blue and purple in color—an old heirloom of no consequence to anyone but me. If you return it you will be richly rewarded with gold.*"

At the mention of the stone, Will again directed a sharp glance at Thomas. Thomas could see others staring at him, too, and one or two glanced curiously at his pouch.

"The letter is signed *Drettroth,*" concluded the duke, "and marked with his seal." He turned to Pisander with a look that spoke of death.

Pisander spat the cloak from his mouth and fell to his knees. "Have mercy, My Lord! I meant no harm—Drettroth misunderstood my intentions."

The duke looked down on him with disgust. "I am no longer surprised that we heard nothing of the Rogandan invasion. It must have taken a lot of effort on your part to keep it quiet. And I wonder about the fate of those agents who mysteriously went missing.

"You'll die for this, Pisander, I promise you. And soon, too. But we'll extract every last detail from you first." He turned to the guards. "Take him to the dungeons!" he ordered.

"I WONDER how Drettroth came to know of your stone?" Will looked at Thomas wonderingly. With the traitor unmasked, the commander had hurried him out of the meeting as quickly as he could.

Thomas shrugged. "I don't know," he said miserably.

"Unfortunately, some of the nobles probably suspect you have the stone that Drettroth is searching for. And after what just happened in there, a few may even guess what the stone is capable of. I regret to say I am not certain they can be trusted to keep it to themselves.

"I am truly sorry, Thomas. It is my fault that your secret has been put at risk."

Thomas could think of nothing to say.

"You are no longer safe here. You know that Rufe and I will be leaving the city soon. I can't command you—you're not a soldier—but I invite you to join us. Our path will be difficult and dangerous, but nowhere is safe in Arvenon anymore."

Thomas brightened at once. It was the best news he'd heard in a long time. "I'll come with you!" he said enthusiastically.

Will looked surprised, but seemed to accept the reply at face value. "Good, that's settled, then. I wanted to ask you anyway, but didn't think it was fair. I will admit that the stone could prove useful to us. And your skill with horses will be very welcome.

"Choose us some mounts, Thomas. There will be seven in our party now, and I need a spare mount, so we will want eight horses. I will join you again later. But first I must speak with the duke."

"IT IS necessary for me to leave again, My Lord." Will stood with the duke on a castle battlement overlooking the city.

The duke sighed. "I have been expecting this conversation."

"The fate of the kingdom will not be decided here. I must get to Ranwood and Stonehold ahead of Drettroth."

"We don't have enough men for you to fight your way through the Rogandan siege, Will. And their commander—Luzik wasn't it?—will be doubly on the lookout now that you've escaped."

"We don't need to worry about Luzik, My Lord. He is dead. I killed him myself."

The duke looked startled. "I suppose I shouldn't be surprised," he finally managed.

"They will not remain leaderless for long, but I am hoping they might be less vigilant than usual. And I think we can arrange a distraction for them at short notice. I am planning to slip past them in the confusion."

"Your departure would be a major loss for us. I imagine Ranauld can take charge of our defense, though. He is a capable man." The duke sounded resigned.

"He would be my choice, too."

"You're right, of course, Will. Your abilities are wasted here. I will quickly draw up letters of introduction. Your appointment as commander of the king's army will not be limited to command at Arnost."

"Thank you, My Lord."

"How many men will you take with you?"

"Just six others. A small group will travel faster and avoid detection more easily."

"Rufe?"

"Yes. And Thomas."

"A wise decision, for his own sake," the duke returned shrewdly.

"And four other soldiers hand picked by Rufe."

The regent nodded his acquiescence. "Be careful, Will," he warned. "No one has unlimited luck, not even you. And we cannot afford to lose you."

Will bowed deeply and took his leave.

THOMAS STOOD BESIDE HIS HORSE, stroking its neck and speaking to it quietly. The animal tossed its head and nickered softly in response. He had chosen a large bay stallion for himself, and he was looking forward to finding some even ground where he could give the stallion its head.

He wore a long waterproof riding cloak and a wide-brimmed leather hat found for him by Rufe. The guardsman told him that the outfit made him look older, and he was trying to effect a manner of casual indifference. He actually felt young and very self-conscious.

Rufe and his four new companions waited nearby. All of them had eaten and drunk their fill and loaded the saddlebags of their horses with supplies. The other soldiers wore swords at their waists and carried long bows slung across their shoulders. Quivers filled with arrows bristled on their backs.

"Who is the spare horse for, Rufe?" one of the soldiers asked.

"I don't know," he replied. "I asked Will the same question, but he wasn't in a talkative mood. I guess we'll find out soon enough."

While they waited, Thomas glanced up at the sky. Clouds covered it completely. Neither the moon nor any stars were visible. It was as good a night as any for sneaking away from the city.

Abruptly Will joined them. "Are you all ready?" he asked.

"Yes," Rufe replied on their behalf.

"Good. Introductions can wait until later. A diversion has been prepared for the benefit of the Rogandans. We will leave soon after it starts. Stay to the right when we pass through the gates, and keep me in sight. If we meet any Rogandans, leave the talking to me. Thomas, please lead the spare horse."

They made their way to the city gates and waited quietly beside them. Before long, fireballs began sailing overhead in the direction of the Rogandan camp. Will had called upon the new long range cata-pults, and the near side of the enemy encampment was under attack. Soon distant cries carried to them on the night.

The sounds of confusion spread, and still Will waited. Then finally he called softly to the gatekeepers, and the gates swung open. The small company rode swiftly through the gates and disappeared into the darkness.

THEIR DEPARTURE WAS REPORTED to the duke as he stood on the battlements. He dismissed the messenger and peered out into the gloom, trying irrationally to catch a glimpse of Will's party in the distance.

After a time he abandoned the attempt and stared off into the west. Would he ever see Erestor again?

The duke sighed and closed his eyes for a moment. War was for the young and the bold, a time for daring deeds and feats of renown. All he wanted was a warm fire and a quiet life in his home far away.

He sighed again, then climbed down the stairs and headed for his bed.

22

Thomas stood up in the saddle, flexing the muscles in his back and stretching his legs. After a few hours on horseback he was beginning to feel stiff. The going had been slow and frustrating, and he found himself longing to break out into the open for a canter.

Once clear of Arnost the riders had briefly swung north and soon found themselves climbing steadily. After about an hour they had swung west, and by the time a couple more hours had passed they were heading directly south. They encountered no one; the Rogandan besiegers seemed entirely unaware of their departure. The almost total darkness had aided their escape, but now it hampered their progress as they picked their way slowly across uneven ground.

Thomas had no idea where they were going, and didn't care. All the ties that bound him to Arnost had gradually been severed. Between the death of Ben, the departure of his mother, and the new coolness between him and his father, he had begun to feel like a stranger in his own city. The upheavals associated with the siege only made it worse. With Will and Rufe leaving as well, nothing remained for him there. The city had become a place of confinement, with growing danger to him both from without and from within. By some mysterious means Drettroth was aware of the stone, and even some of the Arvenian nobles may have seen enough to guess at its secret. No, he was delighted to be gone.

The night was well advanced before Will allowed them to rest. They came to a halt within a stand of pines, although the trees offered little protection from the biting wind. None of them suggested a fire—Rogandan soldiers might be patrolling anywhere, and they could ill afford to take chances.

Once the riders had seen to their horses, Rufe distributed some dried meat, and they huddled together chewing on it and sharing a skin of wine.

"You all know Rufe, and I'm sure you know Thomas, our horse master," Will began. Thomas felt himself coloring at the suggestion that he would be known by strangers. He seriously doubted that these men would ever have heard of him. Thankfully his embarrassment would go unnoticed in the dark.

"Rufe, please introduce our new companions," he continued.

Rufe pointed first to a big man with broad shoulders. "This is Ander. He's from Erestor originally." Thomas couldn't see his features in the dark, but he remembered dark hair and a round face from their time waiting for Will at Arnost.

"Glad to be with you," Ander offered, "and hoping I can be of some use. Once I find out what we're planning to do, that is." He apparently followed his comments with a grin, because Thomas could see teeth glimmering in the dark. Will didn't respond.

After a brief pause, Rufe pointed to a thin man with an angular face and drawn cheeks. "This is Nestor. Everyone calls him Nes. He's from Arnost." Nestor appeared to nod his head by way of acknowledgment, but remained silent.

"And finally, the twins: Rellan and Kuper." He pointed out their lithe forms. "They're also from Erestor."

Thomas peered at them curiously. They had the same lean figures, but from his observations earlier in the evening he would not have picked them as twins. They bowed slightly. Like Nestor, they didn't speak, although Rellan noticed Thomas staring and offered him a grin and a wink. Thomas quickly averted his gaze, embarrassed.

"We're going to rest a while." Will's matter-of-fact tone almost made it sound like a routine training exercise. "Tomorrow a guide will be joining us. He'll ride the spare horse."

Ander spoke up. "A guide? Do we need one? Many of us know our way around. I for one have traveled widely in Arvenon."

"I have also traveled extensively, both within Arvenon and beyond," Will replied. "But this guide is said to be without equal. There may be times when it could cost us our lives if we choose the wrong path. And wasting even a single day could cost the kingdom dearly, if it happens at the wrong time."

Ander said nothing further.

"Rellan and Kuper can take turns at watching. The rest of you get some sleep while you can. We will leave before dawn."

THOMAS WAS unused to sleeping out of doors on hard ground and could not find a comfortable position. The others apparently had no such difficulty; he soon found himself surrounded by the sound of snoring.

Eventually weariness overcame his discomfort, and he felt himself beginning to drift off. To his own great surprise, a single thought dominated his mind as sleep gradually overtook him: he hadn't said goodbye to his father.

THOMAS WAS STARTLED from sleep by vigorous shaking of his shoulder. A rough hand clamped down firmly across his mouth while a voice hissed urgently in his ear. "Sshhhh!"

Instantly alert and dimly recognizing the sharp features of Nestor, Thomas suppressed the urge to struggle against the hand that restrained him. Harsh voices sounded from beyond the tree line—not close, but not far away, either.

He lay still until Nestor released him, then rose quickly and silently and made his way to the horses. Some of them were restless, and he went among them speaking softly to them. The horses settled even as the voices became more distant and faded away. By now his eyes had adjusted to the darkness, but he could still see very little in the pre-dawn gloom.

Thomas headed toward a low mumble of voices nearby. His other companions huddled around Will as their leader fired off instructions.

The meeting apparently finished as he arrived. Seeing Thomas join them, Will turned to him. "Stay with the horses, Thomas—don't let them wander. We will return soon."

With that, Will, Rufe, and the other men vanished into the night. Thomas returned to the horses, and settled down to wait.

The hours dragged by. At one point, early in his vigil, Thomas thought he heard a distant shout, but couldn't be sure. There was no other sign of his companions. Eventually the sky began to lighten as dawn approached, but still there was no sign of the men returning.

Thomas became increasingly anxious as time passed. What if they had all been killed? For the first time in his life, Thomas found himself confronted with the prospect of being totally alone. He had fled with barely a second thought from the only home he had ever known, but he knew he could never fend for himself out here. Without Will and Rufe he would be utterly helpless.

The stone had brought him here. Once again he asked the unanswerable question: why him? Why was he the one who found it? He thought of it as 'his' stone, but he knew it didn't belong to him. It wasn't even his secret anymore. The Rogandan commander at least was aware of it. And wanted it badly.

Did it actually belong to Drettroth? He doubted it. The Rogandan's reference to his 'heirloom' had echoed his own old lie so closely. No, somehow he felt sure that the stone didn't truly belong to anyone.

He understood only too well, though, the desire to possess it, and what it could lead to.

He was struck by a sudden and disturbing thought—was it possible that this whole war was somehow connected to the stone?

THE SUN HAD CLEARED the top of the trees before his companions returned. Thomas was relieved beyond words to see them, but his discomfort did not leave him. The world had become frightening and unpredictable, and he no longer knew his place in it. Surrounded by wide open spaces, all he could see was how small he really was.

Somehow he had to find his way through. Friends counted for something. And Will Prentis and Rufe Sarjant were no ordinary friends.

"What happened?" he asked Will.

"We followed the Rogandans back to the main force. There were a lot of them, and we had to be careful to avoid being seen." Will appeared matter-of-fact about it. "I went in close to hear what they were saying," he added.

"Did you hear anything useful?"

"Not much. It was mostly the grumbling you hear from soldiers anywhere," Will replied, briefly tossing a glance in the direction of his own men. "I did get a rough idea of the direction they're headed in, though."

Thomas must have looked worried, because Will added, "I doubt we'll see anything more of them for a while.

"We need to pick up the pace," he concluded. "They're on foot, but they're moving more quickly than I expected."

THEY RODE HARD MOST of that day. Apparently Will now valued time more than he feared detection, at least for the moment. Their path at last took them across open ground where the horses could run, and Thomas gave the stallion its head. For a time he forgot his troubles as the countryside rolled away effortlessly beneath the hooves of his bay.

By the time the sun had set they were climbing steadily, up and up through a succession of foothills. It was completely dark by the time they ascended a steep and winding path that led to a monastery, set on the shoulder of a small mountain. Seeing what lay before them, Ander mumbled something fiercely under his breath and spat in the direction of the walls.

Will dismounted and approached the entrance. Calling loudly, he banged the pommel of his sword hard on the large wooden gate, barred and bolted against the night.

For a time there was no response. Then a voice called out faintly from within, "Who travels abroad, and why do you disturb the peace of this house of God?"

"Open in the king's name," Will called back. "I am here on the king's business, and it will not wait! The sooner you let us in, the sooner we will be on our way. Open up, I say!"

After a delay Thomas heard the sounds of bars removed and heavy bolts drawn back. Finally the gate swung open, and an old man in the habit of a monk stood before them. A frayed rope belt secured a well-worn robe to his wiry frame, and a long gray beard flowed freely down over his chin. His physical presence might not have been commanding, but a pair of bright and intelligent eyes peered out at them from behind the flaming torch he held before him.

"Welcome, travelers! My name is Brother Elias, and I welcome you to the Monastery of St. Rodrig the Martyr. Come in out of the cold. Enjoy some refreshment before a fire." He bowed and swept the torch inward, pointing toward a group of dark buildings. As they came inside the monastery walls, two monks greeted them and led away their horses to a stable that hugged the wall beside the gates.

They followed Brother Elias to a low structure topped by a large chimney from which smoke billowed forth invitingly. Once they were inside, two other monks appeared and, without instruction, silently set about preparing food and drink while their older companion saw to the comfort of Will's company. They soon found themselves seated on low benches facing a sturdy wooden table beside a roaring fire. They were served bread and cheese along with a thick vegetable gruel ladled from a steaming pot over the fire. The food was very good, and with a full stomach and surrounded by the warmth of the fire, Thomas found his head beginning to sag with weariness.

Brother Elias must have noticed, because he turned to Will and said to him, "Mattresses filled with fresh straw will be brought for you all, and warm blankets. You may spend the night in such comfort as we can offer, here before the great fire."

The monk's offer sounded very appealing indeed to Thomas. He was not alone, either—Kuper visibly relaxed, and Rellan permitted himself a long sigh of anticipation.

Will, though, had other ideas. "I thank you for your kindness, but our business cannot wait. I must speak with Brother Vangellis. I believe he is staying here?"

Brother Elias appeared troubled. "Why do you wish to speak with him?"

"My business is with him alone," Will replied, his face betraying no hint of his intentions.

The monk paused for a long minute, then nodded to one of the Brothers, who disappeared into the night.

They waited for what seemed like hours. Then the monk returned. He bowed to Brother Elias. "I was unable to rouse him."

"Perhaps your business can wait until the morning," Elias suggested, turning to Will.

Will shook his head emphatically. "It cannot. If you are unable to rouse him, I will do it gladly," he said bluntly.

Brother Elias looked alarmed. He turned back to the monk. "Perhaps you could try a little harder," he suggested. The man bowed once again and left the room.

Eventually he reappeared, accompanied by an overweight monk who staggered into the room—awake, but only just. The new arrival stood on his feet unsteadily for a moment and looked about him. He opened his mouth as if to say something, then clamped it shut again.

Finally he slumped down onto a bench, glancing around uncomprehendingly. He was clearly very drunk.

"Allow me to introduce you to Brother Vangellis," said Elias
gently. Thomas glanced at the old monk in surprise. He might have
expected the man to be angry—surely Vangellis was bringing disre-
pute to his order. But instead Thomas sensed only compassion in his
voice. Thomas shook his head. He had never understood the ways of
the religious.

At the sound of his name, Vangellis stood again, attempting an
exaggerated bow before flopping back down onto his bench with a
self-mocking smile. The other travelers gazed at him, some with
amusement and some with disinterest. Ander stood and stared,
making no attempt to disguise his contempt.

Will got up and walked over to him. "My name is Will Prentis," he
said. "I command the armies of the king, and I need your help."

"How...can...such as _I_...help...such as _you_?" Vangellis paused as
though checking to make sure it had come out right, then, apparently
pleased with his efforts, grinned expansively.

"You must come with us, as a guide," Will said.

Vangellis smiled again, weakly this time. "A mish...TAKE. You
have the wrong _man_," he said, slowly and carefully articulating each
word.

"There is no mistake, I assure you," Will replied.

"With regret, then, I musht decline your mosht generous offer."
Vangellis slurred, then paused and nodded, apparently to himself.

Ander could hide his disgust no longer. "You cannot be serious,
Will!" he burst out. "This drunkard? Guide _us_?!" Shocked at Ander's
disrespect toward his commander, Rufe got to his feet and glared at
him. Ander saw it and quickly subsided.

Will ignored him. "We have brought a horse for you," he said to
Vangellis. He turned to the twins. "He may need some help. Get him
outside and onto the horse." Rellan and Kuper got up and moved
swiftly toward the startled monk.

"Wait!" The ringing command from Brother Elias carried enough
authority to halt the twins in the act of lifting Vangellis bodily from

his seat. Elias turned to Will, genuine alarm on his face. "You cannot do this! Surely you can see that the man is not fit to travel."

"He'll soon sober up once he gets some fresh air," Will replied mildly.

"So you thank us for our hospitality by forcibly kidnapping one of our order?" Elias protested.

"I mean no disrespect. But our need is very great." Will spoke with simple sincerity. "Is Vangellis a member of your order, then?" he asked.

"Well, no," the Brother admitted. "Not exactly. He is my guest. And under my care."

Will already knew that about Vangellis. And much else besides. Even without the stone, Thomas could see that. Will did not reserve his tactical skills entirely for the battlefield.

"It makes no difference," Will asserted. "We must all make sacrifices at times, and his skills are greatly needed." His tone was diplomatic, but his words took on an iron edge. "We will take him with us. By force if necessary."

Brother Elias looked from Will to Vangellis and back again. The anguish on the old monk's face made Thomas squirm. But Will was unmoved.

Elias gazed intently at Vangellis for a long moment. Then slowly the tension eased from his face. He seemed to have come to a decision. "God's purposes seem strange to us at times," he said. "But he knows what he is doing." He turned back to Will. "You must allow him a few minutes to pack some warmer clothing and a few possessions. The Brothers will use the time to prepare provisions to send with you in your saddlebags."

Vangellis looked up at Brother Elias as though the old monk had slapped him. Elias came to his side, and whispered in his ear before helping him up and ushering him from the room.

"Go with them," Will instructed the twins. "Stay out of their way, but don't let them out of your sight." They nodded and moved off swiftly.

They were gone for long enough that Will became restless and sent Nestor to hurry them along. Nestor returned a few minutes later, followed soon after by Brother Elias, Vangellis, and the twins. Vangellis was wrapped in a heavy cloak and dragged behind him two bulging saddlebags. His face was flushed and his eyes wide and moist. He looked pitiful. Thomas wondered what had passed between him and Brother Elias. Whatever it was, Vangellis had apparently accepted that he must go.

True to Elias's word, food had been prepared for the travelers. The monks with the provisions accompanied them to their horses. Thomas discovered, to his surprise and delight, that the animals had been rubbed down, fed, and watered. Clearly some of the monks, at least, understood horses. He quietly approached the monks who held the reins and thanked them for their efforts. They bowed silently in response.

The food was stowed, and the riders prepared to mount. All except Vangellis. He shuffled to the gates, clearly expecting to join the party on foot.

"You must ride," Will told him. "We have no time for further delay."

"I cannot...ride a horse," Vangellis asserted. "I will walk."

"What kind of guide is this?" Ander muttered sarcastically.

That earned him a rebuke from Will. "Enough!" the commander growled.

Will turned to Thomas. "He's going to need some help. Make it quick."

Thomas dismounted and went to Vangellis. "Riding is not difficult, with a bit of practice," he assured the monk, drawing the spare horse closer. The horse snorted and shook its head vigorously, pulling against the reins. Vangellis backed away in terror.

Based on his experience at teaching novices to ride, Thomas could see at once that Vangellis would make no progress tonight. Probably not anytime soon, either. He looked up at Will and shook his head.

"Thomas, you're the best rider, and the lightest. He's with you."

Thomas sighed inwardly. Riding double was not going to be

pleasant, especially with an inexperienced rider scared of horses. "Rufe?" he called out hopefully to his friend.

Seeing Rufe approach him with a purposeful stride, Vangellis began to panic. A lot of struggling and yelling followed before Elias intervened. He took Vangellis to one side and spoke quietly to him for a time. Eventually the monk calmed down and submitted to the inevitable.

The saddle was removed and Vangellis hefted by main force onto Thomas's bay by Rufe and Nestor. Before he could fall off, Thomas vaulted up behind him and reached around him for the reins.

That night's ride was a deepening nightmare for both Thomas and the unhappy monk. Controlling the horse from behind Vangellis became more and more difficult as Thomas grew increasingly weary. Vangellis had no idea how to move with the horse and was bounced around unmercifully. Many times he would have fallen but for Thomas. Without a saddle it took a prodigious effort to keep the monk on the horse, heavy and uncoordinated as he was. His wine-induced stupor gradually wore off, or perhaps was relentlessly shaken out of him. He groaned more and more frequently and eventually began to cry out in pain after the worst of the jolts.

Will halted them well before dawn. By then everyone in the party was on edge. Ander was muttering under his breath, and some of the others were noticeably restless. Thomas felt so tired he didn't care. The monk was too miserable to do anything except position himself as far as possible from the others. He limped away clutching his saddlebags and moaning softly.

When dawn came none of them had managed to sleep much. But Will was impatient to be gone. He called the men together, and they huddled bleary eyed around him. "I don't want a repeat of last night's experience," he began. "Thomas, you're going to stay here and teach Brother Vangellis to ride.

"Nes, I need you to stay and protect them. The rest of us will try to get to Ranwood ahead of Drettroth. His main force has been traveling by foot, but they will be getting close now. We've had too many diversions, and now we don't have a lot of time." At the mention of diversions, Ander threw a scowl in the direction of Vangellis.

Will and his party mounted without pausing to eat. "Too bad you're going to miss out on the fun," Ander said to Nestor with a grin. "Enjoy the babysitting," he concluded with a wink at Thomas.

As they headed off Will called back to Thomas, "You have two, maybe three days. Make it count." Then they were gone.

23

S teffan trudged into his apartments and collapsed onto the bed. Once again he had returned completely exhausted after another day of wrestling. The daily struggle around a table with his father-in-law and his nobles did at least have one benefit—it was making the prospect of fighting on the battlefield seem positively appealing.

Istel's promise of support had been entirely sincere, and Steffan had to acknowledge that the Castelan king was showing real energy in raising armies and training soldiers for the defense of the allied kingdoms. The problem was that Istel thought only in terms of defense. Steffan, far from home and cut off from his kingdom, wanted action. He was all for setting off for Arvenon tomorrow with an army at his back.

Istel pointed out that they would be operating blind, with no idea of Agon's intentions. And if the reported size of the Rogandan army was accurate, any false move could prove fatal. Steffan countered that wars were not won by sitting safely inside a fortress while your enemy roamed freely, pillaging your land, burning your crops, and picking off your weaker cities at his leisure.

He had his own soldiers, of course—two thousand of his best. But he knew they were far too few to win a war on their own. He would need Istel's help even to keep his army intact if he wanted to break through the Rogandan soldiers holding the pass into Arvenon.

If only he had brought Will Prentis with him instead of old Olaf. Will would be crafting plans and coming up with ideas. And he had a way of inspiring confidence and hope. Steffan had come to depend on him so much. It was strange to think that he wasn't many summers past twenty years of age.

Will was probably stuck inside Arnost at that moment, unable to do anything useful. That was good news for the capital, of course. Somehow Steffan couldn't imagine it falling to the Rogandans with Will in charge of the defense. But he would have been much more useful here with the king. Now the war would have to be won—or lost, he thought grimly—without Will's help.

Essanda's young face appeared over him, a look of concern creasing her brow. "You are tired, My Lord."

"I told you not to call me that, Essanda!" he snapped irritably. The face abruptly disappeared, and he quickly repented. "I'm sorry. I didn't mean to yell at you."

"That's all right," she said generously. "A king has many worries, I know." She sailed back into view. "What should I call you?"

"You can call me Steffan. But no more of 'My Lord'!" He frowned at her in mock anger.

"I will call you Steffan when it's just us," she decided. Then her mouth formed a stubborn line. "But I will call you 'My Lord' when we are with company."

He smiled at her affectionately. "That sounds like a good compromise, Essanda," he agreed.

She vanished behind him. Then her hand appeared and began to gently stroke his hair and his neck. It felt very soothing.

He sighed in appreciation. "Where did you learn to do that?"

"My mother always stroked my hair when I was sad or upset. It made me feel better. I thought you might need to feel better, too."

"You're a remarkable girl, Essanda."

"'My Lady', if you please," she teased, adding "Steffan" with a self-conscious giggle.

He smiled again, then closed his eyes and allowed himself to drift off as she continued her stroking. It took only moments before he was asleep and dreaming. They were pleasant dreams, without hint of wars or conferences or turmoil.

SEEING that he had fallen asleep, Essanda climbed up onto the bed and lay down beside him. Soon the two of them floated far away, released for a time from the daily troubles of mortal kings and queens.

NESTOR DID NOT STAY with Thomas and the monk for long. No more than two minutes after the others had left, he mounted his horse and disappeared. He returned briefly after a short time. "There's a stream just over that rise," he told Thomas, pointing to a low ridge a short walk away. Then he disappeared again. Thomas headed in the direction he had indicated and found the stream. The water was cool and fresh, and he felt much better after splashing his face and taking a long draft.

When he returned he found Vangellis snoring loudly. He briefly debated with himself about waking the monk, but eventually decided that his new student would learn more effectively if he started the day with a bit of sleep. It also gave him the opportunity to carefully examine his horse. Thankfully the stallion did not seem to have suffered lasting ill effects from the long journey bearing two riders.

Vangellis woke a couple of hours later to find that Thomas had prepared a modest breakfast from bread and cheese he had discovered in his saddlebags. Thomas had also filled a couple of skins with fresh water from the stream.

"Please join me," Thomas said simply. "Nes seems to be off somewhere, so we will have to enjoy breakfast on our own. My name is Thomas. Thomas Stablehand."

"I am Brother Vangellis, as I'm sure you are well aware by now," replied the monk with a self-mocking smile. He sat down very delicately beside Thomas, wincing as he made contact with the ground. "So you're supposed to teach me to ride." He sounded very skeptical about the prospect.

"We won't get on a horse today," said Thomas. "I thought you might be a bit uncomfortable."

Vangellis looked both surprised and delighted. "I doubt that your leader will be pleased," he ventured.

"Will won't mind. He's happy to leave the teaching to me," Thomas replied confidently. The monk looked at him with obvious curiosity. Thomas ignored it and went on. "Getting on a horse isn't the first and most important thing. It's understanding how horses behave, what they like and dislike, what's good for them and what isn't," he explained. "For example, normally I would never ride double. My horse tolerated it last night—we have an understanding. But it isn't good for him, and I wouldn't do it without a reason.

"Last night I put your interests first. We need to get you to the point where a choice like that isn't necessary."

"But I don't like horses. I've been scared of them all my life."

"That's probably because you think they're unpredictable. Or because you had a bad experience when you were young. Either way, I've found that accurate understanding takes away the fear. Once you know why they behave as they do, you can predict their reactions, and avoid situations that upset them. Well, most of the time," he added with a grin.

Thomas began with simple explanations, and demonstrated each point with the help of one of the horses. Vangellis often asked for clarification, and Thomas was surprised by his perceptive questions. Warming to the obvious interest of his pupil, Thomas shared more freely and deeply the important lessons he'd learned about horses. With this new understanding, the monk was able to begin to move beyond his fears, and soon demonstrated a natural empathy for the animals. The horses seemed to respond to him, too. Before the end of the day, Thomas concluded that Vangellis had real aptitude as a horse handler. Possibly more so than any student he had taught at Arnost. It didn't guarantee that he would do well in the saddle. But it was a promising beginning.

From time to time during the day Vangellis had become restless and asked for a short break. He would head off out of sight for a while, taking his saddlebags with him. When he returned he was ready to begin again. The time alone seemed to calm him, so Thomas soon agreed to these breaks without hesitation.

Nestor returned as the sun was setting. He brought with him a pair of hares that he had shot with his bow. He quickly skinned and cleaned the rabbits, and as soon as it was dark he set about building a fire to cook them. Thomas wondered about the wisdom of a fire but did not question Nestor. The location where they had camped was well concealed, and he was sure that their protector would not take unnecessary risks.

"Where have you been, Nes?" Thomas asked him.

"Protecting you doesn't mean sitting here waiting for a fight," he replied calmly. "I've been scouting around for miles in all directions. No one dangerous is anywhere nearby. Once we've eaten I'll smother the fire. It's very unlikely we'll be troubled tonight."

The rabbits were delicious, especially when accompanied by a few drafts from a skin of wine that the Brothers had packed in their saddlebags. Vangellis didn't say much during the meal, but he shared the wine enthusiastically.

The next day Thomas began teaching the monk to ride. By then the monk could tolerate short periods in the saddle in spite of his soreness. Thomas could tell quite quickly if a person was going to be able to ride well; Vangellis would never be among the best, but he had the makings of a competent rider. His natural feel for horses helped him sense changes in the mood of his mount. Now he just needed to learn to respond quickly and appropriately. By the end of the day Thomas was satisfied with his progress, but he became increasingly aware that Will could return at any time.

Thomas woke early on the third day, impatient to resume their lessons. When Vangellis got up, he disappeared as usual with his saddlebags. This time Thomas followed him. Although he felt a twinge of guilt about spying, he was determined to see what the monk was doing. He carefully kept out of sight as he followed deeper into the trees.

Vangellis came to a stop and looked behind him. Thomas barely pulled back out of sight in time. After a pause he peered from behind a tree. Vangellis was pulling a wineskin from one of his saddlebags. His hands were shaking as he lifted it to his lips and drank a deep draft. Then he closed his eyes and sighed deeply. The trembling in his hands ceased.

Thomas remembered a conversation he had overheard between his parents. An old uncle of his mother's had injured his back and could no longer work. The doctors offered no relief, and to dull the pain he turned to wine. Thomas remembered the sadness in his mother's voice as she talked about how far he had fallen. The wine robbed him of so much, but he could not give it up. He was totally and helplessly dependent on it.

Thomas moved slightly, and a twig snapped loudly under his foot. Vangellis started. "Who's there?" he called sharply.

After a moment's indecision, Thomas stepped out from his hiding place. He felt ashamed, but it was the monk who reacted with guilt, trying to conceal the wineskin behind his robe.

"Do you have problems with your back?" Thomas blurted out, immediately feeling stupid for asking the question.

Vangellis sighed and brought the skin into the open again. "No, Thomas," he said sadly. "The wine helps me cope with a different pain." Another twisted smile played across his lips. Then he shrugged and took another short draft before returning the wineskin to his saddlebag.

Nothing further was said by either of them, and Thomas resumed the training as if nothing had happened.

. . .

IN THE END they saw no sign of Will's party for almost four days. Late that afternoon the twins appeared. They had been riding hard, their horses covered with sweat. Nestor was with them. Thomas felt sure their protector had spotted the twins well before they arrived.

"We need to be ready to leave the minute Will arrives," Kuper announced. He glanced over at Vangellis, sitting upright on his horse. "Can he ride?" he asked doubtfully. In response, the monk kicked his heels into the horse's flanks, and they moved away at a trot, the monk moving rhythmically up and down with the horse. "Not bad," Kuper admitted, surprise evident in his face. Then he ignored Vangellis and turned his attention to more pressing matters. "We're going to water our horses. Make sure you're ready."

While Kuper and his brother moved off to the stream, Thomas and Vangellis gathered their few possessions, packed them away and mounted their horses.

Will, Rufe, and Ander arrived only minutes later. "Is he ready?" Will asked Thomas, jerking his head toward the monk. Thomas nodded. "Then let's go. There are fifty Rogandan horsemen behind us."

They moved off immediately. Will did not even look at Vangellis to check his riding skills, and Thomas swelled with pride at the implied compliment to both his teaching skills and his judgment.

THEY DIDN'T STOP AGAIN until it was almost dark. Will would have ridden further if he thought the horses could manage it. But most of the animals had been ridden long and hard, and the riders could ill afford horses pulling up lame. There was no sign of a pursuit. For the moment they seemed to have either lost the Rogandans or left them far behind.

The journey had not been without incident. Vangellis fell twice, and was very fortunate to have avoided serious injury. Considering his lack of experience, Thomas thought he had done well. No one learned to ride well overnight, and they had passed over difficult terrain.

The second fall was especially bad, and Thomas had no doubt that the monk carried serious bruising. They had been riding through a narrow pass when Ander pressed in close to Vangellis, spooking his horse. An experienced horseman would have handled the situation with ease, but Vangellis quickly lost control and fell heavily. Ander cursed Vangellis loudly and repeatedly, blaming the incident on his incompetence. Will, clearly annoyed, had finally cut him off. Ander fell silent, but his antagonism toward the monk was now more obvious than ever. Vangellis said nothing, but, at the first opportunity after they stopped, Thomas was not surprised to see him slip away with his saddlebags.

Once the horses had been seen to, they huddled together around some food and wine packed by the monks.

"Did you get to Ranwood before Drettroth?" Thomas asked Will.

"Yes," he replied. "But less than a day before his army. We arrived early in the morning. I'm not sure the townspeople were happy to see us."

"You can't blame them," Rufe said. "One minute they're happily going about their business, and the next the commander of the king's army rides in and tells them to flee for their lives."

Kuper took up the story. "Will found the local lord and told him he needed to empty the town before nightfall. The lord wanted to call a meeting of the town elders, appoint some scouts to go check for immediate danger, and send out messengers to tell the farmers to sharpen their pitchforks just in case!"

"First time I've seen Will really angry," Ander enthused. "He went to the market square and yelled for silence. Told them the Rogandans were coming and that no one left in town by nightfall would be alive to see the dawn. Ordered them to forget their possessions and run. There was total panic!"

"It did the job," agreed Kuper. "Most of the people were gone within three or four hours. After that it was a few older people who needed help to leave."

"How did the lord take that?" asked Nestor.

"He wasn't happy at first," Rellan replied, with obvious under-statement.

"The lord is a fool," Ander added derisively. "He knew that Arnost was under siege, but did nothing to prepare for war."

"He is not a bad man," said Rufe. "He did everything he could to help the townspeople leave quickly and safely."

"It wasn't his fault," Will agreed. "Good leaders in peacetime aren't always the best leaders in war.

"The town was indefensible," he continued. "No wall, no garrison of any size. It would have been a massacre. And given the location, the Rogandans would have settled in and used the town as a base."

"Not now," grinned Ander.

"What did you do?" Thomas asked. He was entirely captivated by the unfolding story, but tried hard to keep his tone matter-of-fact.

"As soon as people started to leave," Ander responded, "we went through the town and laid out flammables. Dry wood and straw, leaky barrels of oil. Placed them everywhere. The whole place was a bonfire just waiting to be lit."

"Then we found a good spot just outside the town and waited," said Kuper.

They all paused, clearly lost in their memories. Thomas couldn't bear the suspense. "What happened?"

"We waited until the Rogandans arrived," said Rufe. "It was almost dark. They came in, slow and stealthy, and spread out looking around. They couldn't find anyone. When night came on they posted guards, and settled into the houses to sleep."

"We lit fire arrows," Kuper continued, "dozens of them. We sent them sailing in, one after another. It was a beautiful sight! Beautiful and deadly. Once the fires started they spread incredibly quickly. You should have seen the town burn," he said, awe in his voice. "The flames lit up the night sky like it was day."

"The Rogandans knew where we were by then," Rufe said. "The arrows gave us away. We took off in a hurry, but we were close in to the town, so they were never far behind us."

"How many Rogandan soldiers died in the fires?" Thomas wondered aloud.

Vangellis didn't wait for an answer. He got up abruptly and left the group. The soldiers stared silently after his retreating form until well after he was gone.

"We don't know," Will finally replied.

"A lot," said Rufe simply.

Nothing further was said for a long time.

Nestor finally broke the silence. "Where to next?"

"We'll go on to Stonehold," Will replied. "We're part of the way there already."

"There's one road in and out," said Ander. "The Rogandans will use it—they're probably on it already. Even if we can get onto the road ahead of them, we won't be able to use it to get out."

"That's why we brought a guide," Will replied.

Ander grunted dismissively.

Will ignored it. "Ander and Nes, take the first watch. The rest of you get some sleep. We'll be moving out as soon as it's light."

It took Thomas a long time to get to sleep that night. When he slept his dreams were disturbed by images of a burning town and screaming men.

"The Rogandans are on the road to Stonehold in strength," Kuper reported. "We won't be able to get past them. We need to find another way in. And we need to do it quickly."

Will turned to Vangellis. "Do you know of an alternative route?"

"Yes," the monk replied. "There's a mountain trail. I've walked it a couple of times. But it's rough. I don't know if horses will be able to manage it."

"We're about to find out," said Will. "We don't have a choice. How long will it take us?"

"About the same as using the road. It might save us a bit of time. The road winds around a lot because of the landscape. This path is slower going, but it's also shorter because it's more direct. It will depend a lot on the horses."

For the next few hours they alternated between slow, cautious riding and leading their horses on foot. The path was extremely rough, and even when the sun had cleared the horizon Thomas still had to pick his way carefully.

Occasionally the trail widened, and they were able to make better time. Eventually, they crested a ridge, and Stonehold lay below them. The drawbridge was down to provide access across the moat, the portcullis was raised, and people and carts were coming and going. No one at the stronghold seemed to have any awareness of their peril. Thankfully, the Rogandans were nowhere in sight, but Thomas knew that was likely to change very quickly.

Will brought them to a halt. "Rufe, you're with me. The rest of you stay here. Be prepared for a rapid departure," he warned them.

Will and Rufe picked their way down the trail. As they neared the road below, Rellan called down a warning. "Riders! Off in the distance. You don't have long!"

Will and Rufe waved back an acknowledgment as they reached the road below. Then they galloped to the town, crossing the draw-bridge and coming to a halt before the gate.

Thomas was much too far away to hear anything, but it was clear that Will was remonstrating with the guards at the gate. He was pointing repeatedly down the road. The guards were not responding.

From their position high up on the trail, Thomas and his companions could now clearly see Rogandan riders in the distance, approaching at a gallop. If the portcullis wasn't lowered soon, it would be too late.

"Hurry!" groaned Kuper between clenched teeth, tension evident in his voice.

Rufe drew his sword and started waving it around. The guards leaped into action at last and lowered the portcullis to deny Will and Rufe access to the fortress. A few bowmen appeared on the wall, and the two men beat a hasty retreat across the moat with arrows beginning to fall around them.

Just as their horses began clambering back up the trail, the first Rogandan riders appeared. The horsemen quickly clattered across the drawbridge and spread out around the wall, but they soon scattered as the archers on the wall began targeting them instead.

Several of the invaders lingered near the portcullis. Then slowly, ponderously, the drawbridge over the moat began to rise into the air. The Rogandans had no way to prevent it. The last of them fled across the bridge before it could be raised high enough to block their escape.

The invaders spotted Will and Rufe fleeing up the trail, and a sizable group of riders began a vigorous pursuit. Kuper, Rellan, Ander, and Nestor quickly unslung their bows and fired off a couple of volleys. Several pursuers fell to the deadly hail, and the others backed off. It was clear they did not intend to abandon the chase, though.

Vangellis took the lead, and the whole party began hastily retracing their steps. At times they caught glimpses of the Rogandans following them. It was a large group, but they stayed out of bowshot range.

After a couple of hours, the monk turned aside from the main trail and led them onto a hidden path that sloped steeply upward. They climbed for a while, until the path emptied onto a broad plateau. With open ground before them at last, they let their horses run, continuing at a rapid pace for the best part of an hour.

The monk eventually led them off the plateau, and they dipped down out of sight. The path up to the plateau must have been missed by their pursuers, because there had been no recent sightings of them.

Will called them to a halt to rest their horses.

"What happened down there?" Rellan asked.

"Will couldn't convince the guards about the danger," Rufe replied. "They refused to close the portcullis without an order from their local lord."

"How did you change their minds?" Thomas asked.

"Will started yelling at them in Rogandan, and I drew my sword and began threatening them. They finally took the hint."

"Only just in time, as it happened," said Will.

Vangellis took the lead once again when they set off, and they continued until nightfall.

With the sun setting, Will decided they had done enough for one day. They dismounted and shared a simple meal.

"You've led us well," Will told Vangellis. "We couldn't have made it to Stonehold in time without your help. The Rogandans would have captured the town."

The monk dipped his head slightly, but otherwise didn't respond.

Will continued. "We seem to be a long way ahead of them now. We can afford to get some sleep tonight."

"What will we do tomorrow?" Kuper asked.

"I've been giving that some thought," Will replied. "Drettroth undoubtedly had plans once he had taken Ranwood and Stonehold. After the last couple of days, I have a feeling those plans will have changed. I can't even guess at his next movements. He still has his army, though, and there's very little we can do against so many."

"What do you mean?" Thomas asked in surprise. "Look what you achieved at Ranwood. With only five of you!"

"Right. We destroyed one of our own towns."

Thomas opened his mouth to argue, but quickly realized it was wiser to say nothing. He closed it again without speaking.

"Drettroth's had the initiative for too long," Will continued. "We need an army. It's time we joined the king. We ride north for Castel in the morning.

"Get some rest," he concluded. "We will leave at dawn. The Rogandans that followed us from Stonehold will be tracking us as soon as it's light. And if our pursuers from Ranwood ever manage to figure out which way we went, we'll have two groups chasing us."

"Don't you think the group from Ranwood will give up?" Thomas asked hopefully.

"Not a chance," Will replied. "It won't go well for them if they return to Drettroth without us."

24

"Have you been here before?" Will asked Vangellis.

The monk shook his head.

They had been riding for several hours with just two short breaks. They knew that the Rogandans had found their tracks and were following them. They also knew that their pursuers were not far behind.

For some time they had been following an animal trail, but now it branched. One way led down, the other led up.

"Which way should we go?" Will asked the monk.

The downward trail appeared to offer easier going—when Thomas looked ahead along the ascending path, it seemed as if the trees were closing in around it.

Vangellis glanced toward the lower path, then peered thoughtfully for a long time along the upper path. Finally he turned to Will. "The upper path," he said.

Ander grunted derisively, but said nothing.

"The upper path it is," Will ordered without hesitation, pointing along the ascending trail.

"The lower path is the obvious choice. Nes, I need you to make it look like that's the one we took. Rellan and Kuper, go with him."

A low outcrop of rock ran alongside the upper path for the distance of a couple of bowshots. While Nestor and the twins trampled the lower path to make it look as if a group of riders had passed that way, the others dismounted and led their horses onto the rocky outcrop. Ander followed behind to make sure they left no hint of their passing.

By the time Nestor and the twins rejoined them, the sun was well past its zenith. The three soldiers had followed the other trail until they could leave it without their change of direction becoming obvious.

The monk's instinct ultimately proved to be right. The ascending trail continued to climb until they had crisscrossed their way to the top of an escarpment. At the top they once again caught sight of the lower trail. It wound its way into what appeared to be an extensive boggy morass. At that point the trail disappeared. On the other side of the bog, the only way forward led eventually into a box canyon. Riders following the lower trail would eventually be forced to retrace their steps.

They set out to find a place to camp, leaving Nestor behind at the top of the escarpment to watch for any sign of the Rogandans. He caught up with them not long before the sun completely disappeared below the western horizon.

"Did you see them, Nes?" Will asked.

"Yes. They took the lower path."

"How many of them?"

"Almost fifty. It's a large group."

"Have they camped?"

"Yes. Right on the edge of the bog. They'll probably waste most of tomorrow finding a way through it."

"With a dead end waiting for them on the other side," grinned Rellan.

Kuper glanced across at the monk. "We would have been caught in a trap if we'd taken the other path."

"A lucky guess," muttered Ander.

Vangellis said nothing. In the group he never spoke at all unless asked a direct question. He seemed a totally different person from the curious student Thomas had taught to ride.

While Vangellis never obviously appeared to be drunk, it was clear to Thomas that the monk's closest companion was his wineskin. Whenever they stopped, Vangellis wasted no time disappearing off with his saddlebags. If others had their suspicions, nothing had been said. But at the previous stop Thomas had noticed Ander watching the monk closely with narrowed eyes.

THE NEXT DAY they broke camp again before dawn. Will wanted to open up a big lead over their pursuers. They headed west, trying to skirt some rugged terrain that lay directly in their path northward. By the time the sun passed noon, they had made their way down to a succession of low hills covered with tall grass. At last they began to make good time.

Riding in open country again Thomas felt his spirits lifting. He knew that danger could be lurking anywhere—a Rogandan army might be waiting over the next rise for all he knew—but he decided not to think about it. The day passed without incident, and, setting off before dawn once again after another night with too little sleep, they headed northwest.

Will sent Nestor ahead to scout for any sign of trouble. Not long after sunrise he appeared in the distance, riding hard toward them. Wary and alert, they reined in their horses and waited for him to join them.

"Rogandans!" he said urgently. "I almost stumbled into their camp."

"Did they see you?"

"I don't think so."

"How many?"

"It's a big camp. Hundreds of tents."

"They'll have patrols out," Will said. "We can't stay in the open. Vangellis, I need you."

They all dismounted while Will, Nestor, and Vangellis huddled together for several long minutes. Finally Will called them together. "We're heading south. It's the wrong direction, but there's a forest only an hour's ride away, and we should be able to avoid detection there. We'll ride through its outskirts westward until we're clear of the Rogandans."

They set off immediately, riding fast. Time passed, with no sign of the forest, and Thomas became increasingly anxious. He couldn't help looking back repeatedly over his shoulder, half expecting to see an army chasing them.

Being chased by fifty Rogandan soldiers had been frightening. But he had a feeling that Will and Rufe would somehow find a way to outfight, outwit, or simply outrun them. But an entire army?

As he wrestled with his anxiety, memories—unwanted and unwelcome—forced their way back into his mind. He relived the fight at the gates of Arnost. He saw again the Rogandan soldier moving in to finish him off.

There was a time when he had imagined himself as a soldier in his daydreams. It had seemed so exciting. Now he knew better. War was no adventure—it was horrible beyond words.

Within the hour they reached the first outliers of a great forest that stretched east-west as far as the eye could see. Will called them to a halt between two huge trees. They peered back the way they had come, but there was no sign of pursuit. Thomas began to relax a little.

"We'll rest for a few minutes," Will said.

As the words left his lips a faint crack sounded nearby. Every soldier reacted instinctively. Nestor's sword appeared in one fluid movement as he spurred his horse toward the noise. Rellan and Kuper's bows were taut almost before the sound faded away.

A figure detached itself from behind a nearby tree and sprinted deeper into the forest. Rufe got there first and gave chase. He was almost upon the fleeing form when the spy tripped and fell sprawling. Moving with a speed that belied his size Rufe slid from his horse, pinning the figure to the ground with the point of his sword.

A quavering voice said a few words in a language Thomas could not understand.

"It's a girl!" Rufe exclaimed in surprise.

"She's Rogandan," said Will. He rode up and spoke to her, apparently in the same language.

The girl returned a rapid reply, her tone becoming bolder and more insistent with every word. Will spoke again, but she cut him off, impassioned and increasingly shrill.

Rufe dragged her to her feet. She was possibly a couple of years older than Thomas. Between the fire in her eyes and the dark tangle of her long hair she looked quite wild.

"What's she saying?" Ander asked.

"She seems to be some kind of servant who's run away from the Rogandans. She says we must take her with us. Either that, or she insists we kill her right now."

"Those are our options," Ander agreed. "Now that she's seen us she can betray us."

"Safer just to kill her," Nestor said dispassionately.

Vangellis bristled. "Not if you expect to keep me as your guide," he said, his jaw set in a tight line.

Ander opened his mouth to reply, but Will got in first. "Enough!" he said firmly. "She's coming with us. For now, anyway."

To the relief of Thomas they stopped to make camp well before the sun reached the horizon. Will had asked Thomas to ride double again, and the experience had been very unpleasant. The girl, whose name was apparently Elbruhe, had been hefted up behind him with instructions from Will to hang on to Thomas. She had clearly never ridden before and spent much of the first hour alternating between whimpers and squeals of terror. She eventually quietened down, but managed to poke him in the ribs almost continuously in her frantic attempts to hang on.

They attended to their horses and shared a simple meal. Afterward, Will drew Elbruhe aside, and the two talked for a very long time. Elbruhe seemed to do most of the talking. Thomas glanced over from time to time; more than once he spotted the girl sobbing.

Will eventually rejoined the others. They had positioned themselves in a circle as if warming themselves around an imaginary fire. Everyone was there except the girl, who was presumably preparing a place to sleep, and Vangellis, who was off on his own somewhere.

They sat without speaking for what seemed an age. Will appeared more than usually thoughtful.

Eventually Ander broke the silence. "What did you learn about the girl? Will the Rogandans come looking for her?"

Will shook his head. "I doubt it. The Rogandans care more about their animals than their slaves."

"How did she become a slave?"

"She said she's an orphan. That's shameful in their eyes. If the Dark Gods took your parents, they must be angry with you. People follow the example of their gods. I know something of it myself."

"So she ran away?"

"Yes. She decided it was better to starve to death alone in the forest than go on living as a slave. She's witnessed things no one should have to see. And terrible things have been done to her."

Will had nothing more to say, and the conversation ended there.

Later, Thomas lay gratefully beneath his warm blanket, shutting out the cold wind that roared through the tops of the trees above him. He tried to catch glimpses of the stars through the restless branches of the trees, and pondered his own misfortunes. Thanks to the stone he was caught up in events he could not comprehend, let alone control, swept away in a current he could not resist. Not long ago he had never known real danger. Now he flirted with danger every day.

But for all that, the good far outweighed the bad. He tried to imagine the life of the Rogandan girl, and could not. He had grown up with parents—parents who loved him. He knew that even his father cared about him. He had never gone hungry, never been beaten without cause. By the time sleep took him his troubles had given way to a heightened sense of gratitude.

In the morning Will approached him. "We leave within the hour, Thomas. Try to teach the girl what you can about riding. It might make your life easier," he added with a wry grin.

Thomas went over to her. A small stream ran nearby, and she had clearly bathed in it. Her hair was still an unruly tangle, but she seemed more presentable. He beckoned her to follow him, and after a long moment of indecision she did so.

As she followed him to his horse, he decided he couldn't blame her for hesitating. He pitied her for her sufferings, whatever they were, and it felt good to be able to help.

"This is a horse," he said. "Horse!" he repeated in a louder voice, feeling instantly stupid as he realized she couldn't understand a word. She ignored him, moving to the horse's neck and stroking it. The horse responded to her confident touch, allowing her to lean into it.

She couldn't ride, but she clearly knew horses. That should make his task easier. "I'm the horse master. I teach people to ride," he said, trying to sound important but managing only to feel foolish. She continued to ignore him.

His attempts to instruct her turned into nothing more than an exercise in frustration for Thomas. He realized for the first time how much his teaching relied on words. Normally he spoke first, then demonstrated, and followed up with more words to reinforce the lesson. Now he was reduced to the demonstration, and she clearly neither understood nor cared what he was trying to convey.

She soon became bored and wandered off. He coaxed her back, but not for long. Eventually he had almost been forced to drag her back to the horse, and she became very testy. The others stayed away, but he noticed them throwing sidelong glances in his direction, and more than once caught them smirking.

Finally he had abandoned any thought of teaching her to ride. In exasperation he placed himself in front of her and grabbed her hands, showing her how to hang on to him. This drew a mocking laugh from her, which stung and discouraged him.

They finally set off with Elbruhe seated behind him once again. She held on as instructed, but the outcome certainly hadn't flattered his skills as a teacher. The obvious amusement of some of the others didn't help, either.

As the day progressed, Thomas sensed that she was bouncing less and moving with the horse more. She no longer poked him in the ribs, either. She seemed to be learning from him indirectly, copying his movements and becoming better attuned to the animal. Her obvious progress made the journey easier for both of them, but Thomas felt frustrated.

When they camped for the evening, he lay awake trying to make sense of his own reaction. He realized he'd become accustomed to actively participating in the adventure as others learned to ride. On this occasion, they might have been riding the same horse, but the learning process hadn't been a shared experience in any way, and it left him feeling disconnected and dissatisfied. He recognized that it wasn't the fault of either one of them—the absence of a common language was an insurmountable barrier—and he drifted off to sleep having resolved to be less sensitive and more sympathetic to the girl in the future.

A couple of hours before dawn Thomas was awakened by a piercing scream. Every soldier was instantly alert and on his feet. Will appeared in the gloom and moved to Elbruhe, clamping one hand firmly over her mouth and bending low to whisper in her ear. She writhed under his grasp for a few moments, then became still. He released her, whispering again into her ear.

"It was a nightmare. Nothing more," he said to the curious onlookers. "Nes, make sure no one was nearby to hear that. The rest of you get some more sleep."

Thomas couldn't get back to sleep, though. And from Elbruhe's restless tossing and turning, he guessed that she couldn't, either.

The following morning Elbruhe discovered that the monk understood some Rogandan. After that she sought him out whenever they were not traveling. Vangellis, who had made it obvious that he preferred his own company, seemed to accept her presence with equanimity. She prattled away to him almost without pausing for breath. How much he understood Thomas did not know, but he rarely said much in return.

At one point Thomas found himself briefly alone with Vangellis. "How much do you understand of what Elbruhe says?" he asked.

"I understand Rogandan a lot better than I can speak it," the monk replied. "I don't understand everything she says, though. She talks so fast," he added with a smile.

"What does she talk about?" Thomas ventured.

"I don't think it's my place to say," the monk replied.

"Does she talk about...people?" he persisted.

The monk smiled and said nothing.

She fascinated Thomas, and he couldn't pretend otherwise. From the beginning, though, he decided not to try out the stone on her. It probably wouldn't have shown him anything. But even if it did, he knew that spying on her wouldn't have been right. That was a path he'd trodden before, and he wasn't going to do it again.

Clearly Elbruhe had experienced more than her share of pain and suffering in life. The monk had told Thomas that the wine helped him cope with pain. He didn't seem to have meant physical pain. Maybe the two of them understood each other.

THE NEXT DAY Thomas decided to let Elbruhe ride in front, so she could experience riding more normally. He held the reins around her, and found that she was now able to hold herself in position without needing his help.

Sitting behind her he couldn't help noticing the way her hair bounced to and fro in the wind. Her wild appearance was greatly diminished—she'd found a way of removing most of the tangles from her hair—and it felt like he was seeing her for the first time.

As the morning gradually wore away Thomas began to find it unsettling to be sitting behind her. Reaching around her waist with the reins meant his arms bumped against her continually. He couldn't help noticing the soft roundness of her body, skinny though she was. Had she found it distracting to ride behind him, holding him tightly? He hoped so, though he scarcely dared to admit it even to himself. If she did, she showed no sign of it.

At one point they slowed while traveling over uneven ground. His arms swung around more than usual, making constant contact with her. After a few minutes of this, she turned her head and glared at him. Then tossing the hair fiercely from her eyes, she spat a stern rebuke into his face. Finally she paused, before adding "Delou-ahn," sarcastically.

Will, riding nearby, laughed out loud.

"Well, tell us what she said," said Rufe mischievously.

"She said, 'Keep your hands to yourself!'" he replied with a grin. "Then she called him 'Sweetheart.'"

Every one of the soldiers burst out in uproarious laughter. Thomas felt himself coloring beet red.

The remainder of the ride was a nightmare that couldn't end soon enough for Thomas. He tried to hold his arms away from her body, but it wasn't possible to control the horse without touching her at all. Upset with her for humiliating him, he felt tempted to dream up a biting response. But he knew that the language chasm would defeat him even if he found something suitable to say.

It was so unfair. And why did Will have to tell everyone what she said?

The soldiers were still chortling over the incident when they finally stopped for the day. Elbruhe clearly enjoyed the attention, and she looked down her nose condescendingly at Thomas as she dismounted.

Turning her back on him, she went to his horse and hugged its neck, speaking baby talk to it. The horse seemed to enjoy her attentions. Then she walked away without a backward glance.

Thomas turned to the horse and glared at it. "Traitor!" he muttered accusingly. The horse whinnied and shook its head.

The monk unexpectedly sought him out. "Don't take it to heart, Thomas," he suggested gently. "She was cruel, I know. But she's used to being mocked, and I think she enjoyed serving it out for once. She doesn't mean it."

Thomas knew the monk meant well, but it didn't placate him. He decided to avoid Elbruhe entirely. If she noticed at all, it didn't bother

her. She soon sought out Vangellis and chattered away happily to him as usual. The monk listened patiently as always.

Thomas ended the day annoyed with Elbruhe for humiliating him, angry with the soldiers for laughing, and peeved with the monk for being kind to her. The brush down he gave his horse was less enthusiastic than usual, too.

SOMETHING HAPPENED the next morning that caused Thomas to forget his grievances. Not long after Thomas had woken, he was startled by a loud wailing. The haunting quality of the sound sent a chill up his spine. The whole camp was astir in moments. He looked around for Elbruhe, but the noise wasn't coming from her. It was coming from the monk.

To the surprise of Thomas, Will ignored Vangellis and his wailing and hobbled over to Ander. "What have you done?" he demanded, stiff with anger.

The burly soldier's face displayed a hardened wariness. "He's supposed to be our guide. I've had enough of following the advice of a drunk!"

Will approached Ander until their faces were inches apart, and stared him down. "Lay a finger on him or his possessions again, and you'll deal with me!"

Ander could not meet his eyes. He dropped his gaze sullenly to his feet.

"You're on double duty. For the rest of this week. You're getting off lightly, too—don't push me, or I'll come up with a real punishment." Will's tone was even and controlled, but the menace in his voice was unmistakable.

The wailing continued uninterrupted, adding a bizarre backdrop to the confrontation.

Thomas felt completely bemused. What had just happened?

Will headed to Vangellis and tried to talk to him. The monk ignored him.

It was the girl who finally managed to get through to him. She took his arm and led him aside, speaking in soothing tones. A few minutes later the wailing stopped. Thomas could hear the monk quietly sobbing for a while, then that, too, came to an end.

Rufe was standing apart, frowning. "What's going on?" Thomas asked bemusedly.

Rufe nodded in the direction of the monk. "It seems Ander slashed all his wineskins in the night."

"Oh. So you knew about the wineskins?"

"Everyone knew," Rufe replied. "Will didn't mind as long as he stayed alert. He never wanted to be here, and we all thought it would help him stay calm."

Rufe's comments were a revelation to Thomas. He had imagined the wineskins were his secret with Vangellis. He wondered what else might be obvious to everyone. What were they saying about him and Elbruhe? He felt a blush coming on, and quickly excused himself.

They eventually set out much later than usual. Outwardly, at least, the monk seemed calm. This time Elbruhe rode double with him instead of with Thomas. The young horse master felt nothing but relief. He couldn't think straight when she was around.

25

The party had barely departed when Elbruhe called to Will. After a brief exchange they resumed their journey. Just thirty minutes later the girl called out again, more urgently this time. The horse she shared with Vangellis had come to a stop, and she quickly dismounted. The monk all but fell from the horse. He lay on the ground where he landed while Elbruhe fussed around him.

Will rode over and bent low over his horse to examine Vangellis. Elbruhe spoke rapidly and vehemently, punctuating her words with animated gestures. Will replied, pointing firmly in the direction they had been traveling. She became very agitated, waving her hands dismissively toward Will and the rest of the party. She then turned her back on Will and knelt down beside the monk.

Will waved Rufe to his side, and the two of them carried on a conversation in low tones. Thomas could not hear what they were saying.

Finally Will ordered them all to dismount. "Vangellis is not well. We'll stay here for a while until he improves."

"He's faking it," Ander sneered, speaking under his breath so that those nearest him could hear but Will could not.

Rufe heard, though. He pushed himself in front of Ander, towering over him. "If you've got something to say, then say it to Will," he challenged, his voice trembling with anger.

"There's no problem," Ander replied hastily in a tone that suggested Rufe was turning an acorn into an oak tree.

Rufe stared down at him without speaking, then turned on his heel and left. Thomas noticed Ander roll his eyes dismissively at Rufe's back as the giant guardsman moved away. Thomas got up and left, too. He felt like he'd witnessed one skirmish too many in Ander's tireless campaign against the monk.

THE SUN PASSED OVERHEAD and began its journey toward the western horizon, but Vangellis hadn't improved. He was getting worse. When they stopped he had been shaking with fever. Now, several hours later, his fever raged unchecked and the trembling had become more violent. He vomited repeatedly, even though nothing remained to be purged from his stomach.

At one point Thomas spotted Ander stealing a furtive look at Vangellis as he passed by. Thomas wondered what he was thinking. Did he feel remorse for what he'd done? No reasonable person could think that Vangellis was faking his illness. But Ander couldn't be relied upon to be reasonable where the monk was involved.

Elbruhe was tending Vangellis, and Will hovered nearby. Vangellis lay prone, although from time to time he seemed to be seized by some kind of fit. As Thomas contemplated the scene Nestor happened by. "What's happening to him, Nes?" Thomas asked.

"He's got the barrel fever," the veteran replied.

"What's that?"

"He doesn't have his wine anymore. He's come to rely on it," said Nestor. "Now the craving's got hold of him."

"How do you know?"

"Seen it before," he replied.

"What can we do?"

"We can wait."

"Wait for what?"

"To see if he survives. This time tomorrow we should know."

"You can't mean he's going to die!" Thomas protested.

Nestor shrugged. "He might. Seen it before," he repeated.

Thomas couldn't bear the uncertainty. He joined the little huddle around Vangellis to see if there was anything he could do.

Seeing him arrive, Elbruhe addressed him sweetly, ending with a teasing "Delou-ahn."

"Elbruhe wonders if her sweetheart might fetch some fresh water," Will said, managing a tight smile.

Thomas stood there dumbly for a moment, then fled in search of a water skin. A small stream flowed about fifty paces away, and he filled the water skin there and hurried back. Elbruhe ran it over a damp piece of cloth until it was dripping wet, then placed it across the monk's forehead.

She spoke again to Will, a serious look on her face.

"She wants some 'feverwort'. We need to find a way of breaking his fever."

"What's feverwort?" Thomas asked.

"It's a herb used by the Rogandans to treat various ailments," Will replied. "Fever is only one of them. I've seen the plant before; my aunt used to grow it. It has a broad green leaf and a small pale white flower. If we're lucky we might find some near the stream."

The description didn't sound very detailed, but Thomas set off hopefully to look for the herb. Will followed close behind him.

After a long hunt Thomas found something that vaguely fit Will's description. The flower was pale lavender, though, not white. Nevertheless he headed hopefully to Elbruhe to show her what he'd found.

Seeing it set her off on a tirade.

"Well, I don't know what to look for," he said defensively. "I've never even seen it."

Will reappeared, just in time. "Apparently that's poisonous," he explained to Thomas. "The leaf of feverwort is broader, and darker in color. And the flower needs to be white."

Thomas plodded off to have another try. As he passed Elbruhe she poked out her tongue at him and gave him another earful. "Thanks so much for your helpful explanation," he retorted.

Walking past the twins he overheard Rellan saying to his brother, "Listen to them. Just like an old married couple," while Kuper chortled loudly. Thomas scowled at them and walked on, pursued by gales of laughter.

It took him almost an hour, but Thomas eventually found a plant that he felt certain was feverwort. Grabbing two large handfuls, he sprinted back to the camp, and held it out expectantly to Elbruhe. She leaped up excitedly, and, to his complete astonishment, planted a joyful kiss on his cheek. Then she turned away, calling loudly for Will.

Thomas stood there dumbfounded. When he recovered himself he decided to get more water. His cheek still tingling, he set off for the stream, fervently hoping that no one had noticed.

He returned to the camp at the same time as Will, who wasted no time calling for Rufe.

"We need to build a fire."

Rufe was clearly taken aback. "That's a big risk!"

"Nevertheless, we will do it. Avoid green branches. Try to keep the smoke to a minimum."

Elbruhe boiled water over the fire and used the leaf of the herb to make a steaming broth. Then she lifted the monk's head and carefully poured some into his mouth. He sputtered and coughed, spilling most of it. But she gently persisted, returning the broth to his lips again and again, making sure he swallowed a few drops at least each time.

By nightfall there were hopeful signs that the fever might be easing. If they thought he was through the worst of it, though, they were sadly mistaken. The monk's problems were just getting started. None of them got any sleep that night.

It began just after dark. The monk was lying quietly with Elbruhe close at hand to check on his condition. The twins were on watch, and the others had started to think about sleeping.

Then suddenly Vangellis had begun screaming in terror, slapping at himself and rolling on the ground. "Get them off me!" he shrieked.

The camp was instantly in an uproar. Will and Rufe rushed to him, ready to help. But they could not understand what his problem was.

"What is it? " Will demanded. "What's on you?"

He ignored Will and kept screaming, and scratching himself frantically. Great welts appeared wherever he made contact with bare skin.

Will grabbed his head with both hands and forced the monk to look at him. "What...is...the...problem!"

"Insects! Crawling over me!" Vangellis gasped. Then his eyes widened. "Biting, biting!" The screaming resumed, more panicked than ever.

At that point Nestor stepped in and took control of the situation. "Hold him down and cover his eyes! He's seeing things that aren't there. He'll hurt himself if we don't stop him."

"Do what he says," Will ordered.

Rufe, Will, and Nestor surrounded him and tackled him to the ground. His twisting and writhing became frenzied, but they held him down. Thomas tore a strip off his blanket and fashioned a simple blindfold. He fastened it around the monk's face, trying to ignore the madness in his bulging eyeballs.

Will stuffed some cloth in his mouth, and the shouting was reduced to a wild mumbling.

Eventually Vangellis became calm.

Gradually they released him. They began with his mouth, then uncovered his eyes. After a few minutes without further struggling, they finally released him entirely.

Elbruhe spoke to him soothingly, and helped him drink some more broth.

He lay with his head in her lap, entirely spent. In his weakened state from the fever, Thomas could not imagine how he had found the energy to fight so hard.

That had only been the beginning. As the night progressed the monk had to endure further invasions of insects, then snakes, and later rats crawling all over his body. Each time he suffered the indignity of being forcibly restrained.

Thomas and his companions later realized that covering the monk's eyes did nothing to diminish his visions. And nothing could prevent him from feeling the intruders crawling over his flesh. The hours of darkness must have been a waking nightmare to him.

Thomas realized at one point that he hadn't seen Ander at all during the night. He had certainly never approached the monk, and seemed to have stayed well clear of the others. When dawn came Thomas looked around, and couldn't see him anywhere.

Ander reappeared only minutes later.

"Anything happening?" Will called out to him.

Ander simply shook his head. He looked tired, too.

Will must have sent him off scouting. Yet Will didn't seem to have left the side of Vangellis at all during the night. Then Thomas remembered Will talking to the twins. They had disappeared as well.

Thomas hadn't given a thought to security; the drama involving the monk had fully absorbed his attention. Apparently it hadn't distracted Will from his other responsibilities, though. How did he do it?

Elbruhe must have been tired, too. Thomas greatly admired the way she cared for Vangellis. She was tireless, tending to his every need with gentle compassion. He would have admired her even more if she hadn't taken to snapping at him all the time. Thankfully he didn't understand a word, and he was grateful that Will chose not to enlighten him.

Two full days dragged slowly by before the monk's crisis finally appeared to be over. Vangellis was left too weak to move, but both Elbruhe and Nestor now hoped that he would survive.

Thomas thought back to his conversation with Nestor two days previously. The idea that the monk might die had seemed so extreme to him at the time. But the soldier had been right. Life could be far more fragile than Thomas imagined.

In the end they remained at the campsite a further four days.

Even then the monk was barely capable of sitting on a horse. Thomas sat behind him once more, steadying him, and Elbruhe rode alone for the first time. No one questioned her right to join the party or to ride one of their horses. At some point she had crossed a mysterious threshold and become one of them.

KUPER AND RELLAN RODE IN, bringing their horses to a halt beside their commander.

"Any sign of Rogandans?" Will asked.

Kuper shook his head. "No sign at all. We seem to have lost our pursuers. Ander and Rellan and I have scouted far and wide, and no Rogandans are anywhere near us."

"What about the army we caught a glimpse of?"

"Long gone. Their tracks show that they headed west, toward Erestor."

Will nodded. "So there is no immediate danger," he said.

"Has our delay created a problem?" asked Kuper.

Thomas had been asking himself the same question. The commander had without hesitation put the needs of Vangellis ahead of everything else. Perhaps he felt responsible for the monk since he had compelled him to join them. They'd been held up for six days, though, and Will had seemed so determined to avoid wasting time. Thomas had the impression that the fate of the kingdom might be hanging in the balance.

Will shook his head. "I'm not concerned about the delay. My most pressing priority was to prevent Drettroth from carrying out his immediate plans at Ranwood and Stonehold—there was real urgency behind that. We need to find the king, but I never expected we'd be able to reach him quickly. Not with so many Rogandans roaming the countryside."

Kuper nodded.

"Let's keep moving," said Will. "We won't be traveling far today."

Thomas had no idea how Will juggled his various responsibilities. He was simply glad it wasn't his job.

They rode slowly but steadily along the fringes of the great forest for a couple of hours, until Nestor returned from forward scouting and reported that he'd found a village within the forest. A small trail intersected their path about thirty minutes ride away. He had followed it far enough to see it broaden into a well-used road. A goatherd had told him about the village. Nestor guessed it was a couple of hours further on, riding slowly.

Will called them together and announced they would divert to the village. After the unexpected delay they needed to restock their provisions, and it offered an opportunity to warn the local inhabitants about the Rogandan invasion and ask them to spread the word. The villagers might also have remedies to help speed the recovery of Vangellis.

By the time they reached the village Vangellis was close to collapse. They helped him from the horse and stretched him out on the ground while Will sought out the village headman.

The village might have been home to fifteen families, and it soon became apparent that it was poor indeed by any standard. Livestock, normally abundant in a reasonably prosperous village, were hard to find here; a couple of small pigs ran squealing from the horses, and a half dozen scrawny chickens pecked hopefully around a small cluster of rude huts. The children ran around naked, and the clothing of the adults was poor in both quality and condition. The villagers themselves looked thin and weathered, as if worn down by too many cares. Thomas had never seen poverty like it.

No young men at all could be seen. Thomas guessed that the young men would be pressed into the service of the local lord, either as soldiers or working in his fields.

The village lay in a large clearing, well within the boundaries of the great forest. Trees had been cleared on either side of the village and meager crops struggled for life in small strips of cultivated earth. The land had probably been cleared gradually over many generations.

Thomas discovered through Rufe that the village was on the northern boundary of the domain of a minor baron. Most of his holdings lay south of the forest, although a couple of other larger villages lay near at hand to the south and also within the forest.

Will appeared with the headman, who didn't appear to be any better clothed or fed than the rest of them. The fellow looked anxious. Thomas expected a headman to seem more confident and authoritative.

Will explained that the party had a sick man who needed care, and wanted to rest and restock supplies. The headman looked even more worried, but he nevertheless arranged billets for them all. Each of them would be placed in a different household, except for Thomas and Vangellis who were sent off together.

Elbruhe made it clear through Will that she was to be notified immediately of any change in the monk's condition. She had plenty to say, and Thomas nodded wisely and listened intently as if he was hanging on her every word. She was clearly annoyed by his behavior, a fact that brought him considerable satisfaction.

Before they dispersed Will called them together.

"I've warned the headman about the Rogandans. He's sent messages to the nearby villages. He's also sent word to his local lord. We can expect a visit.

"Ander and Nestor, you take first watch. I want to know the minute anyone comes near this village. Something doesn't feel right here. These people are harmless, but they're living in fear. Be ready to be roused at any moment.

"Rellan and Kuper, take over the watch at dusk."

VANGELLIS AND THOMAS had been assigned to an elderly couple, and their hosts ushered them into a small hut. A small fire burned inside on a simple hearth with a rough stone chimney to catch the smoke. The chimney was surprisingly effective, but smoke still filled the hut, and Thomas soon found his eyes watering. Vangellis was too tired to pay any attention to their surroundings. The man pointed him to a small space that had been cleared on the floor, covered by a rough blanket. Thomas helped him to lie down before sitting on a three-legged stool proudly produced by the woman.

Small strings of onions, leeks, and other dried vegetables hung from the roof. The woman slowly retrieved a few and began to prepare a meal. Her husband watched her mournfully. Neither of them said a word, and Thomas found himself unable to think what to say, either.

Not long after dusk the woman indicated that the food was ready to eat. Vangellis was in no condition to join them, so Thomas found himself eating with his hosts, sitting on his stool while they sat on the floor. The meal consisted of a vegetable stew served in wooden bowls and a large slab of dark bread.

The bread had arrived just before they sat down to eat. A young girl brought it to the woman, stretching up on tiptoes to whisper in her ear before hurrying off. The hosts set aside no bread for themselves, but their eyes followed closely every piece on its journey to Thomas's mouth to be chewed. He guessed that the bread had been sent by the headman, intended for the guests only.

The stew was thin and the vegetables scrawny. The bread was tough and strongly flavored, but it was bread. He softened it by dipping it into the stew before attempting to chew it.

The portion served to Thomas didn't go close to filling him, but he didn't ask for more. From the condition of the man and the woman, they weren't used to eating any better themselves.

A portion of bread and stew had been set aside for Vangellis, so after Thomas had finished eating he thanked his hosts and carried the monk's food to him. Tearing off small pieces of the bread and dipping them into the stew, he placed them into the mouth of the prone man. Vangellis moved his jaws half-heartedly a few times before swallowing the pieces whole.

A blanket for Thomas had been placed near Vangellis. He lay down, peering across at the man and woman in the dim light provided by the fire. They had also lain down, but he could see no sign of blankets. He realized that they must have given up their blankets for their guests.

Uncomfortable at the thought of the cold night that lay ahead of them, but unsure about what to do, Thomas lay for a long time unable to sleep. After thirty minutes of restless indecision he could stand it no longer. He stumbled out of the hut in the darkness and made his way to his horse to retrieve some blankets.

Back in the hut again he returned the borrowed blankets to their original owners. They peered at him with wide eyes, saying nothing. But they accepted the blankets without hesitation.

Thomas tucked a blanket around the monk and settled down for the night. He was more tired than he realized, and soon drifted off to the sound of the monk's rhythmic snoring.

Once asleep, he dreamed. He found himself walking alone across a courtyard in the castle at Arnost. Water bubbled merrily from the spout of a fountain and sparkled in the late afternoon sunlight.

Walking beside the fountain, something on the ground caught his eye. Bending down to examine it, he was astonished to discover that it was his stone. He fumbled for the pouch at his belt, anxious to discover how it had fallen out. But his stone was still in its place.

Completely baffled, he opened the drawstring and took out the familiar object. Then he picked up the stone from the ground and compared them. They appeared to be identical.

Abruptly something struck him hard from behind, on the back of his head. He pitched forward, both stones flying from his hand into the fountain. Down, down, he fell. The last thing he saw before blacking out was the base of the fountain. It was covered with stones, every one identical to his own.

Confused and disoriented, Thomas struggled to return to wakefulness. Someone was bending over him, shaking him gently.

Vangellis swam into view. "Sorry if I startled you," he said. "You were calling out in your sleep."

Thomas frowned. His surroundings mingled strangely with lingering elements of his dream, and it was difficult to re-establish reality.

After clearing his head he peered up into the concerned face of Vangellis and realized that the monk looked different.

"Are you feeling better?" he asked. Vangellis looked very pale, but otherwise more normal than he had appeared for many days.

"Yes," he replied. "I think I am."

They were alone in the hut. Vangellis pointed to two small wooden bowls. "Fresh milk," he said. "I suspect this is our breakfast." He drank the contents of one of the bowls and gave out a sigh of satisfaction. A white mustache briefly appeared above his lips before he wiped it away with his sleeve.

The monk studied the hut and its contents carefully. As he did so, a frown gradually furrowed his brow. "I need to speak with Will," he said, and marched determinedly from the hut.

Thomas jumped up from the floor. Gulping down his milk, he hurried out after Vangellis. Elbruhe would have his hide for letting the monk dash around so soon after his illness. He had to run to keep up—the monk was in a hurry.

Vangellis quickly found Will, who stood in the village square talking to the other soldiers. Everyone was there except the girl.

The monk walked up to them and nodded in greeting.

"How was your meal last night?" Vangellis asked. His voice sounded casual, but Thomas detected an edge to his tone.

"I've eaten better," Kuper replied with energy.

"Smallest meal I've been served since I was a boy," Nestor added. "I had to send the woman back to prepare more. Twice."

Others grunted in assent. "A soldier can't fight if he doesn't eat," Ander asserted.

Vangellis nodded his head calmly, but his voice was tight. "We're condemning these people to death."

"What are you talking about?" Nestor demanded.

"We ate as much food in one night as the entire village would have eaten in a week. Maybe more. Food was already in very short supply for them. Another couple of days with us staying here, and they won't make it through the winter."

Rufe waved his hand in denial. "We'll pay them. There's no need for them to starve."

"Pay them with what?" Vangellis demanded.

"With money, of course," Rufe replied, baffled by the question.

Vangellis shook his head, trying to remain patient. "People like this have no use for money."

He looked Will in the eye. "Pay them, and you guarantee their deaths. Their lord will never believe they were given money. He'll conclude they stole it from us."

There was a pause, then everyone started talking at once, but Will cut them off. "He's right," he said.

He faced the monk. "What do you suggest?"

"We need to give them food. Not money."

"We can give them a deer," Rellan suggested.

Vangellis shook his head stubbornly. "They won't be allowed to kill deer from the forest. Deer will be reserved for the lord. Ask them!"

Will held up a hand for silence. "There's no law prohibiting us from killing deer. We will hunt some ourselves," he said. "But we won't give them to the villagers. We'll tell them to invite people from the nearby villages to come to a feast. We'll hold a market. They'll need to bring some food to trade. We'll sell meat in exchange for vegetables, then invite them all to the feast.

"Some of the meat and most of the vegetables will stay here for the local villagers. The rest we'll take with us as provisions."

Vangellis paused for a moment, thinking. He nodded once, tentatively, then again decisively. "I think that might work," he said with a smile.

"That's settled, then," said Will. "It will mean another delay, but we're not leaving until we find out what's been going on in this village anyway. Safeguarding these people is no less our duty than fighting the Rogandans.

"Rellan and Kuper. Go find us two or three large deer. Nestor and Ander, you're on watch. I'll speak to the headman."

Before they could disperse, Elbruhe appeared. She took in the scene with a single glance. Making her way to the monk's side, she took him firmly by the elbow. Then, frowning fiercely across at Thomas, she rattled off a couple of choice phrases, clearly savoring each word as it left her mouth. The sarcasm in her tone required no translation. Finally, chin held high, she took charge of Vangellis and defiantly steered him back in the direction from which she had come.

Her performance was appreciated enormously by the men. They applauded noisily, accompanied by some hooting and hollering. The villagers, hard at work tending their strips, paused for a moment and stared at them all curiously. Rufe, grinning from ear to ear, gave Thomas a wink.

There was no point whatsoever in responding. With a sigh of resignation Thomas turned away and headed off to tend to the horses.

26

Steffan sat motionless on his destrier watching the columns march past. Captain Olaf no longer led Steffan's soldiers to war—advancing years and infirmity had finally caught up with the old veteran, and he was confined to his bed in Castel Citadel. Lord Bottren had taken command of the Arvenian army, at least for the moment. Once again Steffan found himself wishing he had Will Prentis at his side.

Essanda had risen early to see him off. He could still picture her, a thoughtful frown creasing her young face. Steffan had assured her that everything would be fine. He had the feeling she wasn't convinced, but she was trying hard not to show it.

The truth was that he was bursting to go. Careful planning was well and good, but Steffan had long since wearied of the endless round of debate and negotiation. He was longing to do something, to take the fight to the Rogandans at last.

Eventually he had reached the point where he could bear it no more. He sought out King Istel and vented his spleen—at length, and at considerable volume. His father-in-law had taken a long hard look at him, then finally conceded that the time for action had come. Things had moved remarkably quickly after that.

The soldiers were marching on Deadman's Pass, still blocked by the Rogandans who had occupied it on the day of Steffan's wedding. Clearing the pass would present the new joint force with their first real challenge.

Steffan's army was ready to fight, and he couldn't wait to see his men take the initiative. He found it inconceivable that a small band of Rogandans could hold them up for long.

THERE COULD BE no doubt that Will's market was turning out to be a big success. Over two hundred people had appeared from neighboring villages and farms, lured by the promise of trade and especially the report of a feast. It was obvious to Thomas that very little feasting happened around here, so it wasn't surprising that people became enthusiastic once they had overcome their initial reticence.

The twins had returned from the hunt with a large buck and three does. At that moment two of the does were roasting over a fire in preparation for the feast. The buck and the other doe had been carved up and traded for vegetables, cheese, bread and other items of food.

Nothing had been wasted. The hide, the antlers, the bladder, and even the entrails all had their uses and the local farmers had quickly taken up what seemed to be a rare opportunity to trade them. The raw meat had been cut into long strips and wrapped in vine leaves to keep them fresh. Business had been brisk as soon as the meat was offered for trade. The new owners would undoubtedly smoke the strips to preserve the meat. The families in the region would benefit greatly from the additional variety in their diets over the winter months to come.

Will had already turned over generous supplies of food to the headman for distribution to the other families in the village. The man had brightened considerably. In fact, he had almost smiled. And the feast hadn't even started yet.

The villagers were not the only ones looking happier. Thomas had never seen Vangellis so relaxed—he almost seemed normal. Even Elbruhe had flashed Thomas a smile. She also paid him a compliment. At least that's what she appeared to be doing, and Thomas was more than willing to take it at face value.

JUST BEFORE DUSK, with the feast well underway, Will gathered together the members of his party.

"Nestor just warned me that a group of riders is approaching from the south. He estimated there are at least twenty of them. He and Ander will watch them closely to make sure nothing surprising happens.

"Thomas and Vangellis—keep out of the way. I don't want anything to happen to either of you. Make sure Elbruhe stays with you.

"The rest of you know what to do. Don't start any trouble, but if I give the signal, don't hesitate."

Thomas and Vangellis, with Elbruhe following them, withdrew to a suitable spot beside one of the huts. From there they should be able to observe everything that happened without interfering or unnecessarily putting themselves at risk. Vangellis spoke quietly to Elbruhe, who listened intently with a deepening frown.

Will must have warned the headman, too, because the sounds of merriment quickly began to die down, and people scurried away. Soon only Will stood in the open. Flanked by a giant bonfire, he was biting off chunks of meat from a large piece of venison.

Before long a group of riders rode into the village. They were led by a rotund man in late middle age with a long scar across his face. He sent probing glances around every point of the village before approaching Will.

"Who authorized this debauchery?" he demanded.

"I did. Come and enjoy some of the venison—it's very good, and there's plenty here for all."

"Your life is forfeit for poaching the king's deer, fool."

"And who are you to decide matters of life and death on the king's behalf?" Will asked calmly.

"I am Baron Rudungen. I represent the king here."

"I also represent the king. I am commander of the king's armies. My name is Will Prentis."

"Where are your armies, then, Commander?" the baron asked, mockingly searching around him.

"The placement of the king's armies is not a subject for idle chatter in times of war."

"Hah! You talk big, but my men will soon bring you down to size." The baron nodded to the nearest of his soldiers, and they began to close in.

Will raised his right arm, and two arrows flew through the air and buried themselves into the shields of the two men nearest to Will. "Withdraw your men, or next time your head will be the target, Baron," Will called out.

The baron's men halted, peering around nervously trying to spot the archers.

"I see you have been expecting us. Well your bold talk doesn't deceive me," the baron sneered. "My spies report that you have only five soldiers with you. You're badly outnumbered."

"And my spies tell me you brought only twenty men. Some of them are looking a bit pale. I wonder how many have actually fought a battle before. They may discover that parade ground tussles with wooden swords do little to prepare you for the real thing. My men have fought the Rogandans many times, and always against much worse odds than this. I'm sorry, Baron, but if you were planning to pick a fight with the king's commander you should have brought an army."

Will's words had been skillfully chosen and were having their effect. Some of the baron's men appeared nervous and fidgety. Thomas could see that more than a few were indeed looking pale.

The baron said nothing. He was clearly calculating the odds and trying to think of a way to turn the situation in his favor. Finally he came to a decision.

"I see no reason for bloodshed," the baron offered reasonably. "Let's settle this in a more civilized fashion: my champion against yours, hand-to-hand combat with no weapons. If your man wins, I will allow you to leave here without interference. If my man wins, all of you will return with me to my castle in chains.

"Either way, the vermin here who call themselves villagers will learn to regret their little party today."

Will's face became stern. "I guessed that you might have been responsible for the poverty in these parts. It seems I was right.

"I accept your challenge," he continued, "but with one alteration. If my man wins, you will come with us to the king. Bound and as our prisoner. If we make it past the Rogandan army waiting for us, you will get an opportunity to explain your actions today directly to the king. And you will be held accountable for the brutal oppression of your subjects."

The baron laughed, a cruel and mocking sound. "We will see," he said. "Choose your champion." He called to his men, and one of them dismounted and stepped forward. Thomas gasped. He was a big brute of a fellow with a thick neck and a cruel face. The baron rode to his side and bent down to him, whispering in his ear. The man nodded once and began stripping off his weapons.

"Rufe," Will called. Rufe appeared, very close to the position where Thomas and the others were hiding. Will came over to him. "This baron intends treachery," he said, speaking quietly. "Be careful. Whatever happens, this is going to end in a fight, and we're going to need you."

Rufe nodded. He stepped forward, handing his weapons to Will. Ander, Nestor, and the twins were nowhere to be seen.

When Rufe moved into the open the baron's soldiers gasped. Their man might have been big, but Rufe was bigger.

"Let me warn you against treachery, Baron," Will called. "Many of your men will die unnecessary deaths here today if you play me false."

The baron did not bother to reply. He waved his man forward impatiently.

The two men circled warily, looking for an opportunity. Then the baron's man charged and wrapped his arms around Rufe, pinning one of Rufe's arms to his side. He began to squeeze. The baron's soldiers cheered excitedly.

A lesser man could not have withstood the crushing pressure, but Rufe tightened his own great muscles and began pounding his opponent's head with his free fist. After a few moments the man released his hold and stepped back, shaking his head to clear it.

While he was still dazed, Rufe charged him, fists raised, and rained heavy blows to his upper body. The man chopped downward onto Rufe's left arm, forcing him to step back wincing with the pain.

The fight wore on, with both men landing punishing blows but neither able to knock the other from the contest. The baron's champion was not able to deliver an easy victory, and Thomas could sense the tension rising. The baron's men were becoming restless.

Then Rufe's opponent reached behind his back, and knives appeared in both hands. Rufe reacted instinctively, running at him then dropping into a slide that carried him right up to the waiting man. At the last moment Rufe spread his legs enough to encompass the right leg of the other. Even as the man reached down to stab him, Rufe snapped his legs together in a scissor movement. Thomas heard the sickening crack of a leg breaking, and the knife-wielder crashed to the ground with a cry of agony.

After that chaos ensued. The baron loudly called his men to arms, and Rufe and Will were soon fighting for their lives. First two, then three, then four of the baron's men fell from their horses, arrows protruding from their chests or necks. But the remaining soldiers soon located the archers and moved to engage them. The stream of arrows ceased, but not before three more men lay unmoving in the dust.

Small knots of men writhed to and fro across the village square, the dying rays of the sun adding a faint red tinge to the scene. The twins fought back to back, their blades dancing among the many targets around them. Ander and Nestor fought nearby. A couple of soldiers brave enough to test their strength and swordsmanship quickly paid with their lives; others soon learned to stay out of reach. Will and Rufe had likewise fought their way to each other's side. They each accounted for an enemy before the others drew back warily.

So far the baron's extra numbers had made no impact. Half of his men milled around uselessly, the skillful tactics of Will's fighters keeping most of them out of the fight. They got their chance only when one of their own went down.

The baron stayed on the sidelines, shouting instructions in a fury. Thomas could see that some of his men would have turned and run, but they feared their leader even more than their enemies.

The fight had reached a dangerous point for Will and his men. They were visibly tiring. Thomas felt sick to the stomach as he recalled the struggle at the gates of Arnost. Even as he watched, Rellan sustained a heavy blow to his left arm. He was now unable to do more than defend himself. Worse, Ander, who had been fighting ferociously, tripped and went down. Enemies immediately swarmed over him, stabbing downward, until Nestor's desperate swordsmanship forced them back.

The baron's remaining soldiers cheered and joined the struggle with renewed hope and energy.

At this crucial moment, with the balance tilting in favor of the baron, it abruptly shifted again. A ragtag group of men unexpectedly appeared on the fringes of the battlefield, moving steadily toward the struggle. They were farmers, armed with picks, axes, and even rakes.

The baron greeted their arrival with unconcealed rage. In response to his furious instructions, several of his men peeled off immediately to confront the new challengers.

The farmers had no skill at arms; they brought little more than raw courage to the battle. The baron's men, however, knew exactly how to deal with peasants. The soldiers fell on them savagely, threatening an imminent bloodbath. First one, then a second farmer was struck down, and the others showed signs of wavering.

But the looming slaughter never happened. In the first moments of confusion, Rufe glimpsed an opportunity and seized it. Pushing through the distracted opponents that remained before him, he ran to the baron and dragged him from his horse. He threw the noble roughly to the ground, planted a foot firmly on his chest and pinned his neck with the point of his sword.

"Throw down your weapons. Now! Or the baron dies," he bellowed.

The baron squirmed under his foot. But the sharp weapon at his throat left him no choice. "Do as he says," he hissed.

"Speak...LOUDER...Baron," Rufe suggested, poking down with his sword to emphasize each word. "I don't think they can hear you."

"Do as he says!" the baron shrieked.

His soldiers complied immediately.

FEW IN THE village slept at all that night. The baron spent an uncomfortable night trussed up and gagged, guarded by Nestor, who was not gentle with him. The gag had been applied after an incessant stream of threats and curses from the noble.

The villagers gathered the dead and laid them out while the able-bodied among the baron's surviving soldiers, supervised by Rufe and Kuper, labored digging graves in the cemetery beside the village.

Fortunately, Vangellis seemed to have largely recovered from his brush with the barrel fever. During the night he worked tirelessly among the wounded, ably assisted by Elbruhe. Thomas ran errands for them, fetching water and stoking fires. He also searched in the woods around the village for feverwort. The search was difficult and frustrating. He hunted in the dark aided only by the flickering light of a torch, and it took him almost three hours. But he continued until his persistence was rewarded. He handed over the leaves without expecting or receiving any praise for his efforts; all of them were too weary to care about such niceties.

In the morning the headman humbly approached Vangellis and asked him to conduct funerals on behalf of the villagers, who counted two of their own among the dead. Vangellis seemed strangely reluctant, but after some hesitation he agreed, to the

obvious relief of the headman. Thomas was surprised by his reticence—he was, after all, a monk. But there was much that Thomas
found difficult to understand about Vangellis.

Will gathered the villagers. The local families and those from
neighboring villages huddled together. Many of them sobbed and
wailed piteously. The deaths had added further grief to their already
difficult lives. Not all among the visitors were personally affected, but
every one of them appeared downcast. Thomas was not surprised.
They had come for a feast, not a funeral.

Will also gathered the soldiers, both his own and the baron's. The
baron arrived, too, led in by Rufe. The noble glowered darkly but said
nothing. Indeed it was not possible for him to speak. Will had
decided he could not trust the baron to remain silent, and did not
want him disrupting the proceedings. So the man whose pride and
arrogance had led to the deaths stood there with a gag in his mouth,
hands tied behind his back, and a face like thunder.

All of them gathered in the tiny cemetery at one end of the
village, between two deep trenches close by and a larger group of
newly dug graves positioned off to the side. Carefully constructed
wooden crosses adorned the graves of the two villagers. The other
graves, dug for the fallen soldiers, boasted nothing better than rude
crosses fashioned by their comrades from sticks.

Will nodded to Vangellis, and he stepped forward slowly. The
monk seemed ill at ease. He stood with head bowed for so long that
Thomas began to feel uncomfortable. But everyone else seemed to be
waiting respectfully, so Thomas tried to mimic their calm demeanor.

At last Vangellis lifted his head. "All of us must one day face God
to give account. And when we come before him, we do so without the
benefit of earthly rank or status."

Thomas threw a glance across at the baron, who frowned and
mumbled angrily behind his gag.

"All of us have done wrong. We deserve the condemnation of a
just and righteous God," Vangellis continued, coloring as he said it.

"But God offers pardon and hope. Forgiveness, undeserved, and
unearned."

Thomas glanced across at the graves, wondering if every one of the men lying within them was worthy of a free pardon after what they'd done.

The monk walked slowly to the grave of one of the soldiers and lifted the simple cross from the mound, raising it high. "God's gift of life comes through one who was punished in our place. He offers pardon to all who will humble themselves to receive it."

Thomas felt sure he could see tears glistening in the eyes of the monk, but Vangellis again lowered his head, and Thomas could not be certain.

"The promise of resurrection and life forever with God," the monk continued in a low voice.

He uttered some words of ritual, and the mourners filed past the open graves. Then the baron's men were set to work filling them in.

After the last grave had been covered with earth, Will called the baron's surviving soldiers together. Along with the local headman, the headmen of two neighboring villages had been invited to witness Will's conversation. The soldiers stood restless and anxious, uncertain of their fate and bone weary from a night of hard work immediately after a deadly battle. More than half their number now lay under the earth keeping company with generations of departed villagers.

"You have done great wrong here," Will told them. "Not just by attacking the king's commander without reason or provocation, but by actively aiding in the oppression of these villagers. Your duty as soldiers is to protect the defenseless, not to steal from them the necessities of life and rob them of hope. You will carry your shame with you to your graves.

"No such behavior would be tolerated in any soldier of mine. Nevertheless, I recognize that you were doing the bidding of the baron, and it is he who will be primarily held to account.

"All of you have worked hard during the night without shirking or complaint. That counts for something. You have been fortunate to survive. Some of you are wounded, but all of you can ride if you travel slowly. I'm sending you back."

Faces lifted in surprise and relief.

"But you will carry a message to whoever rules in the baron's absence. We will stay here for a time to attend to our wounded. During that period, if any soldier comes within a day's ride of this village, the baron will die immediately.

"When we leave, the baron will go with us. If he survives the journey he will face the king. Our sovereign is a just ruler, and I do not expect him to be pleased with the baron's treatment of those under his protection, nor with the attack on his commander.

"As soon as I have opportunity I will send men to visit this region. If I discover that the abuse of these villagers has continued, I will return. With an army next time.

"Make sure this message is delivered. In full. Do you understand?"

One of the soldiers, an older man, stepped forward. "The message will be delivered, Commander," he said. "I give you my word. We are grateful to you for your mercy."

"Then go in peace," said Will. "Be aware, though, that I will not be so generous next time, if I meet you in similar circumstances.

"May you find yourselves serving a better master in the days to come," he concluded.

With that he sent them off. They left with their horses but not their weapons.

Once they had gone, Will turned to Thomas.

"I have a task for you, Thomas. The baron's former soldiers," he said, jerking his head in the direction of the newly filled graves, "won't be needing their mounts anymore. I'm giving them to the villagers. I want you to show them how to care for horses. There should be time for you to teach a few of the basics of riding, too."

He turned to Nestor. "Have you spent time behind a plow?"

"Almost from the time I could walk," the veteran confirmed.

"Then show the villagers how to harness their new horses to their plows. Maybe we can still bring some good out of this...this nightmare," he concluded, waving his hand vaguely around the village.

Following his gaze Thomas could still see remnants of the recent battle. A few trees bristled with stray arrows, the dirt was stained with dark blood in many places, and discarded shields and weapons lay in piles where the villagers had stacked them. Even a few signs of the feast remained, incongruous amidst the detritus of war and the fresh mounds of earth.

Nestor pointed over to the pile of weapons. "Are you going to give them to the villagers as well? We could show them how to defend themselves."

Will shook his head. "There won't be a future for these villagers if they try to fight their local lord. If they put all of their energy into farming they'll survive. With the help of the horses they might even thrive if the new lord gives them half a chance.

"No," Will continued, "it will be up to us to make sure they're treated properly and well defended."

Elbruhe had not attended the funerals; she remained with the wounded. Vangellis joined her as soon as the ceremony was over.

"Let's go check on Ander and Rellan," said Will, setting off for the hut that had been turned over to the monk to care for the wounded.

Following the example of their commander, Thomas and the others turned their backs on the dead and set their faces toward those who might still benefit from their help.

27

The battle for the village was over, won decisively by Will and his men. The battle for Ander's life had just begun. The outcome of this latest struggle was far from certain.

The monk had been kept busy throughout the night. Rellan's left forearm had been broken in the dying stages of the fight, and Vangellis quickly set it and applied a splint. A few villagers and a number of the baron's soldiers had also required treatment for various wounds.

The best of his attention, though, had been devoted to Ander, who lay unconscious and weak, barely clinging to life. Ander had been stabbed repeatedly before Nestor was able to drive off his attackers, and he had lost a lot of blood.

Vangellis bound up his wounds and staunched the flow of blood. Most of all the monk now feared fever and the wounds turning septic. He brewed a fragrant potion consisting of feverwort and a number of other herbs, and with the help of Elbruhe delivered it persistently into the mouth of the stricken soldier. At least some of the broth went down each time Ander swallowed.

The monk had also prepared a noxious-smelling paste. He

applied it liberally to long strips of cloth which he used as poultices when dressing the wounds.

Thomas, who had come to the hut with the others and contrived to stay on when they left, watched the process as closely as he dared. He knew he would be instantly dismissed if he got in the way, so he sat quietly in a corner and tried to remain as unobtrusive as possible. The truth was that he had never had an opportunity like it to study Elbruhe unobserved, and he watched her delicate movements with wide-eyed fascination as she attended her patient. She was so completely absorbed in the task before her that she never noticed her audience, nor the rapt attentiveness that accompanied her every gesture and sigh.

The young woman in turn, while never neglecting the soldier, seemed to be focusing almost her entire attention on the monk. Neither of them said more than an occasional word, but she seemed to anticipate his needs, handing him dressings or instruments almost before he reached for them.

How had the monk managed to capture her interest so entirely? Thomas felt a pang of jealousy as he pondered this important and seemingly unanswerable question.

His new train of thought caused him to begin studying Vangellis himself. Thomas's own attentions were now divided between Elbruhe and the monk, just as the girl's were divided between the monk and Ander. Vangellis, though, allowed himself no distractions. His attentions were concentrated exclusively on his patient.

It occurred to Thomas that the tireless efforts of Vangellis were bent entirely on the recovery of his onetime persecutor, the man who had so callously plunged him into his own near-fatal crisis. If the monk felt even the slightest animosity toward Ander, he showed no sign of it.

The others occasionally appeared in the room. Most often it was Will and Nestor, and early in the evening Thomas decided to leave with them after one of their visits. He was beginning to feel hungry and tired.

"What do you think, Nes?" Will asked, once they were clear of the hut. "Will they be able to save him?"

Nestor paused for a moment, then simply shook his head.

At that moment animated noises came from another hut where the baron was being held. Will frowned darkly, and made as if to go in there. But with an effort he restrained himself.

"Perhaps our noble guest is less than satisfied with his accommodations," he said tightly. "Could you please take a turn at watching him, Thomas?"

"Yes, of course."

Thomas went to the hut, ducked his head and entered. The interior was illuminated by the red glow from a small fire which provided warmth as well as light. The baron was chained to the central pole of the hut, secured by an ankle iron.

The baron had not been at all pleased about being chained. Thomas witnessed the whole incident. An old woman had produced the chain. She put it into Will's hands and left without a word.

Will sought out the headman, showing him the chain and asking about the woman. "Baron put this on 'er husband as punishment," the headman had explained. "'er man was old and frail, but Baron 'ad 'im chained to a post out in the open. Middle o' winter. When Baron left we built a small shelter round 'im. But Baron's men came back later. Tore it down. Tried to shelter 'im 'erself, she did. But 'e didn't survive for long. The cold nearly got 'er, too.

"No blacksmith 'ere. So we 'ad to cut off 'is foot. To get 'im free, y' see, so we could bury 'im. We never told 'er. Terr'ble sick, she was. Almost died."

Will had clearly been sickened by the cruelty of the punishment. "What crime had the man committed?" he asked.

"'e didn't bow when Baron rode past. Couldn't do it, y' see. Twas 'is back. Gave out years ago. Too long workin' in the fields."

Will said nothing in response. But he gave the chain to Nestor, who was able to release the ankle lock. Then Will took the chain and clapped the iron onto the baron's ankle himself, securing his hands firmly in front of him with a length of rope.

The baron had plenty to say about it. The commander had little patience for his ranting or for his threats. When he showed no signs of subsiding, Will delivered a couple of stinging slaps to his face and stuffed the gag back into his mouth.

Now, many hours later, the baron did not look quite so lordly. His rich clothes were filthy, and his eyes were wild and staring. The gag was still in place. It must have been very uncomfortable.

Rellan sat in one corner of the hut, pale and clearly in pain. If the baron had been hoping for sympathy from him, he would have been sorely disappointed. Rellan had offered to watch the baron for a few hours, since only Rufe, Nestor, and Kuper were now available for patrol. The injured soldier was clearly reaching the end of his endurance.

"Will asked me to relieve you, Rellan. You need to get some rest."

"Thank you, Thomas," he replied wearily, climbing awkwardly to his feet and leaving the hut without a backward glance.

Thomas sat down, and immediately became aware that the baron was urgently trying to catch his eye. He looked everywhere except at the baron, who began jigging around in an almost maniacal fashion to draw his attention. After a few minutes of this, the situation became ridiculous. Eventually it became maddening.

Finally the inevitable could be denied no longer. Thomas looked at him. The look on the baron's face was so ludicrous that a mad laugh burst from Thomas before he could prevent it. The baron's face instantly turned to fury, which caused Thomas to blush and look away again.

For a few minutes nothing happened. Then the baron apparently mastered himself, and the whole pantomime began again.

When Thomas finally made eye contact with his prisoner again, the baron was desperately trying to communicate something.

"Mmm...mmm. Ummh-mmhh!"

Thomas didn't know what to do. The baron started up again, even more urgent this time. "Mmh! HMM!"

Eventually Thomas realized he was trying to communicate that he wanted the gag removed. That seemed like a bad idea. Thomas decided he should ignore it. But then what if the baron really needed to say something—something important? Would Will be angry when he found out?

After agonies of indecision, Thomas concluded that no real harm could come from letting the baron say what was on his mind. He was in charge—he could take whatever action seemed appropriate. Moving to the baron's side, he removed the gag.

"Untie my hands this instant," demanded the baron in a commanding voice.

The baron was so accustomed to giving orders, and Thomas so accustomed to doing as he was told, that he almost obeyed. Then he checked himself. What would the baron order him to do next? And the man was a prisoner—he wasn't supposed to be giving orders at all.

Thomas sat and did nothing. He watched as the nobleman wrestled with his anger before eventually mastering himself.

"I need to relieve myself," the baron said in a reasonable voice. "I can't do that unless you free me. Please release my arms."

The appeal took Thomas completely by surprise. How could he deny such a request? But what if the baron had trickery in mind? A ruse of some kind would be entirely in character for a man like him.

Not knowing what to say he said nothing. The baron waited for a couple of minutes then repeated his request, this time through gritted teeth, slowly emphasizing each word as if talking to the village idiot. Thomas, thoughts churning with indecision, still remained silent.

Abruptly he thought of a way of being certain about the baron's intentions. He reached down to his pouch and fumbled for the drawstring. Then he noticed his prisoner watching him curiously, and memories of the Earl of Pisander flooded into his mind: 'Boy! What do you have in your pouch? Bring it here at once.'

He released the pouch hastily and resumed his confused silence.

Stealing occasional glances at the baron from the corner of his eye, Thomas could sense a storm brewing. Having seen him in action during the battle, it wasn't hard to imagine that the lord was accustomed to instant obedience whenever he uttered a demand. He had now issued a peremptory command and followed it with a polite request. Thomas had not responded to either of them. Predictably, the baron erupted.

Assaulted by a barrage of expletive-laden threats, and alarmed that the yelling would arouse the entire village, Thomas rapidly came to a decision and acted immediately on it. He attempted to stuff the gag back into the baron's mouth. The nobleman clamped his mouth shut uncooperatively. Thomas drew back the gag. The stream of curses resumed immediately.

But not for long. Guessing what would happen and moving like lightning, Thomas jammed the gag into the newly open mouth.

"MMMHHM! UHMMMM! MMWAHHHMM!"

Apoplectic with rage, the baron's eyes opened so wide they looked like they would pop. Thomas tried his best to settle back down and ignore the wild man before him. Many tense minutes passed before the storm appeared to subside.

Then Thomas noticed a dark stain appear on the baron's clothing and slowly spread downward. Startled, he looked at the man's face. The baron had turned beet red and tears of frustrated fury welled in his eyes. Seeing the state of this previously commanding figure unnerved Thomas completely.

It hadn't been trickery. The baron had made the most basic and reasonable of human requests and he had denied it. He knew about the cruelty of the man, and his head told him he deserved this and much, much more. But he was a nobleman. Nobody treated nobles like this and got away with it. What would the king say when the baron told him how he'd been humiliated? What would the consequences be for Thomas? But it was too late to repair the situation now.

The baron finally subsided completely. It was a good thing, too, because Thomas could no longer meet his eye. He didn't dare even to glance at the man. Time continued to pass, slowly and agonizingly.

Will had not forgotten Thomas, though. Eventually an old woman arrived in the hut. She came to Thomas, not speaking, but patting him on the shoulder and waving him to the door. He recognized her as the one who had given Will the chain. Her weathered face crinkled into a sad and toothless smile as he wearily dragged himself to his feet.

As he left he saw her settle herself down. She didn't avoid the baron's eye. She fixed him with a stony glare, and he averted his gaze.

For Thomas, this guard duty proved to be one of the most miserable experiences of his life. It was dark when he finally emerged from the hut, and he looked expectantly to see the first signs of dawn in the sky. He was surprised to learn he had only been in there for three or four hours. The sun would not be rising for many hours yet.

He hadn't eaten, but he didn't feel hungry. He dragged himself off to bed and after tossing and turning for a couple more hours eventually fell into a deep and troubled sleep.

WHEN THOMAS ROSE in the morning he realized that he'd seen no sign of Vangellis, and the monk's blanket did not appear to have been disturbed. No one was in the hut, but once again fresh milk had been left along with a small lump of bread. He gulped down the milk and hungrily bit into the bread as he pushed outside. A dull morning awaited him, with dark clouds rolling across the sky from the west. Ants swarmed on the ground near the hut, anticipating rain.

Curious about Vangellis, and eager to see Elbruhe, he headed for the hut where he expected to find them, carefully avoiding the place where the baron was being held. He hoped fervently that Will would not ask him to guard the prisoner again, and wondered if he could find a way to say no if he was asked.

Nestor was leaving as he arrived. Belatedly, and somewhat guiltily, it occurred to him to wonder if Ander had made it through the night.

"How's Ander, Nes?" he asked.

Nestor screwed up his face and peered up at the sky before turning to him to answer.

"He's alive. Barely. The monk's been up all night with him. Not sure what he's trying to prove. Doesn't owe him any favors."

The soldier spat and glanced at the sky once more before disappearing behind one of the huts.

Before Thomas could step inside he noticed Elbruhe striding purposefully in his direction. He smiled and opened his mouth to greet her, but she ignored him completely, pushing past him into the hut with neither a word nor a backward glance. He frowned, trying to think what he'd done to deserve her reaction. Completely at a loss, he shrugged helplessly, ducked his head and followed her into the hut.

He arrived inside into the middle of an argument. Elbruhe was expostulating fiercely in Rogandan. Her arms were jerking about as she emphatically drove home every point, and her tone was brimming over with emotion. But her voice was lowered so as not to disturb the patient. The scene was almost comical.

Thomas didn't need to understand Rogandan to get the drift of it. Vangellis had been up all night tending to his patient, while Elbruhe finally got some sleep. Now she wanted to reverse the roles. He was politely but firmly refusing to do it. The monk clearly had a stubborn streak, and the girl's best efforts made no difference at all. He wouldn't budge.

Finally, she threw up her hands in exasperation and turned to the patient. Thomas at last remembered Ander, and looked across at the soldier.

What he saw shocked him. If the man had seemed pale and weak before, he now appeared almost spectral. Thomas had seen corpses before, and Ander's sallow complexion reminded him of a corpse.

Vangellis knelt at his head gently mopping his brow. Elbruhe was right—the monk looked close to exhaustion himself. His mouth was moving, but Thomas couldn't catch what he was saying. Was he whispering to his patient? Thomas felt a little stupid when he finally figured it out. The monk was praying.

A life and death struggle was being fought in the hut. Ander's life was a small lamp with its oil almost spent and its wick flickering weakly. Vangellis was protecting the tiny flame, shielding it from the elements. The fact that his task seemed utterly hopeless did not appear to dismay him at all.

The monk's face was lit by a number of candles as well as the fire in the hut. But his face almost appeared to have a light of its own. How was that possible? Puzzled, Thomas stared at him intently. He watched closely for many minutes, and with increasing astonishment. It was true—he hadn't imagined it. The monk was, quite literally, glowing. Thomas gazed at him in wonder, feeling like he had never seen him before.

Something strange and beyond his comprehension was taking place in that room. Thomas was superstitious of course. He had a robust fear of God, sometimes remembered to pray to the saints—especially when he was in trouble—and had enough sense to be terrified of ghosts. What was happening in the hut felt different, though. He was glimpsing something far beyond his grasp, but it made him feel stronger, more hopeful about life.

Although he didn't feel in any way frightened or alarmed, he knew for certain that he did not belong there. His legs carried him from the hut almost involuntarily.

Once outside, the sense of awe quickly began to dissipate. But Thomas had emerged with an unshakable conviction that Ander would recover. He couldn't say why he believed that, and it certainly made no sense. But he didn't doubt it even for a minute.

Humming brightly to himself and with a spring in his step, he set off to check the horses. The sun was setting low in the sky before he realized that Elbruhe had been absent from his thoughts all afternoon, and he hadn't even noticed.

AFTER A DAY and a half of heavy rain the weather cleared. There had been no sign of the baron's soldiers; it seemed that the new steward was taking Will's message seriously. The baron himself was now allowed to spend the daylight hours out of doors. But he was still chained, and anchored to a pole. His gag had been removed on the understanding that he would not speak. He kept his end of the bargain, but his dark looks and threatening demeanor still said plenty to anyone willing to pay attention. As long as he didn't speak, though, Will chose to ignore his behavior.

Many of the villagers avoided him entirely. Even chained he still terrified them. A few paused whenever they passed by and glared at him, though, crossing themselves to ward off evil as they left.

The village was a scene of continuous bustle. Thomas had been teaching the villagers to care for the horses. A few of them could not overcome their fear of the animals, but many others now approached them confidently and were quickly learning how to handle them. In another day or two, Thomas hoped to have three or four of them in the saddle.

Nestor had also begun to show them how to plow their fields behind a horse. The farmers were clearly startled at how much more could be achieved with the help of their new animals. The village was changing before their eyes. The grim faces and the quiet despair that greeted them when they first arrived already seemed a distant memory.

Thomas had not visited Ander again, but he remained eager to know how he was progressing. His companions uniformly predicted a gloomy outcome; Thomas believed otherwise but kept his opinions to himself. Will seemed willing to tolerate a further delay in reaching the king until the situation was resolved. One way or the other it would surely be settled before long.

Late in the second day after Thomas had last seen Ander and the monk, Elbruhe came running out of the hut calling excitedly. No one could understand a word she was saying until Will arrived and relayed her unexpected news. Ander was awake.

All of them ran immediately to the little hut and crammed inside it. Nestor was already there. Elbruhe tolerated the presence of the new arrivals for no longer than a minute before shooing them out again.

They all returned the next day, this time by invitation. Thomas unabashedly pushed his way to the front to get a better look. Ander was not only awake, but sitting up, supported by Elbruhe who had rushed back to his side as soon as her invitation had been delivered. As they arrived she was helping him sip from a bowl filled with steaming broth.

Ander offered them a barely audible greeting and managed a weak smile. The soldiers returned hearty, if muted, congratulations, then lapsed into silence. Thomas could sense their surprise, though. Their companion may have looked frail, but he was very much alive. He even had some color in his cheeks.

Thomas took the opportunity to study the monk closely. He appeared entirely normal. There was nothing unusual about his appearance. Thomas could no longer detect any visible glow from him, but there was a calm composure about his presence that seemed different from before. After a brief smile of greeting he ignored the visitors and quietly went about his business.

The most remarkable change was in Ander. His eyes barely left the monk. Looking at the convalescent soldier, Thomas found himself remembering Ben, his faithful mastiff, lying quietly at his feet attentive to his every movement.

ANDER LEFT the hut for the first time a couple of days later. He was too weak to go far, but everyone was heartened by his obvious progress. Within a week he was able to move about more freely, and Will asked Thomas to assess his ability to ride.

Thomas led Ander to his horse. The animal whinnied in pleasure as its master greeted it and stroked its neck.

"Do you think you'll be able to ride again soon, Ander?"

"My wounds are healing well, but they may open up again if I ride too soon," he replied. "It shouldn't be too far off, though. Maybe three or four days. I'm sure Will is eager to be on the move again."

"Will won't leave until you're ready."

They stood there without speaking for a time. Thomas finally broke the silence.

"It didn't look good for you in there, Ander. But somehow I knew you were going to make it." He wanted to say more, but he couldn't find the words.

"It wasn't good. I was in a very dark place." A faraway look came into Ander's eyes. "I couldn't find my way out. There was a bright light, way off in the distance, but I couldn't get to it. I was lost." Ander paused, remembering. "Then he called me."

"Who?" asked Thomas.

Ander looked at him, uncomprehending.

"Who called you?" Thomas repeated.

"The monk, of course. Brother Vangellis."

Ander turned back to his horse, patting its neck.

Thomas was too shocked to reply. He had never heard Ander even refer to the monk by name, much less use his title.

Before long all the soldiers were calling the monk 'Brother Vangellis'. None of them even seemed aware of the change.

Thomas couldn't bring himself to do it, though. It wasn't any lack of respect. It wasn't actually anything to do with the monk. He'd come face to face with something outside his comprehension, and he couldn't figure out how to respond to it.

If he adopted the monk's title, deep down inside himself he sensed that he would be crossing a threshold. His world would change, and he would change with it.

'Brother Vangellis.' Such simple words. But he couldn't say them.

That left him with a dilemma. He had nothing against the monk, and didn't want anyone to think he was making a point by staying away from his title. He soon discovered, though, that with a little creativity it was possible to avoid referring to a person by name at all.

LATER THAT AFTERNOON they gathered to say goodbye to Rellan and Kuper. Rellan held his arm loosely in a sling. He wouldn't have full use of it any time soon, but he looked a lot brighter even than a couple of days ago.

"Are you sure you want us to leave, Will?" Kuper looked concerned.

"Don't worry about us," Will replied. "With or without you, we can't fight our way through a Rogandan army. And I need you to get to Erestor and find Lord Burtelen. He should have raised an army by now, and we're going to need it.

"Make sure he personally receives the messages I've given you. Hand them over yourself—don't give them to anyone other than him."

"Understood."

Will turned to Rellan and jabbed a finger at him. "I don't want to see you again until you're fully recovered."

Rellan managed a smile. "You'll see me sooner than you think. I won't stay away a minute longer than I need to," he vowed.

The twins eased their mounts forward as everyone called out farewells. As they passed Thomas, Rellan winked at him.

"Stay out of trouble," he grinned, jerking his head toward Elbruhe.

Kuper laughed out loud. Thomas felt a blush coming and hoped no one was watching him too closely.

As THE TWINS spurred their horses and rode out of the village, the baron smirked to himself. This upstart 'commander' didn't have too many soldiers left to command.

Soon they would leave to find the king, and this Will would undoubtedly take him with them. Many long leagues lay between this village and the king, though, and they couldn't expect him to ride while he was chained. An opportunity to escape would present itself, and now there were two enemies fewer to worry about.

He scowled as he thought about his own soldiers. The cowards had made no attempt to rescue him. When he got back to his castle there would be some scores to settle.

His eyes narrowed as he surveyed the village and its inhabitants. They dared to plow their fields with his horses, and stand in judgment over him as they passed by. Their turn would come.

He moved uncomfortably, causing his chains to rattle, which further fueled his anger. So his captors thought they could chain him up like a dog, did they? Commoners and rabble, every one of them. He would find a way to make them pay.

28

A lmost another week passed before they finally left the village. Ander's recovery had progressed remarkably well, and he almost looked his normal self. For his sake, Will refused to consider leaving sooner, but by the end of that time the commander was becoming noticeably restive. He had made certain that all of them were thoroughly prepared in advance so that nothing further would delay their departure.

Although all members of the party now had their own horse to ride, they were still able to leave a dozen animals for the villagers. The locals had selflessly given up some of the horses to neighboring villages. As a result, three villages now had four horses each as well as people trained in the care and use of them. Thomas made sure that each village had more than one mare; in time, small herds could be established.

Adequate supplies of feed would need to be set aside for the winter months, but plenty of suitable fodder grew nearby, and the children could help to gather it. The villagers had already completed the construction of crude stables to shelter their precious new assistants.

Every person in the village turned out to bid them goodbye. By prior agreement, each member of the party had prepared a small gift for their hosts. Thomas gave his favorite horse brush to his hosts. They knew that he was the army's horse master, and understood the value to him of this gift. They thanked him many times.

The old man had a new sparkle in his eyes of late. He came close and pinched the cheek of Thomas affectionately. The old woman embraced him with tears in her eyes. She had spoken several times of her own son, taken from her many years previously to serve the baron. The monk had once asked her if Thomas reminded her of her son, and she readily confirmed his suspicion. Thomas had no difficulty imagining how his own mother might feel in similar circumstances, and he made sure his farewell was warm and unhurried.

All of the villagers approached the monk, bowing and touching his cloak reverently. Some brought children for him to bless. He appeared uncomfortable and embarrassed by the attention. They either didn't notice or didn't care.

As they mounted, the headman approached Will.

"Thank y'. All o' y'," he said, bowing low respectfully. "Don't know 'ow to pay y'. For all y' kindness, y' un'erstand."

"No need for payment," Will replied with a smile. "We're pleased we could do something to help get the village back onto its feet."

The headman bowed low once again.

Then he lowered his voice. "B'ware o' Baron," he confided. "'im'll 'urt y' if 'e can."

"We understand. Thank you for the warning."

Thomas glanced over at the baron, who sat atop his horse with hands tied firmly in front of him and the rope secured to the horn of his saddle. He glared at the villagers and his captors alike with creased brows and open anger on his face. The headman was clearly right. They would need to guard the nobleman like an enemy soldier.

They waved a final farewell, and rode out of the village.

Nestor and Rufe had scouted for many leagues to the north, west and east and discovered no sign of the Rogandans. Based on this information, and after a lengthy consultation with the monk, Will decided to head directly north for Castel to seek out the king. He knew they were very unlikely to be able to avoid the Rogandans entirely. They would need to find a way through Deadman's Pass, and Will fully expected to find it held against them.

The weather remained fine once they cleared the great forest and rode north through open grasslands. For three days they made excellent progress, stopping only briefly to rest their horses and to sleep. They ate and drank during the brief rest breaks, and slept for no more than four or five hours before setting off again before dawn.

By the evening of the third day, both the monk and Elbruhe had become well accustomed to the saddle. Observing them, Thomas felt they looked as though they had been riding most of their lives.

Very little passed between any of them, even when they stopped for the night. Weeks of intensity and high drama had given way to a single focus on reaching the king. Thomas was glad of the respite; he needed time to ponder everything that had happened. His old life in Arnost now seemed like a distant memory. A few weeks ago he hadn't even met some of the people who had now assumed significance in his life—people like the monk, and, well, Elbruhe. He felt himself blushing again, grateful that no one was nearby to notice it.

The baron had scarcely spoken since they left the village. Thomas thought he could see the nobleman's scowl deepening as the leagues rolled away beneath the pounding hooves of their horses. Thomas wasn't the only one aware of it, either—he noticed both Will and Rufe watching their prisoner more closely than ever.

With the forest now far behind them, the riders began to notice a range of mountains off in the distance. The mountains drew ever nearer as they journeyed north. After a few days the terrain was noticeably changing, and there were signs that the grasslands were coming to an end. Before long they found themselves climbing steadily, and encountering isolated stands of trees.

A tree line became visible ahead in the foothills of the mountains and gradually gained definition as they approached. Tall pines stretched east and west as far as the eye could see. Will consulted with Vangellis before deciding that it was time to turn west to find the break in the tree line that signaled the entrance to the pass into Castel.

It was well past noon, with the sun moving steadily across the sky on its way toward the western horizon, when Nestor appeared ahead in the distance, riding hard toward them. It could only mean one thing.

"Head for the tree line!" Will ordered urgently. They turned their mounts north again and dashed for the safety of the trees.

Nestor did not reach them until they had almost made it to the trees. Riders were now clearly visible behind him.

"How many?" Will called as soon as he came into earshot.

"No more than a dozen," he called back. "Others on foot, but far away."

"Follow me!" Will called as they plunged at last into the trees. He led them in deeper until they came to a natural dell, sheltered from sight until they were right upon it.

He called them to a halt, and immediately dismounted. All of them quickly followed his example.

"Thomas, take the horses to the far side of the dell, and try to keep them quiet. Ander, take care of Brother Vangellis and the girl. Take the baron with you. You won't be fighting—I need you to keep them out of harm's way.

"Rufe and Nes, come with me. If they find us, they'll get a warm welcome."

"Commander!" called the baron. "You could use an extra fighter. It's time to put aside our differences for a while. Untie my hands and let me have a sword."

Will turned to the nobleman, and Thomas felt his heart skip a beat. Surely Will would never agree to such an idea.

"When this is over I'll return the sword, and we will continue as before. You have my word. I will put my case before the king."

Thomas glanced from Will to the baron and back again. It was true that they were badly outnumbered, with only three uninjured fighters to defend them all. But surely the baron's promise couldn't be taken seriously.

Will's face set hard. "I don't trust you, Baron. You demonstrated clearly at the village that your word means nothing." He turned to Ander. "Keep him out of sight," he told him.

Ander nodded. "Don't try anything, Baron," he growled.

The nobleman ignored him.

Ander took up a position on the far side of Rufe, directly in front of Thomas and the horses. The baron stood behind Thomas, and Brother Vangellis and Elbruhe positioned themselves at the rear.

Thomas glanced around behind him, eyeing the baron doubtfully. He couldn't help remembering his guard duty in the hut.

Seeing the look on his face, the baron addressed him quietly. "Don't worry, boy. I wouldn't want to see anything happen to you." Then, more quietly, he added "Yet," with a nasty smile.

Thomas faced forward again, sweating uncomfortably and trying hard to convince himself that he could simply ignore the nobleman's words.

They all settled down to wait. Time passed, and Thomas began to hope that they would remain undetected.

Then they heard the voices of their pursuers, calling out to each other as they searched among the trees. Thomas wondered if they would be making so much noise if they had been aware of the reputations of their outnumbered quarry.

The Rogandans drew closer, and one of them soon passed by very close to their hiding place. He didn't enter the dell, though, and Thomas dared to hope the soldier would leave without discovering them.

He stole another glance back at the baron, and was horrified to see the prisoner with a knife, having almost severed the bonds on his hands.

With the Rogandan so nearby, Thomas couldn't call out. Instead, he urgently reached forward to alert Ander.

At that crucial moment, though, Thomas was struck on the head and fell heavily to the ground. Dazed, he picked himself up in time to see the baron mounted, and spurring his horse out of the dell. Clearing their cover the nobleman let forth a shout of challenge that echoed through the trees. The Rogandan immediately turned toward the sound, calling loudly for his companions.

Other soldiers soon appeared. Two of them set off after the baron, whose fleeing form was already lost to sight. The others swarmed into the dell.

One soldier was met by an arrow and tumbled from his horse, dead before he hit the ground. An arrow intended for a second soldier instead took his mount in the neck. The horse screamed and went down, throwing its rider almost at the feet of Will. The commander dispatched him with a single stroke and immediately looked around for new targets.

Another soldier came at Thomas, sword raised to strike. The youth released the horses and threw himself to one side. He escaped the attack, but could only watch helpless as the Rogandan scattered the horses.

The dell soon descended into a chaos of shouting soldiers, flying arrows, and the clash of swords. Thomas remained kneeling where he was, trying to remain inconspicuous.

Nestor got off several more arrows before three soldiers attacked him at once. He was soon fighting for his life.

Another soldier came at Rufe. The giant guardsman ducked under the attacker's wild sword swipe, picked up a branch, and used it to knock the man from his horse. Rufe was on him before he had a chance to get up. He'd barely dealt with this opponent before two more were on him.

Ander also quickly came under attack. He had been assigned the task of protecting the monk and Elbruhe, and he did so with energy that belied his recent injuries. He called anxiously to the monk and the girl, urging them to hide among the trees.

Will much preferred to fight on horseback, and grabbed the reins of a riderless horse and swung himself into the saddle. Rufe soon followed his example, and the two of them rode to the aid of Nestor, who took advantage of the distraction to find a mount himself. Although still heavily outnumbered, they coordinated their efforts to draw the attackers away from Ander and the others. The main conflict soon shifted westward out of sight of Thomas.

The sounds of battle gradually diminished, and Thomas dared to hope that those sheltering in the dell had seen the last of the fighting. He looked around, trying to locate each of his companions. The monk was nowhere to be seen, but he spotted Elbruhe not far away, peering cautiously from behind a tree. Ander leaned on his sword, breathing hard. He had fought bravely and effectively, but it had clearly taken a big toll on his reduced resources.

One riderless horse wandered nearby, and Thomas quickly secured it. He could see no sign of the other horses, but he decided not to go searching for them until the outcome of the battle was decided. They probably weren't too far off. He peered off into the trees to the west, looking for any sign of returning soldiers.

Ander shouted a sudden warning and moved to engage a Rogandan soldier who rode in from the opposite direction. Thomas, still holding the reins of the horse, drew back and watched the conflict from a safe distance. Ander soon showed himself to be the more experienced fighter, but his reactions had slowed, and the other soldier made up for his lack of skills with a seemingly endless supply of energy. Thomas felt confident about the ultimate outcome, but nothing could be taken for granted.

Totally absorbed in the scene before him, Thomas was startled into sudden alertness by a high-pitched cry, "TO-MMAAASSS!" He spun around in time to see a second Rogandan spurring his horse toward him, a spear pointed at his heart. He threw himself frantically out of the way, barely avoiding the spear thrust. Without Elbruhe's warning he could not have escaped.

He scrambled quickly to his feet, ready for a second attack, but the rider had already turned aside to pursue a new target. Thomas watched with helpless horror as the soldier overtook the fleeing form of Elbruhe and ran her through.

Heart pounding and screaming her name, he ran to her side, utterly heedless of his own safety. He reached her in a moment and knelt beside her.

Ander, having dealt with his previous opponent, appeared on horseback and chased the attacker out of the dell. Thomas did not even notice.

Elbruhe lay face down, with blood soaking the clothing on her back around a gaping wound. He gently turned her toward him onto her side. She gazed uncomprehending up into his face for a moment, then life flickered briefly in her eyes. A crooked smile passed across her lips. "Delou-ahn," she murmured.

His anguished tears blinded him as he sat down and drew her to himself. Hopelessly he racked his brains, trying to imagine some way to staunch the bright red flow from her back. But no answers came, and he simply clung to her.

Then he felt her body relax. She sighed, a long and weary sigh, and breathed no more.

A tight knot came into his throat, and bitter tears flowed freely, dripping down onto her face. He sat unmoving, cradling her head in his lap. Entirely unconscious of his surroundings, he saw only her face, peaceful at last, and her empty staring eyes.

HE WAS STILL THERE when Vangellis found him. The flow of tears had ceased, and he sat numb and unmoving, unaware of the world around him, as if frozen in time.

Vangellis drew close, and, reaching down, gently closed her eyes. Thomas started as if slapped, and looked up at the monk. Their eyes met, and, finding compassion and grief in the eyes of another who had truly cared about the girl, he was completely undone. He began to weep loudly.

The monk bent low once more and carefully removed the burden from his lap. Then, drawing Thomas to his feet, he enfolded him in a giant bear hug.

Thomas abandoned himself to his grief then and wept without constraint, his entire body wracked with heaving sobs. Vangellis held him tightly.

In time the torrent ceased, and Thomas, once more calm, stepped back from the monk. He didn't understand how, but it felt like he had been washed clean inside. His grief had not left him, but he was surprised to discover that he felt some measure of peace.

They stood without speaking for a time.

Finally the monk spoke up. "We can't stay here, Thomas," he said. Then almost to himself he continued, "But I won't leave her like that."

He turned to Thomas and asked him, "Will you help me prepare a grave?"

Thomas simply nodded in response.

They set out together to find a suitable resting place. Before long they came upon a grassy sod beside a small stream where wildflowers covered the ground, pale and delicate. Neither of them spoke—they didn't need to. This was the spot.

Thomas returned to the dell and retrieved a fallen spear. He marked out a section of ground and used the spear to begin carefully removing the turves. He put the grass and the flowers to one side and began digging into the moist soil underneath. The monk got down on hands and knees to help him.

After thirty minutes they had laid bare a shallow grave. They went together to the dell and retrieved her body, carrying it to the open grave and lovingly positioning it within. Then Vangellis led Thomas to the stream, and they rinsed their clothes as best they could, staining the clear water bright red. Thomas did it absently, his thoughts far away.

The monk fashioned a small cross from wood, securing the pieces with tough twine torn from a creeper. He placed it into the ground above her head.

"I will not leave Elbruhe to the harsh mercies of her Dark Gods," he said quietly, as if speaking to himself aloud. "She questioned me many times about our own God—he had captured her imagination, and, I believe, her heart, and it is into his gracious hands that I commend her spirit."

He said much more, speaking of hope and of a final resurrection. But Thomas heard little of it. His mind wandered down pathways of the past, remembering an independent spirit, a face framed by wild hair, the lash of a sharp tongue, and the weary attentiveness of a nurse laboring through the night. Most of all he thought about everything she had come to mean to him, and the magnitude of what he had so suddenly and irrevocably lost.

Then they slowly covered her body with the moist earth, repositioning the turves on top of the mound. Thomas could not bring himself to cover her head. He turned aside while Vangellis completed the task.

Thomas lingered by the graveside, unable to will himself to embrace the future. Vangellis disappeared, perhaps wanting to allow him some solitude.

The monk returned after about an hour, holding the reins of a horse.

"I found him wandering nearby," he explained. "Do you think you could find us another one?"

Thomas did not respond immediately, but finally he nodded and accepted the reins offered by Vangellis. He mounted the horse and set off.

He did not want to stop thinking about Elbruhe and his loss, and he felt almost guilty about focusing on anything else. But at the same time it was a relief to have something to do.

He began his search at the dell, carefully avoiding the place where Elbruhe had fallen. A number of bodies lay there, and he belatedly and guiltily wondered what had become of his other companions. All of the slain wore Rogandan garb, which came as a relief to him. Seeing them lying there evoked no response at all in him. That in itself felt strange given the intensity of the grief he had just experienced. He clicked his tongue and guided his horse away from the dell. He didn't look back.

Another horse was grazing quietly not far away, and he took its reins and led it back to the stream. Vangellis knelt beside the grave with his head bowed, apparently praying. Thomas was not willing to disturb him, but one of the horses whinnied and shook its head, causing the monk to look up.

The monk joined him and accepted the reins, swinging himself into the saddle. They both sat silently on their horses for many minutes. Then Vangellis turned his horse's head and slowly headed off through the trees.

After pausing a moment longer, Thomas followed him. *I won't ever forget you*, he promised silently, brushing at the new flow of tears that welled up in his eyes and trickled down over his cheeks.

"THOMAS! LOOK, A RIDERLESS HORSE," Vangellis called. Thomas peered in the direction he was pointing and saw the animal through the trees off to their left.

"We'd better remove its saddle and bridle," the youth replied. "If the reins get caught in some branches the horse will starve."

They picked their way through the trees and emerged into a small clearing.

"We seem to have found its rider," said the monk, pointing to a figure lying face down on the ground.

Even from a distance Thomas could see that it was the baron. At the sight of their betrayer Thomas felt intense anger rising up within him. He wanted to hurt the man, to make him pay.

He dismounted and marched over to the baron, bending down and flipping him onto his back. He stepped back at once, retching involuntarily.

The baron was dead. His killers had not treated him kindly. He lay with his intestines hanging out and the ground soaked with his blood. The look on his face made it obvious that he had died a particularly painful death.

Vangellis came to his side and winced. "They certainly made a mess of him," he exclaimed. "A terrible way to die, poor fellow," he concluded.

Thomas glared at him. "Poor fellow?" he said indignantly. "He deserved everything he got and more! Elbruhe would be alive right now if it wasn't for him!"

To his annoyance, he felt his lower lip tremble uncontrollably as he spoke her name. His own weakness made him angrier than ever. "I hate him! I hate the sight of him," he spat. He turned away and paced up and down restlessly, trying to master his feelings.

After a few minutes he looked back and saw the monk gathering rocks into a pile at the baron's head.

Seeing him looking on, Vangellis paused for a moment. "The ground is very hard here," he said. "We can't dig a grave without tools. I'm planning to cover him with branches. Would you like to help me?"

"No! I won't do anything for him. The vultures can have him if they want. They'll probably choke on him!"

Thomas turned angrily on the monk. "Why are you doing this for him? I know you cared about her." His lip betrayed him again and forced him to silence, tears of frustration welling in his eyes.

"Yes, I cared about her," Vangellis acknowledged. He paused, a thoughtful look on his face. "You're going to have to forgive him, Thomas."

"Forgive him?! Never!" Thomas vowed fiercely. "I'll hate him until the day I die."

"He's beyond your hatred now."

"I don't care. After what he did, he doesn't deserve to be forgiven. Ever!"

The monk did not respond for a full minute. Then he said softly, "Do all of *your* actions deserve forgiveness, Thomas? Have you never given anyone reason to hate you for what you did to them?"

Thomas looked at him sharply, expecting accusation but finding no sign of it in the monk's eyes. If anything, Vangellis looked ashamed.

Thomas opened his mouth to absolve himself, but an image came flooding into his mind. He saw a pitchfork, saw himself lunging with unbridled rage, to hurt, to wound. He remembered the terror in Simon's eyes.

He clamped shut his mouth and turned away.

Somehow his fierce anger toward the baron had ebbed away, but a stubbornness rose up in its place. He would not forgive. He would *never* forgive.

The monk resumed his labors without assistance from Thomas. The youth instead busied himself with the stray horse.

As Thomas waited for Vangellis to finish, the reality of their situation gradually sank in. They had no idea what had become of Will and Rufe and the others. If any Rogandans appeared they would find themselves undefended. Even the baron had been armed with a knife and trained to defend himself; their prospects would be worse than his.

Thomas started to become restless. Vangellis was taking too long.

Finally he could wait no longer. "We need to go!" he said, unable to keep a tone of irritability out of his voice. "It isn't safe here."

The monk must have decided he'd done enough, because almost immediately he ceased his efforts. He stood by the graveside with head bowed for a few moments then turned away and mounted his horse. They picked their way out of the small clearing and resumed their journey. They were heading away from their friends, but Thomas felt confident that Nestor could track them wherever they went. Assuming he was still in a position to do so.

They traveled for about an hour, with Vangellis taking the lead. As much as possible they stayed among the trees, and saw no one. By then the light was fading fast.

The monk brought his horse to a stop and turned to Thomas.

"We have no way of knowing what's happened to Will and the others," he said. "I don't doubt for a minute that they're still alive. And they will come looking for us.

"They will follow us because they feel responsible for our safety. But the truth is that I have become a burden to them. They no longer need my services as a guide. The pass to Castel is somewhere nearby, and they know which direction to take to find it. And once Will rejoins the king he will have his choice of local guides.

"What about you, though, Thomas? I know you have a long-standing friendship with both Will and Rufe, and you are the army's horse master. But why did they bring you on such a perilous journey? Do you have some key role to play that I am not aware of? Or did they bring you away from Arnost to protect you from something or someone?"

The monk's questions shocked Thomas. His guesses were close to the mark—uncomfortably so. Was the reality of his situation this obvious to everyone? Or was the monk simply an exceptionally shrewd observer?

Vangellis had also raised an uncomfortable question. Was he himself also a burden to Will? He knew that Will and Rufe, and the others, too, would defend him without hesitation. Even if it put their own lives at risk. Surely that made him a liability, because he could offer little in return. They had no need of his particular skills with horses. And the stone was of little use out here, even if he could be confident it would work reliably for him.

Then he found himself wondering if he should have tried the stone on the baron. Perhaps he could have anticipated his treachery and saved Elbruhe's life. But even in his grief Thomas could see that playing guessing games with the past was pointless. The past could not be changed. What was done was done.

Vangellis still waited patiently for a response. And Thomas discovered that his perspective had undergone a major shift.

"It isn't just you," he acknowledged. "I'm a burden to them as well."

"Then I have a suggestion," Vangellis told him. "The others will catch up with us tomorrow if we rest tonight, and we will rejoin them and continue to slow them down.

"But there is another way. I know of a remote monastery up in the mountains—we can reach it in three or four days. We'll be safe from the Rogandans there. Our friends will no longer need to worry about us."

"But will they know we've gone somewhere safe?"

"They won't know for certain. I think they will guess, though."

"I hope you're right. Will needs to join the king. He needs an army."

"The monastery, then?" Vangellis asked.

"The monastery," Thomas agreed.

29

"It happened over here." Ander led them to the place where Elbruhe had lain.

"She's been moved," said Will.

"You're right," Nestor affirmed, and immediately set off, head down, following the trail of blood.

They followed the trail for several minutes. "Thomas couldn't have carried her this far on his own," Rufe asserted.

"No," Will agreed. "Brother Vangellis must have been here, too."

They soon found themselves in a small clearing beside a stream, looking at a new mound with a small cross at its head. They dismounted and stood in silence, taking in the scene.

"It was a brutal end to a harsh life."

The others looked at Will in wonder, astonished at the tremulous tone of his voice, and even more surprised to see the tears that trickled down his cheeks.

Finally Rufe spoke up. "They chose a peaceful place to lay her to rest, though," he offered.

"They did," Will agreed firmly, his voice steady again.

They stood without speaking for many minutes.

"Brother Vangellis would have seen her off properly," Ander said finally.

The others nodded their agreement.

Will turned away from the grave. "We can't delay longer. Let's find out what's become of our Thomas and Brother Vangellis," he said.

They mounted and headed off after Nestor who had already found the trail and was following it swiftly on foot, leading his horse.

They followed only for a short time before Nestor halted.

"They turned aside here," he announced, "before continuing on their original path."

They followed him into a small clearing. A small pile of rocks had been fashioned into a simple cairn, and a small mound lay beneath it. A horse grazed beside the mound.

The mound proved to be mostly fallen tree branches and leaves. They removed a few of the branches and found a body freshly laid out beneath the pile. It was the baron.

"Looks like the Rogandans have saved our king some trouble," Nestor suggested dryly.

"This fool has cost us far too much time and loss already. Let's be on our way," said Will, throwing a branch or two back onto the mound.

"The horse?" asked Rufe.

"It can go wherever it wants to," he replied. "Looks like Thomas already removed the saddle and bridle," he concluded, pointing to some items lying on the other side of the cairn.

The afternoon light failed and quickly gave way to dusk, forcing them to abandon the search until daylight. They ate slowly and lay down to sleep as soon as Will had assigned each of them a turn at sentry duty through the night. After the riding and the fighting that lay behind them they were soon asleep.

In the morning Nestor led them on. The trail was going cold, and he consulted with the others more than once before leading them forward. He always found the right path.

The afternoon was wearing on when they finally halted before a rocky incline.

"They're a long way ahead of us," Nestor said. "They must have traveled on during the night."

"The monk knows his way around," Will replied.

"I suspect we'll find that they abandoned their horses here," Nestor suggested. "The trail goes on and up, and they were traveling by foot."

"I think I know where they're going," said Will. "There's a remote monastery somewhere up there in the mountains. Brother Vangellis will certainly know where to find it."

He paused for a moment, then continued. "We're not going to follow them any further. We no longer need a guide, and Thomas will be safer there than anywhere we might take him."

Rufe nodded. "Young Thomas'll be all right. He's in good hands."

"None better," Ander agreed.

"Then let's not delay any longer," Will concluded. "It's time we found the king."

THOMAS and the monk had been climbing steadily throughout the afternoon. Their progress was slower now, since they were traveling on foot.

They had set the horses free as soon as the going became difficult for the animals. Vangellis explained that the monastery did not maintain food or shelter for horses, so there was little point in keeping them any longer than they were useful.

When they paused for a meal late in the day, Thomas discovered to his dismay that they were eating the last of their provisions.

"How are we going to survive without food?" he demanded.

Vangellis, who appeared entirely unconcerned about their predicament, paused in his eating and gazed across at Thomas.

"Three or four days without food would do us no real harm. It might do us some good. Perhaps it would help us remember the lot of those who never have enough to eat."

Thomas colored, remembering the way his hosts in the village watched him eat the bread.

"But you need not worry," the monk continued with a smile. "I have spent many years wandering alone in many different places, and I have learned where to find things to eat. We will not go hungry.

"I also know how to keep us safe from any predators that might be roaming these mountains. Apart from predators of the human variety, that is," he added seriously.

They lit a small fire that night. Vangellis chose dry wood that gave off little smoke, but they had spent the entire day climbing ever upward through difficult terrain, and the likelihood of anyone coming upon them seemed very remote indeed.

Once he lay down, Thomas fell quickly into a deep sleep. He dreamed that he was riding alone across open grasslands. He was going somewhere on an important errand, but he couldn't quite remember what it was. Soon he came to a wide and swiftly flowing river. He could see no place to safely cross it, but for some reason it seemed important to do so.

He dismounted and led his horse down to the water's edge to take a drink. Then he heard a voice calling his name.

"TO-MMAAASSS!"

He looked up, startled, and saw Elbruhe standing on the opposite bank of the river. She was calling to him, urgently trying to tell him something. But he could barely hear her over the noise of the water, and he couldn't understand a word she was saying, anyway.

Impulsively, he mounted his horse and rode it into the river. There was no other way to cross. The horse struck out strongly for the other bank, but they were quickly caught in the current, and swept downstream.

Thomas turned his head to keep his eyes on Elbruhe, but her form dwindled rapidly in size and soon disappeared from sight. He faintly heard her call his name one last time, "Toooommmmaaasss...!"

He woke with a start and sat up, panting for air. The night was cold, but he found himself covered with sweat.

Everything around him was still pitch black. Stars twinkled high overhead, but as yet no glow had appeared in the eastern sky.

Then he heard a strange wailing sound. Could it be Elbruhe calling him? Then he remembered that she was dead. The hairs tingled on the back of his neck.

The fire had burned down, and only coals remained. In the dim light he could see no sign of Vangellis. The monk was not there.

He heard the sound again. This time it seemed more clearly human, more anguished. Had Vangellis gone to identify the source of the noise? He had a feeling that the monk would not be frightened by strange cries in the night.

He got up and crept carefully in the direction he had heard it coming from. Once he was away from the glow of the embers his eyes gradually adjusted to the darkness. He picked his way among the trees until he came to a clearing.

An indistinct form was faintly visible across the clearing from him. Sobs shook the dark frame, punctuated occasionally by a low wailing. He had found the monk.

Thomas stood there for a few minutes, uncertain how to respond. Did the monk need his help in some way? Or would he feel that Thomas was spying on him?

Eventually he took the easiest solution and quietly slipped away. He returned to the campsite and lay down again beside the coals. But he could not get back to sleep. He lay awake, picturing the monk sobbing alone in the clearing, and wondering what could have reduced him to such a state of distress.

The first hint of dawn finally began to glow in the eastern sky. A dark mass of clouds overhead had hidden the stars; the clouds slowly became visible, their outlines tinged with orange and yellow. As the light grew in strength the colors became richer and more varied. Captivated by the display, Thomas for a moment forgot all else in the extravagant dawning of a new day.

The light grew brighter, and the vivid colors slowly yielded to bold whites and grays. With the performance coming to an end, Thomas began to find it increasingly difficult to understand how such beauty could coexist so casually with the pain and loss in the world. How could God send a sunrise like that after the brutality of Elbruhe's death?

The sun had cleared the treetops before the monk returned to the campsite. He showed no signs of his pre-dawn distress. In fact he appeared more peaceful and composed than Thomas had ever remembered him.

"I've brought some berries," the monk announced with a smile, revealing a dark blue treasure trove secreted in a fold of his cloak. "They're delicious," he promised. The blue-stained teeth exposed by his grin amply reinforced his assertion.

Thomas tried one, and they were indeed delicious. The two of them quickly disposed of the pile, and both sat back sighing contentedly.

Vangellis was different—that much was obvious—and Thomas was very curious to know the reason. But he didn't quite know how to approach the subject. After a moment's reflection he decided to ask about something that had baffled him for quite some time.

"Why did Ander hate you so much?" he asked.

The monk didn't answer immediately. He sat gazing up into the sky for so long that Thomas began to wonder if he'd heard the question.

"I'm not sure," Vangellis finally offered. "Perhaps someone he cared about had been treated badly by a member of the clergy. When that happens, it's easy to just lump all of us in together. You find a worm in your apple, and you lose your taste for apples."

He paused again.

"And when he first met me I would have given him no reason at all to question his assessment," he acknowledged with a sad smile.

"He doesn't think that way now, though."

"No," the monk agreed. "He doesn't hate me anymore."

He fell silent again, and his eyes narrowed, apparently remembering the events in the village.

"He couldn't hate you after you healed him."

The monk shook his head. "I didn't heal him. God did that."

Vangellis must have been in a talkative mood, because almost without pause he continued.

"When Ander first woke up, Nestor was in the room. He never says much, as you know. But he had a few things to say to Ander. He told him that everyone else had long since given him up for dead. Said he'd asked me what I was trying to prove, staying up day and night caring for him. Told Ander he owed me a debt he could never repay. Then he got up and left the hut.

"It was nonsense, of course. Ander owed me nothing. And I told him as much after Nestor had gone.

"Ander didn't seem surprised by any of it. He never said a word; he just took it all in. But he followed me everywhere with his eyes. He looked like he was...well, I can't quite describe it."

"I know what you mean," Thomas said. "He was in awe of you."

The monk clearly found that thought uncomfortable. "He came to trust me," he countered. "I think that was the main thing that changed."

The conversation lapsed for a while, and they sat in silence.

After some time, Vangellis turned to Thomas.

"Did I disturb you last night?" he asked directly.

Thomas felt himself flushing a bit, and didn't immediately answer.

"I'm sorry I interrupted your sleep," the monk continued, not offering Thomas an opportunity to deny it.

"Something happened last night," he said tentatively. He paused for a while, then apparently decided to speak more freely.

"A lot has happened to me since Will dragged me from my bolt hole at the monastery. I was very unhappy about it at the time, but I'm grateful to him now.

"To begin with, Ander showed me a great kindness by depriving me of my wineskins. Perhaps kindness wasn't his intention at the time, but the truth is that anything I've done for him since was merely a partial repayment for the greater good he'd already done for me.

"Then we went to the village. I have visited many such villages, and seen similar oppression, although thankfully not often quite that bad. But those people needed help, help that I could offer. Help that I had *vowed* to offer. I managed to escape reality in the monastery, but I couldn't escape it there in the village.

"Then came the opportunity to care for Ander." He paused and gazed heavenward again. "Showing love in practical ways to people who hate you changes you as well as them," he said quietly.

"Then there was the fight. And the loss of Elbruhe. She had suffered so much during her life and received so little. But she gave whatever she could so unstintingly. It was a slap in the face to me. I had tried to escape from the world—to escape something I'd done. I ran away like a coward."

He turned to Thomas, a look of determination on his face.

"I'm through with running. I won't do it anymore."

Thomas didn't know what to say, so he said nothing.

"I need you to understand that, Thomas. Because I'll need to leave you at some point."

At this last statement, Thomas's reaction changed instantly from curiosity to alarm. Will and Rufe were now far away. He had left them out of a selfless desire to release them. But he had done so knowing he wasn't alone. He had lost Elbruhe, lost his friends, and now the monk was planning to abandon him, too.

"So you're going to leave me alone in this wilderness?" he blurted out.

"No, no! Of course not. I won't suddenly desert you," the monk assured him hastily.

Then he sighed. "I suppose I will have to tell you the whole story," he said. "I think after all this time I need to get it out of me, anyway. Are you willing to hear it?" he asked.

Thomas nodded, his curiosity aroused.

"I knew from my youth that I had a calling on my life," the monk began. "My father was a farmer, and he was a good man. But I had no desire to follow him, even though my family had farmed for generations.

"I took my vows on my twentieth birthday, and became apprenticed to an older man who had been serving as a monk all of his life. He was a kind and humble man, and I traveled with him for almost ten years, observing him and learning from him as he cared for the poor and spent his life in service. God was not an idea to him—he was a master like no other and his truest friend.

"I remained with him until he died, full of years and mourned by all who had known him. He had run the race and finished well, and I was filled with the desire to emulate him and his life of service.

"I believe I began well, too. For many years I traveled far and wide, doing whatever I could to care for those in need. There has never been a shortage of such people. I tried to bring God's hope to those who had no hope and to anyone who would receive it.

"I even traveled into foreign lands, learning something of their language and customs. Whenever I was welcomed by a man or woman of peace, I stayed for a time, then moved on."

"Is that how you got your reputation as a guide?" Thomas asked.

"I suppose so," Vangellis replied. "I certainly had opportunity to visit many different places over the years.

"At one time I found myself back in a particular region of Arvenon. People were surrounded by plenty, but suffering greatly. The local lord was not a good man; our own Baron Rudungen was an uncomfortable reminder of him.

"One day I came upon him by accident. A young woman in a nearby town had caught his eye and aroused his lust, and he had waited until she was alone and unprotected. She was little more than a girl. He was intent on taking from her by force what she clearly was unwilling to offer him freely.

"I knew this girl, and I could not bear to see her brutalized. I remonstrated with the nobleman, and he slapped me to the ground, vowing that he would have his way with her. He gloated that he had done the same many times and would do so many more. He boasted loudly that no one dared prevent him, even if they had the means.

"The girl had taken the opportunity to run off, and was nowhere to be seen. He turned his back on me, cursing, ready to set off after her.

"Something rose up in me. I decided that I had to save her, so I picked up a rock and struck him on the back of the head. He went down hard, and didn't get up.

"When I examined him I saw immediately that he was dead. Having cared for many sick people, I knew the signs. So I hid his body and left.

"It was a great mystery to everyone when he didn't appear. The girl was not suspected, since no one apart from me even knew that he had seen her. She wasn't aware of what I'd done. I wasn't suspected, either—none of the people, great or small, imagined even for a minute that I was capable of murder."

He paused and looked across at his companion. "Yes, Thomas," he said sadly, "I'm sorry to say that you're wandering the wilderness with a murderer."

Thomas sat there for a moment, not sure what to say. He simply couldn't see the monk as a bad man. "We've seen a lot of people die," he finally said. "Even a nobleman. Some deserved it, and some didn't. Was it so terrible that this man died? It sounds like he truly did deserve it."

A wry smile appeared on the face of Vangellis. "Are you saying that monks should be allowed to go around killing people, as long as the people are bad enough?"

"No, of course not! But it seems like...well, one mistake destroyed your whole life. Was there no way you could be forgiven? Is murder unforgivable?"

"No, that wasn't it. God can forgive murder. The problem is that I wasn't sorry I'd done it."

He paused for a moment.

"I knew that I should turn myself in," he continued, "but I kept putting it off. I tried to carry on with my work, but my heart wasn't in it anymore. You can't break your vows like that and then carry on like nothing has changed.

"I soon discovered that I'd lost all sense of purpose and calling. My life became a pretense, and my own hypocrisy became more than I could stomach. So I moved on, never able to settle, always restless."

He paused again, for longer this time.

"Then I discovered that alcohol can numb the pain and make you forget for a while. After that my downward slide continued faster than ever. Pretty soon I wasn't recognizable as the same person anymore.

"I'd fallen so far there didn't seem to be any way back. Eventually I ended up at the monastery where you found me. I probably would have ended my days there in a drunken stupor if Will hadn't dragged me away.

"Then came the withdrawals, a severe mercy I have Ander to thank for. It was soon followed by the pressing need to care for the helpless, and for a time I forgot myself as I became immersed in exercising my calling once again. Then there was the shock of Elbruhe's death. It confirmed to me that I had truly begun to care again.

"The death of the baron also showed me that I had been changing. He richly deserved punishment, but this time I had no desire to take it into my own hands. I didn't hate him, so he had no hold over me. And his death reminded me that God does not forget to dispense justice, even if it sometimes seems long delayed.

"Last night came the crisis. All this time I have thought myself incapable of repentance, and therefore lost to forgiveness. But I have changed. I'm sorry now that I took justice into my own hands. I repented of murdering the noble, abandoning my vows, and selfishly escaping into oblivion.

"My innocence is gone forever—I can't undo the past. But I can see now that living without integrity was always a choice. I can have my integrity back. Not for free, certainly, but I'm more than willing to pay the price.

"The amazing thing is that I truly know that I am forgiven. And last night I renewed my vows. I shed some tears, but I also had my first taste of real contentment for a very long time."

Thomas could see that Vangellis was, indeed, a different person. He had never seen him so peaceful, so happy.

"So I hope you understand now why I have to go back," he continued. "I must face justice for the murder that I committed."

Thomas found himself unable to respond for some time. Too many thoughts and feelings churned around inside him, and he had no idea what to say. He didn't want to see the monk go back. And he didn't feel at all like he was sitting down with a murderer. He felt like he was in the presence of the safest person he had ever known. He felt like arguing, but it was obvious to him that sooner or later the monk would leave, no matter what he said.

Ander had seen something unique in the monk. Thomas couldn't quite define what it was, but he could see it, too. And Thomas trusted him no less than Ander did.

Eventually he found his voice. "When will you go back?" he asked.

"There's no point in going now," the monk replied calmly. "The Rogandans almost certainly control that part of Arvenon. I'll need to wait until Will finds a way to remove them."

"He will find a way," Thomas asserted.

"I believe he will, too," the monk agreed.

Thomas harbored no doubts at all on that subject. For the first time, though, he found himself with mixed feelings about it.

"I know all this is a lot for you to take in," the monk acknowledged. "But I want you to know that I won't simply abandon you. I will do anything in my power to help you, Thomas."

Thomas replied without hesitation. "And I will do anything I can to help you, too, Brother Vangellis."

30

The going became easier as Thomas and the monk found their way onto an animal trail that was heading in roughly the right direction. After climbing for much of the morning, they were now following the line of a long ridge, and Thomas appreciated the easier going.

He had a lot to think about. The revelations of the previous day offered a new perspective on the monk's actions and behavior, and Thomas felt better able to understand everything that had happened since Brother Vangellis had joined them. At the same time he was still coming to terms with the death of Elbruhe, and struggling to control the ferocity of his own emotions whenever he thought about the baron. Underneath it all lay a nagging uncertainty about his own future. What would become of him?

Wandering along with his mind in another place, he suddenly noticed that the monk had halted abruptly.

"Move backward, Thomas. VERRRYY slowly."

Baffled, Thomas did not instantly obey. He shot a glance at the monk and saw him standing with his posture relaxed but his gaze fixed intensely. He followed the monk's stare. A huge brown bear faced them, less than a stone's throw off the path to his left. The bear stood tall on its hind legs, towering above them. Its mouth hung wide in a menacing snarl. Then, a growl issuing from deep in its throat, it began moving threateningly toward them.

Unreasoning terror gripped Thomas. Heart pounding, he broke into a cold sweat. His first instinct was to turn and run for his life. He would have done so, too, had not the monk opened wide his mouth and begun to sing. The bear halted in its tracks, head bent slightly to one side. Thomas, in amazement, looked first at the bear, then at the monk, then back at the bear again.

Warming to his task, the monk lifted up his voice and sang with complete abandon. He sang of the mountains and the skies, the forest and the plains, the birds of the air and the creatures of the sea. It was a joyous song, a psalm of praise to the Creator. As he sang he waved his arms above his head and swayed slowly from side to side, entering in wholeheartedly with his entire body. The bear stood perfectly still.

The song seemed to go on for hours, although it must surely have been only minutes. Eventually the joyful strains came to an end. The monk closed his mouth and lowered his arms.

The bear lingered until the last notes had died away. Then it dropped onto all fours, turned its back and disappeared off into the trees. For all the world it seemed as if the creature had waited politely for the song to finish before leaving.

"I think we should move off, Thomas. Mr. Bruin might have liked the performance so much he went to gather some friends for another one," the monk said with a smile.

Thomas needed no urging. They set off at a rapid clip, the youth unable to prevent himself from looking back continually over his shoulder.

"I DON'T UNDERSTAND what happened back there," Thomas began.

They sat huddled before a fire as the daylight dimmed around them. Thanks to prodigious efforts on the part of Thomas, it was a very large fire. He had gathered many loads of dead wood into a huge pile, each time forcing himself to go back for more. Whenever he reached down to pick up a branch, he fully expected a bear to appear from behind a tree and rise up to threaten him. He wondered if singing would work for him as well, and racked his brains for suitable songs just in case.

"This isn't the first time I've encountered a bear," the monk replied. "After I first took my vows I was walking in a forest on one occasion. I thought I was alone, and I was singing heartily. Then I looked up and saw a mother bear and her two cubs. My heart almost stopped beating. My singing stopped, too, and the bears didn't seem at all pleased. So I started up again, and they calmed down. I sang every song I could think of, and they gave me a very fair hearing. When I eventually ran out of ideas, they just left."

"So you were never frightened by bears?"

"Actually, the very opposite was true—I'd always been terrified of bears. From a young age I heard stories of the bear that attacked and killed my uncle. And I knew you can't outrun them. So my first bear encounter frightened and encouraged me at the same time."

"Have you met any bears since?"

"Yes. On two occasions. I serenaded my second bear, and we both left satisfied. The third bear wasn't interested in songs. He was hungry, and apparently I looked like food. As he moved in I lectured him sternly, but he wouldn't listen."

"What did you do?"

"I picked up a lump of wood in each hand and laid into him. For his benefit, I also quoted scripture from the book of Proverbs."

"Are you serious?! What did the quote say?"

"The passage says '*My son, do not despise the Lord's discipline and do not resent his rebuke, because the Lord disciplines those he loves*'," the monk replied with a grin. "I swatted him once for every word. We didn't make it to the end of the passage, though."

"Why? What happened?"

"He had a sudden change of heart, and he repented."

The image of Brother Vangellis sternly disciplining an aggressive bear was too much for Thomas. He couldn't help himself. He burst out laughing. The hilarity was too contagious to long resist—in short order the monk had joined him. Soon the two of them were laughing so hard that tears ran down their cheeks.

"My sides hurt," Thomas complained when they finally stopped.

"Mine do, too," Brother Vangellis replied, wiping his eyes with the sleeves of his gown. After a pause he added, "But I think we both needed that."

The sun had now set completely, and it was getting colder. Thomas threw more wood onto the fire, realizing as he did so that he was no longer anxious about the bears. He felt confident that the monk would keep both of them safe.

They sat for a while watching the flames reach out to embrace the new fuel. A large beetle emerged onto one of the fresh branches and scurried along it to safety. Thomas felt a little like the beetle. He'd barely remained one step ahead of disaster for weeks now.

The monk was studying him closely. "I can see you've been carrying a burden, Thomas," he offered gently.

How does he know? Thomas wondered.

"Yes, it's true," he finally admitted.

"Would you like to talk about it?"

Did he want to talk about it? Thomas stared into the fire, trying to make sense of his own thoughts on the subject. The monk waited patiently, his face outlined by the flickering flames.

"Why do things happen the way they do?" he finally asked. "Why me?"

The monk didn't reply.

Then Thomas realized that he'd made his decision. His long-standing questions about the stone still remained. They were questions that Will couldn't answer—maybe the monk could.

Haltingly at first, he began to tell the story of the stone, starting from the very beginning. This time he left nothing out, not even the incident with the pitchfork.

The monk asked questions from time to time, but mostly just let him speak.

The fire had diminished to glowing ashes before he finally came to an end.

"So no one knows about the stone except you and Will?"

"No one."

The monk reached across to the wood pile and began rebuilding the fire. With no immediate response coming from Brother Vangellis, Thomas began to feel worried.

"Do you think I'm damned?" he asked anxiously.

The monk looked startled. "Why would you think that?" he asked.

"Maybe the stone is evil."

The monk shook his head. "See this fire," he said, waving a branch that had just caught alight. "We use it to keep us warm, to cook our food, and to protect ourselves from wild animals. Our enemies also use it to destroy our crops and to burn down entire towns and villages."

He threw more wood on the fire. "Fire is not evil. It's people who are evil."

Thomas wasn't satisfied. "Well, I've used the stone in ways that are evil. Doesn't that make me evil?"

"All of us do evil things, Thomas."

He stared into the fire a moment before responding further.

"From what I've heard, you did begin badly with the stone. You paid a price for it, too. But I think you have learned from your mistakes. It's been a long time since you abused the gift of the stone."

"Is it a gift? It seems more like a curse!"

"It's a gift," the monk asserted firmly.

"Where did it come from?"

"I don't know. The monastery we are heading for has a library. Perhaps we might learn something there.

"But I have never heard of anything at all like your stone, Thomas. I don't want to build your hopes up."

Thomas sighed. He trusted the monk, and it felt good to have unburdened himself. He now realized, though, that he had irrationally hoped that Brother Vangellis would be able to help him. His wishful thinking simply wasn't realistic. How could anyone under-stand the stone? No one even knew it existed.

Then he remembered that Lord Drettroth knew. Thankfully the Rogandan lord was far away and had no idea where to find either him or the stone.

BY NOON of the next day they had reached the monastery. Built of solid stone, it had been established on a small but fertile plateau, high up in the mountains. Walking toward it they found themselves on a broad path that led first through a grove of apple and pear trees then skirted extensive fields. Brother Vangellis pointed out the care-fully cultivated strips of land and explained that the monks grew corn and other grain crops as well as many types of vegetables. Goats and chickens fled from their approach as they made their way up to the thick stone wall that surrounded the monastery buildings.

The gates of the compound hung wide open. As they passed inside they saw a dozen monks sitting in the sunshine around a wooden table, enjoying a simple meal of bread, cheese, and wine.

Several of them leaped to their feet when they saw Brother Vangellis, greeting him excitedly. They crowded around him, all talking at once. The others hung back, looking uncertain and uncom-fortable.

"What is the reason for all this excitement?" asked an old monk, frowning at them with mock severity. He stepped forward, and the little crowd parted before him. Approaching Brother Vangellis, he reached up and slowly placed a hand on each of his shoulders. Holding him there, he quietly studied his face for a long moment. Then he enveloped the younger man in a warm embrace. Thomas could see tears glistening in his eyes. Drawing back, he studied him once more with a happy smile.

"My friend, it does my old heart good to see you!" he exclaimed. "And it brings me great joy to see the sun once again shining upon your brow."

He turned to the other monks, who still sat silent and awkward at the table. "Why do you hesitate?" he asked, a tone of gentle chiding in his voice. "The return of a prodigal is always a cause for great rejoicing."

They rose and faced Brother Vangellis, who greeted them with a self-conscious bow. They greeted him politely, if not warmly, although a couple of them muttered apologies for their half-hearted welcome.

"And who is this young man that you have brought with you?" the older monk asked. He turned to Thomas, presenting a round and cheerful face surmounted with wisps of snowy white hair.

"This is Thomas Stablehand," Brother Vangellis replied. "He has seen a lot in his young life, and comes to you through great danger. He is horse master to the army of our king. Thomas, this is Brother Beneface, the abbot of this monastery."

"Thomas, you are welcome here," the abbot assured him. "May you find peace and rest in our community and refreshment for your spirit."

"Thank you, Brother Beneface," Thomas managed.

The abbot introduced Thomas to a young monk around his own age.

"Brother Hann will show you around, Thomas. I must borrow your friend for a while—I can see we have a great deal of catching up to do. He will join you later."

With that he took Brother Vangellis by the arm, and steered him away toward one of the monastery buildings.

"Come with me, Thomas," said the young monk. "Are you hungry? I will show you to the kitchen." Then he added eagerly, "Do you really ride horses?"

"Yes," Thomas replied, trying to sound matter-of-fact. "As it happens, I teach soldiers to ride horses."

"Really? I've always wanted to ride a horse. Maybe you could teach me."

"So you have horses here? Brother Vangellis didn't think so."

"No, unfortunately we don't."

"Then it won't be easy to teach you to ride," said Thomas with a grin.

"I suppose not," Brother Hann acknowledged sheepishly.

After a brief visit to the kitchen, from which they emerged laden with bread, cheese, and apples, the two of them wandered around the fields outside the monastery, enjoying the frequent bursts of sunshine through the clouds. They were soon chatting happily like old friends. The young monk's cheerful demeanor and infectious laughter soon put Thomas at his ease. He began to wonder when he had last felt so relaxed. The war with the Rogandans seemed a very long way away.

A bell rang from the monastery.

"I must go to prayers now, Thomas. I will show you to the guest rooms on my way there."

They headed toward a building along the inner wall of the monastery compound.

"You won't be alone, Thomas. We have another guest here already. It's very unusual for us to have guests at all—we're so far away from other people up here. And to have multiple guests at the same time is even more unusual."

He lowered his voice. "The other guest is a bit strange. I think he's suspicious. He's foreign, too."

At this news Thomas at once became alert. A cloud threatened to intrude upon his sunny afternoon.

"It's probably just me, though," Brother Hann added with a smile. "Brother Beneface would say I shouldn't be so quick to judge."

He led Thomas to a long building that hugged the inner wall of the compound. A single corridor stretched along the length of the building and provided access to half a dozen small guest rooms. Large windows along the corridor opened onto the monastery grounds and admitted light into the rooms, each of which had its own door and window.

The monk led Thomas to the first room along the corridor. "The other guest is staying in the room at the far end," he whispered.

Then, speaking more loudly, he said, "Make yourself at home,

Thomas. Come and go as you please. Two bells means that dinner is about to be served in the refectory."

Thomas had nothing to put in his room except the waterproof cloak and wide-brimmed hat he had brought with him from Arnost. He took off the cloak and hung it on a wooden hook in the wall opposite the bed. He placed the hat on a three-legged stool in the corner of the room. Then he left the room and emerged once again into the late afternoon sunshine.

The monks had apparently gathered in a small chapel; the sound of their chanting carried across the monastery grounds. Thomas headed out of the gates and wandered around the outer walls of the monastery, circumnavigating it entirely. The monastery faced north, and he discovered that it was perched almost on the edge of the plateau.

To the left of the main gates he found several large hen houses, a goat pen, and a number of small enclosures that turned out to be a piggery. Beyond them lay the fertile fields that provided crops for the monks.

To the right of the main gates a rocky outcrop separated the monastery buildings from a steep precipice. Far below, at the base of the plateau, Thomas glimpsed a wide river flowing eastward through rugged country.

A bell tolled twice, calling Thomas back to the monastery to join the monks for dinner. As he headed toward the gate he noticed a stranger leaning against a tree, studying him. Seeing that he had been noticed, the man immediately turned his attention elsewhere. Thomas decided to ignore him, and headed through the gates.

When he reached the refectory building he saw that the stranger had followed him in. Brother Beneface greeted Thomas at the door and ushered him inside. A smiling Brother Vangellis stood waiting for him.

The abbot welcomed the stranger at the door.

"Brother Vangellis, Thomas," he said, turning back to them, "I would like to introduce you to another visitor. His name is Harald. He speaks very little of our language."

He indicated a man who was bearded and dark in complexion, and medium in height. The man bowed slightly.

Brother Vangellis addressed him, speaking a few words in a language that Thomas did not recognize. The man's face remained blank, and he shrugged, indicating that he did not understand.

Brother Vangellis then smiled, and returned Harald's bow. Thomas copied him.

They took their places standing behind low benches in front of a long wooden table. As soon as the abbot gave thanks for the food everyone sat down, and a hubbub of cheerful conversation quickly broke out while a couple of monks served the food. The meal consisted of a thick vegetable gruel served hot, along with freshly baked bread. The food tasted very good indeed to Thomas after their limited diet in the wilderness.

Harald sat at one end of the table, speaking to no one. As soon as he had finished eating he stood up and faced the abbot, giving him a formal nod in acknowledgment of his hospitality. Then he left.

"He's Rogandan," Brother Vangellis whispered to Thomas.

"How do you know?"

"I spoke to him in Rogandan. I said, 'May no evil creature shadow your path'. It's a saying among Rogandans—they are very superstitious. The standard response is a special hand gesture to ward off evil. He pretended not to understand me, but his right hand instinctively began the gesture before he could stop it. I'm sure no one else noticed. But I did, and he saw that I did."

A wave of anxiety flooded over Thomas. He had felt sure they would be safe here.

His concern must have shown on his face, because the monk quickly added, "There's probably nothing to worry about. But we should watch this Harald, just in case. I will have a word to Brother Beneface.

"I was planning to share the monks' quarters with them, but I will sleep in the guest room next to yours instead."

Thomas thanked him more than once.

. . .

A SMALL SOUND startled Thomas into wakefulness. He lay unmoving in his bed, his eyes slowly adjusting to the thin strip of moonlight that shone through the heavy curtains across his window. Someone was in his room.

A vague shadow hovered near the opposite wall—the intruder seemed to be groping around inside his cloak. Moments later the figure slipped from the room. The door closed softly, and silence descended once again like a blanket.

Thomas lay without moving for a very long time. Then he got up and stole next door to the monk's room. Rhythmic snoring sounds issued from the prone form of Brother Vangellis.

Thomas shook him gently. The monk mumbled and turned over. Thomas shook him again. He woke with a start to see Thomas holding a finger warningly to his mouth.

"What's wrong, Thomas?" he whispered, becoming quickly alert.

"I just had a visitor," Thomas hissed. "He was poking around in my cloak. Maybe he was looking for the stone."

"You still have it?"

"Yes, I have it. I keep it with me. It wasn't in my cloak."

"There's no harm done, then. Don't assume the worst, Thomas. I doubt that your visitor knows anything about the stone. The man is probably just a common thief."

Thomas did not reply. He stood there feeling tense and unhappy and shivering uncontrollably.

"Go back to bed. I am awake now, and I will get up and watch the corridor here from my room until daylight. In the morning I will speak with Brother Beneface."

IN THE MORNING they set off together to search out the abbot. When they found him, he appeared a little flustered.

"Good morning, Brother Vangellis, Thomas," he said. "It seems that our visitor, Harald—if that truly was his name—is no longer our guest at the monastery.

"Certainly his possessions have been removed from the room he was occupying in the guest house. And I have just been informed that a quantity of supplies have disappeared from the kitchen. Our cook was most indignant."

At that moment another monk appeared, red faced. "The silver chalice we use for Holy Communion has gone missing, Brother Beneface. I can't find it anywhere in the chapel."

"Oh, well," sighed the abbot. "These are the risks you take when you welcome strangers into your midst."

Then, suddenly recalling his audience, he hastily added, "Please pardon me, Thomas. I meant no slight on you!"

Brother Vangellis chuckled. "As it happens, Thomas had a visitor himself last night, Brother Beneface. He woke to someone poking around his cloak in the dark. I suspect that your guest was little more than a thief."

"I fear you are right. We must pray for his soul, poor fellow."

The abbot turned to Thomas. "I am very sorry that your experience of our hospitality has not been entirely pleasant so far.

"I hope we can make amends, though. I will ask Brother Hann to free himself for a few days to keep you company."

Thomas thanked him sincerely, and tried to make it clear that the monks' hospitality had, in fact, been excellent.

They took their leave of the abbot and set off to join the other monks at breakfast.

"I think you can afford to relax again, Thomas," Brother Vangellis assured him as they headed into the refectory. "I suspect we've seen the last of 'Harald'."

31

For Thomas, the loss of Elbruhe lay constantly at the back of his mind, a dark shadow that brooded just beyond the reach of his normal awareness. It nagged incessantly at him until he turned his thoughts inward and dragged it into the open once again. But exposing it never seemed to offer him release.

Fortunately for him, he found the perfect tonic in Brother Hann. It was hard to feel gloomy for long around someone who was so unfailingly cheerful. And the young monk, being unaware of the situation, was entirely unaffected in his communication.

Thomas and Brother Hann found themselves spending every available minute together, and the two of them quickly became inseparable. Thomas had grown up without siblings and with no close friend his own age. In recent times almost all of his significant relationships had been with people much older than himself. The only exception was Elbruhe, but she was different in every imaginable way.

Brother Hann and Thomas were as unalike as anyone might reasonably expect a monk and an army horse master to be. But they made the simple discovery that they enjoyed each other's company. After the recent blows sustained by Thomas, he gradually came to appreciate Brother Hann's sunny disposition as a welcome breath of fresh air. For his part, Brother Hann listened with unfeigned amazement as Thomas told him about his years in Arnost, the Rogandan invasion, and everything that had happened to him since. Separated for a time from the turmoil of the recent past, Thomas found unexpected peace and solace in his days at the monastery, in spite of the grief that gnawed at him.

In the afternoon of their second day at the monastery, Brother Vangellis took Thomas to the library. It was a substantial building located at the southwest corner of the monastery grounds. Shafts of bright sunlight burst into the library through large windows facing directly west. The windows looked out over the edge of the plateau and commanded a magnificent view of mountains marching far off into the distance as well as vistas of the rugged terrain close at hand.

Many books lined a series of wooden shelves that ringed the room. A number of benches with stools stood in the middle of the room, and almost every available surface was covered with books, scrolls and manuscripts. Even some of the stools carried precariously balanced piles of books and papers.

Brother Vangellis introduced Thomas to the librarian, Brother Erastus, a thin man in late middle age with a long nose and sharp eyes. After welcoming Thomas the librarian fixed him with a penetrating gaze for a few moments before turning his attention to Brother Vangellis.

"So you've finally decided to visit an old scholar in his library, eh? If you took more time to study instead of forever scurrying around frantically, you might be better off," he suggested, wagging a long finger at Brother Vangellis. He sounded stern, but the smile creasing his face betrayed his true feelings.

Brother Vangellis ignored the bait. "You are privileged," he assured Thomas, "to stand in one of the largest libraries in the kingdom."

"*The* largest library in the kingdom," Brother Erastus corrected him, "apart from the king's own library in Arnost. *And* we have the biggest collection of old scrolls in Arvenon. We have books on almost every imaginable topic: history, philosophy, science, and, of course, theology, to name a few."

"Brother Erastus is rather proud of his collection," Brother Vangellis told Thomas.

"Rightly so!" the librarian replied with energy.

"Has no one told you that pride is a sin?" Brother Vangellis teased.

The librarian sighed deeply. "I am afraid your friend never was much of a scholar," he told Thomas. "But it doesn't prevent him knocking on my door whenever he needs me for something."

He turned back to Brother Vangellis. "I presume you do have a reason for interrupting my labors."

"Yes. I have an unusual challenge to offer you. I was wondering if you have ever come across any reference to a stone that confers special powers," the monk replied, coming immediately to the point.

"What kind of special powers?" the librarian returned.

"The ability to discern the thoughts of other people."

"Sounds like superstition to me," Brother Erastus asserted.

"Yes, it does," agreed Brother Vangellis.

The librarian turned to Thomas. "May I see the stone, please?" he asked.

Thomas was too shocked to reply. He turned to Brother Vangellis with dismay, wondering how much he had told the librarian.

"I've told him nothing, Thomas!" his friend protested.

"You didn't need to," Brother Erastus said calmly. "Some things are as obvious to me as the very large nose on my face.

"You give me far too little credit, Brother Vangellis," he continued. "Just because I spend so much time reading books doesn't mean I can't read people."

Brother Vangellis shook his head and shrugged helplessly. "He's an old rogue, Thomas," he said. "But I would trust him with my life. It's safe to show him the stone."

Still alarmed at the ease with which his secret had been laid bare, Thomas drew the stone slowly from his pouch and, after a moment's reluctance, handed it to the librarian. Brother Vangellis, who had never seen it himself, peered inquisitively over the librarian's shoulder.

"It's unusual," the scholar observed. "I've never seen anything quite like it. I collect rocks as a hobby, and I can tell you that this stone is made of different material from any of the rocks in my collection."

He handed it back to Thomas. "It might be a sky rock," he suggested.

"What's a sky rock?" Thomas asked, quickly putting it away again.

"It's a rock that's fallen to earth from the heavens," the librarian replied. "Sometimes we see a streak of light across the sky at night. We're seeing tiny stars falling to the earth. Occasionally people find the location where one has landed.

"But a sky rock that gives you the power to see into other people's minds? I don't recall ever reading about such a thing, and I have read almost everything in our library at one time or another. But I am willing to take a fresh look at some of the older scrolls."

"Thank you, Brother Erastus," said Brother Vangellis, making a small formal bow and frowning at Thomas, who belatedly managed to blurt out a mumbled thanks of his own.

"Well, this has been as much excitement as I can cope with in one afternoon," said the librarian decisively. "Off you go, then," he added, shooing them out. "The sooner you leave the sooner I can get started on my search."

As they were moving out he placed a hand briefly on Thomas's shoulder. "You needn't worry, young man," he said reassuringly. "I won't breathe a word of this to anyone."

As the days passed it seemed increasingly unlikely to Thomas that the librarian would be able to discover anything about the stone. He decided to put the search out of his mind and enjoy the unexpected benefits of the sanctuary offered by the monastery. He knew that the war with the Rogandans must surely be continuing and that his friends might well be in peril. He also knew that he could not hide here forever. But each new day brought sunshine, laughter, and contentment in the company of his new friend. For now it was enough.

It therefore came as a shock when, almost a week after their arrival at the monastery, Brother Vangellis sought him out one afternoon and told him that Brother Erastus had uncovered some information about the stone.

The two of them hurried to the library to find Brother Erastus waiting impatiently for them to arrive. With no more than a hurried greeting, he led them to the western wall of the library. Removing a cleverly concealed panel in one of the bookshelves, he revealed a hidden lever. He pulled down hard on the lever, and the bookshelf swung noiselessly to one side, exposing a narrow opening in the floor that led down to a winding staircase.

They followed him down the stairs into a large room lit by wall-mounted candles. He pulled another lever beside the staircase, and the bookshelf above swung silently back into place, sealing the chamber.

Thomas glanced around the room in the dim light. A large table at one end of the room held a small collection of scrolls with a couple of oil lamps for illumination. The walls were entirely covered with small wooden cubicles filled to overflowing with scrolls.

"We keep our oldest scrolls here," Brother Erastus told Thomas. "The even temperature, the dry air, and the absence of sunlight have allowed us to preserve them for very long periods. The only alternative is to copy them. We eventually do that when they deteriorate enough, but it is an immense task."

Thomas had never learned to read and write, and the usefulness of expending such effort on ancient documents was not at all clear to him. However, Thomas guessed that Will might have appreciated this place. Will had learned his letters from his uncle, who was a trader, and had said more than once in his hearing that the skill could be valuable at times. Thomas decided to see it through the eyes of his friend. He nodded wisely in appreciation.

"Not only scrolls have been preserved down here," Brother

Vangellis added. "The monks have retreated here more than once when the monastery was attacked."

"Has the monastery ever been destroyed?" Thomas wondered aloud.

"Yes, once," the librarian replied. "During the Rogandan invasion in the days of King Rufus II. The monks remained hidden, and thankfully almost all of the library was saved."

"Buildings can always be rebuilt, of course. Scrolls are infinitely more precious," Brother Vangellis added with a grin. Brother Erastus ignored the remark.

"Over here, Thomas." The scholar led them to the table. "When I found this scroll I realized that I had seen it before. When I last read it, though, I dismissed it as a fable.

"Not all historians are careful to separate fact from rumor and hearsay," he explained. "It can be difficult to discern old histories from old stories."

"Does it mention the stone directly?" Brother Vangellis asked.

"It does much more than that," the librarian replied. "It offers an entire history for it."

Thomas felt his heart beginning to pound. He felt restless, nervous, and excited in equal measures. "Can you read it to me?" he asked, his voice quavering with emotion.

"Of course," the librarian replied. "I'd suggest you take a seat," he said, pointing them to a pair of stools beside the table. "This is going to take a while.

"This scroll is very old. It is hard to accurately date it, but some clues suggest that it dates back two hundred years at least. The author calls himself Randolf of Clerbon—he is not known to me. And in the early part of the scroll he quotes an even older manuscript by another unknown author.

"This is what it says.

'THREE TALISMANS *of great potency are abroad in the world, uncelebrated, unrecognized, and hidden from any certain knowledge. Perhaps I alone know their true history, long forgotten with the passing of many scores of years. I once learned of an ancient parchment, lost and mayhap forgotten by all save only an aged hermit. The old man had glimpsed it in his youth, and he described it to me as well as his failing memory served him.*

Long did I search for it, and bitter and fruitless my labor seemed. Dark and tiresome would be the full tale thereof. At last, hope having deserted me, I stumbled upon it, the greatest treasure in my possession. Even now I have it before me, a faded manuscript, crumbling with age and arcane in script. Many candles burned to naught ere I found a way to decipher it.

Hear, then, the testimony of a scribe whose witness has been silent for many an age:

Long years have passed away since Goodman Tomas walked upon the earth. A poor farmer and simple he was, yet greatly beloved by all who knew him. He lived in a rude hut in but a small village.

One day his fortunes turned. Though his back had been bowed down with much labor, yet was he seen to stand again straight and tall. Tales grew up around his wisdom, and people journeyed from afar to seek his counsel. His insights failed him not, and his sayings gave birth to a bountiful supply of proverbs.

It came to pass that his village became a town, and the town a city, and he the mayor. His family prospered likewise.

Late in life offered he a gift unto the king of his country. Rude in appearance was the gift but great in effect, and the king, who was a good ruler, handled it wisely. His fortunes likewise changed, and he became powerful even as his kingdom prospered.

The story sprang up and spread abroad that Tomas had received a star from heaven that fell from the sky and landed in the form of a rock beside his hut. Great and manifold were the gifts bestowed by this rock upon its owner—gifts of insight, good health and influence among men. And behold, having received it freely from Tomas, the king rejoiced also in the selfsame gifts. Nor were the benefits denied to Tomas when he yielded up the rock. He continued as before until he had attained a great age.

So Tomas died, full of years, and in time the king also slept with his fathers. The son of the king prospered, too, and increased yet more in power. A subtle, but alas, not a wise king was he, and many enemies gathered themselves against him. The neighboring kingdoms rose up, bound together in hatred for the king and desire for the rock. Nevertheless, try as they might, they could not overcome him, such was his might in arms and his shrewdness in council. Finally, by treachery alone was he brought low, slain by the hand of one he trusted.

Thus lost the son of the wise king his kingdom and his life, all through foolishness and pride. The ruler who wrested control of his kingdom laid hands upon the rock, lusting to command every virtue of which he had heard so much. It benefited him nothing. Years of bitter fortune and failing prosperity passed, until in anger he caused the rock to be smashed into a thousand fragments and cast outside his palace.

And lo, it came to pass that certain peasants, chancing upon the pieces, found them pleasing to the eye. Taking them up, they bore them unto their dwellings. Anon it was seen that some of the virtue of the rock had passed into three of the pieces. One brought health and vitality, a second, great authority, and a third, insight into the hearts and minds of men.

Long and illuminating would be the history that chronicled the fortunes attending those who found the stones. Time revealed that the stones, as likewise the rock vouchsafed to Tomas, lost their virtue entirely when taken by force, at times remaining dormant for a generation. Only when a stone was gifted freely, or found by chance, was the virtue bestowed. The stones together were like the original rock in every respect but one—once a gift had been made of a stone, its virtue was thereafter withheld from the giver.

Some stones passed as heirlooms from father to son or mother to daughter. In time the gift was always squandered through pride or folly, or lost through violence or misadventure.

None can say where the stones are today. Long years have passed since last I heard aught of them. Many say they are lost forever, and some rejoice in their vanishment. Some say they are a gift from God to the wise. Others say they are a tool of the Devil to curse and ensnare all who receive them.

There was a time when one of the stones lay in my hand for a moment. Young and foolish I was, and greatly desirous of possessing it, though every opportunity was denied me. Now I am old, and wiser, and content with my lot in life. Who could envy those who bear the burden of such a gift?

THE WITNESS ENDED THUS. *My account concerning the ancient manuscript is accurate in every particular and my translation faithful and true. I, Randolf of Clerbon, swear it on my life.'*

"THIS 'RANDOLF OF CLERBON' appears to have written the last sentence in blood—most probably his own," said Brother Erastus, distaste plainly evident on his face. "But he continues, once again using ink."

'IN THE UNRELENTING *passage of years since the scribe lived and breathed, many things have changed, and some remain the same. The role of the rock in shaping kingdoms, revealed in the manuscript, has never ceased. The true history of Arvenon and the surrounding kingdoms is incomplete without reference to the stones of power.*

Such fateful talismans—how they haunt my dreams! Ever have I sought them, but alas, thus far to no avail. Much lore have I gathered concerning the three—the Stone of Vitality, that grants well-being and life beyond the span of other men, the Stone of Authority, that bestows power and influence for good or for ill, and the Stone of Knowing, that lays bare the hearts and motivations of others. I record here but a small part of this lore, in order that my labor shall not prove entirely vain, that my research shall not crumble to dust with my mortal body.

What, then, can be said of these stones? They respect neither rank nor status. They surrender their power impartially to saint and sinner alike. Certain boundaries do, however, encompass those who bear them. The potency of a stone is diminished by afflictions of the body or the spirit, especially when a stone is new to the bearer. Familiarity increases their virtue, though bearers assume fearful risks with overuse.

Such is the witness of those who lay greatest claim to discernment about the stones.

Nevertheless, overuse has never been chief among the perils confronting those who bear a stone. The principal danger has ever been the lust of others who desired the stones for themselves.

A stone fails of its purpose if a bearer has been killed to acquire it, no matter who carried out the murder. The same failure ensues if a stone is taken without consent.

Such limitations have never deterred the unscrupulous, though. The most cunning among them have ever recognized the futility of force, and sought instead to obtain the stones using fear and intimidation. That history must needs be told.

First, though, it is necessary to faithfully chronicle the properties of the stones. I will describe each in turn, for though their lineage is common, their likeness and behavior vary considerably.

The Stone of Knowing is said to be little bigger than a man's fingernail, smooth to the touch, and colored brightly with azure and magenta tones. The stone grants admittance—full and unfettered—to thought, intent, and motivation of every person upon whom the eye of the bearer falls. Certain parchment fragments, perplexing in nature, hint that even animals and birds lie within its reach, at least in small measure.

No memory from the past is safe—every secret buried deep must be surrendered to its power. The stone may offer glimpses of what is to come, but with no certain assuredness, since many a fork in the road awaits the traveler who journeys to the future.

An extraordinary weight bears down upon the hand that cradles this stone. It is said that, of the three, the Stone of Knowing holds the greatest potentiality for good or evil, depending only on the character of the one who bears it.

The Stone of...'

"AND THERE THE ACCOUNT ENDS," the librarian said. "The scroll is torn, and the latter part of it is missing."

He took in a deep breath and exhaled slowly as though marking the successful completion of a long and arduous journey. They all sat hushed and still for many minutes.

The scholar eventually broke the silence.

"The writer tells us he is Randolf of Clerbon. I have searched widely, and learned that Clerbon was once located in the region we now call Erestor. I have discovered no reference to this place in the last two hundred years. I therefore believe we can safely conclude that this scroll is at least as old as that."

Brother Vangellis shook his head in wonder. "Astonishing as this tale seems," he said, "it has about it the smell of truth, or something very near the truth. You have done well indeed to find it." He acknowledged the librarian with a respectful nod.

Thomas did not know what to say. Surely he should feel only relief to know where the stone came from. But the history of the stone was alarming, and it was difficult to grasp what it all meant.

Brother Vangellis got up. "I think it's time we went outside for some fresh air, Thomas," he said, looking at his young friend with concern in his eyes.

Brother Erastus put away the scroll and unsealed the entrance to the cellar, and they all emerged into the library. The late afternoon sun flooded the room with golden light; before long it would sink behind the distant mountains. Thomas realized they had been down there for longer than he had imagined.

As they emerged from the building, an agitated Brother Hann ran up to them.

"We've been looking for you everywhere!" He thrust Thomas's cloak and hat into his hands. He turned to Brother Vangellis. "Brother Dannel has your things. There he is now!" He waved frantically, and Brother Dannel ran over and handed over the meager possessions Brother Vangellis had left in the guest house.

"What's going on?" Brother Vangellis asked.

"A Rogandan force has surrounded the monastery," Brother Dannel replied. "One of the Brothers saw them coming and ran to raise the alarm. We shut the gates before they arrived, but feared we had locked you out."

"They're demanding we hand you over, Thomas, and you, too, Brother Vangellis!" Brother Hann exclaimed, unable to hide his dismay. "We have done all we can to remove every trace of you. It's something about Thomas stealing an heirloom belonging to their commander. The commander of their entire army is right here at the gates. His name is Lord Dead Wrath or something."

"He is lying about this supposed heirloom," said Brother Vangellis calmly. "Where is the abbot?"

"He is at the gate," Brother Hann told him. "He instructed us all to hide under the library. But what will happen to him?"

"That is in God's hands," replied Brother Dannel. "We must do as he has said."

THE MONKS and Thomas huddled together fearfully in the hidden room underground, listening to the Rogandan soldiers rampaging through the library above. Brother Erastus sat there with tears in his eyes. He had taken many armfuls of books down into the cellar, and would have gone back for more had they not restrained him. As it was they scarcely closed the opening in time.

The murmur of barely audible prayers filled the room, interrupted from time to time by crashes above as another bookshelf was pulled from the wall.

In the absence of the abbot, Brother Dannel was the most senior monk. He had been praying quietly for some time, but now he lifted his head and turned to Brother Vangellis.

"It is clear to me that you must make good your escape while you still can, Brother Vangellis," he said decisively. "You must take Thomas with you.

"The Rogandans will quickly realize that the river below us offers the only effective escape route from this region. They will send soldiers to watch the river."

"How can we escape from here?" Brother Vangellis asked.

"There is a tunnel down to the bottom of the plateau. It was built by the Brothers who came before us, for just such an emergency as we face now."

From the surprise on the faces of some of the monks, Thomas could see that not all of them were aware of this information.

"We will follow you later, if it proves to be God's purpose," Brother Dannel promised.

"There is a small coracle on the bank of the river below," he continued. "It will carry you to safety. Go quickly now!"

An older monk lifted a flagstone to reveal a large metal ring set into the floor. He tugged unsuccessfully at it. A couple of the younger monks joined in, and soon a piece of the floor pulled free, causing those tugging to fall backward. A draft of stale air rushed into the room, almost extinguishing the candles.

Brother Dannel handed a burning torch to each of them. "May the peace of Christ go with you!" he said fervently. His lips continued to move noiselessly as he breathed a silent prayer over them.

They stepped down onto the first steps of a long and winding staircase that stretched far below them into the dark. Treading carefully they began their descent, Brother Vangellis first, then Thomas.

After a few moments they heard the entrance to the tunnel close above them.

"What are they doing?" Thomas called anxiously. "Why don't they escape, too? How can Brother Dannel say they'll follow if it's God's purpose? Does God want them to die?"

Brother Vangellis did not answer. The monk trod purposefully down, down, not looking back. Thomas hurried after him as quickly as he dared, anxious to catch up.

Once Thomas glanced above him. He could see nothing. As they moved on, the dark closed in behind them, even as it stretched down before them beyond their sight.

Thomas thought about the scroll and the history of the stone. He turned it over and over in his mind, examining it from every angle. Lord Drettroth had surely discovered the truth, too. There must be another copy of the scroll at large in the world.

What if he catches me? But the stone won't work for him if he takes it from me by force! What did the scroll mean by fear and intimidation? Will Drettroth try to frighten me into giving it to him? I must never let him catch me! How did he find me here?

His mind flew from thought to thought while his feet kept moving, down, down, down, ever deeper. In time his mind became numb, and nothing remained except the endless staircase and the unyielding dark.

The story continues and concludes in
The Cost of Knowing,
the second book in Allan N. Packer's
The Stone Cycle

LIST OF CHARACTERS

- *Agon* - king of Rogand
- *Ander* - Arvenian soldier from Erestor; skilled swordsman and archer
- *Axel Stablehand* - master of the Arvenian royal stables at Arnost, and the father of Thomas
- *Beneface* - abbot of a high plateau monastery in Arvenon boasting an extensive library
- *Bottren* - high-ranking Arvenian nobleman and close confidante of King Steffan
- *Burtelen* - high-ranking Arvenian nobleman from Erestor and close confidante of King Steffan
- *Dannel* - monk at a high plateau monastery in Arvenon boasting an extensive library
- *Drettroth* - high-ranking Rogandan nobleman; commander of the Rogandan army
- *Duke of Erestor* - The uncle of King Steffan of Arvenon, and the regent during the king's absence; the senior member of the nobility in Erestor
- *Edgar* - greedy Arvenian soldier
- *Elbruhe* - young Rogandan woman; runaway slave

- *Elias* - abbot at the Monastery of St. Rodrig the Martyr where Brother Vangellis was hiding away
- *Erastus* - librarian at a high plateau monastery in Arvenon
- *Essanda* - Princess of Castel
- *Gordan* - Castelan nobleman and confidante of King Istel
- *Haldek* - Rogandan soldier; stronghold guard
- *Hann* - young monk at a high plateau monastery in Arvenon
- *Istel* - king of Castel, a neighboring kingdom to Arvenon
- *Kuper* - Arvenian soldier from Erestor; skilled swordsman and archer and twin brother to Rellan
- *Luzik* - Rogandan army commander
- *Marya* - wife of Axel Stablehand and mother of Thomas
- *Nestor* - Arvenian soldier from Arnost
- *Pisander* - Arvenian earl and head of King Steffan's foreign spy network; member of the nobility from Erestor
- *Ranauld* - Arvenian count; a confidante of King Steffan
- *Randolf of Clerbon* - author of an ancient scroll
- *Rellan* - Arvenian soldier from Erestor; skilled swordsman and archer and twin brother to Kuper
- *Rudungen* - a minor Arvenian baron
- *Rufe Sarjant* - respected and physically imposing Arvenian soldier; a close friend of Will Prentis
- *Simon* - boy who helps in the Arvenian royal stables
- *Steffan the Second* - king of Arvenon
- *Thomas Stablehand* - possessor of the Stone of Knowing; son of Axel, the Arvenian royal stable master, and Marya
- *Vangellis* - widely traveled Arvenian monk
- *Will Prentis* - young, ambitious, and unusually capable Arvenian soldier; fluent in Rogandan and widely traveled

NOTE FROM THE AUTHOR

Thank you for reading *The Stone of Knowing*—I hope you enjoyed it. Please consider leaving a review. Reviews make a huge difference to authors as well as benefiting other readers. I also very much appreciate feedback from my readers.

The story of *The Stone of Knowing* continues and concludes in *The Cost of Knowing (The Stone Cycle Book 2)*, outlined below. *The Stone of Authority (The Stone Cycle Book 3)* continues the saga.

A prequel to *The Stone of Knowing*, called *The Seer: A Prequel to The Stone of Knowing*, also available from online bookstores, reveals how the stone came to be where Thomas found it. Details below.

To be kept up to date on new releases, sign up to my mailing list at www.allanpacker.com. New subscribers will receive an exclusive bonus novelette, available in ebook and audiobook format. The novelette, *The Rending: A Prequel to The Cost of Knowing*, is described below.

But first, *The Cost of Knowing (The Stone Cycle Book 2)*.

The ripples begin to make waves

Thomas Stablehand's life is not the only thing spinning out of control since he found the stone. Entire kingdoms are now in turmoil.

Will Prentis, newly appointed as army commander, must outmaneuver a growing array of enemies as he prepares for an unequal showdown with Arvenon's invaders. Thomas, hunted unceasingly and aided only by Brother Vangellis, must sacrifice all to safeguard the stone.

The fate of kingdoms soon hinges on them and on Essanda, their new queen, who is easy to underestimate but may have surprises of her own in store.

Together they must confront a ruthless invader hiding a darker purpose.

The odds are hopeless. And for three kingdoms, the stakes are far higher than anyone knows.

How did the stone come to be where Thomas found it? The answer can be found in *The Seer: A Prequel to The Stone of Knowing*, a new prequel to *The Stone of Knowing*.

The Seer: A Prequel to The Stone of Knowing is a novelette, 5 chapters (13,500 words) in length, available in online bookstores. It is a standalone story, and as such can be read independently of other books in *The Stone Cycle* series. The novelette is described below.

Eyes see no more than a glimpse

Sheylha is a seer—a woman with unique and extraordinary abili-

ties. Powerful men want to control her, to use her to dominate others.

Kalvor is a warrior of unusual tenacity, a hunter who never gives up. Driven by his past, he has become a dangerous enemy.

When Kalvor is sent to find and capture the seer, each of them will be tested in ways they could never have imagined.

In time the outcome will determine the fate of kingdoms.

To be kept up to date on new releases, sign up to my mailing list at *allanpacker.com*. New subscribers will receive an exclusive bonus novelette—a prequel to *The Cost of Knowing*. The novelette, *The Rending: A Prequel to The Cost of Knowing*, is a complete story four chapters (13,000 words) in length. It provides additional context to one of the story threads from *The Cost of Knowing* without introducing spoilers for other books in *The Stone Cycle* series. The novelette is described below.

Endings may be beginnings in disguise

Anneka is comfortable and confident, a noblewoman of consequence living a life of privilege. Until the day her world is torn apart.

After losing everything she most cares about, she must abandon her home and her way of life in an attempt to secure the future of those who depend on her.

No one, least of all Anneka, could anticipate a deeper significance to her struggle. Yet her journey will one day influence the fate of kingdoms.

AFTERWORD

The Stone of Knowing is not a children's story, but it did begin life as a bedtime tale I told our children when they were quite young.

In their early years all four children shared a single bedroom, and I began telling them stories before they went to sleep. The stories were mostly serial in nature and typically ran for a few days or weeks. The longest lasted about 18 months. I made them up as we went along, and we journeyed together wherever the creative mood of the moment took us. Usually two or three stories were active at a time, and the children took turns to decide which one they wanted to hear. This process of natural selection helped me discover the style and content that best pleased my audience. The stories were sometimes serious and sometimes silly. Occasionally they offered a useful way to convey a message. Mostly, though, the stories were simply intended to entertain and engage the listeners.

At some point I decided to turn one of the stories into a novel. I chose one of the longest running adventures and began the slow process of fleshing it out. I wrote in bursts, sometimes with long pauses that stretched into years. Life brought many distractions; during this period we moved as a family to the United States, and some years later returned to Australia. The story was placed on long-term hold while I authored a technical book, and further time passed before I found the energy to resume writing. When our children grew up, they embraced the emerging novel enthusiastically, and I returned to it largely because of their insistence that I finish it.

Most of the main characters in the novel appeared in the original story, and many of the major plot elements in both *The Stone of Knowing* and its sequel, *The Cost of Knowing*, also flowed from the same source. The bedtime tale came to an end before it reached the climax that unfolds in the sequel, although in many ways the developing plot anticipated the final outcome.

Although I completed *The Stone of Knowing* more than five years ago, I decided to delay publication until *The Cost of Knowing* had been written. As a result I have not required other readers to share in the long intermission I imposed upon my own family.

I never expected the journey to span 25 years. But I've enjoyed the opportunity to turn the spoken story—long forgotten by all of our children—into something more solid and lasting. And it's helped me relive the days when a line of young faces were turned attentively to mine, as eager as I was to discover whatever might happen next.

Allan Packer
Adelaide, South Australia
2019

RESEARCH NOTES

Spoiler Alert!

The reader is advised to avoid this section before finishing *The Stone of Knowing*.

Mystery Plays

The guild-run mystery play / morality play in Chapter 9 was inspired by theatrical equivalents in medieval Europe.

From https://en.wikipedia.org/wiki/Mystery_play:

"By the end of the 15th century, the practice of acting these plays in cycles on festival days was established in several parts of Europe. Sometimes, each play was performed on a decorated pageant cart that moved about the city to allow different crowds to watch each play, and provided actors with a dressing room as well as a stage."

Delirium Tremens

Alcohol withdrawal, as experienced by Brother Vangellis, is today managed by drugs, but in the days before modern medicines the symptoms could be quite severe. The most severe form of withdrawal, sometimes referred to as Delirium tremens (DTs), usually occurs 24 to 72 hours after alcohol intake ceases. It can involve a range of symptoms including disorientation, tremors, and visual and auditory hallucinations. In the worst case, seizures can lead to death. For a discussion of signs and symptoms, refer to:

https://en.wikipedia.org/wiki/Alcohol_withdrawal_syndrome.

Encounters with wild bears

Some advisors recommend a vigorous defense should a bear decide to attack.

From http://www.bearsmart.com/about-bears/dispelling-myths/:

"If a bear attacks (particularly a black bear) in an offensive manner and physical contact is made, fight for your life. Kick, punch, hit the bear with rocks or sticks or any improvised weapon you can find."

The same site offers the following advice: "Warn bears of your presence by talking calmly and loudly or singing, especially in dense bush where visibility may be limited or around rivers or streams where bears have trouble hearing you coming. Your voice will help identify you as human and non-threatening."

I have personally heard a naturalist describe the beneficial effect of singing to a bear during an encounter in the wild.

Real-world religious elements

It isn't original in a fantasy story to include religious features that are recognizable from the real world—William Morris did the same in *The Well at the World's End*, published in 1896. It is, however, unusual in a modern fantasy, where religions are typically either absent or entirely invented.

Many of the religious elements in *The Stone of Knowing* stemmed from the original tale I told our children, and found their way into the written story for that reason. The end result may please some readers and disappoint others. Either way, it is worth noting that any religious components of the story, both recognizable and invented, are intended to be incidental. *The Stone of Knowing* is an epic fantasy adventure, not a religious allegory.

ACKNOWLEDGMENTS

First and foremost, I would like to thank my wife and children for persisting in encouraging me to keep at the story, and for being willing beta readers at various stages of the journey. My son-in-law Ray also engaged enthusiastically with the story in the latter years of its development. My wife, Merilyn, was my most committed supporter throughout, and reliably provided worthwhile feedback whenever it was needed.

Special thanks to my beta readers, Merilyn, Stephen (who definitely wins the prize for the most completions of the manuscript), Deborah, Melanie, James, Ray, Marc, Jen Neal, Brian Plush, Francie Hardy, Cherilyn White, Ali, and Llewelyn Hoy. Their feedback and suggestions led to improvements in a number of areas.

In the earliest stages I benefited from input and encouragement from a number of established authors. My father, Ken Packer, gave specific assistance in various technical aspects of writing. Roger and Sandra Carter also provided valuable feedback and urged me to keep going.

I am indebted to Brian Plush for the awesome map—he took my rough draft and created a work of art.

I would also like to express my appreciation to my developmental editor, Mary Novak. I received a great deal of valuable constructive criticism from her, all of which has improved the flow and polish of the story.

I am grateful to Deborah for her thorough proofreading, completed in spite of many worthy life distractions.

The responsibility for remaining flaws lies solely with me.

Thanks, too, to my daughter, Melanie Cellier, who drew upon her considerable experience as an indie author of young adult fantasy and fairy tale retellings to offer advice around presentation and release practicalities.

Finally, thanks go to God, who has always provided joy and purpose in living, comfort in times of sorrow, inspiration for creativity, and so much else besides.

ABOUT THE AUTHOR

Allan Packer is an emerging author of epic fantasy. *The Stone of Knowing* is his first novel.

Allan grew up surrounded by books and became an avid reader during his childhood. In his university years fantasy displaced science fiction as his favorite genre, thanks primarily to J. R. R. Tolkien. He later shared this love with his four children by reading *The Lord of the Rings* to them aloud—a three-month marathon he completed twice during their formative years.

Born in Australia, Allan has lived and worked on three continents, and spent one quarter of his working years abroad. Having worked as an IT professional throughout his career, he was first published as a technical author.

Today he lives with his wife in Adelaide, South Australia, near their children and a small but growing band of grandchildren.

Allan is currently working on his second epic fantasy series.

www.ingramcontent.com/pod-product-compliance
Lightning Source LLC
Chambersburg PA
CBHW020653110726
47901CB00001B/165